PUFFING BILLY, 1813, GREAT BRITAIN

DANGEROUS LEGACY

GORDON RYAN

SHADOW MOUNTAIN
SALT LAKE CITY, UTAH

To new beginnings . . .

Library of Congress Cataloging-in-Publication Data

Ryan, Gordon, 1943–
    Dangerous legacy / by Gordon Ryan.
      p.   cm.
    ISBN 0–87579–905–1
      1. International relations—Fiction. 2. Nuclear disarmament—
Fiction. 3. Mormons—Fiction. I. Title.
PS3568.Y32D36   1994
813' .54—dc20   94–26638
                                                                     CIP

Printed in the United States of America

10 9 8 7 6 5 4 3 2 1

AUTHOR'S PREFACE

My sincere appreciation is expressed to those persons who have contributed to *Dangerous Legacy,* both morally and professionally, including my mother, Eleanor Hansen Ryan, who taught me to read before the age of five and thereby instilled in me a love for books; Colleen, my lovely wife, who believes in results and does what she can to help achieve them; Kate, my wonderful and loving daughter, who just believes, always; Bill, whose friendship throughout my adulthood has made him my only brother and whose professionalism and staff loyalty throughout his career helped me formulate some of the lead characters; and to our grandchildren, whose contribution is known but to Colleen and me.

I am deeply indebted to Richard Peterson, Deseret Book editorial assistant, who saw the potential and saved me from the slush pile; to Richard Tice, associate editor, for his patience and clarity in helping me to produce a readable novel; to Michelle Eckersley, assistant art director, for her creative contributions; and to Sheri Dew, Vice President, Publishing, at Deseret Book, without whose courage, perserverance, and sponsorship I would not have been able to claim the privilege of being an author. She helped me realize a new horizon, for which I will be eternally grateful.

PROLOGUE

Moscow, USSR
1963

HE HAD BEEN PUBLICLY HUMILIATED before the whole world and before his satellite puppet governments, for whom this perceived weakness might give rise to rebellious behavior. But more important, he had been humiliated before the political vultures who constantly circled, looking for some flaw that would enable them to pick his bones before the last breath of air had left his body.

Blast that Kennedy! He wasn't supposed to have the guts to stand the test. That's what his advisers had told him, that's what he had believed, and that's what he had acted upon. The place-

1

ment of short-range missiles in Cuba, right in the front yard of the Americans, was to have been another communist victory in this bloodless war that had been waged since the end of World War II. When the installations were prematurely discovered, Fidel Castro had been useless, and the entire effort had left the central communist power looking to the world like a toothless bear. He had to do something if he were to retain any semblance of world control, much less retain power in his office. He would yet teach that young upstart in the White House a lesson in global politics.

He had, of course, no knowledge that Cuba had sounded his political death knell and that in less than eighteen months he would be removed from office, having his powers divided between Brezhnev and Kosygin. He would live out his life in relative obscurity in a small country dacha, however preferable that was to the fate of many of his predecessors. He also had no foresight to know that in seven short months, his chief protagonist in the world theater would succumb to an assassin's bullet.

Nikita Sergeyevich Khrushchev had no illusions about the use of power. He had learned at the feet of some of the world's masters, both while serving them, as he had Stalin, and while fighting to keep them from overpowering the Rodina, as with Hitler. Human sacrifice was a small thing compared to keeping power. As he sat at a small conference table in a closet-sized room, looking around at the small assemblage of loyal followers, he was determined to do what was necessary to achieve his objectives, whatever the cost. This small group was to develop a plan that would humiliate the Americans and weaken the NATO alliance. Their recommendations four months later, presented in the form of basic objectives, surprised even the hardened Khrushchev.

Silent Wind Objectives
(Top Secret)

A. Place the USSR in the strategic position of controlling events that would subject the U.S.A. to public castigation and potentially force withdrawal from occupied territories.

B. Destroy the image of the U.S.A. as
   having secure and safe control over
   their nuclear weapons in friendly territory.

C. Design the operation for high public
   exposure and criticism, with minimum
   loss of life. (Low-yield device with
   limited range.)

After lengthy debate, Khrushchev dismissed the committee
and called for Marshal Orchenko from the Third Directorate,
which dealt with covert operations. Orchenko was more astonished at the boldness of the plan than Khrushchev had been, but
he undertook the assignment to prepare an operational outline,
delivered thirty days later.

Silent Wind Operational Plans
(Top Secret)

1. Five teams of trained KGB agents (one
   in reserve) will be selected to
   covertly place small, tactical nuclear
   weapons in close proximity to U.S.
   installations known to house nuclear
   weapons.

2. Four tactical nuclear devices, in the
   25 kiloton range will be placed near
   U.S. military installations. Targets:
   Japan, England, Spain, and U.S.A.
   (U.S. base to be decided.)

3. The U.S.S.R. will create incidents
   that will cause the U.S. to place
   their military on higher alert,
   requiring them to bring their weapons
   delivery systems to a ready state.

4. During the alert, Soviet agents will
   recover the hidden nuclear weapon in
   the selected country and detonate near
   the U.S. base.

5. Soviet and world media will portray
   the incident as representative of the
   lack of control exerted by the U.S.

over their nuclear safety program, and
pressure will be placed on the U.S. to
remove weapons from all bases.

6. The target country will be selected by
the Committee as political concerns
dictate.

Kennedy's assassination, occurring in the midst of their operation, did not change their resolve. In fact, once the cowboy from
Texas became president, they went forward with even more determination. Had their plans become public knowledge, the Soviet
Union might have been brought down thirty years earlier. As it
was, in October 1964 only Khrushchev and his immediate cronies
came down as a result of the Cuban fiasco, but not before "Silent
Wind" had been conceptualized, planned, and implemented.

Somewhere in South Vietnam
September 1966

Three minutes after the 405th Search and Rescue Squadron
received the alert at 0415 hours, 1st Lt. John Stanicich was in the
cockpit of the helo, designation Fox One, determining coordinates. Chief Warrant Officer (CWO) Jason "Tex" Miller, copilot,
advised Lieutenant Stanicich that their door gunner, Staff
Sergeant Lopez, was down with hepatitis. Just as they were about
to advise flight control to get a replacement ASAP, Spec5 Clinton
Michael O'Brien, avionics maintenance technician, jumped
aboard, requesting permission to fill in for Lopez. Although not
designated flight crew, O'Brien had taken every opportunity to
accompany rescue missions and had participated in several successful efforts. Stanicich grunted his approval for O'Brien to fill
in and notified flight control that Fox One was prepared for departure.

O'Brien had been in the U.S. Army only six years. Born and
brought up in New Zealand, he had married a young American
woman he had met while she was on holiday in New Zealand.
They had moved to the States, where O'Brien entered the military to take advantage of its university program. Little had he
imagined then that he would be fighting in an Asian war in the

service of his adopted country. O'Brien had two sons and three daughters, and he was looking forward to seeing them again when his tour was up. Due to rotate to the States in about forty-five days, he was ready to return to "the world." Prior to arrival in Vietnam, O'Brien had managed to obtain over one hundred hours bootleg instruction on the UH-1B Iroquois and intended to apply for army warrant officer flight training; that is, should the good Lord allow him to survive this hot hole.

Five minutes out Lieutenant Stanicich called for O'Brien to check guns and keep his eyes open. He made contact with a flight of Air Force F-4s assigned to cover the rescue effort. Their arrival was anticipated in about thirty-five minutes. Direct contact had not been made with the downed pilot, call sign Beaver Four, and Stanicich's flight of two helos would be the first on the scene.

As Fox One arrived in the projected area of the downed pilot, they noticed ground activity and made a few passes to determine size and disposition of the troops, drawing sporadic fire in the process. They were unable to make contact, and ninety minutes later they advised the F-4 cover flight of their departure for refueling.

Once back at the 405th, they refueled, discussed with Fox Two a new grid search pattern, and prepared to return. O'Brien knew that darkness would quickly follow this next mission, and with it the chances for a successful recovery were reduced significantly.

Thirty-odd minutes later, they reached the new search area and began sweeping the grid. On the third pass, the radio crackled, "Rescue, Rescue, I say again, this is Beaver Four, over." The voice was desperate.

"Beaver Four, this is Fox One," Lieutenant Stanicich replied. "We hear ya, buddy. Give us a fix!"

The relief the downed pilot felt was enormous. Since punching out of his aircraft, he had felt his chances of rescue were minimal unless he could make contact quickly. An inner voice kept telling him his time had not yet come, although with a broken leg and a pain level that indicated several cracked or broken ribs, he had to admit that his prospects looked grim. He knew the NVA were in the area, but as yet they had not located his hiding place. His F-4E Phantom had gone down miles away, and he felt certain no one would have seen his ejection the previous night. In spite of hearing helicopters earlier that morning, he had not been able to make contact with the rescue team and had resolved to save his locator beacon and radio until he knew for certain rescue teams were close at hand.

––––––––––––

"Fox One, thank God. I hear you approaching from the east but haven't spotted you yet. I'm on the east side of a small knoll, two clicks south of the three tall peaks. There's a small clearing about three hundred yards east at the base of the knoll. Leg's crippled, unable to make it to the clearing, over."

"Roger that, Beaver Four. We've got the peak in sight. We'll keep approaching from the east. Advise when you spot us. Hang in there, Beaver Four—we'll have you home in time for dinner."

Lieutenant Stanicich turned slightly and called out, "O'Brien, look sharp back there and watch for Charlie. Let me know if you see anything. Looks like you're gonna have to go get him."

"Roger, L.T.," O'Brien replied. This wasn't the first time O'Brien had gone into the bush to bring out a wounded crew member. It had instilled in him an appreciation of the fear the downed airman always felt. It also provided exhilarating euphoria when successfully achieved, when all were safely away.

"Fox Two, this is Fox One. We're going down for a closer look. Fly cover. LZ looks clean, but watch the tree line to the south."

"Roger, Fox One. Take it easy."

CWO Miller first spotted the clearing seconds before the downed pilot came over the radio again: "Got you in sight, Fox One. Ground seems clear from my end. Can you come and get me? Over."

"Roger, Beaver Four, we're heading in for a look-see. One sweep around and we'll touch down."

Fox One proceeded to traverse the area, and O'Brien spotted no activity on the ground. They all knew the dangers at this point. When Charlie spotted a downed airman, he would often set up an ambush, just waiting for the search-and-rescue helos. That way, he had a chance to get the entire crew as well as the downed airman. It had worked successfully on many occasions. If Charlie had Beaver Four's general location, he would use the airman as bait. The Fox One crew knew the risks, but that was the purpose of their mission.

"Fox Two, we're going in. Continue your cover and advise movement." Turning to his copilot, Stanicich said, "Miller, when we touch down, get back and man O'Brien's weapon. OK, O'Brien, get your running shoes on and get this guy. We've got about forty minutes of daylight."

"Can do, Lieutenant," O'Brien replied.

The stationary hover is the most difficult maneuver for helicopters, and Lieutenant Stanicich wanted to avoid holding in place for any length of time. Fox One was about fifteen feet off the ground when Charlie opened fire. Small-arms fire began coming from southeast of the clearing and immediately struck the helicopter. O'Brien began to return fire, and Stanicich tried to lift off. One round caught Stanicich in the left temple, killing him instantly. CWO Miller never had time to regain control, and they went straight in from about eighteen feet, landing with a jolt. Miller tried to recover control of the still-functioning aircraft to lift off, but he caught two rounds in the chest. O'Brien continued to return fire, while Fox Two, flying cover overhead and visually aware of the situation, also began to return fire at Charlie's location.

As soon as O'Brien saw there was a problem with Stanicich and Miller, he grabbed the medical pack he was going to take to the downed airman and went forward to assess the damage in the cockpit. He quickly ascertained that Stanicich was beyond help and turned his attention to Miller. Miller was still conscious, gasping for breath, and O'Brien adjusted the man's position and applied some compresses.

"Can you hold on while I get Beaver Four?" O'Brien asked Miller. He nodded, and O'Brien grabbed his M-16 and bolted from the aircraft, making for the tree line to the west. Fox Two gave covering fire, and shortly the ground fire from Charlie's position ceased.

O'Brien reached the tree line and almost immediately spotted the pilot against the base of a tree, holding a pistol ready. His flight suit was shredded, and O'Brien could see the compound fracture of his left leg, with bone protruding. The airman had wrapped a tourniquet above the injury to restrict bleeding, but he was obviously going nowhere. For that matter, O'Brien decided, neither was he. Miller was in no condition to fly them out, and for the first time O'Brien realized that he was the party needing rescue.

O'Brien keyed his portable unit. "Fox Two, this is Fox One on the ground. Stanicich is dead, and Miller's critically hit. I'm in the trees west of the clearing. I've located Beaver Four, over."

"Roger, Fox One, we seem to have cleaned out Charlie. If we wait for backup, you're going to be here overnight. Can you get Beaver Four to the clearing?"

"Fox Two, roger that. Can you pick up?"

"Get on your horse, O'Brien, we're coming in."

O'Brien assessed the wounded man's condition and tried to reassure him. "I'm going to lift you and make for the clearing. If we take any fire, return it as best you can with your pistol." O'Brien lifted the man onto his shoulders in the fireman's carry, one arm between the injured man's legs, holding the man's wrist in front of him. O'Brien had always tried to keep in shape, and the pilot wasn't a large man, but a two-hundred-yard run carrying a full grown man was difficult under any conditions.

O'Brien paused at the tree line, but he could observe no movement from the surrounding area. Fox Two began their descent to land between Fox One and the two men's position at the tree line. O'Brien started his run.

The NVA Captain had planned it well, placing his troops on

both sides of the clearing and holding fire from the second group to avoid retaliation during the first effort. Fox Two was about thirty feet off the ground when Charlie opened up from the north side of the clearing.

Several rounds immediately killed the engine, and Fox Two met the same fate as Fox One, though crashing much harder to the ground. The copilot of Fox Two was killed on impact, and the door gunner was hit several times in the lower abdomen, but not before he had placed accurate fire into Charlie's position, killing the automatic weapons crew.

O'Brien was caught between the trees and Fox Two, with Fox One about sixty yards away. He saw the pilot trying to lift the gunner out of the aircraft, which was beginning to burn. O'Brien raced past Fox Two, shouting for them to get out and make for his aircraft, whose rotor was still turning. It was their only hope for the moment.

About forty yards short of Fox One O'Brien felt the impact of bullets striking his legs, and he went down instantly, bringing a scream of pain from the downed airman. Almost simultaneously, Fox Two exploded in flame, seconds after the pilot extracted the gunner. O'Brien began to crawl toward Fox One, dragging the injured airman with him. He reached the aircraft and hefted the man into the rear, placing him up against the aft bulkhead. O'Brien limped forward to see how Miller was but discovered him lifeless. The helicopter engines were still running, and the rotor was still turning.

Enemy automatic weapons fire had nearly ceased as a result of Fox Two's gunner, but small-arms fire continued to impact the fuselage. O'Brien knew that if they didn't get off soon, they would be guests of Charlie for a long time—if they weren't killed outright. O'Brien went to the side door to check the progress of the crew from Fox Two and spied them lying on the ground about twenty yards out. He climbed out of the helicopter and half-crawled, half-scrambled in their direction, returning fire with his M-16 as he went.

When O'Brien reached the crew, Charlie began to increase fire, hitting the gunner in the back of the head, killing him instantly, and wounding the pilot in the chest and right shoulder. O'Brien took another hit, with the round passing cleanly through his side, entering from the rear and passing out the right side of his waist.

O'Brien staggered to his knees and dragged the pilot back to Fox One, lifting him inside. There, he told O'Brien that his co-pilot had been killed on impact. O'Brien went forward and removed Stanicich's body from the pilot's seat, climbed in, and hoped his bootleg flight lessons would serve him well. It was their only chance, and O'Brien knew well the consequences of failure.

He increased power to the cyclic, and when he cleared ground effect, he lowered the nose and applied forward thrust. Clearing the trees, he could hear additional rounds hit the helicopter. Several seconds later, the gunfire ceased—they were beyond Charlie's visual range. O'Brien felt unsteady from loss of blood and concentrated on retaining consciousness. He tried to contact Fox Control, but the radio was nonresponsive.

He headed for home, praying that the aircraft had the ability to keep them aloft for the thirty-minute flight. In sight of the field, O'Brien began to get hazy and felt a loss of coordination. On instinct, he brought the UH-1B toward the field and put it down roughly, astride the runway, and finally lost consciousness. Field medical personnel took over from there.

Lt. Col. John Redding, downed pilot of a Phantom fighter, and 1st Lt. Mike Farley, helicopter pilot, would both go on to live long and prosperous lives, aware that but for the efforts of Spec5 Clinton Michael O'Brien, theirs would have been a different fate. Redding often found himself wondering if the lives of four men were worth his rescue, a question that many men had found it necessary to live with for the rest of their lives.

Washington, D.C.
The White House Rose Garden
April 1967

President Lyndon Johnson presented his usual down-home image as he congratulated 1st Lt. Clinton Michael O'Brien on his achievement. The war effort in Vietnam was becoming ever more unpopular, so President Johnson relished the opportunity to publicize the heroic efforts of the few who rose above and beyond the call of duty. Lieutenant O'Brien had achieved—*"with great distinction and concern for his fellow man, and with complete disregard to his personal safety"*—the nation's highest commendation. The president was determined to give the widest possible coverage of the award of the Congressional Medal of Honor to this newly commissioned army lieutenant, risen from the ranks to receive a battlefield commission.

Lieutenant O'Brien, for his part, remembered distinctly both the fear he had felt and his comrades still lying somewhere in Vietnam, whom he had been unable to rescue. The fact that they were already dead when he left them only softened his sorrow. They deserved to come home too.

Kathleen Heather O'Brien—Kate to her family—and her children stood proudly by Clinton O'Brien as the president of the United States and the nation Lieutenant O'Brien had chosen to serve honored his efforts. As proud as Kate was to be an American, she also knew that her husband was equally proud to be a Kiwi, a New Zealander. She wondered how he felt receiving his adopted nation's highest award, equivalent to the United Kingdom's Victoria Cross. But Kate knew her husband well, as did their boys. For him, courage and service to others had no political or geographical boundaries. Lt. O'Brien had simply exhibited the characteristics he had learned as a child growing up in New Zealand.

The oldest son, Zach, just turned ten, looked up at his father. His heart nearly burst within him. Zach had always looked upon his father as the model hero his mother had repeatedly taught him about from the scriptures. Doing what was required to the best of one's ability had been instilled in him by his father. To Zach, with his childlike faith, his father had entered the lion's den, vanquished the foe, and had emerged victorious. It was great to know that the president acknowledged his dad, but Zach had known all along what kind of man his father was. Zach had been taught by his parents that if one lived righteously, the Lord would reward him with the opportunity to serve others. That service would bring its own reward.

The men Clinton O'Brien had rescued—John Redding, lieutenant colonel, USAF, retired, and Mike Farley, first lieutenant, U.S. Army—would surely agree.

CHAPTER ONE

———————

South Pacific Ocean
Between Tonga and New Zealand
February, mid-1990s

TRIPLE DIAMOND SAILED GRACEFULLY through light swells and under clear skies. After a six-week interisland vacation, and now five days out of Tonga, Rossiter was confident he would sight land in the morning and reach Auckland by the following evening, wind conditions holding. The South Pacific was beautiful and generally peaceful at this time of year. *Triple Diamond* was a forty-two foot Farr design that had been built only eighteen months earlier in Auckland according to his personal specifications. She had the finest navigational equipment available, weather-sensitive radar, and all the necessary automated gear to support solo travel. After making separate trips with her to Australia, Fiji, and now Tonga, and after weathering several storms in the process, he was justifiably proud of her ability.

Cameron Sterling Rossiter was sailing alone and enjoying the solitude, which was about to end with his arrival in Auckland. Rossiter had lived his whole life in New Zealand, but in recent years, as he had begun to expand his business holdings, he had traveled widely and had seen a world beyond the peaceful shores of New Zealand. Had it not been for business demands, he would have preferred to remain living in New Zealand and sailing these translucent waters forever.

Born in Christchurch, New Zealand, he was several generations down the line from the original founders of this largest of the South Island communities. The original immigrant, Peter Rossiter, arrived with the famous "First Four Ships" in 1850. As with many in New Zealand, Cameron's nautical heritage came easily, but unlike many, he could afford his love of sailing. The long struggle of his father to acquire financial independence through a hard-earned network-marketing system had paid off by the time Cameron was a young man. New Zealand was a country of just over three million people, and consequently the unlimited market potential that existed in the United States, fostering many network-marketing schemes, did not provide similar opportunities in this nation of do-it-yourselfers. Cameron Rossiter recognized early on that only so many could reach success in what was essentially a financial pyramid, and only those who had entered on the ground floor as his father had would make the grade. His father's rise to "Triple Diamond" status was followed by Cameron's astute entry into the importation of computers and Japanese electronics.

Intending to deal internationally, Rossiter had continued his education, eventually earning an MBA from the University of Auckland. Shortly thereafter, he had served as a junior member of the committee that designed the consolidation of local government bodies and had come to the attention of Sir Geoffrey Holden, chairman. Sir Geoffrey had been impressed both by Rossiter's ability to sort through the mundane issues that obfuscated the overall objective and by his proven ability to recognize business opportunities. With some connections opened by Sir Geoffrey, Rossiter had quickly developed a nationwide chain of personal computer stores that catered to small business concerns and home-based computers.

While Rossiter had gained his business acumen from his father, he had gained his lifelong love of sailing and the sea from his mother, and vicariously from a grandfather he never met. Seven years before Rossiter was born, his grandfather, Phillip Nelson Sterling, had been killed at the helm while competing in the 1957 Fastnet, a yacht race held every year off the coast of England and Ireland. The sailors had experienced the most violent weather on record for this race. Rossiter's grandfather had been the consummate Kiwi yachtsman, commodore of the Royal Canterbury Yacht Club, round-the-world crew member, and twice winner of the Sydney-to-Hobart yacht race. Grandfather Sterling had never achieved the financial status enjoyed by his grandson, but the legacy he left provided worthy goals for his descendants, which Cameron Rossiter knew could not be met by acquisition of wealth alone.

At sea Rossiter felt he could understand his grandfather's legacy, and Cameron's ambition was to equal his grandfather's yachting stature. His ultimate goal was larger, however, and should his fortune grow sufficiently to support such an endeavor, he wanted to have a go at the Yanks to bring home the America's Cup. Sailing alone over the past several weeks, Rossiter had been able to contemplate his life and the direction it was taking. At twenty-nine and single, he had much to look forward to. But his arrival in Auckland tomorrow would end the peaceful solitude that Rossiter found only at sea. He would again be "corporate," and although he knew his seafaring life would be limited without the financial support of his corporate endeavors, he longed for a way to eliminate the one and give life to the other.

Persian Gulf
USS **Enterprise**
February

Lieutenant Savini enjoyed the catapult launch the way some people enjoy Space Mountain at Disneyland. The F-14 Tomcat literally jumped out of its resting position, and then it was all go. From the first time he had seen the old movies about early naval aviation, he had wanted to fly off the deck of a carrier, and when he had earned his naval aviator wings, his dream had come true. Lieutenant Vincento Savini, or Vinny, had been a naval aviator for all of eighteen months. He was the first pilot in a family three generations removed from Italy, a family who was probably proud of him, though he might never know, for his father had kicked him out for joining the navy, disappointed that his son had thrown away a career in law. Nevertheless, flying provided everything Vinny wanted in life, and in return he gave his full effort to the job.

Though part of the original deployment for Desert Shield, the international military response to the Iraqi invasion of Kuwait, Vinny was the newest member of his squadron. Quick with a quip, Vinny had been called a wise guy on his very first day. Vinny immediately adopted the personal call sign "Wiseguy," in much the same way police departments twenty years earlier had adopted the term PIG, which hippies used to refer to police, and had made it their motto, "Pride, Integrity, Guts." "Wiseguy" suited Vinny, and no one used it derogatorily, at least not twice. Forty-eight hours after Desert Shield became Desert Storm, Vinny had become the first in his squadron to claim a Mig-26 in aerial combat.

Now, nearly a year after the war had ended, he was still flying as wingman to Commander Nelson on routine observation patrols, primarily designed to keep the Iraqi leader, Abdul Salimar, honest. Small incidents had occurred over recent months, but no aircraft had come up to challenge U.S. air superiority. Today's mission would take the fighters along the northern "no fly zone," where trouble with the Kurds kept the Iraqis involved. Previous flights had occasionally spotted helicopters but had taken no action other than to report the observations.

"Should be a milk run again, Vinny," Commander Nelson called over the radio.

"Right, Skipper. The last thing I ever wanted to be was a farmer," replied Vinny.

"Roger that." Commander Nelson changed frequencies and called the *Enterprise* flight control center. "Dugout, this is Shortstop. How do you read?"

"Shortstop, this is Dugout. We read you five by five."

"Dugout, Roger. On track and beginning run. Anything from Skylight?"

"Negative, Shortstop. All clear."

Skylight was an AWACS E-3A Sentry overhead that kept track of all aerial movement in the sector. It had replaced the World War II version of the combat information center, which had received information from ground spotters. Skylight could keep track of multiple aircraft over several hundred square miles and could vector friendlies toward enemy activity.

Shortstop, a two-plane flight of F-14s, flew across northern Iraq nearly to Syria and turned back to retrace the northern "no fly zone." It spotted little activity other than quick emissions from ground radar stations occasionally firing up their radar systems to harass the flights. Tracking by ground radar and "locking on" was not permitted under the surrender conditions, and on several occasions ground stations had come under attack as a result. The minor harassment was just one part of Salimar's attempt to divert attention from the United Nations inspectors still in Iraq looking for nuclear or biological capability and other war materials.

Commander Nelson advised Dugout of their course reversal and began the home leg. Almost simultaneously, they came under radar observation from two ground locations.

"Skipper, we're being probed from both north and south. Fairly steady transmission."

"Roger, Vinny. I've got it." Still on frequency for the *Enterprise,* Nelson transmitted, "Dugout, be advised, we have two ground installations emitting radar tracking. No action noted."

The *Enterprise* responded, "Shortstop, this is Dugout, we copy. Maintain course and keep us advised."

A new voice came on the air with a sense of urgency: "Shortstop, Shortstop, this is Skylight. We show two, repeat, two SAMs launched. Advise evasive action immediately."

"Roger, Skylight. Vinny, split formation and watch your screen."

"I've got 'em, Skipper." Moving right and up, Lieutenant

Savini watched his screen as the upcoming missiles searched for their target, attempting to lock onto the heat trails and emitting a radar pattern guided by the ground station. Voice rising in emotion, Vinny reported, "They've tagged me, Skipper. One of 'em's locked on. Taking evasive action . . . still got me, can't shake it." Lieutenant Savini jinked the Tomcat all over the sky, but the SAM continued its closing battle until it flew right up the tailpipe of the Tomcat.

"Punch out, Vinny, punch out!" Commander Nelson cried.

Wellington, New Zealand
The Beehive
February

The New Zealand prime minister was not known for his punctuality. Sir Geoffrey Holden waited patiently in the outer office, not quite sure why the prime minister had invited him to the capitol, affectionately known as the Beehive. Since the election, no one really knew for sure what to expect. For the first time, two independent parties had prevented National or Labour from winning a clear majority of seats. The new prime minister had once belonged to one of the established parties, but he had spoken out of turn once too often. The party hadn't counted on his popularity with the public. Now the lack of a simple majority found New Zealand requiring a coalition government. Other countries had dealt with such a division of policy, but New Zealand was going to have to feel its way through this one.

Sir Geoffrey was no stranger to government service. He was quite proud of New Zealand's political heritage, starting with being the first nation in the world to extend the vote to women in 1893. He had actually worked his way up the establishment through local and regional council bodies. He had chaired the government restructure committee formed when New Zealand had mustered the courage to consolidate many local autonomous bodies into the current, more manageable shape of local government. Moans and groans had accompanied the process, but the loudest of the voices had come from those elected officials who faced the prospect of losing their seats.

Sir Geoffrey was also instrumental in the development of New Zealand's nonnuclear policy, the side effect of which was to anger the ANZUS participants and to cause the Americans to pull back on economic development. However, New Zealand had seen no drastic economic liabilities since the American policy was only given lip service by those international corporations for whom New Zealand was a burgeoning market. As the government moved to privatize government functions, including, to everyone's surprise, the postal and communications services, plenty of international companies were standing in the wings to buy into a newly developing and potentially lucrative market.

Several years before, the former prime minister had met with President Bush and begun the process of reestablishing ties with the United States. However, President Bush had not seemed inclined to compromise to any great extent. For all of its beauty and charm, New Zealand had not played a major role in world affairs, a condition Sir Geoffrey desired to correct. As he often stated, "Consolidation of purpose can achieve what narrow-minded people have overlooked." At least that was the phrase that usually accompanied one of his luncheon speeches.

Perhaps Sir Geoffrey's greatest achievement had come late in his career. As a successful barrister in Auckland, Sir Geoffrey had often resolved his cases through negotiation and persuasion, facilitating an out-of-court settlement. He had developed the idea that New Zealand, like Switzerland, was ideally positioned philosophically to function as an international conflict arbitrator. He had cofounded the Organization for International Conflict Resolution, OICR, and had begun to achieve success in helping to resolve disputes. Initially they had been multinational corporate disagreements, but as of late, diplomats from other nations had called on OICR for assistance, hoping to avoid having to put their case before the World Court in The Hague. Establishing New Zealand's position as an international arbiter was Sir Geoffrey's crowning ambition, and through his efforts, OICR had gained momentum, and he could see his plans coming to fruition.

Prime Minister Peter Onekawa entered the room amid a flurry of reporters, who enjoyed a much closer access to their government officials than did the media of many other democratic countries. "A direct access to the public" was the way one government official had put it. Onekawa saw Sir Geoffrey and turned to address the reporters, nodding privately to his secretary to show Sir Geoffrey into his inner office before the press could include him in their questions. What he didn't need right now was speculation on why Sir Geoffrey was coming to see the prime minister.

In his usual jocular manner, Onekawa bandied questions and moved to wrap up the reporters' never-ending inquiries. He left with a wave of the hand and a laughing comment about "we'll have to see what the people want," which had become his basic response instead of "I'm not sure what I'm going to do yet."

Once in the office, Onekawa said, "Sir Geoffrey, good of you to come so soon after the school holidays. How are Mildred and the children?"

"They're fine, Prime Minister. It's good of you to ask. School holidays seem more important to my grandchildren now than they did to either Mildred and me or our children. We took a week for ourselves, just the two of us, and spent some time up in the Bay of Islands. Such a peaceful place, don't you think?"

Sir Geoffrey knew that Onekawa's boyhood home had been in the Bay of Islands and his Maori lineage had come from the top of the North Island. Some of Onekawa's ancestors had been involved in the original treaty negotiations with the British and the signing of the Treaty of Waitangi.

"Mildred requested that I bring back a report on this new carpet we've been hearing about," Sir Geoffrey commented. "It seems the press has limited your honeymoon to the shortest on record. Once again, they've gone straight for the issues vital to the nation: new carpets, furniture, and fixtures. Of course there's plenty of time to address unemployment, inflation, and the world price for wool, right, Prime Minister?" Sir Geoffrey had a public posture of serious contemplation, but within the company of his peers, he demonstrated a sharp wit, generally used to relax the situation rather than attack or insult.

Onekawa laughed, but he knew the accuracy of the comment,

however glib. Fully a third of his time was spent fending off questions and comments relevant to no pressing national or economic issue. That was politics, and he had become a master at the mundane response, a politician's stock in trade, as it were.

"Please, be seated, Geoff. I know your schedule is tight, and I appreciate your coming on such short notice," said Onekawa. "I'll get right to the point. New Zealand is going to receive a seat on the Security Council this year. As you know, since the breakup of the Soviet Union, the veto power of permanent members of the council plays less of a role than in past deliberations. New Zealand can contribute to the world forum somewhat more independently than during the days when we were required to follow the party line."

Onekawa watched Sir Geoffrey Holden for response, not sure if Holden had accurately guessed why he had been invited to the Beehive. Sir Geoffrey gave no indication of surprise, or for that matter agreement. Onekawa continued, "I'm sure you can appreciate that we need someone with your experience. We'd like you to fill that seat. How do you think Mildred would like living in New York?"

Sir Geoffrey had not risen to prominence by accident. He thoroughly understood the world of politics. "Seldom do the purposes for decisions conform with the reasons presented" was another of his oft-quoted sayings. Where logic would dictate one course of action if the reasons presented were valid, another course of action would perhaps be necessary if the actual grounds for action were known. Sir Geoffrey had learned to handle that dichotomy best by searching for the facts and determining his own reasons for action. In this case, he already knew several pros and cons that this ambassadorship would entail.

First, his career was coming to a close. A crowning achievement was possible, albeit at risk with the potential failure of government-sponsored actions in the world body. New Zealand seldom had taken the initiative to propose significant actions to the General Assembly, but during the period while they were to serve on the Security Council, they could. A position on the council added considerable stature to their presence, and governments

were known to reach beyond their capacity in such circumstances.

Second, the United Nations was being called upon more and
more often to provide policemen for the vast array of "neighborhood fights" that had developed around the world. With the
stature of Security Council member, New Zealand might well be
called upon to provide troops in foreign locations beyond those
medical personnel who had served with distinction in Desert
Storm. The ambassador would be called upon to take a position
with regard to such requests, and he could well find himself at
odds with his government. He did not want to conclude his career
by resigning his ambassadorship in opposition to government policy.

Third, this appointment offered the opportunity for Sir
Geoffrey to find the means to mend the ANZUS fence. He knew
that military alliances were far more important globally than the
mutual protection they ostensibly provided. He had felt for some
time that with the demise of major world tensions and the reduction, if not complete elimination of a communist military threat,
the United States was in an excellent position to concede to
smaller nations on issues that had become less important to the
survival of America.

Sir Geoffrey knew, as all Western governments had known
for over half a century, that the United States would not let a truly
democratic country fall to the threat of communism. Certainly
they had broken faith with Asian allies in the past, but those
nations had never been democracies in the first place, and they
had been supported primarily as a result of their anticommunist
stance. When that stance waned, so did American resolve to stand
by them and shed young American blood in the process.

New Zealand and other Western allies had been able to politically posture regarding their sovereign right to exclude nuclear
weapons and oppose other policies of the major powers, but
everyone knew that if push came to shove, all would coalesce into
a unified body against the foe. After all, when the U.S. Marines
had landed in Wellington in 1942, had anyone been on the docks
to ask, "How big are the bombs on your ships?"

And finally fourth, he wanted to develop the cause of his Organization for International Conflict Resolution. What better forum than the United Nations?

No, Sir Geoffrey Holden did not at present know what Prime Minister Onekawa had used as his true criteria for the selection of a new ambassador, but he knew he would accept. There was yet, however, the terms of appointment to negotiate and some measure of autonomy to be achieved. For that to be accomplished, he would have to show a degree of reluctance. He could guess the end result, however, and he was pleased with the prospects.

CHAPTER TWO

Dublin, Ireland
February

ZACH O'BRIEN CROSSED THE ROAD in front of the U.S. Embassy toward the New Jury's Hotel, anxious to meet his wife for dinner. As he stepped off the curb, a black Mercedes pulled up sharply, startling him and causing him to jump back. The back door opened, and a large, red-faced man quickly got out. "Care for a lift now, O'Brien?" he asked in a rural Irish accent.

Caught somewhat unawares, O'Brien hesitated momentarily before deciding not to dash toward the embassy or the hotel. If they had meant to harm him, they would have already done so. "Do I have a choice?" he asked rhetorically. The red-faced man smiled and gestured toward the rear door. As O'Brien slipped into the back seat, another man on the far side slid over, making room for O'Brien in the middle, and just as quickly, the red-faced man climbed back in, and the car sped away. O'Brien flinched when the second man pulled out a blindfold.

"Just a precaution, mind you," the man said. "We can't have you telling the Guarda where to pay us a visit, now, can we?"

"My wife is waiting in—"

"She'll be told," the red-faced man said. "Not to worry. We're just after having a little chat about you, O'Brien, and we thought you could add to the banter. You're a popular lad." O'Brien rode the rest of the way in silence.

———————

The dining room in the New Jury's Hotel, Ballsbridge, was ornate. Zach's wife, Alison, and his three children were waiting to have dinner to celebrate the conclusion of a great two-week holiday in Ireland. The previous fall, O'Brien had been on assignment in Dublin when the hotel ballroom had been the scene of the annual United States Marine Corps birthday celebration, hosted by the Marine security detachment from the embassy just across the street. During that visit he had decided to bring his family here on vacation.

"Mrs. O'Brien?" the well-dressed man queried.

"Yes?" she responded, concern rising.

"Please pardon the intrusion. Major O'Brien has been unexpectedly called to an urgent meeting, and he has asked that you be informed. He suggested you go ahead and order dinner without him, but please, not to worry. He'll be only an hour or so, and then he will join you. May I be of any assistance?"

Alison was pleased that it wasn't notification of an accident or problem, as she had first thought. "No, thank you very much. We'll be fine. Thank you for informing us."

"My pleasure, Mrs. O'Brien. And a good day to you." He left, nodding slightly to make eye contact with the brunette sitting in the hotel lobby. Alison entered the restaurant with her children, and the brunette stayed in the lobby throughout the evening, unobserved.

———————

Twenty minutes into the countryside, Zach O'Brien allowed his thoughts to drift to his original Irish connections. Often he had wondered what he would be doing if his ancestors had not immigrated to America and New Zealand. The great potato migration had sent Irish all over the world. O'Brien's father, Clinton Michael O'Brien, a retired American army colonel, had been born in New Zealand of Irish stock, and as a result Zach O'Brien, born in the U.S., held dual citizenship in both New Zealand and the United States. He was proud of his Irish and New Zealand heritage.

As a young girl, O'Brien's mother, Kate, had lived in Ireland when her father, Thomas Flynn, had been assigned to the American embassy staff. Grandfather Flynn, during his time in Ireland, had compiled the family genealogy and left his children and grandchildren with a good knowledge of who they were and where they had originally resided. As Zach O'Brien and his children walked these lands, he had felt a sense of pride in his heritage and the sacrifices his family had made. Now after two weeks of visiting their ancestral homeland, he was pleased that his children now had firsthand knowledge of their ancestors.

O'Brien's great-grandfather had been Catholic, as were most Irish, but his great-grandmother was Protestant. His maternal grandfather, Thomas Flynn, however, had made one major departure from the basic Irish traditions. As a young man in Texas, he had left his Catholic origins and embraced the Mormon faith. Investigating religion as a young man, he had felt something call him to a different path, and he had found a fulfilling spirituality within The Church of Jesus Christ of Latter-day Saints. The result had extended four generations to O'Brien's children.

As a young man, Zachariah O'Brien had been brought up with the premise that to serve others was the highest goal one could achieve. As he matured, Major O'Brien had come to an understanding that religion served no purpose if it was theoretical, or merely "Bible thumping." To be practical, religion had to be applied in one's life and in the service of others. Such had been the case nearly twenty-five years earlier when O'Brien's father, as a new lieutenant, had received the Congressional Medal of Honor from President Lyndon Johnson.

"Here we are now," the red-faced man announced. Helped

out of the car, O'Brien was led inside a building, and once the door was closed, the blindfold was removed. Although the room was fairly dark, O'Brien blinked a few times before his eyes adjusted to the dim light. He quickly recognized one of the men seated at the table. Two men sat on either side of the room, and the two from the car stood to the rear.

"So you *have* had access to my dossier?" the man at the table queried. O'Brien didn't respond. "Come now, O'Brien, you recognized me right off. Let's not be coy. Neither of us has much time this evening, and we don't want to keep your wife waiting, do we?"

"I know who you are, Donahue, if that's what you're asking," O'Brien allowed. Kevin Donahue was a brigade commander in the Provisional Wing of the Irish Republican Army, better known as the Provos, and O'Brien had read his file before coming to Ireland.

"Now we're getting somewhere. I hope Fergus was courteous with his invitation," he said, referring to the red-faced man who had met O'Brien outside the embassy.

"No complaints," O'Brien replied.

"Good. Very good. We couldn't have anything happening to our American tourists, now, could we? Think of the economy."

"Not to mention the contributions from the Boston faithful," O'Brien added. Donahue just smiled.

"I understand you've been putting out feelers for a face-to-face, Major O'Brien. Please accept my apologies for the tardy reception, but my duties have kept me somewhat busy. How can we be of assistance?"

"It's more likely we can be of assistance to you. It's our understanding your link to Libyan arms has dried up."

Donahue's eyebrows moved slightly. "Not sure what you mean."

"Your November shipment fell into the wrong hands. Perhaps you weren't aware of who the eventual recipient was." Without seeing any response from Donahue, O'Brien continued, "Seems a South American group has had a recent increase in supplies, courtesy of your Tunisian contact. Hope you hadn't already paid for those weapons."

"Is that the message, Major?" Donahue asked curtly, obviously beginning to get agitated.

"Plus a request. As he is of no use to you, other than perhaps an object lesson to others who might consider double deals, we'd like to have a stab at locating him. Any ideas?"

Donahue thought for a moment before responding. "What's in it for us?"

"A chance to rid the world of a bad person," O'Brien jested. Donahue just smiled, regaining control of his anger. "And perhaps," O'Brien continued, "unimpeded access to the Boston faithful."

"Surely you don't think we still get substantial funds from those pub crawlers in Boston, do you?"

O'Brien also smiled. "Not in dollars, but in public esteem their link is invaluable. They still think you're heroes, and they let the rest of America know it."

Donahue looked at his watch before responding. "We'll be in touch, O'Brien. Better get you back to the Mrs. before she panics and calls the embassy." Donahue rose and came around the table. "Too bad you've crossed over. We could use a good inside man, faithful to the old sod, of course."

Again O'Brien smiled. "But I am, Donahue, I am. It just depends on one's point of view, doesn't it?"

Turning toward the red-faced man, Donahue put his arm around O'Brien. "Take good care of our man, Fergus, and see that he arrives in time for dessert with his wife." Looking into O'Brien's eyes, Donahue took his measure. "We'll meet again, O'Brien. And I'll consider your request."

On the drive back, once again blindfolded, O'Brien reflected on how the American Irish viewed the IRA and their fight with Britain for independence. Americans had a soft spot for almost anyone claiming to seek independence, and the IRA had held a favorite spot with many for a long time. But heroes they were not, thought O'Brien. As he again began to hear city traffic, he flashed on his mother's early teachings about heroes.

Kate O'Brien felt it necessary for her sons to have ideals, and ideals were best expressed by real people. If the public media and their exposé mentality would not allow her to stand the examples up before her sons for fear that their faith would be shattered by the hero's ultimate, and perhaps undeserved, demise, she would use heroes from the past and from the scriptures who were safe from discredit. Such heroes could safely be emulated.

As a lad, O'Brien's favorite story involved young war heroes. In the Book of Mormon, the story was told of several generations of warriors who, after God had supported their victory, covenanted with him to fight no more. But as is often the case, the bad guys came again a generation later, and the fathers were unwilling to break their oath, even to defend their families. The sons came forth to pick up the banner and preserve their liberty.

They were called the "stripling warriors" and came to be known as the "Sons of Helaman," after the general who led them. Two thousand young men followed Helaman into battle, and not one was lost. Kate explained to young Zach that their faith had preserved them, and while the righteous were often called upon to sacrifice their lives in the cause of good, on this occasion, the Lord protected those young men. As a boy, Zach embraced this belief with all his heart, and episodes like his father's rescue of two wounded men only served to reinforce that belief.

Zach had felt the need to follow in his father's footsteps, so after returning from two years of missionary service in Japan, Zach O'Brien entered a service academy. As the son of a Medal of Honor recipient, he was entitled to appointment to any of the academies. Zach had found himself torn between the United States Military Academy at West Point, in honor of his father's service to the army, and his personal desire to attend the Air Force Academy at Colorado Springs, Colorado.

Counseling with his father, Zach chose the Air Force Academy. He graduated in the top 5 percent of his class of 1982 and was accepted for flight training, eventually becoming a qualified F-15 fighter pilot. After several assignments, by 1988 Captain O'Brien found himself working in Washington, D.C., for Lt. General William Austin, deputy director, Intelligence,

National Security Agency. Over the following four years, O'Brien learned a great deal about the international intelligence business. He didn't think of himself as a hero, but he did take seriously his responsibility for serving others and taking part in the war to stop terrorism.

Zach was jolted back to the present by the abrupt stop of the car and the removal of the blindfold. "Have a good evening, Major O'Brien," Fergus offered. "Not everyone who makes these rides gets a chance to have dinner afterwards, you know."

O'Brien made no comment as he departed the vehicle, which quickly sped off. Zach entered the hotel, not noticing the brunette sitting in the lobby. He made his way into the restaurant, spotting his family at a table in the far corner. Alison saw him first, smiling broadly at his approach. "Zach, I wasn't sure whether to call someone or what."

"It's OK, sweetheart. Just someone wanting to say good-bye, Irish-style."

"Well, you're back now," she said, taking his hand. "Why don't you try the lamb? It's very good."

London, England
Strategic Security Group, Ltd.
February

Years of planning, in fact over thirty if truth be known, had gone into the preparation of this operation. If the original planners had been present, they would have agreed completely with the intended use of their elaborately designed operation, for if successful, it would achieve the exact objectives the originators had intended so many years earlier. Perhaps that alone said something about the nature of world politics and the continuity of purpose.

Gregory Farnsworth-Jones, born to Randolph Farnsworth-Jones and Pamela Leicester, was the chief executive officer of Strategic Security Group. SSG was an international consulting and management firm dedicated to solving the security problems of multinational corporations and designing the systems necessary to assure confidentiality of corporate information and the personal safety of senior executives. At least that's what the corporate prospectus said. SSG went far beyond that mandate, as several African and South American dictators could attest. SSG had for years functioned as a highly technical "soldier-of-fortune" and provided the assets countries needed to achieve their objectives, provided of course, the price was right.

Randolph Farnsworth-Jones and his wife, Pamela, had died in an automobile accident many years previously. Once again, if truth be known, three-year-old Gregory Farnsworth-Jones had also died in that tragic accident. Some twenty-two years later, Gregory Farnsworth-Jones had been reborn. Farnsworth-Jones reflected on how this had all come about and pondered the end result. For over twenty-five years he had lived under the identity he now found comfortable. His rebirth, however, had not erased the memory of his first life. Born Gregorio Valasnikov in Leningrad, Union of Soviet Socialist Republics, the son of a minor diplomat, he had been reared abroad wherever his father had been assigned, spending most of his middle years in England and obtaining most of his education in British public schools.

At nineteen, his father had been recalled to the Soviet Union to assume a new post, and Gregorio had enrolled in the Moscow Polytechnic Institute, taking a degree in theoretical physics, followed by graduate study in nuclear physics. He accepted a commission in the army, which assigned him to the war plans section, general staff, where he came under the watchful eye of Marshal Orchenko.

In 1963 at age twenty-six, Captain Valasnikov became the junior member of Marshal Orchenko's staff, assigned to a small and highly confidential committee formed by Premier Khrushchev. Within eight months their plans, designated "Silent Wind," had been implemented, and Gregorio had been placed in London under deep cover, assuming the identity of Farnsworth-Jones. He had been placed in charge of a consulting business that acted as his front, with funds secreted in Swiss accounts only he or Marshal Orchenko could access. The local Soviet embassy was not informed of his presence.

Of the original Silent Wind committee, only three members knew the total extent and overall scope of the plan, Khrushchev,

Marshal Orchenko, and Captain Valasnikov. Specially trained
KGB field teams in five separate groups, including Captain
Valasnikov, who commanded team four, were under the direct
and sole command of Marshal Orchenko. The KGB field teams
had each been told that five teams were training, but only one
would carry out the final mission. In fact, one team had been the
backup, and four teams carried out a similar mission, each in a
different part of the world, with each thinking the other four
teams had been backup. Three days after the completion of their
missions, all five teams and three members of the central planning committee were assembled and ordered to Moscow for
debriefing and reassignment. The plane carrying the teams
exploded in midair, killing all the KGB team members and the
three committee members, plus the crew, leaving only Captain
Valasnikov, who had, quite fortuitously, just missed the flight.

Marshal Orchenko died of a heart attack eight months later,
leaving Captain Valasnikov on his own, with no one aware of his
existence except Khrushchev, who elected to keep this knowledge
to himself. Valasnikov had reported directly to Marshal
Orchenko, and with the death of Khrushchev in 1971, only
Captain Valasnikov, now Gregory Farnsworth-Jones, knew the
legacy they had left the world. By 1992, Captain Valasnikov had
essentially been a sole operative for over twenty-five years, with
no one in the Soviet Union aware of his placement in London.
Over the past three years, as he agonized over the demise of the
Soviet Union, he had formulated a plan to resurrect Silent Wind
to bring about the change that, in his opinion, the world desper-
ately needed.

Next week he would meet with representatives of a Middle
Eastern country whose objectives closely matched those of
Farnsworth-Jones's former leaders. These men were every bit as
ruthless as Khrushchev in their purpose of humiliating the United
States. Implementation of the plan Farnsworth-Jones was about
to put to them would dramatically aid their cause and, in no small
measure, assure his financial well-being. Gregory Farnsworth-
Jones had in fact restructured a Silent Wind committee, and the
ghosts of the past were about to rise from the dead. The box they

would open contained considerably more than Pandora had ever dreamed!

Auckland, New Zealand
The Pulham News Hour, TV One
February

"Good evening, ladies and gentlemen. Tonight we have several stories for you, including a visit to Otago to talk with New Zealand's Olympic hopeful, Andrea Carlson, our best chance for a medal in the singles rowing event. Continuing on sports, we'll visit with a couple of the Going brothers, hopefully to discover what makes one family produce so many world-class athletes.

"But first, we'll visit with New Zealand's newly appointed ambassador to the United Nations, Sir Geoffrey Holden. Stay with us, and we'll be right back after these messages."

During the break, Jeff Pulham chatted with Sir Geoffrey, as much to ease the nervousness as to put Sir Geoffrey off guard. For several years Pulham had been doing his evening news-and-information program immediately following the six o'clock news. He sometimes made his political guests feel as if they were on trial for some crime by his "What now, Minister?" comments, especially when it seemed to Pulham that the public didn't like the guest's policy and Pulham's position would be supported by his viewers.

Pulham's objectivity had been somewhat eroded by his desire for one-upmanship in his discussions with guests. Indeed, watching him made one feel that his visitors were opponents rather than guests to be interviewed. Nevertheless, his style had remained somewhat more cordial than certain other political reporters in New Zealand, and his show enjoyed significant popularity.

"Welcome back, and a very warm welcome to you, Sir Geoffrey," greeted Pulham.

"Thank you, Jeff. It's good of you to have me on your show."

"Congratulations on your appointment as New Zealand's new ambassador to the United Nations. This will be one more in a long series of honors afforded you during your career. Tell us, Sir Geoffrey, has the prime minister given you any particular agenda for your first year, and if so, do you feel New Zealand can command the necessary influence to achieve that agenda?"

"Thank you for your compliments," Sir Geoffrey responded. "I'm sure Mildred deserves more credit for our family achievements than I could ever hope to claim. In answer to your first question, yes, Prime Minister Onekawa has assured me that we will seriously consider each issue that comes before the world body and develop a position relative to New Zealand's interests."

"Surely, Sir Geoffrey, you are not going to New York just to see what comes before the United Nations, and then spend some time thinking about it."

"No, Jeff, of course not. There are many current events on which New Zealand has developed a well-thought-out position, and we intend for our voice to be heard. Remember, the United Nations is a deliberative body in the truest sense. This assures the member nations of due caution, discussion, and time to deliberate issues without reaching impetuous decisions. A consensus has to be formed that will provide benefit to all concerned before acceptance can be anticipated."

"Sir Geoffrey, with all due respect to your ambassador's role, that sounds like so much poppycock. Our viewers have a right to know New Zealand's objectives in this appointment and how you intend to carry them out."

Television news was a visual media. As such, it afforded the participant, whether interviewer or guest, the opportunity to present one's case physically while saying something quite opposite. Sir Geoffrey nodded his head, presenting body language of complete agreement with Pulham's position, but he answered, "Deliberately, very deliberately."

"What about our new seat on the Security Council? Surely that will give us some additional clout? How do you intend to use that visibility?"

"No, Jeff, the Security Council seat doesn't provide its incumbent member 'clout,' as you call it, but instead, it requires considerable additional responsibility to assure that all votes tendered are done with the interest of the overall membership. It is an important responsibility, and one that New Zealand does not take lightly."

"Ambassador, please," an exasperated Pulham said, "we must recognize that the superpowers have thrown their veto power around in the Security Council for years in sole pursuit of their own interests. Surely New Zealand doesn't intend to simply rubber-stamp their proposals."

"You raise a good issue. The use of the veto by permanent members of the Security Council has been an integral part—"

Pulham interrupted roughly, "Excuse me, Ambassador, but you're not speaking to the issue. A history lesson on the role of the veto would take too long for our show. Could you please consider our viewers and help them understand why we apparently have no established plan of action for your term of appointment to the United Nations?" Pulham had often found success with guests by accusing them of positions, or lack thereof, which required them to rebut the statement by answering the original question rather specifically. Sir Geoffrey, however, was not such an inexperienced guest.

"Jeff," Sir Geoffrey said pleasantly, "the prime minister has many times, including on your show, advised our nation of our objectives in the world setting. We will, of course, consult with ambassadors from other nations with similar objectives and see what consensus can be reached."

"Well, Ambassador, if you can't or won't tell us about our agenda issues, can you at least discuss your intentions regarding New Zealand's posture with the newly developing Organization of International Conflict Resolution? Will this appointment enhance New Zealand's role in helping to resolve world conflict? Are your personal goals at stake here?"

"Thank you again for another excellent question. Yes, indeed, the OICR has worked hard to position New Zealand in the role of international arbitrator, and certainly our visible posture on the Security Council will help to enhance that role. As you know, New Zealand is an excellent choice for nations seeking to obtain an outside, objective, and nonthreatening advisor. We are capable of providing very able assistance to these governments."

Pulham felt defeated, but as always, he had the last word, which, when used judiciously, could leave his viewers with the impression that he had won. "Thank you, Sir Geoffrey. Hopefully next time we speak, you will have had time to formulate your ideas about the intended role New Zealand will play on the Security Council. We look forward to our next visit," Pulham, said, slightly raising his eyebrows and expressing an aura of res-ignation and disappointment, designed more to transmit a mes-sage to his viewers of disdain for the current guest than to reflect his actual feelings. This physical posturing clearly left the viewers with the impression, regardless of what was being said, that Pulham felt, "Sure, and pigs might fly too."

Jeff Pulham knew well before the show that political responses would be guarded and cautious. If a political guest said it would be sunny and it turned out to rain, Pulham would roast him on the next show. The weatherman might get away with inaccurate projections, but public figures had learned, especially on shows like *The Pulham News Hour,* to generalize and avoid specifics.

Jeff Pulham understood this concept, and that's why, to some extent, his show took on a "theater" perspective. Every theater needed a show, and every show needed a star. And the star could-n't be allowed to be the guest on *The Pulham News Hour,* could it? Therefore, it had to be the host. News was entertainment, was it not?

Persian Gulf
USS Heritage, *Guided Missile Cruiser*
February

The yeoman approached the captain and waited for him to recog-nize his presence. "Sir, this 'operational immediate' just came in."

The captain took the message, scanned it briefly, and in an agitated tone stated to no one in particular, "Get the XO to the bridge, now!" Captain Wilson Richards, United States Naval Academy, '68, wanted action, and his crew knew what he was like when he didn't receive the response he expected.

The deck officer went to the comm and keyed the mike, "XO to the bridge, immediately. XO to the bridge, immediately."

"Mr. Henry, you have the conn," said Captain Richards, leaving the steering of the ship to the officer's charge. "When the XO arrives, have him step into my sea cabin."

"Aye, aye, sir," Mr. Henry responded.

"Captain's off the bridge," barked the Marine security guard. Naval tradition required the announcement of the captain's arrival to or departure from the bridge.

Within two minutes Commander Bernard Johannsen knocked on the captain's door and entered. He didn't speak but waited for Captain Richards, who seemed lost in thought, to start. From his desk chair, Richards looked up at Johannsen and said, "Salimar's out of his cage again, Barney. This time he got one of the Tomcats from the *Enterprise.* The pilot's wingman saw two chutes, and the *Norfolk* picked up both crew by rescue helo. That guy never seems to learn, and he's got more lives than the proverbial cat."

Captain Wilson Richards was boiling mad. Ever since the end of the Gulf War, Iraq had continued to harass Allied overflights monitoring the conditions of the surrender. Once the bulk of ground troops had left the Middle East, Iraq had quietly disavowed the surrender and continued to pursue their objectives, including military action in the north against the Kurds, designated enemies of the current regime. The Gulf War, if it could be called that, had overtones of Vietnam for Richards, and that was not a pleasant song.

During his academy days, Richards had earned the nickname "Bull," both for his tenacity and, less flattering, for his unwillingness to blindly accept what he was told. Ensign Richards had immediately been assigned to a destroyer on Yankee Station, the U.S. designation for the coastal waters off the coast of Vietnam. Johannsen had followed him, three years later, class of '71.

On that destroyer, Richards had learned that modern wars were fought from the seat of political power and no longer by the commander on the scene, regardless of what he had learned at the academy. Instant communication had allowed the politicians, or "armchair admirals" as they were called, who had never seen the inside of a warship, much less knew anything about the strategic lessons taught in the classroom or on the battlefield, to direct the action vicariously. The common military metaphor had become "fighting with your hands tied." Such a physical posture limited one to butting heads and an occasional well-placed kick, but it didn't allow for the fight to end conclusively.

In the end, Vietnam was a military disaster, but the politicians chose to make it palatable, the way most politicians do. Eventually, both sides simply declared victory and went home. As soon as the Americans were home, the North Vietnamese resumed play, and they won the ball game in overtime.

The Gulf War, which to Richards' way of thinking was still going on, had been different, and they had actually had the opportunity to win it conclusively. They had in fact demolished their opponents, in the air war by modern technology and the default of the Iraqi Air Force, and in the ground campaign by brilliant strategy. Yet the armchair admirals and politicians, in an attempt to appease their world counterparts, had once again snatched defeat from the jaws of victory.

What angered Richards so much was poignantly stated in a novel he had just read, *Honour among Thieves* by British author Sir Jeffrey Archer. In short, Archer's theme had been, "Gorbachev's gone, Bush is gone, Thatcher is gone. Look who's left." Richards knew who was left. Just the Butcher of Baghdad! Why had we brought nearly a half million men, from an international coalition of sixteen countries, if not to do the job completely? There was no justice, it seemed, but Richards, Johannsen, and thousands of others like them had always been ready to spill their own blood to extricate their nation from the foibles of well-meaning, well-intentioned fools! What angered him most was that they had to keep doing it over and over, for the same reasons.

In spite of his views, Richards had excelled at his chosen profession, gaining his fourth stripe, signifying full captain, in fifteen years at age thirty-seven, and now at forty-six he was about to get his first star. Admiral Designate Richards was still boiling mad.

"Read this, Barney," Captain Wilson Richards said, handing Johannsen the "operational immediate" communication. "He may have brought down a Tomcat to parade around Baghdad, but we've just been authorized at 0445 tomorrow morning to shove six Tomahawks down his throat. Make ready, Barney, and keep me advised of progress."

Johannsen stood straight and replied, "Aye, aye, Captain." As he left, he turned in the doorway and added, "We'll kick his teeth in, Bull."

CHAPTER THREE

Auckland, New Zealand
March

A SMALL REGATTA WAS FORMING out on the harbor this clear Friday morning, and Cameron Rossiter felt the stirrings, but he tried to put the temptation aside. He reviewed his desk calendar, just as his secretary, Jenny, entered his office.

"Mr. Rossiter, Ms. Duffield is here for your eleven o'clock appointment regarding the upcoming managers seminar. Should I show her in?"

"Yes, of course, Jenny, please."

Michelle Nicole Duffield entered Rossiter's office, carrying a leather attaché case, a tubular case about one meter long containing possible seating charts and classroom arrangements, and sporting a bright smile. She was dressed in a black-and-white dress, slightly above the knee, over which she wore an Eisenhower-length black jacket. She capped off the ensemble with a colorful cravat around her neck. She stood about 5'3", had short dark hair and dark brown eyes, and was in her mid to late twenties. Her overall appearance was extremely attractive yet quite professional.

"Good morning, Mr. Rossiter, Michelle Duffield," she said as she presented her card. Her voice was pleasant, but what impressed Rossiter initially was her dazzling smile. Rossiter was pleased, and a idea began to formulate in his mind.

"Good morning to you, Ms. Duffield. Thank you for coming so quickly." His thoughts were coming together, and he decided to make the pitch. "Ms. Duffield . . ."

"Excuse me, Mr. Rossiter, please call me Michelle."

"Right, thank you. Cameron's my name. Tell me, Michelle," he said as he turned with a sweeping gesture of his arm toward the window overlooking the harbor, "what do you see out there?" Rossiter's office window wrapped completely around the corner of his office, and the view was spectacular, spanning over 180 degrees.

Michelle moved to the window, slowly taking in the panoramic view while trying to imagine what Rossiter was actually seeking. Perhaps this is part of the test, she thought. She had come following a call from his secretary asking about her company's services and capabilities to arrange a management seminar for several days for his store managers. The purpose of the seminar was to provide a forum for the initial stages of his restructuring, and he purportedly wanted to take the staff away somewhere quiet to formulate their objectives. Michelle looked at the harbor and the yachts, remembering that she had read something about Rossiter and his recent cruise through the islands. Perhaps that's what he's seeking, she thought.

"I see people going about their lives, Mr. Rossiter, commerce in action, enterprise, and I see New Zealand's future. I also see about a dozen high-rise office buildings, most of which are owned by Chinese, Japanese, or Malaysian investors. One could see anything one wished out there, Mr. Rossiter, but perhaps what I see most is the reason I love New Zealand so much. I see the call of the sea."

Rossiter's eyebrows went up. She's either on to me, or she's

worth further investigation, he thought. Either way, we'll combine business and pleasure, and we'll have an enjoyable afternoon. He was sure of his plan now.

"Are you capable of being a spontaneous person, Michelle?"
Rossiter watched her eyes for reaction, sure that she felt completely befuddled by this approach to what was supposed to have
been a business presentation on seminar options. Rossiter continued, "Let me rephrase that. Is there anything we have to discuss
that couldn't be accomplished outdoors on such a beautiful day?"

She looked back toward Rossiter, thinking quickly. "No," she
said somewhat hesitantly, "we have only to consider your requirements regarding meeting facilities and dining accommodations
and to discuss—"

"Great," Rossiter interrupted, "how would you feel about
lunch on the water? If you have early plans, I could have you
back by four if necessary."

"Mr. Rossiter, I'm not dressed for boating. I—"

"Twelve o'clock, slip thirty-five at the Royal New Zealand
Yacht Squadron." Again he watched her reaction, this time to see
if she exhibited any caution or reluctance at this impromptu offer.

Seeing her hesitate once again, Rossiter stepped to the door
of his office. "Jenny, would you please come in here for a
moment?" He took Jenny by the arm, leading her to the window
where Michelle was still observing. "Ms. Duffield is considering
the pros and cons of going sailing with me this afternoon and conducting business on the water. Would you be so kind as to reassure her that my intentions are honorable and that she will be in
no danger?" Michelle looked at Cameron, who had broken into a
broad, rather sheepish smile, giving him a disarming, boyish
innocence.

Cameron's actions took Jenny off guard and flustered her, but
she smiled at Michelle, who was looking a bit ruffled by the
events of the past five minutes.

Michelle spoke first, "Is he always this flamboyant and
impetuous, Jenny?" Turning to Cameron, she said, "You are a
most unusual and interesting man, Mr. Rossiter."

"Cameron. If I can call you Michelle, you can call me Cameron."

Michelle was sure all this was a test, perhaps of her company's flexibility, or of her quick thinking. Whatever it was, this was certainly the most unusual contract she had sought in recent memory. Turning back to Jenny, Michelle added, "Jenny, should 'Captain Hook' manifest himself through Mr. Rossiter while we're gone, I'll depend on you to call for help from Peter Pan." She smiled pleasantly at a very puzzled secretary.

Michelle Nicole Duffield, seven minutes after meeting Cameron Sterling Rossiter, picked up her attaché case, turned toward him, and offered her hand. Giving him a firm business handshake, she briefly locked eyes, offering her brilliant smile, and said, "Until 12:30, Cameron."

Back at her office she explained to Jean, her associate, what had transpired.

"You mean to say he invited you out on his yacht in three minutes?" Jean asked incredulously.

"Probably less. I think he was testing me."

"What for?"

"I'm not sure. Maybe to see if I could innovate, think on my feet, who knows? I really don't need this interruption. I wanted to develop the presentations for the Pan Pacific and Sheraton next week. It's going—"

"Get home and change, Michelle. This sounds better than daytime television. Don't worry, I'll take care of the remaining preparation for the hotels."

Michelle hugged Jean and gathered her purse and briefcase. "It has been a long while since playtime for either of us, hasn't it?" With an impish grin, Michelle added, "Actually, I rather like his impetuous nature."

"Stick to business, partner," Jean cautioned with a smile.

"Yeah," Michelle answered, turning toward the door.

Driving home, she ran over the past hour in her mind. Jean's right, she thought, business first. I've got to show him I'm a professional, an equal. But then again, a girl's got to look her best.

She glanced at her nails and mentally ran through her wardrobe. What to wear . . .

At 12:35 Cameron saw Michelle walking down the pier dressed in white cotton slacks, a blue-and-white Canterbury jersey, and a pair of dark blue Docksiders. She carried a blue-and-white waterproof Hood sea bag.

"Well, here I am, for better or worse," she said.

Cameron looked her over and thought to himself, Well, she certainly knows the proper gear. "Stow your gear below, Michelle, and then loose the bow lines, please. We'll get underway."

Michelle quickly put her bag and jacket below, returned to the deck, and went forward to the tielines. "Ready forward," she called out.

"Right, cast off and hop aboard." Cameron had the engine going and began to back slowly out of the slip, turning to move through the marina toward the open harbor. Once into the harbor entrance, Cameron turned *Triple Diamond* due east. He activated the automatic sail furl, and the mainsail opened to take the breeze. Michelle was amidships and began to trim the sails.

For the next twenty minutes not much was spoken between the two as Cameron piloted the yacht clear of the mounting regatta and headed out into the Hauraki Gulf. Michelle continued to crew without direction, a feat that thoroughly convinced Cameron that her "call of the sea" comment in his office was sincere. It seemed to Cameron that Michelle Nicole Duffield was indeed worth further investigation.

Once *Triple Diamond* was clear of the regatta and settled into a northeast tack, Michelle came aft to the wheel. She sat down on the high side, once again smiling at Cameron and basking in the bright New Zealand sun while silently observing Rangitoto, the dormant island volcano in the harbor. "This is the way to conduct business, I would say," she commented to the sea.

Cameron merely grinned. "Something tells me you didn't just run over to the library during the past hour to study sailing."

"No, I've been out before," she said, still smiling at him.

"Someone special?"

"Very . . . " She paused for a moment to allow him to wonder, and then concluded, " . . . my father."

"Did he teach you to sail?"

"Me and my younger brother, Graham. Dad had Graham out by the time he was three. I was four years older than Graham but wasn't willing to go until I was about twelve. By then, Graham was pretty knowledgeable and tried to lord it over me. We fought all the time. Come to think of it now, I guess we made Dad's weekends on the yacht miserable."

"Where's Graham now?" Cameron asked.

"After Dad's death—I guess Graham was about fifteen—we didn't sail together for some time. Graham sailed occasionally with his mates, but not on Dad's yacht. Mum sold the yacht the following year." Michelle paused, lost in reflection. Cameron watched her for what seemed like several minutes before she continued, "Anyway, after a couple of years, Graham got me to go out with him one Saturday, and we spent hours remembering Dad and our times together. It sort of bonded us in the memory of what we had shared with Dad. Since then we've sailed whenever we've had the opportunity. Graham is a signal officer in the Navy now, stationed in Auckland."

"Well, we should have him along sometime, don't you think?" Cameron offered.

Michelle surveyed the boat and, with a sweeping gesture of her arm, said, "He'd kill to get aboard a yacht like *Triple Diamond.*"

Over the next several hours they learned more about each other, and by four o'clock, they found themselves approaching Pakatoa Resort, an island about thirty miles from the Auckland Marina.

"Michelle, it seems I'll have difficulty keeping my promise to get you home by four."

Michelle smiled. "Is this where I meet 'Captain Hook'?"

"We could put in to Pakatoa and have a great dinner. They also have nice resort facilities, and I could get you a room, my treat, of course, since I kept us out so late, and I'll sleep on the yacht. Or I could drop you off on Waiheke Island, and you could catch the late ferry back. Your choice, Michelle."

"Sail on, Captain. I'm not prepared to mutiny yet."

Over dinner Cameron caught himself looking into Michelle's eyes almost to the point of being embarrassed. "I seem to have forgotten our business discussions this afternoon," Cameron stated sheepishly.

Michelle picked up the opportunity. "I assumed that you had made your decision, and we were found acceptable."

"That, and more," Cameron allowed.

After dinner they returned to *Triple Diamond,* anchored at the pier, and went aboard. Cameron brought a couple of small chairs on deck, and they sat to watch the sun set.

For the next half hour they silently took in the fading rays staining the harbor and the distant skyline of Auckland. Michelle spoke first. "Why the name *Triple Diamond?*"

Cameron hesitated, and Michelle flashed her lovely smile.

"Does your smile always win the day for you?" Cameron asked. Michelle didn't respond.

Cameron looked seaward for a while, thinking how much to reveal. Cameron had seldom felt the necessity of letting anyone share in his dreams, and as yet he had not found the person with whom he felt sufficiently comfortable to allow such openness.

As Michelle gazed at the sky, she felt she knew his thoughts, and they were probably similar to hers. What he was willing to reveal would be an early determinant of their budding relation-ship. This was their first day together, yet already she wanted to know what made this man tick.

She felt comfortable and was aware without compliment that she had passed the seafaring test. At present she had no one spe-cial in her life, but she actually wasn't looking for anyone either. After several years of working for a large hotel chain, arranging conference accommodations and seminar bookings, she had taken the plunge and opened her own office to offer the same services. For two years she had struggled, and only recently had she begun to achieve some success. Much work was in store if her venture were to succeed, and a relationship took time, time she didn't feel she could spare.

Her father had taught her much, including how to work hard for what one wanted. Her pride in his accomplishments was tarnished only by the limited time he had been given to enjoy them. Eight years earlier, just before Christmas, Michelle's father had been sailing with friends when he was unexpectedly killed by a freak accident at sea. Michelle had consoled herself that he would have preferred to die at sea, but it didn't make up for the second half of his life that he had missed, not to mention the loss of his companionship, advice, and comfort. Eventually she had come to feel that her father's memory was closest to her when she was on the water. There would be time to tell these things to Cameron should the moment arise, and should she feel he was the one to listen.

"*Triple Diamond,* you say," Cameron finally said. "Well, it's a long story. My father started on a shoestring, with no real job prospects. After he married my mother . . . "

Several hours later, long after dark, Cameron rose to walk the length of the vessel, checking moorings. The tide had turned, and *Triple Diamond* was pulling in the opposite direction. Their discussions had ranged far and wide, and Cameron felt that this woman, who had so boldly walked into his office less than twelve hours before, had begun to play a part in his life. Her history, including the loss of her father, paralleled his grandfather's story. Cameron knew that there was a lot to learn about Michelle. She was intelligent, confident, attractive, and, of course, seaworthy— all in all, a combination he felt compelled to explore further.

"I'll walk you back to the cabin," Cameron offered, "and I'll sleep on the yacht. A good night's rest will do us both good, and then we'll have Saturday to consider."

"I'll accept the Royal Suite for the evening," Michelle said teasingly. "Breakfast at eight, if you please, Higgins."

Cameron and Michelle spent much of that night in their respective accommodations reflecting on the day's events. Their day had not gone as either had planned, but it was a welcome change for both. For her part, Michelle was totally confused by her willingness to open up to this man, for she fully had intended to not reveal much. What was there about him that had prompted her soul searching? She would have to be more careful, she cautioned herself.

The next day, the morning sail stretched into the afternoon, then turned into a weekend away. Two days later, on Sunday evening as they sailed into the Auckland Marina, they both had reached a point where they felt that their lives had changed. The future looked brighter somehow.

Washington, D.C.
National Security Agency
March

Lieutenant General William Austin, USAF, head of Intelligence, National Security Agency, looked through the overnight message traffic, paying particular attention to dispatches from military components remaining near the Saudi Arabian Peninsula. Abdul Salimar had continued to bluster about American attempts to destroy his peaceful efforts to rebuild his country. Lately, Salimar had taken to announcing in his nightly diatribes that the American warmongers were searching for an excuse to use tactical nuclear weapons on his country. This was a new approach for Salimar, and General Austin considered what implications it had for Iraq's future actions. What General Austin had learned not to do was underestimate Abdul Salimar!

"Alice," General Austin said to his secretary, "please see if Major O'Brien is available about ten o'clock."

"Yes, sir, General, I believe I saw him this morning over at 'Image Retrieval.'"

Alice had served with General Austin nearly eleven years. In 1970, at the young age of thirty-five, she had found herself widowed when her husband, Major John O. Henderson, had been shot down over North Vietnam. When Alice had moved to Washington, D.C., to work for General Austin, she had taken to eating her lunch in the park not far from the White House. She had found the Vietnam Memorial comforting, even fifteen years after John's death.

This loss is perhaps what helped her serve General Austin so faithfully. The general's son, Lt. Wesley Austin, USMC, had been killed in Vietnam in 1969 in one of the nameless ground assaults that had gained the disputed territory, only to give it back weeks later. They had never spoken directly to each other regarding their respective losses, but she knew he understood. Alice was a Vietnam War widow, and General Austin was more than a Vietnam veteran, he was a Vietnam parent. Yes, they did indeed understand one another.

At ten, Alice stood in the doorway, smiling, "General, Major O'Brien is here to see you."

"Thank you, Alice, have him come in."

Zach O'Brien was in civilian clothes, a usual routine for the National Security Agency. NSA officials frequently dealt with other government departments, and they had realized that uniforms sometimes put them at a disadvantage in dealing with civilians. The use of civilian attire had also reduced the military post atmosphere that existed at the Pentagon. The NSA sought for a different image, which sometimes irritated those at the Pentagon.

O'Brien had not served General Austin nearly as long as Alice, but he knew the general was a tough taskmaster. They had gotten along well since General Austin had recognized in O'Brien some of his own traits. O'Brien was a hard worker, generally put in more than was expected, and could be depended upon to produce a final product greater than that requested. The general felt he could ask no more of subordinates, and he was certain of O'Brien's loyalty. Having security clearances was one thing, but with some individuals, the loyalty exhibited to one's superior was often subordinated to the personal career of the individual concerned.

General Austin had on several occasions seen O'Brien carry out his orders, perfectly legal, which, should they have not been completed successfully, would have impeded O'Brien's progression. That kind of loyalty was rare. Even rarer was the kind of loyalty General Austin felt for his staff. Some superiors, even those for whom O'Brien had displayed the same kind of loyalty, had turned it to their advantage and taken personal credit for success. It took all kinds, O'Brien knew, but General Austin was the kind of leader men would follow into danger, and not only in the battlefield sense.

Zach O'Brien walked into General Austin's office and stood before his desk. "Good morning, General, it looks like Salimar gave his new lecture again last night." O'Brien knew that General Austin had begun to express concerns about Salimar's new charges. The general looked up at O'Brien with a smile that said without words, "Reading my mind again, Zach?"

"Yes," General Austin said, "and he keeps throwing the same pitch. What do you make of it, Major?"

"General, we know that for all of his rhetoric he seldom develops an idea or makes a play to his audience without some purpose behind it. Yet, we have absolutely no intel that indicates he has come into possession of or has a firm source for nuclear capabilities. His thrust seems directed toward getting his third-world allies to consider pressuring us to reduce actions against Iraq."

Among the third-world countries, and especially within the Middle East, Iraq actually had few allies in the true sense. Most of the other countries felt the fear that comes with an unpredictable bully in the neighborhood. Yet they were all content to let Salimar fight their war, either rhetorically or physically, against the United States. Salimar had become the de facto point man for the real and imagined grievances held against the U.S. With the Soviet Union no longer supporting terrorist groups or governments supportive of Soviet desires, a vacuum had been created that smaller despots had moved to fill. Iraq had been leading the pack for some time, and Abdul Salimar's simple survival was testimony to his resilience. General Austin was right. He was not to be underestimated.

His ability to directly confront the major powers was severely limited, but he was a master at playing the part of the aggrieved relative. His victories were public in the sense that even supporters of a major league ball team achieve some satisfaction in seeing the underdog bang one out of the park occasionally. Though Salimar had tried direct military action with disastrous results, he

was still preaching to the converted while other political "ministers" whose leadership had been demonstrated had been ousted
by their congregations. In Iraq, the "religion" of obedience to the
leader was mandatory!

"Major O'Brien, I want you to develop some analyses of
Salimar's intentions," General Austin directed. "What purpose
does this new 'nuclear rhetoric' hold, what are some of his possible intentions, and where might we expect it to lead? Got the
picture?"

"Yes, sir. How long do we have, General?"

"Two weeks. If he acts in the meantime, you're too late."

"Right, General. I'll get my team right on it."

"And Major, one other thing. An assignment right down your
alley. The State Department has asked us to provide someone to
liaise with the new ambassador to the United Nations from New
Zealand. He's been floating a couple of trial balloons about
ANZUS policy changes in New Zealand. Set up a meeting with
him and see what's on his mind. This is an old horse, Major, but if
we could make some inroads here, it would please our British
brothers. Dust off your Kiwi passport and put on your charm for
the ambassador. Your Kiwi citizenship may come in handy on
this one."

"Yes, sir," replied O'Brien, turning to leave. O'Brien left
General Austin's office with two more assignments than when he
had entered. The first required his section, Office of Strategic
Analysis, to come up with an option list covering Iraq's purposes
behind Abdul Salimar's charges that the U.S. was considering
using nuclear capabilities against his peace-loving country,
accompanied by possible courses of action each purpose would
generate, and the second entailed devising an appropriate U.S.
response to each potential action, preferably proactive to reduce
the impact of whatever movement Salimar was planning, and not
reactive to Salimar's *fait accompli.*

To accomplish this first assignment, Major O'Brien would
call upon the "Irish Mafia," as O'Brien's team was called. The
section was comprised of three military officers, one Air Force
chief master sergeant, and O'Brien's secretary. The designation

of "Irish Mafia" had come about when the third officer had
arrived late last month. Most of the team had Irish ancestry, but
the new boy on the block was Italian, Lieutenant Vincento Savini,
or Vinny, a naval aviator and a veteran of the Gulf Storm campaign with one kill to his credit. That achievement was no small
accomplishment against an Iraqi air force that had made a short
career of giving away their planes to a former enemy so they
wouldn't be blown out of the sky by coalition forces. Savini had
been shot down while on routine patrol one month earlier and,
during ejection, had injured his back, requiring a temporary
assignment. Considering his personnel and academic record,
Major O'Brien was glad to get him.

Lieutenant Savini had joined the existing cadre of Air Force
Captain Shelly Molloy, Ph.D. in political science with a Middle
Eastern specialty, and Marine Corps Captain John Francis
Murphy, former commander of Baker Company, First Recon
Battalion. During Desert Storm, Captain Murphy's company had
been instrumental in convincing the Iraqis that a direct sea assault
was imminent, when in fact an "end run" was in progress, which
resulted in complete surprise to the vaunted Republican Guard.

It was actually Chief Master Sergeant Franklin Harrison who
had coined the team name, following the arrival of Savini. Sergeant Harrison, somewhat tactlessly, had commented one day
shortly after Savini's arrival that O'Brien, Molloy, and Murphy
could have been running guns for the IRA back in Oliver North's
day, and Savini had just showed up with the family historical
know-how to accomplish it. It looked like an Irish Mafia to him,
Chief Harrison had commented.

Major O'Brien's second assignment with the New Zealand
ambassador would be more enjoyable. He held a deep love for
New Zealand and had pleasant memories of sailing off the coast
and fishing in the magnificent mountain streams and lakes. His
father and mother had retired to New Zealand, and they lived at
the top of the North Island in an area called the Bay of Islands.
O'Brien thought it was one of the most tranquil places he had
ever seen. O'Brien didn't know Ambassador Holden personally,
but he looked forward to the meeting.

New York City
United Nations
March

Sir Geoffrey rose to greet O'Brien as he entered the New Zealand delegation suite at the United Nations. Sir Geoffrey was about sixty, over six feet tall and still trim, with the look of a former athlete. Zach was familiar with his stature as one of New Zealand's former cricket greats, with three "centuries" in test cricket to his credit. He was assured a place in New Zealand history, both athletically, which Kiwis revered, and politically, which they tolerated because of his sports stature. Zach had often met with senior foreign-government officials, but as yet his duties had not provided him the opportunity to meet with New Zealand government officials.

Immediately, Sir Geoffrey put him at ease. "So, Major O'Brien, which of you will I be dealing with today, the Yankee or the Kiwi?" he said amiably, referring to O'Brien's dual citizenship.

O'Brien smiled at him and replied, "The choice is yours, Ambassador, and whenever one cannot provide suitable answers or approval, we'll call upon the other for advice. Fair enough?"

"Excellent, Major. I'm going to like you, Zach—may I call you Zach?"

"Certainly, Ambassador."

"Please, that always sounds so formal. Call me Geoff or Geoffrey."

"Suppose we compromise and I call you Sir Geoffrey? A good compromise is a great way to start any political meeting, wouldn't you say?"

"Yes, I would. We are indeed going to get along. Now, let me explain why I requested this meeting through our embassy. As you know, New Zealand has, for some years now, precluded American naval ships from visiting our ports due to your nuclear weapons and our nuclear-free zone. We understand, of course, that not all of your ships have nuclear weapons on board, but your defense policy of not declaring weaponry requires us to assume that they all do and thus to deny entry."

"Yes, sir, I'm familiar with the policy and New Zealand's reasons for implementing it, including the French nuclear testing in the Pacific that exacerbated the situation."

"Quite right. The French testing certainly had something to do with our desire to reduce or, more accurately, eliminate such testing from our country."

"Sir Geoffrey," O'Brien injected, "New Zealand incurred certain responsibilities in becoming a member of ANZUS, and the feeling here has been that the New Zealand government has essentially tied the hands of one of its partners and prevented us from honoring our obligations to assist the treaty nations in their defense."

"Yes, obviously that is our policy's weakest point. We understand that. But the world has changed considerably now, and we would like to propose that those changes facilitate the resurrection of a cooperative relationship between the United States and New Zealand, both of which you call home." Sir Geoffrey smiled broadly, knowing he was playing on O'Brien's dual loyalties.

"Go on, Sir Geoffrey. You've enthralled this 'Yankiwi' with your proposal."

"In all seriousness, I believe the reduction of world communism has significantly reduced the tension and provided the United States an excellent opportunity to reply in kind, in ways designed to demonstrate the United States' desire to join these peaceful changes, without harming its defense interests. In return, we could define our nonnuclear policy to apply specifically to nuclear weaponry and thus allow nuclear-propelled craft to visit our shores. Can you see my point, Zach?"

"Yes, I can, Sir Geoffrey. If we relaxed our stance and agreed to 'declare' the status of our naval vessels, we would have essentially complied with the wishes of a small, peaceful, and supportive nation, which also had the strength to refuse the United States entry into their country under the previous conditions. Thus we would afford our nuclear-propelled ships access to New Zealand harbors. Yet should the need arise, we could revert to our policy of nondisclosure. Is that about the gist of your proposal?"

Sir Geoffrey smiled even more broadly. "Well done, Major

O'Brien. You've summarized better than I had proposed. Can I count on your support?"

"I don't carry much weight, Sir Geoffrey, but the proposal sounds like a win-win solution, and my boss loves those. I'll present your views to him, and I feel confident he will discuss it with the national security advisor and the president."

"Thank you, Zach. You'll be in touch?"

"As soon as I have some answers." O'Brien paused momentarily, thinking, "We'll call this the 'The Kiwi Initiative.' Does that meet with your approval, sir?"

"Very well, thank you. Until next time, then," the ambassador said, offering his hand. "It's been a pleasure meeting you, Major O'Brien. Perhaps we can meet again as we bring this to successful completion."

"I hope that will be possible, Ambassador. Thank you again for your hospitality."

On the shuttle flight home O'Brien contemplated the issues surrounding Sir Geoffrey's proposal. Of course, the Pentagon wouldn't like it. They seldom liked anything that curtailed their prerogatives or placed restrictions on them. However, Zach thought, that was why the Constitution required civilian leadership of the military. Yes, he thought, the Kiwi Initiative had promise. He would put it to General Austin.

CHAPTER FOUR

Baghdad, Iraq
April

EXCELLENCY, AMBASSADOR HAQUIM ADVISES that negotiations have gone well with the man who calls himself Mr. Wyndham. We have not yet learned his true identity. He assures us that all necessary preparations can be accomplished by July or, at latest, August." General Alihambra was, of necessity, deferential to the Leader and tried to evaluate his mood.

"How much?"

"Excellency, Mr. Wyndham has requested fifty million U.S. dollars in his Swiss account by May 1, and a further twenty-five million for each incident we require, as it is accomplished."

"Have you confirmed his reliance, *personally?*" The Leader emphasized "personally," thereby assuring General Alihambra of his early and untimely demise should the plan fail. General Alihambra knew this point of any plan well. The Leader would take full credit from the Revolutionary Council for all successful operations, but he would disavow any knowledge regarding approval for any plan that failed. This assured, to those fearful for their lives, which included anyone with whom the Leader had contact, that they would put forth maximum effort to succeed. Many generals who had merely followed the Great Leader's military strategy in the recent "Mother of all Battles" were no longer present to explain why "their" plan had failed.

"Your Excellency, our agents have confirmed prior accomplishments claimed by Mr. Wyndham. We have yet to confirm the existence of, or Mr. Wyndham's accessibility to, a weapon of the magnitude we require. We are seeking assurances of that as we speak." General Alihambra was concerned that delivery would even be possible, but he knew His Excellency was committed, and the die was cast. He would succeed, or Mr. Wyndham would die before him. "What is your command, Excellency?"

"Proceed!" After a suitable pause, during which General Alihambra had not felt dismissed, the Leader looked directly into General Alihambra's eyes and added, "You will *personally* take charge of this operation, General, assuring the people of your undivided attention to our success!"

"Yes, Excellency. One other item, Your Excellency, regarding Ambassador Haquim. He advises of certain new proposals from the ambassador from New Zealand that he feels are worthy of Your Excellency's consideration. Ambassador Holden, the representative from New Zealand, has had initial discussions with the Americans, requesting the U.S. to consider a change to their public policy of neither confirming nor denying that nuclear weapons are present aboard U.S. vessels. Ambassador Haquim seeks permission from Your Excellency to approach Ambassador Holden and offer support for this peaceful proposition, to further solidify our small alliance with New Zealand."

Salimar thought for a few moments, considering what potential this situation offered. Quickly his eyes lit up, and he looked at Alihambra. "Proceed," he directed.

"Yes, Excellency."

New York City
United Nations
April

Ambassador Haquim finished his address to the World Health
Organization Food Committee, having expressed his deep and
genuine concern for food distribution among the starving Kurdish
people in northern Iraq. These were the same people against
whom, the month before, President Abdul Salimar had launched
a quick and ruthless ground offensive, inflicting massive casualties in the process. He gathered his materials and started out the
door. Coming through the foyer, he arranged to cross paths with
Sir Geoffrey Holden, the ambassador from New Zealand.

"Ah, Sir Geoffrey, it is so good to catch you. Might we speak
a moment?"

"Certainly, Mr. Ambassador, how may the people of our
small South Pacific nation be of service to the people of Iraq?"

"Perhaps we could move to my humble office where you
could tell me about this beautiful land I believe the Yankees call
'Down Under,'" Haquim said with a smile, taking Sir Geoffrey
by the arm.

They continued walking down the corridor and entered the
elevator. Haquim had been Iraq's ambassador for seven years, and
he knew that Sir Geoffrey had only recently arrived to represent
New Zealand. He wanted to take the measure of the man and
attempt to see where he stood on issues regarding the Middle
East. Haquim knew that New Zealand had sent medical personnel
to the war against his country, but he felt perhaps the choice of
medical rather than combat troops was a reflection of New
Zealand's reluctance to punish Iraq. Did that signify some agreement or areas where mutual agreement could be reached?

Sir Geoffrey had expected to be lobbied by third-world countries not associated with the major powers. New Zealand played
an interesting role inasmuch as they could perhaps be written off
as puppets of the British system, which only followed the
American's lead, but then again New Zealand had hung out the
"No Visitors" sign to the American navy. That seemed to indicate

that New Zealand was willing to take a stand in opposition to the U.S.

Haquim also had direction from his government to develop an alliance with Sir Geoffrey's new proposal to the Americans. As yet Haquim did not see where this would benefit Iraq, but he would follow through and report.

Washington, D.C.
National Security Agency
April

"G'day, Alice. How's it go'n, mate?"

"Major O'Brien, each time you go to New Zealand, you sound more and more like 'Crocodile Dundee.' What is it, the water you drink down there?" asked an exasperated Alice.

Zach O'Brien smiled boyishly and said, "Alice, you're just going to have to come with me some time and find out. Who knows, you might like it. I've never met anyone who didn't. You might even find some rich old Kiwi looking for a Yankee lass to tame, and you could spend the rest of your life waiting on him hand and foot."

Alice rose from her chair and with a lifted eyebrow said, "If I remember the stories you've told of your Kiwi grandmother, the proper response is 'Wash your mouth out.'" Alice had heard many stories of Major O'Brien's early years in New Zealand. His step-grandmother had been a young widow and had married again to Zach's Grandfather Flynn. Major O'Brien had described her as a caring woman who loved both the children and grandchildren from her first marriage and the children and grandchildren of her second husband, which included young Zachariah O'Brien. Family members had teased her about starting another family with her new husband, and thinking she had done her bit, she had replied emphatically, "Wash your mouth out."

"The general's waiting, Major O'Brien. Please try to maintain the proper decorum of this respectable organization." Alice had developed a sincere liking for Major O'Brien. She knew him to be a faithful husband to his wife and caring father to his three children, that alone being something she had not always observed in others. Equally important in her list of priorities, she saw the service and loyalty he provided to General Austin.

General Austin was just back from three days of strategic planning and evaluation with the section chiefs from CIA, NSA, and DCS Intelligence of the Joint Chiefs of Staff. They had used Major O'Brien's analysis of Abdul Salimar's new verbal direction as a basis for discussion of his intentions.

"Good morning, Major O'Brien. The president and the Congress of the United States, along with 280 million taxpayers, hope you were comfortable and secure in your recent excursion to the lower hemisphere, at their expense of course," General Austin said with a gleam in his eye. He had overheard the closing of Major O'Brien's comments with Alice and decided to take up the action.

"Well, sir, I felt it only fair to the peace-loving and trusting citizens of New Zealand that they receive the benefit of the wisdom and training the United States has seen fit to provide for one of their own. In that regard, sir, my presence was highly desirable both to myself and to the government of New Zealand. Of course, my parents were somewhat enthusiastic as well.

"In all seriousness, General, thank you for the assignment. My father sends his regards, and my grandmother sent scones."

"You're quite welcome, Major. I often think of the first time I met your father."

"Yes, sir, he's told me. I believe he was a guest speaker at the Air Force Academy while you were deputy commandant."

"That's right. We had several Vietnam veterans speak to our escape-and-evasion classes during the year, and on one of his visits to the United States, Colonel O'Brien consented to appear. You can understand how impressive the blue ribbon with the white stars is to young cadets. They get few opportunities to meet a live recipient of the Medal of Honor, much less the recipient and the person rescued at the same time. It was a very emotional moment for all. Colonel Redding was present, and your father had not known he was coming. They had not seen each other since President Johnson made the presentation. When they met, Colonel O'Brien struggled to maintain his Kiwi reserve."

General Austin knew the esteem in which Major O'Brien held his father, and Austin understood that reverence. He had often wished other sons could acknowledge their fathers in such a way. He envied Major O'Brien that, while at the same time he sorrowed for the loss he had experienced with his own son, whom he had never really gotten to know as a fellow warrior.

General Austin continued, "Yep, Colonel O'Brien was masterful in his presentation that day, and like most Kiwis, very humble in the process. I'm sure he transmitted some of that humility to you, Major, but it must have been your mother or your Yankee grandfather who slipped in a bit of brass, eh?"

"General, in all humility, I am grateful for everything my wonderful progenitors have contributed toward the development of the fine specimen you now have under your command," O'Brien said with a straight face.

Austin held Major O'Brien's eyes for a moment, reflecting the pride he would have liked to have displayed for his lost son. The general finally motioned for O'Brien to sit down. "To business, Major. How did it go with the Kiwis?"

O'Brien accepted the exchange as one more indication of the kind of man General Austin was. He could take pride in another man's accomplishments and recognize the merit in their achievements. Seating himself, he said, "I believe they have a good case, General, and should we prove accurate in our concerns about Iraq, the Kiwi Initiative could be an excellent counter move, especially for world opinion."

"Explain."

"Yes, sir. If Salimar continues to bluster about U.S. tactical nuclear weapons in theater operations, he will eventually raise some concerns, even among our allies. Our historical naval policy has served us well to deter the knowledge of which ships the Soviets should target first. That policy decision, supported in its day by the constant tension, has considerably lessened in the face of today's requirements."

"What are the Kiwis proposing?" General Austin asked.

"I met with Ambassador Sir Geoffrey Holden in New York in March as you directed. This last week I accepted his invitation to fly to New Zealand, where we met with Prime Minister Onekawa, U.S. Ambassador John Huston, Sir Geoffrey, and Admiral Sir Trevor Pottsdam, chief of the New Zealand defense forces."

General Austin had been unaware until O'Brien had phoned him from the embassy in Wellington that the meeting would be at the top level, and in fact Major O'Brien had not known it himself until several minutes before the meeting when Sir Geoffrey advised him they would meet with the prime minister. If they had known, General Austin would probably have included a more senior officer, or perhaps would have gone himself.

"The prime minister feels that the United States is in an excellent position, especially with a country as supportive to Western policies as New Zealand has always been, to grant this concession and reschedule naval visits. On their part, they would concede that ships under nuclear propulsion would be acceptable. He feels both sides have something to gain in the exchange, while both, of course, will receive flack from detractors for whom any nuclear affiliation would be unacceptable."

"What are your *American* recommendations, Major, as opposed to your Kiwi bias?" General Austin asked with a smile.

O'Brien chuckled at that question. "General, Ambassador Holden asked me basically the same question, but he wanted my *Kiwi* support and my *American* connections." O'Brien found being viewed by each side as "their" representative put a new and humorous light on negotiations. "I truly believe we have a lot to gain. We could put a stopper in Salimar's tirades about the use of nuclear forces against Iraq. The world would see a small country bringing the United States to their way of thinking, without lessening the security aspects of our standing policies. I think it can be win-win."

Major O'Brien knew that General Austin was a strong proponent of the win-win negotiating philosophy, which maintained that each party "win" something in an agreement. O'Brien continued, "Better someone like the Kiwis turn us around than some third-world country demanding it, where we would just hunker down and not budge. It would also demonstrate to the world that the U.S. is aware of and supports the policy decisions of friendly nations, even when they don't completely agree with our stance."

"OK, Zach, you've made a good case. I'll consider your views. Put them on paper, concisely please, and I'll run them up the flagpole to the boss. The president has been looking for some opportunities to win. He certainly hasn't had many lately, even where we're trying to provide secure food distribution to starving people. He just might go for it.

"Oh, by the way, at our seminar, your Iraqi options proposal was considered. About fifty percent were in agreement, forty percent were supportive but not convinced, and the other ten percent, as usual, didn't even know it was Tuesday. Well done, Major. I'll have Alice copy you on my notes so you can consider their comments. Put your staff on it, and work up some recommendations resulting from the seminar input."

Major O'Brien started to leave but turned in the doorway when General Austin attempted a faulty Kiwi accent, "Oh, 'n' Major, I'll have a couple of y'r Grandmother Flynn's scones for mornin' tea, if you please."

Auckland, New Zealand
April

Cameron Sterling Rossiter gazed out the window of his corner office. Was it only one week since he had been at the helm of *Triple Diamond?* It seemed like months. From his office on the twenty-sixth floor of the Fay Richwhite building on Queen Street, Rossiter could look over the Auckland Harbor, from the bridge crossing the harbor to the North Shore, out to the entrance of the Hauraki Gulf. When he permitted himself the luxury of day dreaming, he could get lost just watching the myriad of yachts on the water. Auckland was aptly called the "City of Sails."

Since returning from his six-week cruise throughout the South Pacific Islands in January, he had immersed himself in restructuring his business holdings. ConnectAbility, Ltd., had grown fast. He now had outlets in seventeen New Zealand cities, and recently he had gone international, opening four outlets in Australia. He had developed contracts with over thirty companies to provide their PC work stations and service contracts. Rossiter had a head for business and, like his father, he was making the most of it while young. Still, it never made any sense to him. While you were young, you should be out enjoying life, worrying about financial security only when you got older. Life was reversed in its priorities. His mental reverie was interrupted by his secretary on the intercom.

"Mr. Rossiter, Sir Geoffrey Holden's secretary is calling from New York. Would you like me to put him through?"

"Yes, please, Jenny." Rossiter had worked only once with Sir Geoffrey, serving as one of several assistants on the government reorganization study. Though Sir Geoffrey had taken an interest in his career since, it was unusual for Sir Geoffrey to call personally.

Rossiter picked up his extension, "Good morning, this is Cameron Rossiter."

"Good morning to you, Mr. Rossiter," said the ambassador's secretary. "Sir Geoffrey will be right with you."

After a few seconds' pause, during which Rossiter continued to speculate on the reason for the call, Sir Geoffrey came on the line.

"Cameron, how's the business mogul?"

"I'm well, Sir Geoffrey. How is everything in New York City? Been mugged yet?"

"Not so you'd notice, Cameron, but then most of the mugging at the UN goes on behind closed doors. I've got a little favor to ask of you, and I hope you'll be able to assist."

"Anything within my power."

"There's a young chap I've been dealing with here on an issue of importance to New Zealand's relations with the U.S. I think you know I've been working on the naval visitation issue, and I believe we're coming to some agreement."

"You've certainly generated discussion here, on both sides of the fence. How can I be of help?"

"This young air force officer, O'Brien is his name, Zach O'Brien, will be coming down to formulate a plan of action with our naval boys at Devonport. Actually, Cameron, O'Brien is also a Kiwi on his father's side. His parents now live in the Bay of Islands, but he will need to be near our naval base at Devonport. I called to ask if you could put him up in that palatial abode you call home over on the North Shore."

"Of course, Sir Geoffrey. That's a simple enough request. Anything special I can arrange for him?"

"He's a keen sailor as well, although I doubt he's in your class. Perhaps you could take a few days and show him around the local islands. It would be most appreciated, dear boy."

"When will he arrive?"

"I'll have my secretary get back to you. It should be within the next six weeks or so. I hear you've branched out over to 'Oz' to make a few dollars. How's it going?"

"Very well so far. Glad to be of service, Ambassador. Please be assured we'll treat the Yank right."

"I know you will. My sincere thanks. Think about stopping in on one of your next expeditions to the States. I'd love to show you New York. Might even arrange to get you mugged if we work it right. Cheerio."

"Good day, Sir Geoffrey. My regards to Lady Mildred."

Rossiter replaced the receiver and resumed his gazing out the window. Sir Geoffrey had plenty of contacts in Auckland who could have arranged for O'Brien's lodging. It seemed clear Sir Geoffrey wanted him to meet O'Brien, but as yet Rossiter didn't know why. Time would tell, and for the moment he had other issues requiring his attention.

CHAPTER FIVE

Geneva, Switzerland
May

THE FLIGHT TO GENEVA HAD BEEN PLEASANT ENOUGH, especially for someone who would be fifty million U.S. dollars richer when he returned. Where much could be gained, however, much could be lost. Dealing with these people concerned him. There was no honor to be found in such an alliance. Each had his motivations, and each would look out only for himself.

Stephen Wyndham was traveling alone. He had spent the weekend in Stockholm and two days in Berlin. His flight to Geneva on Swiss Air would be less than an hour, and he didn't intend to be in Geneva long. Before meeting with his contacts, he had two appointments to keep. The primary purpose of clandestine visits to Switzerland was generally financial, and this was no exception. Wyndham had two appointments with banks, one to confirm a recent large deposit and to transfer the funds to another account, and another to arrange for a detailed document to be placed in a safety deposit box. Once both missions were accomplished, he was prepared for his meeting.

Ambassador Haquim had traveled to Geneva from New York and had been in meetings with the World Health Organization, continuing his quest for food for the starving people of northern Iraq, for whom he continued to portray his government's desperate concern. Haquim had arranged to meet Wyndham in a small hotel away from the downtown area, and he had taken three different taxis to arrive.

General Alihambra had been waiting none too patiently in the hotel room since his arrival early that morning. The meeting was set for two P.M., and Haquim was late. Alihambra didn't like having this politician be part of the plan. He would have preferred to limit the knowledge to those he could trust, or at least to those he could control. He had learned well from Salimar, but he also knew if he could not contain control of this project, he would learn one final lesson from the Great Leader.

General Alihambra's career had risen in much the same way as had Abdul Salimar's. A trail of death and deception lay behind his promotions. He comforted himself with the knowledge that were they not dead, he would be. Iraq's political system offered little opportunity for the faint-hearted. Certain of those who no longer threatened him had died at the request of the man he now served, His Excellency, Abdul Salimar.

As Alihambra pondered his situation, Haquim knocked on the door. As the general opened it, he said with a gracious smile, "His Excellency sends his warmest wishes and asks after your health." The little game of "who is closest to the Leader" was often played by those in power, and if you were able to convince your opponents that you had the president's ear, most certainly they would listen.

Haquim was not fooled. He knew that General Alihambra would have preferred to remain completely out of this risky venture and merely continue in his previous role, well established and totally in control of those around him. "It was good of you to come, General," Haquim said as he took a seat. "Are preparations complete?"

"Yes, Ambassador. Funds have been deposited to Wyndham's account. All is prepared, and His Excellency is waiting for our contact following this meeting. He is pleased with your progress at the UN and the opportunity you have provided for this small alliance with one of the Western governments."

Haquim paused, reflecting on Salimar's appointment of him to the United Nations. He had been a loyal Baath Party member and had shown the proper respect to the Leader throughout his career, but one never really knew the purposes for which Salimar selected people to his government. When they were given assignments abroad, however, they almost always had family in Iraq. This assured Salimar of some degree of loyalty, interpreted to mean obedience. During his time at the United Nations, Haquim had met many people seeking an insight into Abdul Salimar. He had always replied with the most flattering and complimentary responses. He had also been approached by those he felt were feeling him out for defection. Haquim was caught in a dangerous game of knowing whom to trust, and many souls with whom he had served over the years were now able to trust completely, in the presence of Allah.

"General, tell me about this Wyndham. Can he deliver?"

"Our agents have reviewed his past performance with 'friends,' and they have been well pleased with his results. His venture last year in stealing an entire shipment of arms from Rasuli in Tunisia, which Rasuli had already sold to the Irish group, was, to say the least, impressive. Rasuli is not an easy man to fool. He comes highly recommended, but the task we have prepared for him will tax his resources. Such goods as we seek are closely guarded, and the technology required is also limited. Where he might procure—"

A knock interrupted General Alihambra in midsentence. Before moving to open the door, he checked the pistol he had placed alongside the cushion in his chair and a second in the rear waistband of his trousers.

"Ah, my dear Wyndham, please come in. You have met Ambassador Haquim, have you not?"

"Once, earlier this year in New York. How is your charity

fund developing, Ambassador? I hope our small contribution was of some assistance."

"Certainly, Mr. Wyndham, all is well, and the peoples of Iraq thank you most sincerely."

Wyndham took a seat and surveyed the room. Months before he had received a notice in one of the post boxes arranged for surreptitious contact, known only to those for whom he had already provided services. Following receipt of this notice, Wyndham had contacted Ambassador Haquim's office at the United Nations and met with the Ambassador to discuss a corporate donation to the charity for which Haquim was then soliciting. The result had been a further contact from General Alihambra, which had culminated in a meeting two months earlier in Zurich. Wyndham waited for the general to begin.

"Did you find our arrangements to your satisfaction, Mr. Wyndham?" Alihambra said, emphasizing the term *arrangements.*

"Yes, indeed, General. I have confirmed your deposit. Only a few details remain to be accomplished. I am prepared to discuss these with you to assure your satisfaction."

For the next half hour, Wyndham proceeded to outline the proposed project, leaving out all essential details regarding locations and personnel involvement. The entire operation would be directed by Wyndham and, with one exception, would use only personnel selected by him. General Alihambra seemed pleased with the proposals, adding some small measures that he felt would justify his report that he had been instrumental in planning the operation. Success was the only outcome that concerned Alihambra, and should they succeed, he wanted to assure the Leader that he had been responsible for all aspects of the plan. Should they not succeed, it mattered little what part he had played.

Concluding the meeting, Wyndham advised General Alihambra on one additional requirement, which only the general could provide. He explained his need, and Alihambra, without hesitation, said it would be no problem.

"Mr. Wyndham, what may I inform His Excellency will be the proposed date of execution?"

"Twenty-five to thirty days following departure," replied Wyndham. "I will notify Ambassador Haquim's office of the day of departure." Wyndham stood, prepared to leave, and said, "Gentlemen, we shall not meet again prior to implementation. Following successful completion of this assignment, I will expect an additional twenty-five million U.S. dollars to be deposited into the same account. Should you require additional assistance as you have indicated, the ambassador can post the usual request for donations to previous donors. Someone will then be in touch."

Wyndham then left the room, leaving Ambassador Haquim and General Alihambra at their most vulnerable stage. Fifty million U.S. dollars of His Excellency's money was in Wyndham's bank account, and they had little idea where to find him other than the charitable mail-out that they had used the first time, as instructed by one of Wyndham's earlier clients.

Ambassador Haquim and General Alihambra had no way of knowing that Gregorio Valasnikov, alias Gregory Farnsworth-Jones, alias Stephen Wyndham, was, to Valasnikov's way of thinking, fulfilling his destiny. He would only be carrying out his own objectives, as well as theirs, and getting paid handsomely for it in the process.

To Gregorio Valasnikov, alias Gregory Farnsworth-Jones, it only seemed appropriate that a new member should join the team and that "Stephen Wyndham" should be the tool by which Silent Wind was resurrected.

Woodbridge, Virginia
May

"Oh, and would you pick up some sweet corn as well?" Alison called out to Zach as he left the kitchen. "You know how George likes his corn."

"And you know how important corn is to me too, don't you?" Zach said, wrapping his arms around Alison, who responded by leaning her head back into his shoulder.

"I seem to vaguely recall something about it, way back when," Alison teased.

When Zach first saw Alison Williams, nearly fifteen years earlier, he had been fresh out of the Air Force Academy and had gone to visit a friend at Brigham Young University. He was shopping in a grocery store when he spotted her, long blonde hair hanging past her shoulders. She was selecting corn on the cob from the produce aisle. He literally bumped into her, causing about a dozen cobs of corn to fall on the floor.

"Oh, excuse me, I wasn't watching where I was going," Zach lied.

"Well, at least you can help me pick these up," Alison had said, exasperated.

"Why so much corn?" Zach asked.

"My roommates and I are having a barbecue this afternoon with some friends over." Alison looked more closely at Zach as he placed the corn back on the counter. "Do you attend the Y?"

"No, no, I've just graduated from the Air Force Academy."

"Well, we clipped your wings this year, didn't we?" Alison taunted, referring to the BYU-Air Force Academy football game.

"Yeah, I must admit we went down in flames. Such a gracious loss, however, must be deserving of a free meal to the losing team, wouldn't you say?" Zach was amazed at himself for being so bold.

"Well, I don't know, I—"

"Just two more lonely lads, one from BYU and one from, let's just say one more who loves corn"—Zach paused—"and blonde hair with green eyes."

From that afternoon on, no one else had ever been under consideration by either of them. All during Zach's air force flight training in Arizona, he would take every opportunity to drive the long weekend up to BYU to be with Alison. They had been married exactly ten months after they met, right after Alison completed her undergraduate degree in child psychology.

Kissing the top of Alison's head, Zach stepped back. "Right," he replied, "sweet corn it is. Be back in a couple of hours." Zach had his chore list, and once again Saturday golf was not on it.

Alison had invited George and Wendy Gresham, their neighbors, over for barbecue this evening, and Zach was looking forward to the evening. Ever since their chance meeting in the store and the subsequent afternoon of grilled corn, barbecues had held a special place for the O'Briens. Fourteen years they had been married, and he still thought he'd got the best of the bargain. He loved, or perhaps, as he sometimes thought of it, cherished, this woman who provided for him so much of the purpose and meaning his life required.

"C'mon, Michael. You going with me?" he called out to his young son.

"Coming, Dad," Michael replied. Michael was the O'Brien's middle child and only son. At seven, he was all boy and was fully involved in keeping ahead of his sisters. In three weeks, Michael would be eight. They climbed in the car, and Zach backed out of the driveway. Patricia, twelve, came running out of the house. "Dad, will you be going near Thrifty?"

"We'll be in the mall for a while, Pat. What can I get you?"

"I need some Clearasil."

Surprised, Zach responded, "But you have lovely skin!"

"Oh, Dad, look at it!" She thrust out her chin, pointing to a microscopic red spot. "It's Gi-nourmous. If Greg sees me like this, I'll just die. Really, pleasssse."

Smiling, Zach surrendered. "OK, Pat." He winked at his son. "We'll do what we can to save your life, won't we, Michael?" Greg was George and Wendy's thirteen-year-old son, and of course he would be over for the barbecue this evening. Greg had a paper route, and on weekends he delivered the paper about six A.M. For the past seven weeks, Pat had been up by six o'clock so she could just happen to be the one who opened the door when he rode his bike by the house. Zach and Michael backed out of the driveway and headed for the freeway.

"Dad, why are girls so stupid?" Michael queried.

"What makes you say that?"

"Well, we're always late for church because Pat has to fix her hair, or paint her nails, or do some other stupid thing. Now she's ga-ga over Greg Gresham."

"Well, Michael, I suppose that does seem pretty stupid. But I think you might have a slightly different view in a few years."

"No way."

"It usually happens as you grow. Speaking of growing, you'll be eight soon. Are you ready for your baptism?"

"Yeah."

"Have you been learning about the Savior in church?"

"Yeah."

"And?" Zach elicited.

"And other stuff."

As usual, Zach would have to pry information out of his son. "I mean, what have you been learning about the Savior?"

"Oh. That he died for us."

"Do you remember why he died for us?"

"Yeah, ummm, I think so, ummm . . . I can't remember."

Zach began to feel like a dentist pulling a couple of stubborn teeth. Trying a different tack, he changed direction. "Are things going well in school?"

"Sure." Michael knew how to change direction too. "Dad, can we go to McDonald's for lunch?"

Zach just shook his head and wondered how old kids had to be before they reached a five-minute attention span. "Sure Michael, after shopping."

Driving along I-95 toward the shopping center, Zach began to think about their upcoming trip to New Zealand. Ambassador Holden had arranged for him to meet with New Zealand naval officials to coordinate the forthcoming visit by an American ship. The whole O'Brien family would be going because the kids hadn't seen Zach's parents for nearly two years. Zach was pleased that he had been involved in developing this new change in American policy. Perhaps the world was changing after all, and nations could turn their attention to solving human tragedies rather than expending so much on defending what they already had. Turning off the freeway toward Capitol Faire Mall, O'Brien felt hopeful about the visit.

"Dad, I know why."

Jolted out of his thought process, Zach wondered what Michael was talking about. "What? What was that, Michael?"

"I said I know why Jesus died for us. He died for us because he loves us."

Zach pulled into a parking space, turned off the ignition, and turned to look at his son. "Michael, if you already know that, then you know the most important lesson we ever learn in this life. I'm very proud that you're old enough now to be baptized and that you understand about the Savior. We are all proud of you, even your 'stupid' sisters. All of us love you. Now, let's go get those chores done. I can already taste my Big Mac."

"Can I have a Happy Meal, Dad?"

"Absolutely, Michael."

A few hours later, as Zach was working on the barbeque to get the coals just right, Alison came out to see if the grill was ready. This was their first outdoor barbecue of the summer, and everything had needed cleaning.

"Every winter I say I'll wrap this barbecue in plastic or tarp and keep it in good shape for the next spring, but each year it's filthy."

"It's OK, dear. It needs a good cleaning each year anyway."

Giving his wife an obvious visual check, he whistled, "You're looking pretty good, Mrs. O'Brien."

"Why thank you, sir. I'll bet you say that to all the ladies."

"Well, yes, I do, but to the very special ones, I mean it."

Alison cocked her eyebrows in a questioning manner, reaching up to give him a little kiss.

"Hallo, anybody home?" the voice of George Gresham boomed down the driveway as he and Wendy and their four children made their way around the back of the house. "Is this the place?"

"George, good to see you. Come on in." Zach shook George's hand and gave Wendy a peck on the cheek. George wrapped his arms around Alison and lifted her partially off the ground.

"Put her down, George," Wendy admonished. "He embarrasses me so much. He's a menace to all he meets."

George laughed. "True, true. Well now, what's for dinner? Something worth staying for?"

Wendy shook her head. "For you, baked crow."

"I like mine medium rare, without feathers."

"Americana," Alison quickly added. "Hamburgers, hot dogs, corn on the cob, watermelon, and then ice cream, homemade of course."

"Reminds me of my misspent youth in Texas," George replied. "Texans are big on Americana."

Alison knew, despite Wendy's seeming disapproval, how much Wendy loved George; in fact, everybody Alison knew loved George Gresham. His love was evident for all, and he showed it in his everyday actions. George had spent his early years practicing law, and fifteen years ago he had been appointed by Virginia's governor to the circuit court. He had been on the bench ever since, and he had a reputation for fair and equitable distribution of justice.

George took a root beer from the iced tub and sat in one of the lounge chairs, while Wendy and Alison went into the house to complete preparations. "What's new at the NSA, Zach?"

"I'm sorry, George. We have a Democrat for president now, so I'm not allowed to discuss national policy with Republicans."

"Oh, it's OK, Zach. I've had two seminars in 'Down Home' talk, and I know all that 'good ole boy' stuff."

They both had a good laugh. Washington, D.C., was surrounded by thousands of political appointees from both parties who were either in or out of favor, depending on who was in the White House and Congress. George, and Zach as well, were basically Republican, although Zach, as a member of the military, was prohibited from taking a public stance or campaigning for any partisan office candidate.

"We're coming to an understanding on what we've called the Kiwi Initiative. Basically, the Kiwis want us to recommence naval visits, which will require some concession regarding our nuclear declaration policy. You know, weapons on board and such."

"And you are, of course, unbiased in all this?"

"Absolutely . . . not," Zach said with demonstrable pause. "I want it to succeed. I think it would be good for both countries." Moving to the back door, Zach called out, "Dinner's ready. C'mon kids and ladies, before George gets it all."

After the Greshams had left and the kids were tucked in, Zach and Alison went back out on the patio to enjoy the cool evening air. Zach thought Alison looked radiant in the early moonlight as she lay back on her recliner, her hair flowing over the edges of the cushion.

"That was fun tonight, Zach," Alison commented. "I really like the Greshams."

"So do I. They're a good family. Speaking of good families, how are the O'Briens doing?"

"What do you mean?"

"I mean this is my infrequent husbandly 'check in.' I'm gone so often on assignment, I fall behind somewhat. Pat needed Clearisil this morning so Greg wouldn't think she was a total loss."

"Oh, that. Well, your daughter's growing up before your eyes. Or maybe I should say, 'in your absence.' I wouldn't worry about it too much, sweetheart. They know you love them."

"And you?" Zach said reaching for her hand.

"This lady feels the same way."

"Sometimes I wonder, is it all worth it? My job takes me away so often. There are only so many years available to us to teach our kids and be with them."

"That's true, but what you do is important, Zach. When you're gone and I'm alone with cuts, bruises, and heartaches from newly developing teenagers, I remind myself that what you do makes a difference. Maybe we can't always see it immediately, and possibly much of the world will never know, but *we* know."

Zach faced Alison and softly brushed her cheek with his hand. "Have I told you today how much I love you, Alison?"

"Today? Here it is evening, and you haven't even said it once." She looked at him, radiating love in her eyes. "You're a good father, Zach, and the best husband I could hope for. If this is, as you said, your husbandly 'check in' time, then know this: your family loves you, they pray for you always, and your wife loves you with all her heart, and equally important, she knows you love her. And one more thing. Your Heavenly Father loves you. Rest assured he's told me that many times in answer to my prayers."

This woman, Zach thought, is all that a man could hope for and more than he deserved.

Wellington, New Zealand
The Beehive
May

"I have Prime Minister John Blankenship's secretary on the line. She would like to put the prime minister through to you."

"Good," said Prime Minister Onekawa. "I'll take it in my private office."

"Yes, sir. Putting him through now."

Onekawa sat behind his desk in a small side office off his main suite and lifted the receiver. "Prime Minister, how are you this morning?"

"Peter, we'd better get off this prime minister bit or we'll spend half our time on the phone, calling titles," John Blankenship commented.

Onekawa laughed and replied, "Right you are, John. How can we be of assistance today?"

"Just a short call, Peter. Her Majesty has advised us that she would like to send Prince Andrew to represent the Crown at the upcoming visit of the American naval vessel. Do you foresee any difficulty with arranging that?"

Onekawa immediately saw it as a bit of flag waving, designed to publicize the Royal commitment to the Commonwealth. Stopping the infection, so to speak. Over the past couple of years, Australia had been proposing withdrawal from Commonwealth membership and formation of an independent republic. More than a political ploy, it was drawing positive support from the population as well as in the parliament. The Crown didn't want it to spread across the Tasman to New Zealand.

"That would be wonderful, John. We can arrange that. Would he be here long?"

"Probably not. His schedule is always tight, and we are essentially adding this at the last moment. He will arrive in Auckland first, and then he would actually like to fly out to the ships a day or so before they arrive, coming in with the vessels. Naval protocol, I should think."

"We'll handle it. I presume the admiralty will be in touch?

"Yes, Admiral Sir Reginald Johns will coordinate the visit."

"Fine, John, fine. I'll alert Admiral Pottsdam of the visit. Thank you so much for the call. We'd like to see you at some point, John," Onekawa offered.

Blankenship laughed. "I'd love it, Peter, especially the trout fishing, but I might not have a seat in the House when I got back." He laughed again.

"Well, we could always use another conservative POMy bloke out here." British subjects in the South Pacific were often referred to as POMs, stretching back to the time when most people sent from Britain to Australia were "Prisoners of Her, or His, Majesty," POM for short.

"I think I'll keep riding the whirlwind here, Peter, but thanks for the offer."

"And a good day to you, John."

Returning to his office, he called out to his secretary, "Get Admiral Pottsdam on the phone would you, please?"

"Yes, sir. Right away."

Persian Gulf
USS **Heritage**
May

Captain Wilson Richards had just concluded a staff meeting in the officers' wardroom, and the junior officers had filed out when Richards asked his executive officer, Commander Bernard Johannsen, "Ever been to New Zealand, Barney?"

"No, Captain, never had the pleasure. I've visited Australia and some of the Pacific Islands, but unfortunately I missed New Zealand."

"This communication just came in. Seems the chief of naval operations wants you to take a look down there. Think you could work that in to your schedule?"

"Got any idea what the CNO wants me to do in New Zealand, Captain?"

"From the thrust of this message, he wants you to wave the flag a bit. Seems you'll have to go on another ship as well. Let's see . . . " Captain Richards paused momentarily and tried hard to keep from smiling. "Oh, yes, here it is, USS *Cherokee*."

Johannsen was beginning to get a bit suspicious by this time. "The new Apache class nuclear-powered guided missile cruiser. She's just off the dockyards. The last I heard, she was about to finish sea trials, berthing out of Norfolk."

"Yeah, I've been following her progress," Richards said. "Seems New Zealand wants to invite the navy back, and the president thinks this is a good time to restore relations. Auckland used to be a great port to visit."

"Sounds like we're trying to mend some fences that have been down for a while. I could think of worse duty."

"Well, in any event, *Cherokee*'s short one crewman for this publicity tour. It'll include a few stops down the South American east coast, sail around the Horn, and berth in Auckland. The CNO thought you could lend a hand." Richards watched his XO carefully as he added the next part: "Oh yes, the last line of the message. I nearly forgot. Something about a fourth stripe . . . "

Captain Wilson Richards stepped toward Commander Bernard Johannsen as the XO registered shock. Pumping his hand, Richards said, "Congratulations, *Captain* Johannsen. A very well-deserved promotion and long overdue. Barney, it's been my pleasure to serve with you, and the *Heritage* will miss you. God speed on your new command."

Richards and Johannsen had served together for three years and knew each other well. Admiral Designate Richards and Captain selectee Johannsen were academy men and, as such, had only one specific goal: command of their own vessels. Now it was Captain Bernard Johannsen's turn.

CHAPTER SIX

▬▬ ▬ ▬ ▬ ▬ ▬▬

Northern Japan
Small Private Cemetery
June

TRANSLATED, THE JAPANESE TOMBSTONE READ:

TOSHAMATSU
Husband born 3 February 1910
Wife born 18 November 1914
Our loving parents died
12 December 1963

Mr. and Mrs. Toshamatsu watched quietly as the workers
excavated the cemetery plot. Though most Japanese chose cre-
mation for their dead, a few chose burial. Mr. Toshamatsu had
received permission from the proper authorities to relocate his
parents to their new home in the south of Japan. Finally the
workmen reached wood and began the process of gently lifting
the caskets to the surface. Both parents had been buried doubled

up in the same plot, a common practice in a country where space was at a premium.

Upon completion of the task, the caskets were washed down and loaded into a waiting hearse. The couple thanked the workmen, got in their car, and followed the hearse out onto the motorway. About fifteen miles down the road, the hearse pulled off onto a side road and stopped. The Japanese couple followed, parking immediately behind the stopped hearse. A man from the hearse got out and walked back to the car, handing the Japanese man an envelope containing five thousand U.S. dollars, after which the couple drove away.

The hearse continued down the side road, meeting a moving van about five miles further on, and stopped again. Four men were waiting. They opened the rear door of the hearse, removed the caskets one by one, and transferred them to the enclosed van. The van and the hearse then left in opposite directions. Had the authorities felt to open the caskets, their discovery would have surprised them. The bodies of Mr. and Mrs. Honaka Toshamatsu had been cremated over thirty years earlier, one day short of their funeral. The resurrection of Silent Wind had begun.

New York City
Crossfire, CNN Television Network
June

"Welcome back, ladies and gentlemen. We've been at it hot and heavy over this latest issue of U.S. naval warships declaring nuclear weapons. To refresh everyone's memory, New Zealand, because of their nonnuclear stance, has not permitted our ships to visit for over ten years. U.S. defense policy would not allow us to declare that visiting ships were not carrying nuclear weapons, so New Zealand has excluded all U.S. ships. The United States has now rescinded this policy, and the first visit to New Zealand is planned sometime in July or August.

Our guests tonight have been discussing the merits of this policy change. On my right is Sir Geoffrey Holden, New Zealand's ambassador to the United Nations, and on my left is Senator Henry Walenski, Democrat from Pennsylvania."

"Sir Geoffrey, before the break you were telling our audience why this change was mutually advantageous to New Zealand and America. Please continue."

"Thank you, Tom. As you know, New Zealand has been a strong supporter of most U.S. policies around the world for many years. This exclusion policy was adopted by our government during a period when nuclear power was receiving worldwide press coverage. We determined that it was in our interest to preclude the development of nuclear power in New Zealand."

The moderator intervened at this point to remind the audience that the nuclear accident at Three Mile Island had happened concurrently with debate in New Zealand.

"Ambassador, New Zealand is a country blessed with abundant hydroelectric resources also, is it not?"

"That's exactly right, Tom. It was not necessary for us to consider nuclear power generation as an option, and so we discarded any further consideration." Sir Geoffrey continued to provide background, including the fact that the French had been conducting nuclear testing in the South Pacific for years, against the desires of all the nations within geographical proximity to their testing. Greenpeace had been strongly protesting such testing, and French intelligence agents had brazenly planted a bomb on the Greenpeace flagship, *Rainbow Warrior,* and sunk her in Auckland harbor, with loss of life. Sir Geoffrey concluded, "Basically, all the factors combined to present a negative case, and consensus was easily reached. No nuclear visitation."

"Ambassador, that's quite a history, but is it not true that now New Zealand has reversed her position on nuclear propulsion?" Tom turned to his other guest. "Perhaps we should hear from Senator Walenski."

"Thanks, Tom. My constituency includes the Three Mile Island community, and so we have the benefit of extensive postaccident research. I serve on the Armed Forces Committee, and it is well known where I stand on this issue. I believe the U.S. has no business declaring to the world what types of weapons we carry on our ships. It will diminish our security capability and allow those who oppose us to have more information than we want them to have.

"We don't need to visit New Zealand, Tom; they need us. So many of these little countries rant and rave about their rights and try to tell the U.S. what to do, but they're all standing in line when the Foreign Aid Committee debates who to assist."

"Senator," Tom queried, "isn't it possible that with the reduced tension in the world since the collapse of the Soviet Union, we might benefit from some reduction on our part? Certainly, it would offer some comfort to our allies that the U.S. is also looking for ways to reduce the possibility of conflict."

"We must ever be vigilant, Tom, and never let down our guard. Just because the Soviets are gone doesn't mean there are no bad guys left. The U.S. is, and always will be, the guardian of freedom, and we must be prepared to defend our smaller allies, including New Zealand, even if they disagree with our policies."

Sir Geoffrey interjected, "Tom, if I might add . . . "

"Please, Ambassador, go right ahead," said the commentator.

"New Zealand appreciates the role the United States has played during this century of turmoil, and we are grateful for the assistance, although we have never found it necessary to join the queue for economic assistance." Smiling at the camera, Sir Geoffrey continued, "This agreement between the United States of America and New Zealand has received wide support in the United Nations and has demonstrated to that body the sincere intent of Americans everywhere to join their neighbors in peaceful propositions. All of us want to move toward a twenty-first century free of the fears and catastrophes of this century. I for one applaud the courage and foresight of President Eastman as he makes such decisions."

With Sir Geoffrey's rebuttal, air time ran out. "Thank you gentlemen for your contribution to our program this evening. Good-bye until tomorrow, when our guests will be the foreign minister from Bosnia and Congresswoman Stratford. Our guests this evening have been Sir Geoffrey Holden, ambassador to the United Nations from New Zealand, and Senator Walenski, Democrat from Pennsylvania."

Once the policy had been announced and visitation scheduled, talk shows around the country carried the subject, with opinion about evenly divided. The president had taken the opportunity during a commencement address at the United States Naval Academy to announce the New Zealand visit of the nuclear-powered USS *Cherokee,* on which four members of the graduating class whom he was addressing would be serving. He hailed it as another breakthrough for peaceful coexistence in a world finally outgrowing its need for belligerence.

New York City
United Nations Building
June

"Good Morning, Iraqi delegation, Ambassador Haquim's office, how may I help you?"

"Ambassador Haquim, please."

"I'm sorry, sir. The ambassador is out of town for several days. May anyone else be of assistance?"

"No, thank you very much. Is it possible for you to get a message through to the ambassador?"

"Certainly, sir."

"Please inform the ambassador that the departure date for his expected delivery will be July 9. Would you please repeat that back to me. The message is urgent, and the ambassador is waiting for the details."

"Of course, sir. 'The departure date for his expected delivery will be July 9.' May I tell him who called, sir?"

"Mr. Wyndham."

"Yes, thank you, Mr. Wyndham, I'll advise the ambassador today."

Baghdad, Iraq
Military Headquarters
June

Once Ambassador Haquim had arrived back in Iraq, the old fears returned. Each time ministers serving abroad were summoned home, they never knew if it was to be their last visit. Salimar had seldom given warning of his displeasure and had even called gov-

ernment officials to his headquarters to receive honors, immediately prior to their disappearance.

For the time being, Haquim felt he was safe, at least until the
success or failure of the current operation was concluded. He had
received Wyndham's message, and the clock was now running.
With a July 9 departure of the ship, execution date was approximately early August. To a large extent, his and General
Alihambra's fates were in the hands of a man they knew little
about.

Wyndham concerned Haquim considerably less than the
immediate danger. He was meeting with Salimar this afternoon.
Haquim knew there was more to the plan than Salimar had
advised. There always was. His long association with Salimar
brought many memories, none of them comforting to Haquim as
he approached old age. Of course, merely approaching old age
was in and of itself something to be appreciated.

As Haquim recalled Salimar's rise to power through intimi-
dation and murder, he recalled sitting in a cabinet meeting during
the Iran-Iraq war, which was going badly for Iraq. Salimar suggested to those who were present that perhaps he should resign
for the good of the country. Most ministers were too astute to fall
for this trap, but Salimar's health minister agreed and offered to
accept Salimar's resignation. Salimar dragged him into the next
room and shot him, then dismembered his body and had it
returned to his widow. At times Salimar had purged members of
the Revolutionary Council by having those remaining in favor
form the firing squad, thereby assuring both loyalty and shared
responsibility.

Haquim was clearly aware that Abdul Salimar set no limits
to achieve his objectives. Haquim now wondered what the next
phase of this dangerous plan would be. What had already been
implemented would terrorize the heart of any sane person, but,
Haquim thought deep in the recesses of his mind, perhaps the real
problem was whether or not Salimar was a sane person, and there
was only one answer to such a problem.

The car arrived for Haquim promptly at a quarter to four. He
rode silently in the back, mentally preparing his report for

Salimar. No written accounts of these proceedings would be allowed, and reports were to be given in person with no notes for summary. Upon arrival at party headquarters, Haquim quickly rode the elevator to the lower levels where he entered the cabinet room. General Alihambra was already present. They shared non-verbal greetings and waited for Salimar. No other cabinet members were present. Since the inception of this operation, only he, Salimar, and Alihambra knew the plans. Haquim was also sure that only Salimar knew the overall objective, which certainly would not be revealed during this first stage in progress. Merely humiliating the Americans did not provide the strategic objectives that Salimar continued to pursue. Ever since the Gulf War, as the West called it, Salimar had renewed his plans to achieve the unification of all Arab brothers, with Salimar as the focal point.

Salimar appeared in the doorway, and Haquim and Alihambra immediately stood. He moved wordlessly and with no acknowledgment or greeting to the head of the table. Once seated, the other two resumed their seats, and Salimar gave a slight nod of his head to General Alihambra, giving permission to start the briefing.

"Excellency," the general began, "I am pleased to report that your plan is progressing right on schedule. The U.S. Navy warship will leave Norfolk, Virginia, on July 9, making several stops in South America and arriving at our designated location within the first ten days in August. Mr. Wyndham has assured us that all aspects of his operation are in hand and also on schedule."

Salimar turned his attention to Haquim, who began to describe recent developments in the UN, "Excellency, the New Zealand ambassador has succeeded in his mission to schedule this visit to New Zealand. As you directed, this objective was supported by our delegation to the UN and by several other delegations. In fact the New Zealand proposal acquired support from most delegations, including those usually in disagreement. Your plan was bold and imaginative, and when we succeed, it will prove inspired. Others will quickly see the wisdom of your peaceful proposals."

Salimar considered these comments before speaking. He

stood and began pacing the room. "Instruct your staff to begin release of statements charging the presence of nuclear weapons on U.S. vessels in our nearby waters and condemning the potential for disaster. Assure the world that the peace-loving people of Iraq simply wish to unify their country and bring peace and stability to the region."

Salimar continued his pacing, pausing occasionally to consider his intentions. Twenty minutes later, he had completely outlined his directions for the events up to the planned incident in early August. He concluded, "Haquim, you will continue to approach governments both friendly and neutral to enlist their support in this peaceful venture."

"Yes, Excellency," Haquim replied.

"General," Salimar addressed Alihambra, "yours will be the mission of contacting Wyndham again. Advise him that we will have additional need for his services. Advise him that he is to be ready to act within three weeks of notification. To assist in his preparations, inform him that the second incident will be in England in November and that we will provide further information regarding the third incident. Advise him of these facts immediately *following* completion of the first incident, not before. Understood?"

General Alihambra stood to attention and replied, "Yes, Excellency."

Salimar once again turned his attention to Haquim and said with a brief smile, "That will be all, Ambassador. Keep me advised of your progress and responses from other governments. We must always know our friends from our enemies, Haquim, is that not so?"

"Certainly, Excellency, most certainly."

Haquim departed the room and Salimar turned to Alihambra. "Summon the general staff tomorrow morning for briefing. You know who to preclude from attending."

"It will be done immediately, Excellency."

Salimar sat and dismissed Alihambra with a wave of the hand. He remained sitting and thinking for the next half hour, contemplating the formulation of his plans, all of which seemed to be developing so well. These Americans possessed all the military capability in the world but so foolishly lacked the resolve to use it. They were so predictable.

Washington, D.C.
The Pentagon
Office of the Chief of Naval Operations
June

Captain Bernard Johannsen admired the new stripe on his sleeve as he completed uniform preparations for this morning's meeting with the CNO. He had departed the USS *Heritage* only a week earlier and had been in Washington the past two days being briefed by the Joint Chiefs staff and Air Force Major O'Brien from the NSA, who had arranged the visit with the Kiwis. How the air force ever got involved in a naval visit, Johannsen didn't know, but O'Brien had seemed like a nice-enough guy, and he hadn't tried to tell him what needed to be done. This morning with the CNO would be a different story. He fully expected the complete drill about crew relations while ashore in New Zealand and the expected repercussions should anything unseemly occur. The CNO had to see the challenge. After all his crew of 470 were not comprised of Sunday School boys.

As Captain Johannsen drove his rental car into the Joint Chiefs parking area, he looked for a visitor's space, finally finding one about six rows out. This was one place he had never sought a tour. If they kept him at sea for the remainder of his career, he would be quite happy. Entering the building, he provided his identity card to the sentry, who found his name on the expected visitor list. After receiving a visitor pass, Johannsen was escorted to the CNO's office suite. The female lieutenant junior grade asked him if he would like a cup of coffee, which he declined. He was eight minutes early and sat down to wait.

In a few minutes, the LTJG advised him that the chief would see him now. Captain Johannsen rose, placed his cap under his arm, and entered the admiral's office, coming to a position of attention eighteen inches in front of the desk.

"Sir, Captain Bernard Johannsen, reporting as ordered."

Admiral Charles "Chuck" Hansen, United States Naval Academy, '56, looked up from behind his desk and examined Captain Johannsen. Hansen had thirty-six years of active service and was a rated pilot, as well as a proponent of nuclear propulsion. He had served under the legendary Hyman Rickover, whose reign in the nuclear navy was unparalleled. Having served such a tough taskmaster for nearly nine years gave Hansen an appreciation for the tradition and formality associated with reporting to a senior admiral. Hansen, however, had never assumed the brusque and often tactless demeanor for which Rickover was noted.

"At ease, Captain. Please be seated." Hansen gestured to the small seating area around a coffee table. "Lt. Pickering, please have a pot of coffee sent in and ask Commander Benton to join us."

"Aye, aye, Admiral," Pickering replied.

"Congratulations on your new command, Captain Johannsen. Captain Richards tells me it's well deserved and his only concern is breaking in a new executive officer."

"Thank you, Admiral. It was a pleasure to serve with Captain Richards. He'll make a fine admiral, but I know he'll miss the bridge."

"Don't we all?" sighed Admiral Hansen. "The joy of seeing the next generation like yourself take over sea command is tempered by the fact that we have those years behind us."

"I understand, sir."

"No, I doubt you do, Johannsen, but perhaps you will some day." Hansen turned to the door as Commander Benton entered.

"Good morning, Admiral, you sent for me, sir?"

"Yes, Commander, I'd like you to meet Captain Johannsen. You saw the orders assigning Johannsen as skipper of the *Cherokee*. Please be good enough to brief the Captain on what we can expect from the Kiwis."

Johannsen stood and offered his hand to Benton, who reached across the coffee table to accept the handshake. "It's a pleasure to meet you, Captain, and please accept my congratulations on your new command. The *Cherokee* is first class in every respect." The two sat down, and Benton began his briefing, "The expected routing is down the East Coast, through the West Indies, and on to South America. Brief stops have been planned in Rio de Janeiro and Buenos Aires. Then you will proceed around the Horn, coming to a northwesterly heading. HMNZS *Northland,* a Kiwi frigate, will come out about a thousand miles to accompany you in the rest of the way. Detailed briefing documents will be a part of your orders for arrival in New Zealand. There will be three stops, in Christchurch, Wellington, and Auckland, and you will spend about two weeks in New Zealand."

Johannsen looked at the admiral and asked, "Admiral, the trip sounds quite routine. Any particular political considerations I should be aware of?"

"There is one recently added wrinkle. A member of the British royal family, Prince Andrew, will be visiting New Zealand to coincide with the arrival of *Cherokee,* and he will most likely fly out a couple of days before. He will probably be berthed on the *Northland,* but the details have not been worked out yet. He is a fully qualified naval officer, with a helicopter rating. You just need to be aware that there is this new political dimension."

"Will we have any American political dignitaries aboard, sir?"

"Not at present, although they will be at the receptions in the three major cities you'll visit. Actually the New Zealand ambassador to the United Nations, Sir Geoffrey Holden, initiated the whole thing, and the National Security Agency developed the concept. Frankly, Captain, there are still those at the top who are not happy about this change in policy. To reveal armament goes against the grain."

"Understand, Admiral. We'll do our best to make a good presentation."

"Fine, Captain Johannsen. If there are no further questions, Commander Benton will provide you with the necessary background on the Kiwi commander who will rendezvous with you after you round the Horn. Best of luck on this mission. And again, enjoy your time at the helm while you can. It goes all too quickly."

Johannsen and Benton both stood, coming to attention while

Admiral Hansen returned to his desk. They turned to leave, Johannsen following Commander Benton. For the remainder of the morning Benton advised Johannsen of several considerations of this visit. During the process, Johannsen came to the conclusion that Benton was one of those who regretted the decision to declare weaponry publicly before entering port. Change always arouses the fear of those who are unwilling to seek new horizons, Johannsen thought.

CHAPTER SEVEN

━━━ ▬ ▬ ▬ ▬ ━━━

Auckland, New Zealand
International Airport
June

Cᴀᴍᴇʀᴏɴ Rᴏssɪᴛᴇʀ sᴀᴛ ɪɴ ᴛʜᴇ sᴍᴀʟʟ McDonald's annex down-stairs in the arrival area of the international airport. He had been there since 6:30 ᴀ.ᴍ., even though the flight from San Francisco via Hawaii was not due until 7:05. The flight eventually arrived ten minutes early, but it was now 7:40, and passengers were just beginning to come through the entryway following customs clear-ance. Rossiter was meeting Major Zachariah O'Brien. Rossiter knew that O'Brien's parents were somewhere in the crowd, since he had indicated he would be bringing his wife and children on this trip as well. His parents would take the children back to the Bay of Islands for several days, while O'Brien and his wife, Alison, would stay with Rossiter at his home on the North Shore.

Rossiter had spent his time privately guessing which couple were O'Brien's parents. He had narrowed the choices down to two couples in their fifties or sixties. He knew from Sir Geoffrey that O'Brien's father was a retired U.S. Army colonel, even though he had been born and raised in New Zealand. He also was aware that Colonel O'Brien had won the American Medal of Honor, the Yank's equivalent to the Victoria Cross. These few facts had led Rossiter to focus his attention on the tall, stately gentleman with an erect bearing. His wife was also a tall woman, at least 5'7", with a round face.

Rossiter was just about to approach the elderly couple and ask if they might be the O'Briens when they moved quickly toward the reception area, smiles appearing on their faces. They went to greet a family—a man in his midthirties, a woman of the same age, and three young children. Rossiter was sure he had been right. This was certainly the O'Brien clan. Major O'Brien wrapped his arms around his mother and lifted her off the ground, while his wife gave Colonel O'Brien a warm embrace. Hugs and kisses followed all around for the grandchildren, and Rossiter stayed clear for several minutes, allowing the family to enjoy their reunion. Americans always seemed to have a need to physically demonstrate their affection, and although this family possessed a strong Kiwi and Yankee mix, clearly both cultures had melded, and they felt comfortable with one another. The family greeting made Rossiter think of his newly developing relationship with Michelle Duffield. He had to admit, he had found it quite appealing to have his arms around her as well, even if it wasn't in the airport foyer.

After several minutes had elapsed and Rossiter saw the family chatting, he noticed O'Brien start looking around as if to locate someone else. He walked up and introduced himself. "Major O'Brien?"

"Right. You must be Cameron Rossiter."

"Yes, welcome to New Zealand. Sorry, on second thought, that probably sounds a bit trite since you most likely are as comfortable here as in the States."

"I love them both. Please call me Zach."

"And please call me Cameron."

"Let me introduce my wife, Alison, and these are my parents,

Clinton and Kate O'Brien." Rossiter was greeted by the elder O'Briens and Zach's wife while the children just looked on.

Rossiter spoke first to Colonel O'Brien. "It is my pleasure to meet your family, sir. I've read about your exploits, and I'm honored to make your acquaintance."

"That was a long time ago, young man, and I was very lucky. We've read somewhat concerning your yachting success as well. If you're ever in the Bay of Islands, please honor us with a visit. We'd love to have you and your wife."

"Thank you, Colonel. When I find a young lady who would be willing to have me, I'll certainly let her know of the offer."

Kate O'Brien smiled at her husband and took his arm. "See, dear, aren't you lucky? You found someone who would have you a long time ago."

"Mom," added Alison, "I think you're both pretty lucky."

Major O'Brien was beginning to feel that Rossiter would be overwhelmed by this mutual appreciation society his family presented and nodded to his father.

"Right," the elder O'Brien said, "let's get this show on the road. Kate, we need to take these kids home and get some marmite stuck into them to put some meat on their bones. What do you say?"

"Yuck," Michael piped up. "I don't want none of that stuff. Grandpa Flynn says that all it's good for is caulking windows."

Zach O'Brien brought a close to the fun and games by assigning each child to carry one bag out to the car. Speaking to his father, he said, "Dad, Alison and I will go with Mr. Rossiter. I have a meeting tomorrow with the commander at the Devonport Naval Station. We'll spend the weekend with Rossiter, and then I have a couple of meetings till about Wednesday. We should be up to see you and Mom by about Thursday. We're scheduled to fly back a week from Thursday."

"That's fine, Son. You take care of your responsibilities, and we'll take care of these little Yankiwis."

Zach put his arm around his mom, and they all started to walk to the car park. Grandpa O'Brien said, "Come on, Michael, give your grandpa a hand with these bags, and we'll see how strong you are. If they're too heavy, you're going to need some marmite, young man."

"Gross, Grandpa. I want McDonald's."

After the family said their good-byes in the parking lot, Rossiter took Zach and Alison O'Brien to his car, a shiny black BMW, and they left for his home. Crossing the harbor bridge, Alison remarked how beautiful this view of Auckland always seemed—the bridge, the harbor, a large marina, and dozens of yachts in the harbor, with a background of the downtown Auckland skyline. Rossiter exited the Motorway at Takapuna and turned right toward Devonport. In about ten minutes, they drove up the driveway of an elegant home, obviously recently built. Set on the side of a hill, it was a three-level home in the popular white Mediterranean look, with glass surrounding all sides, providing extended views.

They carried their bags into the home, going straight through to the rear of the house, which contained a large wraparound lounge with sliding glass doors all across the rear. Outside the windows was an enormous deck that included a barbecue pit and a large, covered spa. Immediately below the deck was a full-size swimming pool, connected to solar heating panels on the north-facing roof of the home. The most beautiful aspect of the home, however, was the commanding view of the Auckland Harbor and the sea, from the bridge on the right, clear around to Rangitoto, the island volcano in the harbor to the east.

The house was extremely well sited, and Alison whistled appreciatively to express her admiration. "Cameron, finding a woman who would be willing to have you shouldn't be too hard a task, I should think. This is an absolutely lovely home."

"Thank you, Mrs. O'Brien. My parents came from Christ-church during some of the building, and my mother offered some suggestions."

"Please call me Alison. It's so kind of you to offer your home for our stay."

"No problem at all. Zach, let me show you your room, and then I can show you the maps I've outlined, showing where you need to go. You probably know Auckland pretty well already, don't you?"

"Most places, but I've never been out to the naval base."

"It's less than five minutes. In fact, you can see a couple of the ships from the deck. After I show you around, I'll run back downtown to my office. Please make yourselves at home—take a shower, or sleep if you'd like. I've made arrangements for dinner this evening in Auckland. I hope you don't mind, I've asked a friend to join us."

"So," said Alison, "someone has begun the conversion process?"

"I must admit," Cameron responded with a sheepish grin, "I'm a bit more confused than usual, so perhaps you can help me shed some light on the matter."

Alison smiled. "There never was a woman who was not completely willing to relieve a handsome man of his fears concerning a permanent relationship."

"One step at a time, one step at a time," Cameron said, laughing. "Zach, I've left the keys to my Commodore station wagon on the kitchen table. It's in the garage, and it's yours for the duration of your stay. If you need anything else while I'm gone, please phone my office. The number is also on the kitchen table. Well, I'm off. See you around six. Our dinner reservation is for eight."

Zach walked Cameron to the door, "Thank you again, Cameron. It's very considerate of you to take strangers into your home."

"Not strangers, Zach. Prospective friends, I suspect. Sir Geoffrey is seldom wrong in his judgment."

"I'll grant you that, and he's quite an exceptional diplomat as well. See you this evening."

For the rest of the morning Zach and Alison O'Brien settled into the Rossiter household, unpacking and cleaning up after the long overnight flight from the States. As for the O'Brien children, they were asleep in Grandpa O'Brien's car before they had even crossed the bridge, with four-year-old Kate cuddled in her grandmother Kate's arms. The oldest daughter, Patricia, twelve, had stretched out on the back seat, while Michael, eight, lay on the blankets in the back of the station wagon. Kathleen Heather Flynn and Clinton Michael O'Brien had raised eight children, all of whom were married and who were expanding the O'Brien clan. They now had seventeen grandchildren. Kate and Clinton had been married over forty years, and they still held hands as Clinton drove the three hours from Auckland to the Bay of Islands. Clinton and Kate were never happier than when their children and grandchildren were home.

Cameron Rossiter arrived home about 6:30 that evening. Major O'Brien had already been out scouting the area, making sure he was familiar with the territory for his early appointment tomorrow. He had called the base commander's office to confirm his appointment, and he was told that Captain Graham Duncan was expecting his visit, scheduled for 9:00 A.M.

Shortly after Cameron arrived home, the telephone rang. "Hello," Cameron offered.

"Hello, yourself. Are you prepared to feed a hungry working girl?" Michelle asked.

"Is that a trick question?" Cameron bantered. "I'm learning to be prepared for anything when I'm with you. Have you had a good day?"

"Busy. Trying to wrap it all up early. I've been invited to spend the weekend with some guy and his Yankee friends out on a yacht. Sounds boring to me. What's your advice?"

"I'd suggest you give it a go. Remember what your mother always said, 'Every opportunity you miss is one you won't get twice.' Opportunities of this caliber don't come along every day. Besides, working girls shouldn't be so choosy."

In an affected, upper-class British accent, Michelle responded, "Oh my, perhaps I should have attended Rangi Ruru after all. I'll have to speak to Mummy about my upbringing." They both had a laugh, and Michelle closed, saying, "I'll be around in about an hour."

"Right. Any longer and I might have to call 111."

Michelle replaced the receiver and went to the shower. She had known Cameron Rossiter only five weeks, yet her thoughts were constantly revolving around the *what ifs* of a new relationship. Her sisters were still living in Christchurch, and none of her local friends had acquired the position of confidant. She was feeling her way through the dark this time, going on basic instincts alone.

As she dressed, she knew two things for certain, she was attracted to this man, and so far he had made all the right moves. The worst part of experiencing euphoria in a new relationship was the letdown when some major issue arose that foreshadowed disaster. One felt so depressed after something like that occurred. It tended to make one cautious, which, of course, was not a bad thing. From the first time Cameron had swept her away on *Triple Diamond,* she had cautioned herself to listen and not speak, but each time she had revealed more of her inner self to this man. She had to admit, Cameron had opened his feelings to her as well, so she could at least hope that the affliction was mutual.

When Michelle arrived at Cameron's, she was introduced to Zach and Alison O'Brien. Alison was a lovely woman, about thirty-four, five feet five inches, and Michelle was surprised to learn she had three children. Alison had maintained a slim, attractive body, or perhaps, Michelle thought, she had regained her slim attractive body. It certainly didn't return on its own. Michelle had always been impressed by how her own mother had retained her youthful figure, and even now in her early fifties, she still turned heads when she went out. Marriage and children need not be end of femininity, if one took care. Alison's hair was shoulder-length medium blonde, and her eyes were green. Michelle liked her almost instantly, and she saw in Alison's smile a knowing look that she was going to have to investigate. Had Cameron been talking?

Zach O'Brien was over six feet tall and about thirty-five. He had dark brown hair, blue eyes, and a warm smile that invited conversation. He looked fit, very much a military man. They seemed like a nice couple, and she began to warm to the idea of a weekend with them. She had been a little concerned about this weekend. Cameron had mentioned that the O'Briens were Mormon, which had raised a caution flag for Michelle, yet in spite of her concerns, she was determined to accept them at face value. Michelle's mum had become Mormon sometime before her father's death, but Michelle had avoided any further investigation. When her mum had remarried, her new husband was also Mormon, and she couldn't even attend the wedding in their temple. It had angered her.

Michelle put those thoughts aside as the four of them left the house and drove to the end of the Devonport pier, where Cameron bought tickets for the twenty-minute ferry ride over to Auckland. On the harbor, Alison snuggled up to Zach and watched the lights of the skyline approach as they crossed the water. Alison apparently loved Zach—that was clear in her every contact. Michelle watched the couple and thought how lovely it would be to express heartfelt emotions to another human being and to continue to have such feelings after fourteen years of marriage. Clearly Zach was immersed in Alison, and their marriage had a solid base. Michelle decided that over this weekend she would try to sort out that base and determine how they had acquired it.

After dinner in the city, they took the ferry back across the harbor to Devonport and drove back to Cameron's home. Michelle left for home, and Alison prepared for bed. Rossiter and O'Brien went out on the deck for a while, giving them an opportunity to chat.

"Cameron, you recall this morning that you welcomed me to New Zealand, retracting it by saying I was probably as comfortable here as in the States?"

"Sure. I guess I wasn't thinking quickly enough."

"No, you were right," responded O'Brien, "I am as comfortable here. Sometimes when I visit, I wonder why I go back. I have a deep love for both places, and of course my parents and aunts and uncles live here as well. Each time I return to New

Zealand, I'm amazed at how lovely it is." Zach looked out over the harbor at the Auckland skyline and was briefly silent.

After some reflection, Zach continued, "I've been nearly all over the world, and I've never found another place that possesses such diversity of land and sea within such a small area. New Zealand has the fjords of Norway, the mountains and snow of Europe or the American West, pastoral scenes like Ireland, and the trout fishing is nearly as good as Alaska, yet it seems to remain the best-kept secret of the travel industry. Yes, you could say I love it here. Part of my heart lives here."

Cameron considered Zach's comments and perhaps understood somewhat why Sir Geoffrey had wanted him to meet O'Brien. Certainly there was more to it than a mutual appreciation of their country, but that was a good start. Cameron was pleased to find an American who didn't think everything was bigger and better in the States.

"Well, it's under the sheets for me, Zach. We'll get off about one tomorrow. Will that give you ample time to conduct your business at Devonport?"

"That should be just fine. Thank you again for your gracious hospitality. It was a great evening."

They walked inside, meeting Alison in the hallway coming out of the guest bathroom. She smiled at Cameron. "I really liked Michelle, Cameron. You should bring her over to the States sometime and let us show you the sights. I have this instinct that she'll be around a while."

"Thanks, Alison," responded Cameron. "I'll just go to bed and give it some thought."

Auckland and Hauraki Gulf, New Zealand
Triple Diamond
June

The following morning, Zach met with Captain Duncan at the Devonport Naval Station. Pleasantries were exchanged, and details were arranged for the three-city tour. HMNZS *Northland* was going to accompany USS *Cherokee,* putting out to sea to meet them just after the *Cherokee* rounded the Horn. The added

impact of Prince Andrew's presence assured that all concerned
would work to make this a letter-perfect performance. Captain
Duncan assured O'Brien that all preparations had been arranged
and that the American navy had flown in a Sea King helicopter
for the prince's flight out to the *Cherokee.*

The Kiwis had done all the local planning, and the politicians,
including the American ambassador and the prime minister,
would present mutual comments in Wellington, the second city
to be visited. Monday, Zach would fly to Wellington and meet
with the U.S. Embassy staff to coordinate arrangements, but it
looked like all was well in hand. Zach expressed the appreciation
of the United States for the cooperation of the Royal New
Zealand Navy and advised them he would return several days
prior to the actual visit.

About twelve o'clock, Cameron returned from work and collected Zach and Alison. They drove by Michelle's flat and headed
for the Marina. Zach was quite impressed by *Triple Diamond,* and
when they stowed their gear, he helped make ready for sea.
Alison explained that they would have to make do with three
deck hands, since she was a landlubber at heart, but she was quite
ready to sign on as cook if they were willing.

For the next two days good weather prevailed, which had
been a concern to Cameron considering it was the middle of winter. They sailed out to Great Barrier Island, taking the bus tour
and remaining overnight in a small inlet at the north end of the
island. Michelle and Alison spent considerable time together forward, which allowed Zach and Cameron to learn more about one
another as well. They struck up a friendship based upon an appreciation of sailing and their love for the beauty of New Zealand.
Cameron had met many Americans before, and most of them
glossed over the positive aspects of New Zealand, preferring to
focus on the things that were absent from their pampered world
back home. Zach saw beauty in the variety to be found in New
Zealand, and Cameron was pleased to find that Zach had traveled
from top to bottom and was conversant with the varied topogra-
phy of New Zealand. Most visitors were lucky to get more than a
hundred kilometers outside Auckland, and accordingly they

missed the beauty to be found, especially in the South Island where Cameron had grown up.

Cameron told Zach that he was going to England in late July to compete in the Fastnet, part of the Admiral's Cup yacht races. He would not be in New Zealand when the U.S. Navy arrived, but Zach was quite welcome to avail himself of Cameron's house again on his next visit. Staying with Zach's parents in the Bay of Islands was beautiful, but it was too far to commute to Auckland for the ceremonies that would be part of the visit. Cameron also extended the offer to Zach to include Zach's parents so they could join their son in Auckland.

Michelle was thrilled with the trip. Her appreciation for Alison had grown, and Alison's perceptions were insightful. On Saturday evening, Alison had been watching the sunset with Michelle while the men had gone ashore to bring back fish and chips. It had been quiet for some time, when Alison said, "I believe he loves you, Michelle."

Michelle didn't respond at first, but she allowed herself to think that possibly he did. "It will be difficult for him," Michelle explained. "One, he's quite successful and therefore careful to assure that the woman is not after his possessions, and two, he's a Kiwi. They can't seem to get the words past their lips." She smiled, and the two women continued to reflect on their men until Alison broached the question.

"And you, Michelle?"

"Yes, I'm afraid I'm similarly afflicted!"

On Sunday afternoon as they approached the marina, Cameron manned the tiller with Michelle leaning up against him. Zach and Alison watched the approaching skyline of downtown Auckland from the foredeck. Cameron pulled Michelle tighter and spoke, close to her ear, "Do you think you could get away long enough to join me in England for the Fastnet?"

Michelle thought about accepting but felt that she ought to consider the offer for a while and allow Cameron some time to think about it. "I could speak to Jean. The work load would put quite a burden on her." She looked up at him and gently kissed his lips. "I'll try," she promised.

They tied up *Triple Diamond* and packed their gear in the car. Cameron dropped Michelle off at her flat, kissed her good-bye, and drove off for Devonport. Zach was going to fly to Wellington in the morning and back in the afternoon, and Alison would spend the day in downtown Auckland, having arranged to meet Michelle for lunch on Queen Street.

That evening Michelle had just settled into bed with a novel she was reading. Michelle had read everything she could get her hands on since she turned ten. Her knowledge was broad, and she was an excellent conversationalist on most subjects. In spite of his MBA, Cameron had often found himself ignorant of subjects with which Michelle was thoroughly conversant. She had just reached the end of the chapter when the telephone rang, about eleven. "Hello," she answered.

A quiet voice spoke, "Are you aware that I love you?"

"Yes," she responded softly.

"Goodnight, Michelle."

"Goodnight, Cameron."

Sleep came more comfortably that evening for both of them. Michelle knew she would love England.

South Pacific Ocean
Kamitsu Maru, *En Route to New Zealand*
June

The *Kamitsu Maru* was south of the Solomon Islands by late June and right on schedule. Her cargo contained computers and other electronic gear destined for New Zealand. She had been at sea since early June and had a tight schedule to keep. Her other cargo, kept separate in hold #6, consisted of two older model caskets, from which had been removed all the necessary components of a small nuclear device of early '60s vintage. By modern standards it lacked sophistication, but it was adequate for the task that had been assigned to it.

Only Stephen Wyndham and Roger, an expert in explosive devices, were allowed in hold #6. Wyndham had spent many hours in the hold during the first two weeks of their journey, during which he completed his work, but now he seldom entered the storage area and didn't allow anyone else the opportunity.

They were scheduled to arrive in Auckland about July 2, unload in twenty-four hours, and put back to sea immediately. Timing was important on this trip, and weather was a concern. Winter sailing in the South Pacific could be treacherous. For the remainder of the voyage, the crew would be bored and restless, but they were all well trained for their mission. An experienced master seaman would never have taken this crew for deckhands. All were professional in appearance and spoke with multiple accents, and several were highly educated. For all but two, it was their first time on a freighter, and they hoped it would be their last.

Auckland, New Zealand
June

The four men were dressed in casual sporting attire as they loaded their gear into the rental van. Two of them had arrived earlier that morning at Auckland International on separate flights and had cleared customs without incident. The two others had arrived several days before, making all necessary arrangements beforehand.

They drove straight to the Auckland Marina and began to load their equipment onto the yacht. They looked like an ordinary group of businessmen, two Europeans, one dark Middle Easterner, and one Japanese. They worked without much communication, as if they were in a hurry. By 9:00 A.M. they had everything stowed on board. One of the Europeans told the other to return the van to the hotel rental service. He left, while the others prepared to get underway. When he returned twenty minutes later, they quickly moved out of the slip and maneuvered their way into the harbor. Using engine alone, they turned southeast and headed for the Hauraki Gulf.

It seemed as if *Triple Diamond* knew the way. In fact, unknown to the men who had chartered her, she had been through this exact routing several days earlier, but by sail. Within eight hours they were clearing the Great Barrier Island and heading out to the open sea. Once again, the winter weather had cooperated, and they had smooth sailing. They had encountered no contact since leaving the marina other than the initial traffic in the harbor. The charter was for two weeks, and two of the crew had presented sufficient credentials to the marina charter service to demonstrate their prowess in sailing this class of yacht. All had gone smoothly.

Under sail now, they placed *Triple Diamond* on a heading of 090°, due east. Allowing for tacking, they would maintain this general heading for the next several days, moving straight out into the South Pacific, bound for Chile if they sailed far enough. They had told the charter service they would be cruising up through the Bay of Islands and around the northern bays. They would not be missed for at least ten days, and perhaps not until the chartered time was over, if their luck held.

They settled into a routine, two men on and two off, in six-hour shifts. Had another joined their crew, he would have wondered why four men who didn't particularly seem to enjoy each other's company would choose to spend two weeks together in the confined spaces of a yacht. Even though *Triple Diamond* was large by private yacht standards, it required a reasonable degree of intimacy to share quarters for any length of time. These men kept to themselves. If an observant detective had been aboard, he would have immediately noticed that they didn't always respond immediately when someone called them by name, as if they didn't recognize their names, which was the case since none of the four went by their true names. They had met only once before, three weeks earlier when they had assembled in Japan and the man who hired them had briefed them on the mission. Three of them were present for that briefing, and two of them had a long association with the briefer, Stephen Wyndham, although they did not know each other well. One other was new to the group.

The fourth man had been recruited quite differently. Riaz Khalil, known on this voyage as Rio, had learned of his part in this venture five weeks earlier. Since that time he had been committed. Rio lived in a small village several hundred miles south of Baghdad, Iraq. While still a young man, Rio had lived in Kuwait and had worked for several of the wealthy Kuwaiti families. He had learned how to sail as crew on their pleasure craft and had enjoyed the open waters. He became quite adept at sailing and regretted the necessity of returning to his village at the behest of his father. He had remained in the village, continuing to assist the family until his father's death several years later. He had gotten married there, and over the years the couple had had five children. After his father's death, Rio was conscripted into the Iraqi military during the war with Iran and had somehow survived that conflict.

During the Gulf War, Rio had served with the 146th Artillery Battalion. They had practiced and drilled for months for their part in the glorious reclamation of Kuwait as part of greater Iraq. When the Americans had appeared from behind them, his unit completely disintegrated. They surrendered without firing a shot. Their total battalion was taken prisoner, and their weapons destroyed. Following repatriation, he was informed that their officers had been summoned to Baghdad, and they were never heard from again. For himself, he had been unable to obtain employment again, and whenever army units passed through his village, he was treated as a traitor and coward, as had others from his battalion. Life had not been easy for Rio since his return to Iraq. He had watched his children slowly starve and his wife plead for food with those who passed through the village.

When the Republican Guard colonel had arrived, Rio was resigned to his fate. He felt that they were systematically eliminating the former battalion members, and his turn had come. He kissed his wife and children good-bye and left with the colonel. In Baghdad he was interrogated about his sailing knowledge and informed that the Great Leader was giving him the opportunity to redeem himself and perform a heroic act for his people. When General Alihambra and His Excellency actually appeared before him one day, he was astonished. To be in the presence of the Great Leader and to be offered the opportunity to serve the people was more than he could have expected. He was assured that his family would be provided for and that they would have more food than they would need. Rio wept with relief, and from that time he knew he was destined to accomplish this great deed for his people, even though it meant meeting Allah for his reward.

What Rio would never know was that his wife and five children had been taken from the village one day after he left, and they had not been seen since. No trail was desired, and none would be found.

Triple Diamond continued east for two days and was well beyond sight of land. Occasional aircraft flew overhead, but little traffic was spotted at sea. They constantly monitored their radio and, with the use of the radar, kept well away from any other vessels. They had only to wait now, keeping close to their intended rendezvous, 177°30'E, 36°20'S.

CHAPTER EIGHT

Auckland, New Zealand
HMNZS Northland
July

As THE *NORTHLAND* PREPARED TO GET UNDERWAY, Captain Duncan, commanding officer of the naval station, met with Commander Alistair Campbell. Captain Duncan had laid out the route that would take *Northland* considerably further out to sea than would normally be necessary to escort a visiting vessel into Auckland harbor.

"This has become sort of a political circus, Commander, as you can well imagine. On the return, when you get about three days out, His Royal Highness, Prince Andrew will fly out to board. He will be aboard an American Sea King chopper, and they'll have refueling capabilities overhead, just precautionary. He plans to spend the first night aboard *Cherokee* and the final two aboard *Northland*. Let's just keep things shipshape, Commander. His presence will be awkward on the bridge, but alert your crew to the appropriate protocol."

"Yes, sir."

"Alistair, we need to show all appropriate courtesy to the visiting crew, but during your return trip, I want you to monitor emissions from *Cherokee* to ascertain whether her nuclear propulsion emits any trace elements. We have no reason to believe any problems will occur, but you can rely on the fact that Greenpeace will also meet you a few hundred miles out, and we don't want them being the first to discover any detrimental readings."

"Understood, Captain. We'll be underway by 1800 hours."

"Good luck, Alistair, and keep us informed."

Though *Northland* and her crew of two hundred and forty got underway later than expected, the ship was well out to sea before dawn, and about eighteen hours ahead of the small freighter that was traveling a slower but parallel course. They would never meet, and the *Northland* would never even know of the existence of the *Kamitsu Maru*.

Auckland, New Zealand
Kamitsu Maru
July

The *Kamitsu Maru* had arrived in the small hours of the morning, and by noon the wharfies were busily unloading its cargo, among which were several hundred computers destined for Connect-Ability, Ltd. Cameron Rossiter had purchased this lot at excellent prices, despite the requirement that a specific vessel deliver the shipment. Rossiter had generally shipped with Burlington and had always been satisfied with their delivery. He had been told that the manufacturing company had overproduced for a contract that had fallen through. He was being offered the opportunity to claim the excess at good prices. If true, it was a way to make good on someone else's contract failure.

This was a "one off," as he saw it, and it certainly provided good profit margins, so he came himself to determine as best he could that the product was indeed legal and not a stolen lot hijacked somewhere along the line. Rossiter arrived at the dock within several hours of being notified of arrival. The lot numbers seemed to be in order with his manifest, and he had already checked with the manufacturer regarding their legality. Everything seemed in order.

The added benefit, of course, was that the man who had contacted him for this contract had also requested direction to a yacht charter service. After ascertaining the potential crew's sailing skills, Cameron had arranged for his contact to charter *Triple Diamond,* since he would be away in England for the Fastnet yacht races. All in all, this had turned out to be an excellent business deal.

Kamitsu Maru was completely unloaded by eight that evening and was ready to get underway again—unloaded except for the cargo in hold #6. Fortunately for the nearly one million residents of Auckland, upwards of forty or fifty thousand within a two-or three-mile radius, nothing untoward happened on board the *Kamitsu Maru* that evening. Those New Zealanders went to bed, peacefully sleeping in their "nuclear-free" island, blissfully unaware of the devastating potential lurking within their harbor. About two hundred and forty of them aboard the *Northland* had just missed the opportunity to sleep close to potential disaster, but tragically they would have another opportunity to be concerned, however briefly, about the cargo now in hold #6.

The captain indicated to the dock agent that he had a cargo waiting in Samoa and would run empty till then. The shipping agent offered to find them a cargo for Samoa if they could lay over two days, but the captain advised that his customer in Samoa needed them to be on time. At 10:30 that evening, *Kamitsu Maru* left, minus one crewman who would be flying back by a different route. At 5:30 that evening, Stephen Wyndham had left the ship to catch the Aerolineas Airgentinas flight to Santiago. After a few days stopover, he would then fly on to Buenos Aires.

Auckland, New Zealand
July

Arriving back from lunch, Michelle sat at her desk, ready to begin an afternoon of scheduling room assignments for her upcoming seminar. Within ten minutes the fax phone rang, and she could tell by the number printed on the read-out display that the fax was coming from the United States.

Dear Michelle,

All has settled back into the normal routine once more, and as I go through the day taking care of the children and the daily household tasks, I find my thoughts straying to our lovely week-end with you and Cameron on the boat. It seems like another time, another place, almost like I dreamed it. Michelle, I just wanted you to know how much Zach and I appreciated that time spent with you both. It was very therapeutic for Zach and I to be able to spend some time together doing something so very different.

I believe our marriage and relationship were strengthened by seeing a couple just on the verge of loving one another, and so we were able to reinforce our own commitment. It seems that no matter how much in love a couple are with each other, they need to take time to remember and to constantly keep love alive in their marriage. The weekend on the boat certainly contributed to our marriage in this area.

Michelle, you asked me some rather deep questions on the deck that evening, and so many times since then I have gone over the replies I should have given. I feel a little like I do when I have just finished a long distance call to a loved one. I remember all the comments after I have hung up and then have to sit down and write a very long letter to cover what I should have said. I am sure that Cameron loves you, he exhibits all of the signs of a man who has found the woman he wants to spend the rest of his life with. I know too that you are in love with him, but I also feel that you are holding back, afraid perhaps of the commitment. The chemistry between you is apparent. Cameron knows his mind and is just waiting for you to come to the same knowledge that he has. He doesn't want to pressure you in any way and seems slightly out of his depth in a situation where he cannot take charge. I guess in his business and personal life he rarely comes upon a dilemma of this nature, he is used to being at the helm.

Some of the questions you asked that night I know have arisen because you want to be absolutely sure before you make a commitment. "How do I know that Zach loves me? How do I know that I love Zach? What makes our marriage so different from other marriages you have seen? How come we still carry on like lovers after three children and fourteen years of marriage?" I know the answer to all of these questions, but just how to incorporate it in my letter is something else. Still, I will give it my best shot.

I know Zach loves me because he makes me feel like the most special and cherished woman in the world. I know because of the way he looks at me, the way he is more concerned for my welfare than his own. I know because I feel it in my heart and in my soul. When he leaves a room something feels different for me, and when he returns my whole life lights up. I know I love him because he is everything to me, he is my lover, my very best friend, the very best father our children could have, and he is so gentle and caring with them that I fall in love with him all over again when I see him with them.

When I met Zach all other experiences in my life paled into insignificance, and it seemed like my life had only just begun from that moment. I care more for his well-being than my own. I live for the moment he walks through the door after being on assignment—my day brightens so much when his car pulls into the driveway. And I feel like a queen when he holds me and looks into my eyes. That is how I know I love him.

Why is our marriage so different from so many others? That is more difficult to answer as marriages vary according to the two individuals who participate in them. All marriages are different, but I will try to tell you our commitment and the covenants we have made with each other to keep our marriage alive and thriving, and maybe that will answer your questions. Firstly, we try to always stay in love. We try not to be overcome by the responsibilities of parenthood and all of the strains that little children can place on a marriage. We take time for just the two of us to be together and to remember why we chose each other in the first place. Just like the time spent on the boat with you and Cameron.

Second, we spend time together as a family enjoying each other's company and getting to know one another so that we might be the best of friends. One night a week we do nothing else but family activities together. That way each member of the family knows that the time belongs to us and nothing else is more important. I know that this has a very positive influence in our marriage and in our family.

Third, Zach and I decided when we were first married that nothing else would ever be so important that it came before our marriage and our commitment to each other. We covenanted with each other to keep the other party honest about this and to remind the other party if we felt they were getting off on the wrong track at any time. Needless to say, both parties have had the odd reminder or two along the way, but we don't get our feelings hurt because we know that it is the top priority in our lives, and so we respond as best we can to eliminate whatever is causing the problem.

Fourth, I also believe very strongly that our religion plays a very large part in our marriage and our commitment. Michelle, I am not even sure of whether religion is a factor with you and Cameron, but I know with Zach and I it is so very important. As we go to church on Sundays, we are constantly taught principles which help us to make commitments and to keep them. Gosh, I hope that makes some sense to you. It is so much a part of my way of life, but when I actually come to put it down on paper, I have to really think about it.

I guess in summary you could say that all that Zach and I are and what you see in our marriage and family life comes from our commitment to living our lives as the Lord would have us live them. There is no room for selfishness, and we constantly receive so much help that our marriage is blessed. Michelle, I think selfishness is the most common cause of dissent in marriages these days. Everyone tends to want to "do their own thing" and be looking out for their own interests instead of the interests of those they love. Marriages are breaking up all over the place, and some marriages which should be are not even getting started because of selfishness. People love self or money or both more than they love the other person.

In my experience, when I put Zach first and he puts me first, then we both have our needs more than taken care of, and we are in a pretty good position to take good care of our children. Children need to know that their parents love each other and to see that love expressed every day. Our children take it for granted that we love each other and are somewhat surprised when they visit with other children from school and find that their parents seem angry with each other and do not even like one another, let alone love each other. They are not at all at ease with this and have commented on it more than once.

Well, Michelle, I feel like I might be beginning to sound like a preacher . . . certainly not the intention, but I did want to respond to the questions you had raised and try to answer them as honestly as possible. I know you are in a turmoil, and hope that something I have said might be of help to you. Once again thank you for the super weekend and know that you and Cameron have contributed to keeping our marriage alive and well.

Love,
Alison

South Pacific Ocean
Triple Diamond *at Rendezvous with* **Kamitsu Maru**
July

Triple Diamond picked up the *Kamitsu Maru* on radar and made one quick single sideband radio contact to confirm identity. They would rendezvous just before dawn. When *Triple Diamond* appeared out of the mist, *Kamitsu Maru* slowed and came to a full stop. *Triple Diamond* was maneuvered alongside, and immediately a crane lowered two straps, each about eight inches wide. These were placed evenly, one over the stern and one over the bow. They were jostled back and forth around the hull until they were about a third of the way in from each end. The crane began to hoist *Triple Diamond* slowly until it was certain she was balanced correctly.

The crane lifted *Triple Diamond* clear of the water and onto the deck into a prepared place, where the *Kamitsu Maru* crew strapped her down and covered her with canvas that completely obscured all but the mast from view. Western Samoa was on a bearing of 022°, NNE. *Kamitsu Maru* got underway immediately after loading *Triple Diamond,* and the captain gave the new heading, 120° ESE. The weather was still holding, but as *Kamitsu Maru* made headway, a "Silent Wind" was brewing on the horizon.

Auckland, New Zealand
July

"I'm ready on time. Aren't you pleased?" Michelle said, beaming.

"Astonished," replied Cameron. He looked at her with undisguised affection. "But if you had been late, it would have been worth every minute. You look great."

Michelle was inwardly pleased. Cameron was really an unusual man, she thought. She could count the times on one hand when prior boyfriends had even noticed what she was wearing, much less complimented her on it. "Thank you, sir. It behooves a lady to honor her gentleman when he is so considerate," she commented formally.

Cameron let Michelle into the car, and they drove off toward a small restaurant north of Auckland. "I've chartered *Triple Diamond* while I'm gone to England," Cameron said. "A couple of businessmen wanted to cruise the Bay of Islands. It's the same guy who sold me the computer load earlier this month."

"*Triple Diamond?* Your baby? I didn't think you'd even let her out of your sight."

"Neither did I, but when you find a good woman, you've got to trust her out of your sight, don't you? Anyway, it was a good offer, and he has his master's papers. He should know what he's doing."

They drove north through Albany out to Orewa and a little restaurant Cameron knew that overlooked the bay. They sat inside near the window on this cold and wet winter night, looking out over the water. Michelle started the conversation. "I had a fax at work yesterday, from Alison O'Brien. She asked that I thank you again for the wonderful weekend yachting. She hasn't had the opportunity to do that before, and she really enjoyed herself."

"You liked her, didn't you?" Cameron asked.

"Yes, very much. She's easy to like and not judgmental at all. We had a great talk while we were anchored at Great Barrier. She's responded to some of my concerns and questions after some thought."

Cameron's eyes grew a bit larger. "Anything I should know about?"

"Why, Cameron, whatever makes you think we were talking about you?" Changing the subject, she said, "Look how hard it's beginning to rain."

"Right," he allowed. "What shall we have for dinner?"

"I'm in your hands, so to speak. No shellfish though."

Cameron ordered dinner, and they just watched the small harbor at Orewa for a few moments. "I liked Zach too," Cameron said. "He seems to have developed the ability to appreciate someplace other than America. He's also a fair sailor, considering he flies jet fighters for a living."

"What struck you about their relationship, Cameron?"

"What do you mean?"

Well, I saw them, what shall I say . . . united, I guess would be a good word. Did you feel they were happy with each other?"

"I guess I wasn't looking at their marriage particularly. I just enjoyed them individually."

"Did Zach tell you anything about their religion?"

"Not really. He explained why they didn't drink coffee."

Michelle was quiet for a while as the waiter delivered their first course. "Cameron, have I ever told you that my mother joined the Mormon church some years ago?"

"No. How long ago?"

"Oh, sometime in the late '70s I think. My father didn't join, and neither did I or my sisters. It really knocked my dad for a loop. It put a real strain on their marriage for several years, and then I guess my dad came to an accommodation, and they built their lives around it, sort of an unspoken issue. It put a rift in their unity, though, after fifteen years of what seemed to us children a very happy relationship."

"What happened after your father died?"

"Mum was single for a couple of years and then married another Mormon. An *American* Mormon," she said with a hint of disdain.

"Did you support her decision?"

"We never had the opportunity. She just married him and told us about it afterward," Michelle replied with some bitterness.

Sensing a confusion over this issue that he had been unaware of, Cameron just watched Michelle as she wrestled with her thoughts. "Seems to be some unresolved feelings," he commented.

"I suppose. Actually I've resented the Mormons, not their beliefs necessarily, but the division it caused in my parents' marriage. All their friends, I'm talking about school friends and life-long associates, avoided them after Mum joined the church. She stopped drinking, smoking, and doing all of the social things that they had enjoyed with their friends together. When she stopped, it confused their friends, not to mention her own children, and Dad suffered the loss of his friends, even though he hadn't changed. It was unfair."

"How do Zach and Alison fit into this?"

"Well, I had Mormonism figured out, or maybe I should say, eliminated from my mind. When Mum married again, her relationship with her new husband wasn't as good as I remembered my parents' being. They fought a lot. As an American, he was rather abrasive. My sisters thought the same thing. Of course Mum is no pushover when she gets her Irish up."

"It was their second marriage, right?" Cameron asked.

"Yeah."

"And you say you weren't really supportive of them?"

"What are you getting at, Cameron?"

"Nothing really, Michelle. But second marriages are tough enough on their own. When family baggage adds to the pressure, it can become untenable. How are they doing now?"

Michelle thought for a while looking out the window. "First they lived near his children in the States and then for a year near us. Since then they've moved to a 'neutral' city, and they seem to be getting along fairly well."

Cameron just let that analysis sink in for a while as dinner was served and they began to eat. They participated in small talk during dinner, and as dessert was served, Cameron reopened the subject. "These unresolved issues, Michelle. Are they important to you?"

"I don't know. Really, I haven't given them much thought until recently."

"And Zach and Alison made the difference?"

"Perhaps. They seem totally united in their purpose and their feelings for each other. Alison said in her letter that she attributes it primarily to their unified direction in life. She didn't specifically mention spiritual beliefs, but she did say they believed the same thing."

"Could that have been the wedge driven between your parents? Your mum changed direction."

"Yeah. But Dad was the loser, and he hadn't done anything wrong."

"Do you think your mum did?"

"Well, she's the one who changed direction. They were all right until the Mormon religion became her way of life. That's what it is you know. They don't just go to church for a couple of hours on Sunday. They have something going all week long. It's truly a way of life. That's the only way I can put it."

"What did Alison say about all of this?"

"I haven't told her anything yet. On the yacht I just asked her some general questions about what made her marriage seem so unified. I guess it's been on my mind since she wrote, because she basically said that their common belief was the basis for their relationship, and I found it angered me somewhat to hear that given as the reason because my feelings had been just the opposite. You know, because of what I saw it do to my parents."

"Perhaps you should try to separate the two, Michelle. Look at the O'Briens' marriage on its own. Maybe they do have something worth investigating. Your parents and your mum's second marriage carries with it a different set of criteria. It's not my place to interfere, but maybe you should give some thought to your mother's side of the issue. I haven't been particularly religious either, at least not in the sense of regular church attendance. But my parents taught me that there was a value system higher than most humans practiced. My dad firmly believed that people should recognize and accept the value systems of others, while, and this is important, remaining faithful to those values that they themselves held, whatever they were. If your mum discovered a new value system that changed her life, she couldn't deny it, and perhaps she felt she ought to have been able to count on her family's support, even if they didn't subscribe to that new value system."

"Cameron, are you taking her side?"

"Not at all, but you are much closer to this issue than I am, and I can see it troubles you greatly—perhaps even more than you admit to yourself. If your mum faced such opposition from her family—from those she loved the most—in this new religion she found, it must have taken some degree of strength to persevere, wouldn't you say?"

Michelle didn't answer, but Cameron could tell from her faraway look that he had given her something to consider. "Michelle, I truly don't want to interfere, but our relationship . . . " He paused, trying to think what to say.

Michelle gave a slight rise of her eyebrows. "Yes, you were saying . . . "

"Well, you understand, I hope we can begin to confide in one another and progress. You know how I feel. Tomorrow, I'm off to merry old England, and in a couple of weeks you'll join me. Perhaps this time alone for you, without me demanding all of your time, will give you some freedom to think about these things. If you feel confident enough in Alison, why don't you pose these questions to her? Maybe she can shed some light, as an outsider."

Signaling the waiter for the check, Cameron looked back at Michelle. "Do you think we have a common direction, Michelle?"

Avoiding the answer, Michelle turned back to humor. "Now there's food for thought."

Cameron rose and picked up Michelle's coat, helping her place it around her shoulders. Driving back to Devonport, they were quiet much of the way, just holding hands and listening to the radio. Stopping at Michelle's, Cameron got out and came around to her side to assist her out. "Care to come in for some coffee?" Michelle offered.

"I'd love too, but I've still got to pack, and I've got two meetings early to finish before I leave tomorrow night."

Michelle rested her head against his chest and said, "Cameron, I do want us to have a common direction. Will you think about it also while you're away?"

"Of course. I'm beginning to think about you constantly, in whatever direction I'm moving."

Michelle smiled. "Good," she said softly.

Cameron ran his fingers through her hair and held her face between his hands, pulling her up to look at him. "The O'Briens have nothing that we can't find for ourselves, Michelle. I agree with Alison though; it is important to have a unified basis for love. We have a pretty good start, don't you think?"

"Umm," she replied and kissed him, placing her hand behind his head and holding him tightly. "You're an unusual find, Cameron Rossiter. Please don't let my confusion confuse you too."

"I understand, Michelle. Pick me up for the airport tomorrow?" he asked.

"Taxi service at your call. 6:30 sharp, sir."

Washington, D.C.
National Security Agency
July

Lieutenant General William Austin was listening to Major Zachariah O'Brien as they drove the short distance from the White House to the Pentagon. They were on their way to a Joint Chiefs of Staff briefing, and Major O'Brien was one of the presenters. O'Brien wanted to be sure he covered the material to General Austin's satisfaction and included all that he felt was pertinent. It had been a long three days since the rhetoric emanating from Abdul Salimar and his staff had risen to a fever pitch.

"General, it's got to tie in with the New Zealand policy decision. Salimar must feel that somehow he can force removal of ships, or at least get us to declare weaponry on board."

"Let's see what the Joint Chiefs have that we might not be aware of before we present. Limit your presentation to the major points. Speculation at this stage would be counterproductive, but clearly Salimar's got something up his sleeve. We've got to get his shirt off and find out what it is."

They arrived in the Joint Chiefs' area, were cleared by security, and proceeded to the conference room in the E wing. Each service was represented, as well as the CIA and General Austin for the NSA. The chairman of the Joint Chiefs opened.

"Gentlemen, as you are aware, for the past two months the Iraqi news media and those whom they can influence to carry their stories have been filling the airwaves with scare mongering about our intended use of tactical nuclear weapons. At first we thought their intention was to provoke an incident, and when they shot down the F-14 Tomcat off the *Enterprise,* we felt that Salimar had played his hand. Since our barrage of Tomahawks, however, we have experienced no more additional damage to targets we felt were important. No physical incidents have occurred at all." The chairman looked around the room preliminary to soliciting comments.

"We'll start with a summary of existing conditions." Turning to the army chief of staff, he said, "General Cagney, what are the ground dispositions at this time? Any unusual movements or deployments?"

"Thank you, General. No unusual movements have occurred in the past thirty days. Routine troop movements in concert with exercise maneuvers continue, but they do not present a threatening posture. Aerial recon has kept us abreast of unit displacements."

The chairman turned to the navy. "What do you show, Frank?"

"General, since the incident in February, we have seen little resistance and virtually no radar tracking. Our overflights have gone off unimpeded by any form of challenge. It all seems to be verbal abuse at this stage. Hard to put a purpose behind it."

"Gentlemen," the chairman continued, "we know Salimar does little without purpose. Our job is to find out that purpose and quick. Salimar has seized our New Zealand initiative with a vengeance, as if it portrayed a positive opportunity for him. I just don't understand how he feels the issue applies to his part of the world. No parallels at all. General Austin, how does NSA summarize all this?"

"Thank you, sir. Several developments over the past few months show a consistent pattern. However, as you have stated, the objective still seems obscured. Major O'Brien has compiled a short briefing. Major, if you please?"

O'Brien stood and moved to the head of the table, surveying the room to acknowledge each senior officer. O'Brien was by far the junior officer in the room. He proceeded without notes, pausing to answer questions as they arose. "Mr. Chairman, gentlemen. As we know, in February the Iraqis came at us in the usual way, with their radar-tracking stations locking on to overflights, which resulted in the late February downing of a Tomcat. We responded in like fashion. We believe this method of tit for tat has not enabled Salimar to progress on the chess board. He well knows that he can't match us shot for shot and that we will always triumph in that arena.

"He seems now to have moved to public castigation, which also is not new, but which has taken on a new dimension. Three salient points have surfaced as possibilities. Please recognize, gentlemen, trying to identify the objectives of someone as irrational as Abdul Salimar is like raking up leaves on a windy day. The pile continually needs to be restacked. We do however have some starting points.

"One, shortly after Sir Geoffrey Holden arrived as New Zealand's ambassador to the United Nations, he made inquiries regarding the recommencement of U.S. naval visits to New Zealand. I have spoken with Sir Geoffrey several times. His objectives are quite clear. He would like to mend the ANZUS fence and repair relations with the United States, but he feels that New Zealand cannot afford to simply rescind their stand on nuclear issues. He made it clear in his General Assembly address that world tension, in the global warfare sense, has reduced and that New Zealand applauds the Russians and the United States for their efforts to reduce the potential for world catastrophe.

"Privately he has stated that the United States and the United Kingdom, being the only remaining superpowers with such devastating nuclear capability, could gain significant world esteem by publicly showing their willingness to reduce that tension. The United States could be seen agreeing to the request of a small, peaceful country to exclude nuclear weapons from their territory. His position made a lot of sense to the White House. Certainly naval visitation to New Zealand is not paramount on our strategic interest list. However, we often take a posture precluding us from acquiescing to our opponent, so that compromise, with a win-win negotiating posture, is rendered nearly impossible.

"Sir Geoffrey believes he has offered a way for the United States to be seen giving in, without really losing anything of strategic importance. The White House agreed, and as you know, the USS *Cherokee* is underway to arrive next month for the first visit in over ten years. We have openly declared that no nuclear weapons exist on board the *Cherokee*, while the Kiwis have openly accepted the concept of nuclear propulsion as nonbelligerent."

At this point a discussion ensued regarding politicians and military decisions. After a few minutes, O'Brien tactfully moved to get the briefing back on track.

"Second, Ambassador Haquim, Iraqi's ambassador to the United Nations, met privately with Sir Geoffrey to ascertain New Zealand's position on this issue. We believe the Iraqis have taken this issue as a focal point, and the recent tirade of media coverage has been a result of Iraq trying to link this policy change to the U.S. naval vessels in Middle Eastern waters. So far only the usual supporters of Salimar have agreed with his stance.

"The Israelis still believe that Salimar has been able to secretly maintain the development of rudimentary nuclear capability in spite of the inspections of UN observers. No Western intelligence agency has been able to either confirm or deny the existence of such a development, and indeed, if it does exist, Iraq does not have the capability to create a sophisticated weapon or a reliable delivery system. Nevertheless, it is a short distance to Israel, and they continue to be concerned.

"Third, and perhaps most important, time is not on our side. The longer we continue to patrol the Persian Gulf and conduct overflights of Iraq, the more opportunities arise for incidents to occur. Each incident, no matter how favorable the military outcome may be for the United States, continues to erode our welcome in the area. The coalition formed with such delicacy by President Bush does not continue with the same allegiance. It was shaky from the start, and when cousin fought against cousin, it left scars, which the local family members will remember.

"In short, gentlemen, the longer we are there, the more opportunity for incidents. The rate of incidents is inversely proportional to the level of support we can expect in the area. It is somewhat like the general public saying to the police, 'Keep the peace, but don't harass anybody.' Are there any questions?"

Major O'Brien, with General Austin's assistance, continued to answer questions for some time. The attitude ranged from the expected "We won the war, and they'll do what we say" to a lengthy discussion of changing the rules of engagement under which a local commander may engage the enemy. That discussion engendered a heated debate over the necessary decision-making ability of the field commander versus the Joint Chiefs' control of operations as far down as the platoon level. It was an age-old discussion, exacerbated by the instant communication ability that provided the ability to control operations from a central point. Field commanders hated the extraction of their prerogatives, and senior commanders removed from the action hated to give up control of the situation. The discussion detracted from the central issue of this briefing, and finally the chairman brought an end to the meeting.

On the way back to the NSA, General Austin complimented O'Brien on the briefing but admitted that they were no closer to understanding what Salimar was thinking. O'Brien still felt that Salimar's public posturing had a purpose other than to hear himself speak. He would keep working on it.

CHAPTER NINE

Woodbridge, Virginia
August

Dear Alison,

It was great to receive your letter and to have you respond so sincerely to my questions. I hadn't realised that I had been so probing that evening until I read your reply. The other evening I had dinner with Cameron just prior to his departure for England. I shared some of my concerns with him, a tough decision, I might add, and he surprised me by taking a very objective view. He even suggested that I confide in you, since perhaps you had knowledge of others in like condition, so here goes.

I have found myself constantly thinking about your comments as I try to discern just what it is I want out of life and exactly which road I wish to take. I know in my heart that I love Cameron, and I am sure that he loves me, but is that enough, Alison? So many of my friends are opting for relationships without marriage, those who have married are wishing they hadn't, and some have even parted in less than amicable ways. All around me I see people I care about in situations I would hate to be in myself, and I wonder just what it takes for a relationship to make it through the difficult as well as the joyous times. With you and Zach I saw something of what I would like to achieve in a marriage, and when you wrote me the reasons, I couldn't help but reflect back on my own parents' marriage.

Alison, my parents were very happily married for about fifteen years. It was obvious to all those around them that they were the very best of friends, and as their children we had a very full and happy life. We didn't realise it at that time—I think as most children do we just took it for granted, even though we were aware that some of our friends were not happy in their home environment and preferred to be at our house. We had fabulous Christmas holidays in the Marlborough Sounds, yachting, power boating, water skiing, barbecuing with other families, and during the winter months we would holiday at Lake Tekapo and go snow skiing and ice skating.

My Dad was very much into boating, and so we moved in circles where others shared his love of these interests. We seemed to be always planning a holiday and deciding which of our friends to take with us. When we were not on holiday our parents entertained a great deal at our home, and we always had friends coming for dinner parties, barbecues, or Sunday morning "elevenses." Elevenses is the slang term for the morning after a party, when everyone adjourns to the same house next morning to demolish the remaining food and drink. It usually goes on all day Sunday, and all the children would come with their parents and we would have great fun. These friends of our parents had known each other since their school days, and they all had children. We became very close, almost like extended family. We would take vacations with them, the children always staying over at each other's houses, and we would just generally have a fun time together. Everyone brought their own food and wine, and so the families took turns about hosting the party.

Then one day my Mother did something which stunned this whole crowd, including my Father and us . . . she became a Mormon!!! She had never ever professed any religious thoughts or feelings, and as far as we were aware she had no religious upbringing. All of a sudden, she changed dramatically. She would go to Church on Sunday instead of coming boating and skiing. She was always reading the Bible or other Scriptures, and most noticeable was the fact that she gave up drinking alcohol, tea, coffee, and smoking. Dad thought she was having a nervous breakdown as he had tried to get her to give up smoking on many occasions, but she had never been interested in stopping. Now suddenly she stopped doing all the fun things and insisted on drinking only lemonade when we were out socially.

Our friends were totally confused because Mum had always been the life and soul of the party, and in our crowd religion had never been discussed. They were amazed that Mum would get baptised and become so serious about it. Our friends were very uncomfortable with this turn of events and waited to see if it was a passing fad, but it got worse. My Dad did everything in his power to talk my Mother out of it, demanding to know why she needed this when he had given her everything he could. I talked with my Father about the changes as I was thirteen at the time and noticed that it was causing a great deal of anger and confusion in my parents' lives. My Dad was totally against it and could not understand why my Mum would do something that did not include the whole family. My Mother would say that she had had a spiritual experience and that she knew for sure that she needed to make these changes in her life.

My parents' social life began to fall apart. They still went to the parties, but Mum did not drink anymore, and she was the only one who did not. It made all of our long-time friends very uncomfortable, and soon they stopped inviting my parents. Dad felt that was unfair, he had not changed. He still wanted to do all the things he had always done, but because of Mum's actions he was being punished. Yachting suffered as we could no longer go for whole weekends away because Mum wanted to be home for church on Sunday. Dad began taking us children, and everyone would embarrass him by asking, Where is your wife? We children realised that our Dad needed our support, and so we joined forces and made it pretty uncomfortable for Mum. To our surprise she just kept on going to church. She seemed to be very happy with the changes she had made but seemed very disappointed in the actions of friends and family.

I remember Dad saying that he went to the pub one Saturday with Mum's father, and while they were having a drink together, he asked Granddad why he thought this had happened. You see, three of his six children joined the Mormon Church. Another daughter had joined in America where she had moved with her American husband some years earlier. Another daughter also subsequently joined just four months after my Mother did, so my Father asked Granddad if maybe it was hereditary. Granddad had been an atheist all of his life and was just as stunned by it as others and told my Father so. He had no idea why it had happened or what to do about it.

Alison, my parents subsequently lost all of their friends because of my Mother's new religion. They now argued a great deal as my Father was always trying to get my Mother to go back to how she used to be. She would come along, but he always said it was not the same as she did not participate much. What had been a very happy marriage and family life became very tense and strained, and I know my parents almost went their separate ways on three or more occasions. It was only because they really loved each other and us that they could not do that, but they seemed to be going in totally opposite directions. Dad had forbidden us to have anything to do with the Mormons. Mum went to church but could only participate to a degree. She could not participate socially and was always trying to keep Dad happy and live her religion as well. Dad was very stubborn and refused to have anything to do with the Church. Once or twice he came home and the Elders were at our house, and he was really mad, so Mum very quickly stopped that. I was very angry at my Mother for doing something that changed our lives and made Dad angry. I questioned why she had to go and do something like that—weren't we more important?

Dad would ask why if she needed to go to church couldn't she go to one that just had a meeting on Sunday. His argument was that the Mormon church was not a religion, it was a whole way of life. He noticed that my Mother made many changes in her life and was really involved in this new religion. Instead of it passing as he had thought it would, it seemed to become more important with every passing day. I think Dad was ashamed that Mum had become a Mormon since most people knew very little about it and had heard strange things about Mormons.

My Mother stayed true to this new religion and way of life for the next seven years, and my Father stayed true to having nothing whatsoever to do with it. But somehow through all this they stayed together and still loved each other. I know that was not easy, and many times they were both very lonely. But they did it and just enjoyed the times they could as a family. I noticed that my Dad did much more by himself and seemed to gather with a group of guys who went off on skiing trips without their wives and families. If Mum complained, he would say, "Well, you changed the rules, not me."

Seven years after my Mother joined the Mormon Church, my father was killed in a yachting accident, and our lives changed dramatically. My Mother took over the family business and ran that for a couple of years. Then she went to visit with her sister in the United States (the one who joined the Mormon Church) and got engaged to a man from your church. She subsequently married him and moved to America for about three years before returning to live in New Zealand. She is still married to that man, and they are still both Mormons. As you can see, my feelings for the Mormon Church are not great. Though they advocate that families are a priority, in our case it divided our family irreparably.

Alison, you attribute your closeness with Zach and the love you have for him to your participation in your church. You are both

Mormons, so maybe you can help me to understand why this caused so much dissension and heartache in my own parents' marriage and why my Mother would do such a thing when my Father obviously was unhappy with her involvement. If family is so important, why would she do something that made her own family so unhappy? Here I go asking you all these questions again. Seems I can't help myself, but I would like to understand as I know my parents had a great relationship and a marriage to be envied before she became a Mormon. I know you and Zach have a marriage to be envied, but I cannot quite reconcile the two.

Looking back over this, I seem to have poured my heart out and addressed things I haven't even thought about, or perhaps admitted to myself for a long time. I hope I haven't bored you with this family history. Thank you for listening, Alison.

Warm regards,
Michelle

South Atlantic Ocean, near Cape Horn
USS Cherokee
August

"This your first time around the Horn, Ensign?" asked Captain Johannsen.

Ensign William T. O'Malley, U.S. Naval Academy, replied, "Yes, sir."

O'Malley had been present several weeks earlier when President Eastman had addressed the graduating class of the Naval Academy and announced the visit of the USS *Cherokee* to New Zealand. O'Malley had already received his orders and knew his assignment. Three other new ensigns from his graduating class were also aboard the *Cherokee*. Over the past several weeks the *Cherokee* had sailed steadily south on her journey to New Zealand. They had put in for thirty-six hours each in Rio de Janeiro and Buenos Aires.

Johannsen checked the weather sheet and was pleased to see the forecast for smooth sailing. Going around the Horn at any time was dangerous, but during winter it could be treacherous.

Johannsen had always admired those "iron men and wooden ships" who had made the voyage against prevailing winds and who had often sailed weeks to gain fifty or sixty miles. The *Cherokee* would roll and pitch in heavy seas if the weather were bad, but she could still make headway without concern for wind conditions. Johannsen was glad he had been born in this generation and not one hundred years earlier. Maybe he would have been a farmer, he thought.

"Keep us on 185°, O'Malley. I'll be in my sea cabin."

"Aye, aye, sir."

"Captain's off the bridge," bellowed the Marine guard.

Woodbridge, Virginia
August

"Patricia, you know exactly what time to put the kids to bed, right?"

"Yes, Mom. You've told me twenty times. Really, I'm not a kid anymore. I'll be thirteen in four months."

"I know, sweetheart. Here's the number for the temple. If you have any problems, call Mrs. Gresham."

"C'mon, Alison. We'll miss the session if we don't get a move on."

"Coming, Zach. Bye, Patricia. Remember, no more candy."

Patricia just raised her eyebrows and thought to herself, Really, Mom, you treat me like a child. But she just nodded.

"Did you finally get the kids settled?" Zach asked as they drove away.

"It's Pat's first time as the baby-sitter, Zach. I just wanted to be sure she understood everything."

"I'm sure she'll handle it all just fine. I'm really looking forward to the serenity of the temple tonight. Since we missed last month, it seems quite a while, doesn't it?"

"Yes, it does. I had a letter, or I should say, a faxed letter from Michelle today. She was responding to my letter last week thanking them for the weekend on the yacht. Did you know her mother was LDS?"

Zach's face registered some surprise. "No. She never mentioned anything about it during our trip."

"I gather from her letter that she wanted to keep it to herself. When her mom joined the Church, none of the rest of the family did, and you know how that can make for strained relations. I think she carries quite a bit of anger towards the Church. She was very complimentary about our marriage though. I think it's been on her mind because she's thinking seriously about Cameron."

"They'd make a great couple, don't you think? He's got plenty of money to make them happy."

"Zachariah O'Brien," Alison exclaimed, "since when does money make people happy?"

"It doesn't make them happy, Alison," Zach said with a grin, "it just gives them more opportunities to not be sad."

"Do you envy Cameron his lifestyle, the yacht, successful business, and all?"

"You commented on his home yourself. Do you mean to tell me you wouldn't accept such an opportunity if it came along?"

Zach was flowing along in the early evening traffic, heading north for the Washington, D.C., beltway and the LDS temple, northwest of downtown D.C. Changing lanes, two young men in a Porsche whizzed past. "There's an example, Alison. Those two probably didn't earn the money for that Porsche, but they're enjoying the lifestyle nonetheless. I can't say I wasn't impressed by *Triple Diamond* and Cameron's house. He had all the entrapments, BMW, etc."

"Zach, the scriptures don't say money is evil as most people quote, but the love of money. Let's consider for a moment if we had those resources. How much would you say Cameron's yacht would cost, in U.S. dollars?"

"Probably a hundred, maybe a hundred and twenty-five thousand."

"Exactly. As much as some homes cost people. And if we had one, how often would we use it?"

Zach thought for a moment. "Actually, you've triggered a memory I recall from something my Grandmother Flynn told me when I was younger. Her first husband used to live for boating—

first power boats and then yachts. She said they would pack up early Friday, leave about noon, and not come home until late Sunday evening, then she would spend all day Monday washing and cleaning up from the event."

"That's my point, Zach. It's not wrong to have money, but it brings with it some, what did you say earlier, entrapments. They can become as important as our church lifestyle is to us. Tell me, of the Saturdays you've been home this year, how many have you had free, not involved in Scouts or priesthood assignments?"

Zach thought it over for a moment and said, "I'd be lucky if four Saturdays out of the past six months have been totally free for us."

"Absolutely right. What would we do with a yacht like that or, for that matter, any other expensive plaything that required its own dedication? These things take us away from the things we have determined to be important in life. Can you see that?"

"Of course, Alison. But think of the challenge and opportunities we could face together. Finding ways to spend huge sums of money and still remain faithful."

"Now you're just pulling my leg. I can never get you to be serious about these things."

"Sweetheart, I understand what you're trying to say, and I agree. It just seems that of the people we know, some of them have been able to achieve it both ways. I'd like to try," he said with another big smile. "Besides, you don't want to teach Cameron about the Church and tell him he'll have to sell his yacht, do you?"

"No, I don't and you know it. But Michelle has developed some serious questions, and I'm trying to figure a way to answer her and help her reach some conclusions. I like her, Zach. She's a really good person."

"I agree, sweetheart, and we're about to go to the right place for you to find some answers."

Alison reached for Zach's hand and leaned over to kiss his cheek. "You're right, Zach. I'll know what to tell her tomorrow."

South Pacific Ocean
Kamitsu Maru
August

Rio's time had come. During the voyage he had kept to himself and in turn had not been bothered by the crew. They knew his mission was a one-way trip, and while they didn't give it much thought, they did grudgingly admire his dedication. Years before, the South Pacific had seen another generation of his kind, not this far south of course, but further north toward the equator. Hundreds of young men had risen to the challenge of sacrificing their lives for the emperor and, in the process, taken American, Australian, and New Zealand boys with them. Whatever language it was in, *kamikaze* was not a new concept.

At dawn they hoisted *Triple Diamond* over the side, released the straps, and delicately lowered the special cargo to the deck, where mountings had been fabricated to ensure it would not be lost over the side. To come this far and be thwarted by a fluke accident would be disastrous. The captain of the *Kamitsu Maru* bid Rio farewell as he boarded *Triple Diamond,* casting loose the lines. He had several days to wait and would spend those days in contemplation and prayer to Allah. He would ensure his place in Iraq's history and provide security for his family. Rio started the engines and slowly moved off.

Kamitsu Maru commenced to get underway and set a heading of 035°. She would be in Colombia in several days, and then *Kamitsu Maru* would cease to exist. Colombian drug runners would be glad to come into possession of the newly designated *Emiliano Zapata.*

Southwest of Santiago, Chile
Lear Jet over the South Pacific Ocean
August

Wyndham had arrived from Auckland several days earlier and had spent the time leisurely enjoying the sights of Santiago. He chartered a small Lear jet under his own flight credentials and filed a flight plan for Lima. He dropped off the radar screens north of Santiago and proceeded out to sea, turning southwest.

Wyndham flew to the approximate area he expected USS *Cherokee* and began a search pattern. It didn't take long to spot the targets: HMNZS *Northland* had joined *Cherokee,* and they were sailing several hundred yards apart. The two ships were on course and seemed so small from this altitude. This reconnaissance was specifically to pinpoint position and direction in the final hours. Once spotted, the plane flew northwest for about fifteen minutes until the second objective was sighted.

Triple Diamond received the brief message on a secured channel and made a slight adjustment to her course and direction. Tomorrow morning should put her in position to initiate the plan. The Lear jet turned east by northeast and returned to Santiago, declaring a problem with compass headings and advising the charter company of the problem.

Wyndham boarded his local flight to Buenos Aires and departed Chile.

Isle of Wight, Southern England
Admiral's Cup Yacht Race
August

Cameron Rossiter had been in England for two weeks practicing for the Fastnet, one of four races in the Admirals Cup Series. The race would be held in four days, and he had participated in several practice runs. The Fastnet had a history as a grueling ocean race, and no family had given more than Rossiter's. In 1957, his grandfather, Phillip Nelson Sterling had captained the New Zealand entry. The weather developed into the worst on record for the race, yet those dedicated yachties had not shrunk from the elements. His grandfather had recorded in his journal just prior to departure, "Gale winds, force 7 or 8; seamen will prevail on this day!"

Sterling had been right. Driving into strong seas and headwinds all the way to Fastnet Rock, the entrants who had made it to the turnaround point were required to tack downwind on the return voyage, as the wind had been so strong it had burst the spinnakers. Of forty-one starters, only twelve yachts completed the course. Sterling had never returned, lost overboard in the storm. The New Zealand entry finished last, limping into port after her crew had valiantly scoured the raging sea for hours, searching for their captain. Rossiter had always admired the courage of his grandfather, and he was determined to perform up to his heritage. As grueling as it could be at times, racing was in his blood, and he loved it.

He had taken time off to drive up to London to meet Michelle, who was arriving at Heathrow. Other than the dinner the night before he left, they had been apart since the weekend trip with the O'Briens. It had been too long. His hotel phone bill would attest to that. During his time away Cameron had come to realize how much Michelle had become a part of his life. He thought about her constantly, even while he was aboard *Pacific Challenge,* the New Zealand entry in the Admiral's Cup Series. Though his concentration had not suffered as a result and though the boat was doing well in preliminaries, Cameron knew something in him had changed. He was reluctant to admit to himself that it might be permanent. He had told Michelle that he loved her, and she had returned the confession. They had not spent much time talking about the future, preferring to deal with today. There was plenty of time for the future, wasn't there?

Driving into London, Cameron wondered how long they would each be content to continue with an unstated relationship. He loved Michelle, and no matter how long he pretended to himself that it didn't require action, privately he knew she would want to secure the relationship. He was nearly thirty. It was time.

Auckland, New Zealand
August

Dear Michelle,

How are the plans going? Zach and I would not have been surprised to hear that you and Cameron had just decided to take off somewhere and just get married. I have found myself once more pondering your questions and trying to sort out in my own mind just what the answers are and how to give them.

Michelle, I was very surprised to learn that your Mother is

Mormon. I had no idea. It certainly sounded like a tough issue for all of your family, especially your Mum and Dad. I'm sorry to learn that you lost your Father in a yachting accident. That probably explains some of your hesitations as far as Cameron is concerned. It must be difficult for you to go boating with Cameron and not be filled with thoughts of another time and place with your Dad and your family.

With regard to the religious issue it certainly sounds as though your Mum was converted and discovered for herself the truth about her spirituality. It must have been difficult for your Dad to understand these changes and no doubt he felt that his way of life was threatened. Without knowing the more intimate details of their relationship, it is very difficult for me to know just what to say. I do know that there are many members of the Church in similar situations and that they struggle with this issue. Like any-thing we do in life, if we are united in purpose and direction we get there in good shape, but if we are not and pull in opposite directions then we make very little headway. It sounds to me like your Mum and Dad began to take different roads and encoun-tered all of the conflicts which are a part of that. I feel for your Mum because I know how much I rely on Zach to support me in my role as wife and mother and just how much we share on the spiritual side. He strengthens me and I him and that works for us. It must be extremely difficult to go in different directions and still be united in marriage.

I don't think there is any one answer. I feel for your Father because all that he knew and was used to in his life was dis-rupted and, as he put it, someone changed the rules. All I can say is that sometimes life is like that, someone changes the rules. We have to make choices, things don't always stay the same or go the way we would like. In those instances it is what we do about the challenge that counts. I think your Dad was a very proud man and did not want to make changes to his life, but they came any-way and he opposed them. Without knowing what he really felt it is hard to know why he felt as he did about the Mormon Church, but he certainly felt threatened by it. He saw it as something he could have no control over and men usually like to be in charge of their own situation. I also feel for you and the other members of your family as it must have been a challenge to you to have your comfortable enjoyable life disrupted in that manner.

I have heard it said that the same power that is a wonderful uniting force can be just as divisive when two people are not one. This is what happened in your parents' case. I admire the fact that they worked at their marriage because they loved each other and their children. That is so important these days when people seem to give up for much less reason than your parents had. Many would say that they had every reason to part company and go their separate ways, but they didn't and their children are the beneficiaries of that decision.

I don't think either of them were wrong, they both had decisions to make and probably made them to the best of their ability. I am sorry that it left you with such feelings for the Church though, as I have such great love for the gospel and my involvement in it. It saddens me to know you feel as you do. Try to see that your parents were faced with a dilemma that was probably bigger than either of them. Your Father could not give way as he felt he had always been that way, and your Mother was faced with new happenings and new knowledge in her life and could not deny it. A really hard decision, don't you think? One that would stump the strongest of people. Be pleased that they stayed married and that when your Father died you were still together as family.

You didn't mention how your Mother managed after your Father died. Did she stay strong and keep the family together or did you drift apart? How are family relationships now that she is married to someone from the same Church? Are they happy? Try to work out just what you and Cameron want and map out a course about which you are both happy to follow and then pursue it together. Be aware that if changes come along you will be able to face them together and that the challenges your Mum and Dad faced were theirs and theirs alone. Yours will be different and only you and Cameron will have what it takes to overcome them.

I feel like a marriage guidance counselor, Michelle, always giving advice on how to make it. Who is going to give me advice when Zach and I have problems and don't see eye to eye? We have moments when we are angry with each other, you know. We don't always act like teenagers in love, but we are happy most of the time.

Take care, Michelle, and we look forward to being able to spend time together again in the future. I know that you will make the right decisions and that you and Cameron have a great future together.

Love,
Alison

CHAPTER TEN

Over South Atlantic Ocean
British Airways Flight to London
August

GREGORY FARNSWORTH-JONES SAT in first class reviewing the events of the past two weeks. He had literally been around the world. His first trip to New Zealand had been frantic and left no time to see the country. He thought that when this was all over, he would have to go back and leisurely tour both islands. There was time enough for that, and plenty of money to assure first-class accommodations.

The plan had gone like clockwork so far. Within twelve hours, phase one would be complete. Farnsworth-Jones expected a firestorm of public recriminations. If only Comrade Marshal Orchenko could be alive to see his plan carried out. Orchenko would be pleased with how well Captain Valasnikov had innovated a new concept yet had retained the original purposes. Even after thirty years, Farnsworth-Jones, formerly Valasnikov, could still recall the original outlined objectives.

These objectives were to be achieved by the plan that ulti-
mately came to be known as Silent Wind. It was to be carried out
in several stages. Farnsworth-Jones recalled how they had overcome one of the primary concerns in the early planning stages.
Getting the weapons of a small size into each country proved no
problem at all. Where to hide them securely for an indefinite
period was the concern.

He felt justifiable pride when he recalled how, as a young captain among all those senior officers and Politburo members, he had
suggested burying them. The idea was rejected at first since they
felt someone might accidentally unearth the weapons, perhaps in
constructing new buildings or a road, until Captain Valasnikov
explained. Graves are seldom molested, he had said, and he left
his point to be considered. His ideas were accepted, and over the
next five months, one episode of double funerals occurred in each
of the four countries selected. In each case the nature of the deaths
precluded open caskets, and in actuality the deceased persons had
been cremated a day or two before the funeral.

Yes, Farnsworth-Jones felt they would still be pleased with
the results. Phase one was ready to implement, and the subsequent media barrage and condemnation would closely parallel the
original thinking. Politics really didn't change much. Silent Wind
needed only another dictator ready to use the forces placed at his
command. Since the Gulf War, and in fact during the Iran-Iraq
war, Farnsworth-Jones had felt the time was once again propi-
tious, and Abdul Salimar had jumped at the chance to use this
plan to his ends. The next several months would prove quite
unsteady for world leaders. Perhaps at the other end, a shift of
power would occur. Gregory Farnsworth-Jones felt in control,
and he liked the feeling.

Auckland, New Zealand
Devonport Naval Station
August

The American Sea King helicopter sat on the tarmac with the
crew standing alongside, clothed in color-coordinated flight suits.
An American, British, and New Zealand flag were posted to one

side of the entry hatch, and a New Zealand Navy honor guard were lined up in front of the entrance. The navy band had played several more tunes than originally planned because the mayor of North Shore City had not arrived. In the interim, the local officials had taken their opportunity to meet His Royal Highness, Prince Andrew, as he prepared to depart for the rendezvous with *Cherokee* and *Northland.* Admiral Pottsdam, chief, New Zealand Defence Forces, was clearly displeased by this delay to His Highness's schedule, and Captain Duncan, Devonport Naval Station commander, had been unable to discover the problem. Finally the mayor arrived, very apologetic, and made her brief introductions to His Highness.

As they climbed aboard, the three American crew, Prince Andrew, and Commander Peterson, New Zealand Navy, prepared to leave. "Devonport Naval, this is Sabre One. Request departure clearance."

"Roger, Sabre One, you are cleared for departure. Wind is southwest at six knots, altimeter two nine eight six. You are cleared to climb to five zero. After clearing outer marker, switch to frequency one six one point nine."

"Roger, Devonport. Sabre One taxiing."

The Sea King moved clear of the people in the reception area, increased power to the rotor, and gently lifted off, then swept laterally across the runway until they were clear of the obstructions, rising as they crossed over the harbor. Climbing through two thousand feet, the Sea King turned south-southeast. "Devonport, this is Sabre One at four zero feet, heading one three five."

"Copy that, Sabre One. Good flight."

"Thank you, Devonport. Sabre One out."

Overhead, a flight of three New Zealand Air Force fighters flew cover and would accompany the Sea King part of the way, turning back several hundred miles off the coast of New Zealand. Out over the South Pacific, a U.S. Air Force KC-135 refueling tanker lazily circled in the sky, waiting for the opportunity to participate in this political flag waving. His Royal Highness, Prince Andrew, fourth in line for the throne of England, settled back and prepared for the long flight to his new, temporary vessel.

Over North Atlantic Ocean
Air New Zealand Flight to London
August

Had she completed everything? Mail, newspapers, arrangements to feed the cat? She had even stolen the time to compose a rather lengthy letter to Alison about her fears and concerns for a future with Cameron. It was such a mess to go away from home. Michelle always had the feeling that something had been left undone, but then, didn't everyone? Michelle's brother Graham worked at the Devonport Naval Station, and she had called him several weeks earlier to see if he could keep an eye on her house while she was gone.

"Sorry, Michelle," he had said, "they've pulled me off shore duty to stand in for the signal officer on the *Northland*. We're putting to sea tomorrow, and we'll be gone for two to three weeks." Finally Michelle arranged for her next-door neighbor to look in and feed the cat. She had rearranged some of the seminars she was teaching and had rearranged her work schedule, pleading with her business associate to take the remaining seminars so she could be free to go to England. She would have gone anyway.

For the entire flight, Michelle had agonized over the developing relationship with Cameron. It was at a dangerous stage in terms of future directions. At their dinner several weeks earlier as Cameron was leaving for England, he had actually asked her if she thought they were moving in the same direction. She had avoided the question, but it still lingered. Both of them knew the relationship would take a turn one way or the other fairly soon. This trip to England had her worried. Just by going she had shown considerable commitment. She really didn't have any idea how serious Cameron was or what his intentions were. He had said he loved her, but what did that have to do with commitment?

Forty-five minutes out from Heathrow, the pilot announced they would begin their descent and asked passengers to please collect their headsets and pass them to the center aisle, where they would be collected by the flight attendants. Michelle performed this ritual absentmindedly. If the flight attendant had asked Michelle how she had enjoyed the movie, she would have responded, "Excuse me?" Michelle couldn't even have told her the movie title.

She looked out the window and tried to focus her thoughts. It's time to take stock of your life, Michelle, she decided. What are you doing twelve thousand miles from your home, flying off to see someone you just met? He's been away three weeks and probably been thinking only about the yacht races. Why are you making a fool of yourself? Why did you tell this man you love him? Because he told you? Because you want to love someone? Because you're getting close to thirty and the clock is running?

The plane landed without incident and without the frequent requirement to "stack up" over London. Michelle walked down the concourse toward customs, presenting her New Zealand passport to immigration officials. She had ticked "pleasure" on the arrival form where it had asked the purpose of her trip. Would it be pleasurable, she wondered, or would she end up with egg on her face? It had all gone so fast her head was swimming. Enough was enough, she told herself. I've got to tell him that we need to slow down and sort things out. Give ourselves time to make rational decisions. We'll have a nice holiday, and I'll keep things under control.

Clearing customs with her luggage, Michelle pushed her cart through the green-arrow corridor and began to scan the crowd. He probably was busy with the yacht preparations. If he's not here, she thought, how am I going to get down to the coast? What if I can't find where he is? I could take a taxi to the train station and find a trai—! Her thoughts stopped, and she froze in place as she spotted Cameron coming through the crowd, a bright smile on his face. As he reached her, he embraced her fully and held her tight. Michelle felt his arms go around her as he held her close. The tears welled up in her eyes, and she didn't want to let go for fear he would see, or worse that he would disappear. She clung to Cameron, and he felt no desire to release her. Michelle knew why she was here. She no longer had any doubts.

South Pacific Ocean
USS Cherokee, *HMNZS* Northland, Triple Diamond
August

Since joining with the Kiwis, Captain Johannsen had reminded his crew of their responsibility to develop good relations. About twenty-five crew members from each ship had transferred across to experience operational life aboard the opposite vessel. It had proven a positive experience. Both executive officers had exchanged ships for the few days it would take to arrive in Christchurch. Johannsen liked his new Kiwi XO, Commander Reginald Heaps. Below deck on the *Cherokee,* Signal Officer Graham Duffield was learning the differences in communication gear aboard an American vessel. As one of the twenty-five exchange crewmen, he had been on the *Cherokee* for two days now, and he would remain on board until they arrived in Christchurch.

Captain Johannsen was on the bridge, anticipating the arrival of Prince Andrew shortly after daylight. "Any word from Sabre One, Commander?" he asked his Kiwi XO.

"Not yet, Captain. The tanker reports they are still about two hundred miles out. Should hear shortly."

Below, Graham had just begun to receive the first communication. "*Cherokee,* this is Sabre One, how do you read?"

"Sabre One, *Cherokee.* Read loud and strong. Over."

The pilot of the Sea King leaned over to his copilot, not using the microphone so Prince Andrew couldn't hear over the engine noise, and said, "Sounds like the limeys have taken over the *Cherokee* as well, Dan."

"Well," he intoned, "if I recall our history correctly, before the war of 1812 they used to 'impress' our American seamen into their service, Major. Maybe we've turned the tables."

Keying his mike, the pilot again made contact. "*Cherokee,* Sabre One here. We're approximately a hundred and seventy-five miles out. Should be coming up on your radar horizon shortly. ETA about forty minutes. We've got daylight just breaking dead ahead."

"Roger, Sabre One. Preparations for arrival underway."

On the bridge, Commander Heaps took a message from communications and passed it on to the captain. Johannsen read it and tucked it into his pocket. "Ever met Prince Andrew, Commander?" he asked his XO.

"No sir, this will be my first royal acquaintance," he said, smiling.

Aboard *Triple Diamond,* Riaz Khalil had completed his personal preparations. The evening before, he had gone over the instructions given to him by Mr. Wyndham, and everything was ready. About 3:00 A.M. he had spotted the two images on his radar, which he quickly shut down. Now his job was to prepare for rescue. On deck Riaz climbed to tear the sail, leaving it ragged and useless. He partially flooded the lower deck, causing *Triple Diamond* to list even though she was not under sail. All preliminary arrangements for the weapon had been accomplished, and all that remained was to set the ten-minute clock. He would do that just before actual contact.

With little daylight available during the winter, Riaz waited until about 9:30 A.M. to send his radio message. He connected the radio to the depleted set of batteries and using a prerecorded tape with an American accent, he began to transmit: "This is the yacht *Happy Holiday* calling anyone on this frequency. Yacht *Happy Holiday* calling anyone on this frequency. Respond please. Yacht *Happy Holiday* experiencing difficulty. Adrift with no power. Require assistance. Please acknowledge."

Signal Officer Duffield on USS *Cherokee* picked up the weak signal and sent it up to the captain. Turning to his Kiwi XO, Captain Johannsen asked his opinion of the distress message.

"Don't get many yachts out this far, Captain. Bearing is dead ahead. We should be spotting him as soon as we get a bit more light."

"Mr. Heath," Johannsen said to the deck officer, advise communications to contact the yacht that we are in receipt of his distress signal and are proceeding to assist. Inquire as to the nature of his emergency." He continued as an afterthought, "Advise *Northland* of our action as well."

"Aye, aye, sir. Should we notify Sabre One of the event, sir?" Mr. Heath queried.

"Not just yet, Mr. Heath. Let's find out a bit more first. All ahead one third, steady as she goes," directed the captain.

"All ahead one third, steady as she goes. Aye, aye, Captain," responded the helmsman.

For the next ten minutes, *Cherokee* proceeded with caution. The deck officer had doubled the lookout and cautioned them to be alert for a vessel in the water. About 9:45, with the first rays of light breaking behind them, the forward lookout spotted what appeared to be a small vessel, dead in the water.

About fifteen hundred yards off, Captain Johannsen ordered, "All stop," coming to a standstill about five hundred yards short of the yacht.

"Lower the boat, Mr. Heath, and see what assistance is required. Take the corpsman with you."

HMNZS *Northland* was standing off about eight hundred yards east, prepared to render assistance if required. As *Cherokee* came to a stop, *Triple Diamond,* using her engine, slowly moved toward *Cherokee,* maneuvering between *Cherokee* and *Northland.* Captain Johannsen halted the longboat when he saw the movement from the yacht, assuming she had mobility and could bring herself alongside.

Cherokee's communications gear began to pick up another signal, much stronger this time, coming across on *Cherokee's* emergency channel: "Mayday, Mayday . . . der assistance. Trouble with . . . gine room, fire below dec . . . USS *Cherokee.* Mayday, Mayday. Reactor involve . . . der assistance. Trouble with . . . gine room, fire below dec . . . USS *Cherokee.* Mayday, Mayday. Reactor involve . . . "

"Captain," Mr. Heath reported, "Signal coming in, much stronger this time. Captain, it's on our frequency and being repeated over and over. It's garbled, sir, but it includes a Mayday using our designation."

"What's going on here? What's the source of the communication?"

"It's coming from the yacht, Captain."

Riaz had maneuvered *Triple Diamond* to within one hundred and fifty yards of *Cherokee.* He had also initiated the timer, and the dial now read 00:03:35. After raising a flag up the mast, he had gone to the deck. Now, facing east, he positioned himself prone on a little mat that he used for his prayers. Riaz thought of his family and his children and exhorted Allah to be merciful.

The starboard bridge lookout noticed the flag and brought it to the attention of Captain Johannsen. Johannsen raised his field glasses to observe and see what was going on with this yacht. As Johannsen scanned the deck, he saw a man apparently injured, lying prone. As he continued scanning, he caught the flag on the mast. It had three horizontal stripes, red on top, black on the bottom and white with three green stars in the middle.

"That can't be—" Johannsen blurted out, the adrenaline beginning to pump. "Break out small arms and prepa—" The last thing Captain Johannsen saw before the blinding flash of light was the tricolored flag of the nation of Iraq.

Within half a second, everything flammable incinerated, and approximately two seconds later, the extreme temperature disintegrated what remained. The vessel components—steel, aluminum, and other nonporous matter—took a couple of seconds longer to vanish. Below decks, Signal Officer Graham Duffield heard the first syllable of a communication from Sabre One before he died, the heat in his compartment instantly rising to the temperature of the sun. He didn't have time to consider that he would never again sail with Michelle, and he was completely unaware that less than one hundred yards away had been the *Triple Diamond,* the very yacht Michelle had hoped he could one day sail.

On the USS *Cherokee* four hundred and sixty-eight officers and crew never knew what happened, while on HMNZS *Northland* the two hundred and forty-two officers and ratings of Her Majesty's Royal New Zealand Navy had approximately three nanoseconds to evaluate what happened to *Cherokee.*

In the most lopsided military engagement since the "Mother of All Battles," seven hundred and ten men and women of the United States Navy and Her Majesty's Royal New Zealand Navy and one solitary soldier of the 146th Iraqi Artillery Battalion ceased to exist. The two ships disappeared in one minute and forty seconds.

Silent Wind had begun!

South Pacific Ocean
Sabre One
August

"I say again, *Cherokee,* this is Sabre One." No response.

A brilliant flash lit up the early morning haze, lighting the interior of the Sea King as if it were an operating room in a well-equipped hospital.

"What in the world was that?" blurted the pilot.

Prince Andrew had been casually reviewing his notes regarding the crew of the *Cherokee* when he looked up to see the pilot and copilot stare incredulously at the brilliance on the horizon. Looking at each other momentarily, instinct took over for Major Hortense, pilot of Sabre One. He brought the Sea King around and called out to his crew, "Brace yourselves, we're going to receive a shock wave." He dove for the deck to get as low as possible before impact. At about fifteen hundred feet, the shock wave from the nuclear detonation impacted Sabre One, shaking her as if a monster had picked up a toy and flung it across the room.

"I can't control her," Hortense called out to his copilot. "I've lost control of the rudder."

"Major, engine readings erratic," called the copilot. "Oil pressure dropping."

"Mayday, Mayday, this is Sabre One calling Pitstop. Do you read?" There was no response from the refueling tanker several hundred miles behind them headed in the direction of New Zealand.

"Pitstop, this is Sabre One. Engine cutting out, no contact with *Cherokee.* We're going down. Pitstop, do you copy? I say again, Sabre One is going down. Do you copy?"

London, England
Heathrow Airport
August

Stephen Wyndham stood in the queue to clear customs, returning from his holiday to Buenos Aires. As he left the customs area and proceeded to claim his baggage, he also reclaimed his English identity of Gregory Farnsworth-Jones. People were gathered in front of the television monitors, listening to the BBC special broadcast. He caught pieces of the report, something to do with a large explosion. As he waited to leave the customs area, he heard one traveler say that the BBC was indicating that the French had conducted another nuclear test in the South Pacific, while his wife said she had heard on CNN in the coffee shop that a ship had sent a distress signal and then blown up.

Out in the general arrival area people were clustered in front of the television sets, trying to make sense of the initial reports. Holding hands, a young couple walked up to see what all the commotion was about, taking up a small place next to a distinguished-looking gentleman in his midfifties.

"Excuse me, sir," the young man said. "Have you any idea what the news is about?"

"Yes, it's terrible. Something to do with an explosion in the South Pacific. CNN has just reported a nuclear explosion has sunk two naval vessels on patrol, an American and a New Zealand ship."

"*What?*" the young woman shouted. They looked at the television as CNN continued.

" . . . that's correct, Tom, we have had a confirmed report from our Auckland affiliate, Sky News, that the USS *Cherokee,* a nuclear-powered guided missile cruiser, en route for an official visit to New Zealand, and the *Northland,* a Royal New Zealand Navy frigate, have been sunk with loss of all hands in the—"

"*No! No!* Please, God . . . not Graham . . . not again," Michelle exclaimed, dropping her bag as she collapsed in Cameron's arms.

The distinguished-looking gentleman moved away from the young couple and proceeded out the automatic doors to the loading area. Gregory Farnsworth-Jones hailed a taxi and headed for his office. He had plans to formulate and another twenty-five million dollars to make.

CHAPTER ELEVEN

Global News Coverage
August

WITHIN MINUTES THE AIR WAVES were filled with the story. CNN, NBC, CBS, and ABC from the United States and the BBC from London gave every possible tidbit of available information on the mysterious explosion and the missing ships. The BBC in particular intoned continuously about the possible fate of Prince Andrew, missing but known to have not reached the ships before the explosion. A U.S. Air Force tanker had picked up their Mayday signal, which advised that the helicopter was going down but gave no coordinates. A massive air search had subsequently been undertaken.

In Auckland, continuous broadcasts from TV One replayed the history of the *Northland,* interrupting with CNN coverage whenever special news updates were available. All the major networks and their local affiliates were scurrying to find their "expert" to explain to the public what had happened and what the result would be.

Abdul Salimar had planned well for this event, and his media barrage was intended to portray the worst-case scenario and to demonstrate to the world that the Americans had failed to protect the innocent citizens of the world from their vast nuclear arsenal. Even as they spoke, Iraq's news anchors said that the innocent people of Chile were beginning to suffer the consequences of the fallout from this nuclear disaster. When Abdul Salimar came on the air to deliver his version of what had happened, CNN broadcast his tirade live, with simultaneous translation.

Around the world, those governments supportive of the United States were calling for restraint until it was discovered what had caused this catastrophe. The explosion had been reported by the satellite tracking stations at 1855 Greenwich Mean Time, which made it 1355 in Washington, D.C., and 0655 the following morning in New Zealand. President Eastman was in a meeting with several bipartisan representatives of Congress on his budget proposals when he was informed. He excused himself immediately and called a meeting of the Security Council. Prime Minister Onekawa was having breakfast when he was advised by his aide of the reports coming in over the Cable News Network. Virtually ignorant of any factual data with which to respond, the prime minister found himself besieged by media upon his arrival at the Beehive. The one thing that both the New Zealand prime minister and the American president had in common was their complete and total ignorance of facts from which to draw conclusions.

When British prime minister Blankenship was informed of the status of His Royal Highness, Prince Andrew, he had the unenviable task of reporting to Her Majesty that while His Highness was not aboard the vessels when they were destroyed, his helicopter was reported missing approximately one hundred and fifty miles from the scene. A search was underway.

The world's ability to report the occurrence of events had far outstripped the ability to evaluate what had happened, but the media demanded complete and accurate response. Over the next several hours the inability of both governments to provide clarification only fed the rumor mill. By the six o'clock evening news from New York, it was being claimed that an "unconfirmed" report indicated that a United States nuclear submarine had been running practice drills against the *Cherokee* and that either the submarine or the *Cherokee* had accidentally launched a tactical nuclear weapon of small size that resulted in the destruction of both the *Cherokee* and the *Northland.*

This speculative analysis angered the president, who knew he would only be able to control the events by speaking directly with the press, but he had to have more facts. To put some restraint on the rapidly developing situation, he called a press conference for seven P.M. that evening, which was delayed twice until nine P.M. The press prepared themselves like vultures for the slaughter.

Moscow, Russia
September

Maria Koslov watched the Russian newscast with horror as it reported that a large nuclear explosion in the South Pacific had taken the lives of over seven hundred men and women on the USS *Cherokee* and HMNZS *Northland.* Immediately following that broadcast, Maria left for the outskirts of Moscow, to the house she had shared with her widowed father until his death so many years ago.

About an hour later, she was climbing the stairs to the attic of the old, decrepit family home. There she searched through a half-dozen trunks until she discovered the books she was seeking, untouched for nearly thirty years. Something her father had told her as he lay dying in the Moscow hospital from a heart attack. Something he had told her to share with no one, unless . . .

It had not made sense at the time, but her father had said she was to get his diaries to his brother if war were to occur between the United States and the Soviet Union. Six years after his death, his brother also had died, and the diaries had remained until now, except . . . except for the time she had read them right after her uncle's death. She didn't understand the abbreviated entries and some of the references, but the story of Khrushchev's bold plan had been clearly described, including the four obituary notices included in his papers.

Maria Orchenko Koslov knew what she had to do. She would follow her father's instructions as closely as she could. They were not at war, but her cousin would help her. Her uncle, a former Politburo member, had left one son, Vasili Orchenko, nephew to her father, former Marshall Orchenko, director of the Office of War Plans, under Khrushchev. Vasili was now an admiral in the Russian navy, Maria thought, and he would know what to do. Surely he would know what to do.

Washington, D.C.
National Security Agency
August

Throughout the afternoon, the staff at the NSA had been glued to the televisions located in the building. Notwithstanding the vast array of intelligence-gathering systems available, linking the NSA to every other Western intelligence agency in the world, at this moment the staff were obtaining their knowledge in much the same way as nearly three hundred million other Americans— from Cable Network News, Atlanta, Georgia. While the world-wide military and security network of satellite coverage was able to report on the fact that something had happened in a given place at a given time, it remained for the reporter on the ground, at the right place at the right time, to bring in the hard news.

Lieutenant General William Austin was visibly upset. Major Zachariah O'Brien walked into the room, followed closely by Captain Shelley Molloy, the section Middle Eastern specialist.

"Major O'Brien," General Austin began, gesturing toward his telephone, "in less than fifteen minutes that telephone will ring and the national security advisor to the president will demand some answers, which she will then be directed to provide to the president. The president has already spoken to Prime Minister Blankenship about Prince Andrew, and that issue is paramount to resolve. All things considered, it's chaos. Am I getting through to you, Major?"

O'Brien could understand why General Austin was unusu-ally brusque. He needed answers now, but none were forthcom-ing. As for the national security advisor, Clarene Prescott had served under several presidents in differing capacities. She had even succeeded in crossing the sacred barriers of partisanship. Two presidents under whom she had served had been Democrats, and two had been Republicans. She had served in successive order as an undersecretary of defense, a deputy secretary of state, and as ambassador to the United Nations. She now served President Eastman as national security advisor. No one in either party doubted her ability or her penetrating logic. She was often abrasive and direct, but she was, to her detractors' dismay, usually correct in her appraisal. General Austin had worked with her for just over one year and had earned her trust and admiration, something which did not come lightly, for Clarene Prescott did not suffer fools.

"General," O'Brien began, "the KC-135 was able to provide coordinates on Prince Andrew's helicopter just prior to the Mayday message. New Zealand had the closest forces, and they have a massive search underway right now. The Chileans have also launched a search-and-rescue operation. We expect word shortly. On the explosion, we do have some theories. Captain Molloy has been working on this issue for several weeks. Using as her basis the notes you provided from your security conference back in June, she has compiled several possible scenarios, one of which we have come to agree is the most compatible with the actual events of the past sixty days."

In June, General Austin had attended a security conference of senior intelligence agency representatives, at which they had discussed possible reasons for the increase in Iraq's posturing about nuclear weapons in his theater of operations. Major O'Brien had provided a position paper for the conference titled Iraqi Options Proposal, which his staff had nicknamed Desert Boomerang, inasmuch as it called for American forces to leave the Persian Gulf and also developed a movement plan for rapid return in the event of renewed hostilities. It had become the central focal point for the debate, and while not everyone at the meeting had agreed with O'Brien's conclusions, they had provided sufficient thought to stimulate the further development of ideas.

Major O'Brien and Captain Molloy had developed those conclusions into a workable scenario.

"Zach, if we don't have some solid answers for the president by the time his press conference convenes, the media will generate a barbecue like he never saw in Florida. Just give me the highlights, and after I brief Prescott, we'll meet again to evaluate our options."

O'Brien began with a quick summary of Salimar's actions in the seventy-two hours prior to the detonation. He explained that certain of Salimar's accusations were too specific to have come from an intelligence analysis, and the timing of his presentation was phenomenal. The conclusion was that he had to have known what was going to happen.

General Austin interrupted, "Major, you're telling me that Abdul Salimar either directly or indirectly has access to nuclear capability. You'd better have some hard data to support that conclusion."

"General, our conclusions are based upon close observation the past several months and an analysis of what we know for certain versus what we don't know. By the process of elimination, what we have left remains the only possibilities. No one else has any possible motive for such a significant move, and independent terrorist activity, the most likely alternative, is highly improbable, given the nature and setting of the attack. State-sponsored terrorism remains the only probable answer. Who has the strongest reason at present to perpetrate such an act?"

"Major O'Brien, that's thin. Extremely thin! You expect me to advise the national security advisor and the president that in the absence of any other information it is our considered opinion that we should blame Iraq!"

"General, the few facts we do possess speak for themselves. One, we know positively that no nuclear weapon was on board the *Cherokee*. Two, less positive but reasonably certain, no submarine of any nation with nuclear capability was in the area, and three, Abdul Salimar was on the air within fifteen minutes, claiming that a tactical nuclear weapon of limited size was part of the armament of the U.S. ship. Too specific, General. He knew well ahead of time, he just knew!

Austin walked over to his window and paused to look out at the afternoon traffic and the Washington population beginning to head home at the end of their work day. They would all be glued to their televisions tonight as the networks replayed, ad nauseam, the events of the day. He reflected momentarily on how many fine and capable people had occupied this office and the various situations they had found themselves called upon to address. Historians had the advantage of hindsight, a luxury that never availed itself during the process of making decisions. For nearly thirty-five years, Lieutenant General William Austin had been called upon to make decisions, some of which had caused other men and women to place their lives in harm's way, and, he thought somberly, some of which had required those same men and women to trade their future lives for eternal placement of their names on the Wall across the street in the park.

Yet, standing here in this office, he knew that a life's work could often be erased by one act of providing erroneous advice to the president, even when based on the best information available. If the advice proved wrong, it was simply wrong. No excuses and no justification. If a batting average had been compiled for making correct decisions under fire, General Austin would by now have made the Hall of Fame at Cooperstown. Unfortunately, he knew it only took one strike-out with the bases loaded to lose the game. He also knew one other thing that had always stood him well. In the end, you had to trust your people. Once you had chosen those people and tested their capabilities, it was foolhardy to discount their advice. O'Brien had proven himself time and again. He never failed to take the heat when his section was wrong, and he never failed to share the credit with his staff when they were right. They knew what was at stake as well as he did.

When the telephone rang, Austin crossed to his desk and picked up the receiver. "General Austin speaking."

"General, the president requests the pleasure of our company," Clarene Prescott said without emotion, "and since he and I have recently been discussing the Iraqi Options Proposal, prepared by Major O'Brien, I would suggest you have him accompany you."

"We're on our way, Ambassador," replied Austin. In the absence of the usual title of madam secretary, or madam chairman, Clarene Prescott had retained the title of ambassador from her United Nations appointment.

General Austin hung up the phone and spoke directly to Captain Molloy, "Have you anything to add, Captain?"

"General, I support Major O'Brien's conclusions. We are quite certain who, we're fairly certain why, and the only question to answer is how? We need a bit more time to discover the answer to that question."

"Thank you, Captain. I share your confidence in Major O'Brien. However, should he prove wrong, I believe the president will ensure that we'll have all the time we need during our early retirement to discover the truth about O'Brien's trout-fishing stories from New Zealand." He added as an afterthought, "That is, if the New Zealand government will let us in." Reaching for his hat, he looked at O'Brien. "Major, the pleasure of your company has been requested by the president of the United States and the national security advisor. Get your hat, Zach. You are about to discover where the buck stops."

South Pacific Ocean
Kiwi Seven, *New Zealand Air Force Orion*
August

For six hours the crew of *Kiwi Seven* had been on patrol, looking for signs of survivors of Sabre One. Everything flyable had been provided for this massive air-and-sea search mission in an attempt to rescue Prince Andrew and the crew of the Sea King helicopter. U.S. aircraft stationed in Christchurch assigned to Operation Deepfreeze had been provided, and that added several C-130s and two C-141s that happened to be on the ground in New Zealand at the time. Deepfreeze was a long standing resupply mission, headquartered in Christchurch, in support of U.S. facilities in the Antarctic.

"Captain, I have a faint emergency channel signal, locator beacon frequency, on a heading of zero nine seven."

"Roger, Mac. Coming around to investigate."

For the next several minutes, *Kiwi Seven,* one of the Orion patrol craft airborne for this mission, continued on a heading of zero nine seven. "Signal getting stronger, Captain. Dead ahead now." The search-and-rescue effort had been severely hampered by the winter darkness, not providing much daylight search time, and by the fact that a heavy mist had settled in over the entire portion of the ocean being searched.

"Did you see that, Chuck?" the pilot asked. "Looked for a moment like a flare." They both continued to stare through the mist and fog, trying to spot anything unusual.

"There! There it is again, at eleven o'clock."

"Got it, skipper. Let's take her down on the deck and see if we can spot 'em," the copilot suggested.

"Signal much stronger now, Captain. Definitely locator beacon."

"Got 'em," the copilot shouted. "Two torches shining directly at us." The Kiwis used the term *torch* to designate a flashlight beacon.

"Right," the pilot said, "we'll come around and put the landing lights on to signal we saw them. Signal Auckland and give our coordinates. Tell them we'll remain on station until relieved."

Three helicopters were in the general search area, being refueled by tanker in the hopes the survivors would be spotted, and HMNZS *Canterbury* was steaming en route, though still eighteen hours away.

"Captain, Auckland reports helicopter forty minutes out and heading our direction."

Forty-five minutes later, Prince Andrew and his Kiwi aide, plus the three American crew, were being winched aboard the helicopter. Fifteen minutes later, they were en route to HMNZS *Canterbury* for a brief medical check, after which they were flown directly to Wellington. To Prime Minister Peter Onekawa fell the pleasant task of advising British Prime Minister John Blankenship, who then had the greater pleasure of calling Her

Majesty to advise of the safe rescue of her second son. They had been on the water in the life raft nearly nine hours, but within six additional hours, the five occupants of Sabre One who had come within twenty minutes of joining the fateful crews of *Northland* and *Cherokee,* were safely ashore in Wellington, with press clamoring for firsthand accounts.

Questioned by local authorities in New Zealand regarding what they were able to see, they advised that they had been approximately one hundred and sixty miles distant when the flash occurred and had not yet spotted either ship, and no other vessels had been present to their knowledge. Fortune had smiled on Prince Andrew and the crew of Sabre One that day in the form of a late-arriving dignitary at the ceremonies in Devonport prior to takeoff. That thirty-minute delay provided the difference that eventually saved their lives.

Washington, D.C.
The White House Oval Office
August

General Austin was well known to the Secret Service agents who guarded the president, but a few moments were required for Major O'Brien to be identified and passed through into the Oval Office. President William Eastman, former industrial magnate, grandson of an Alaskan pioneer who struck it rich in the gold fields, and Florida senator for twelve years prior to his election to the presidency, was seated on a lounge chair positioned in front of his desk, talking with Clarene Prescott. Seated around the room were four other general officers and the chief of naval operations. Including Austin, exactly twenty-three flag officer's stars were represented by the six men, with a combined service to their country of nearly two hundred and fifty years. Major O'Brien felt humbled and privately reminded himself to remain silent.

No one rose as they entered the room, but the other generals acknowledged their arrival by eye contact and several brief greetings to General Austin. The flag rank officers in the room represented all four branches of the military service. The chairman of the Joint Chiefs was an Army armor officer, as was his immediate

army subordinate, General Cagney. Admiral Fitzwilliams had
served nearly all of his thirty-eight years on aircraft carriers and
was a rated pilot, having in the process of his career spent four
years in the Hanoi Hilton as the guest of the People's Republic of
North Vietnam. General Hammond, the senior Air Force officer,
had compiled over one hundred combat sorties during Vietnam,
with his combat service dating back to F-86s in Korea. But it was
the commandant of the Marine Corps, General Jeremiah Jones,
who commanded O'Brien's attention.

If ever there was a legend in his own time, "Jumping Jerry"
was it. He had enlisted in the Marine Corps at fifteen, lying about
his age, and shortly after his sixteenth birthday, he became part
of the U.S. Marine Corps Pacific Island–hopping campaign to
recover the ground taken by the Japanese early in the war.

At sixteen years and one month, Private Jeremiah Jones
found himself lying face down in the sand of Tarawa Atoll as his
fellow Marines tried to dig a hole and crawl in during the beach
assault. A private on one side and a lance corporal on the other
had remained on the beach that morning for the burial detail.
Private Jones, his platoon pinned down, with the soldiers dying
one by one, had found his way around a machine-gun nest, jumping from foxhole to foxhole and earning the nickname that would
stick with him for the rest of his career. He killed eleven Japanese
soldiers in the process, while receiving three wounds. His lieutenant recommended him for the Medal of Honor, which he had
received the following month from Admiral Halsey.

It wasn't until several months later that his true age was discovered, and those in charge decided that "for the good of the
naval service," Lance Corporal Jones's age would be overlooked.
What else could they have done with an underage kid who quit
high school to join the Marines and who had been awarded the
Medal of Honor? For nearly fifty years, General Jones had served
his country, and on hundreds of occasions he had wondered why
he was able to walk away from the beach on Tarawa while most
of his squad had remained forever.

O'Brien took his seat, determined to stay in the background
of this impressive gathering. President Eastman stood and

addressed the group. "Gentlemen, Ambassador Prescott, thank you for coming so quickly. I think we understand the nature of this gathering and the importance of reaching some immediate conclusions." He paused to be sure they understood that this would be no contemplative think-tank session. He needed answers, and he needed them now. "First and most important if I am to retain any credibility whatsoever, I need to know the absolute truth about the nature of armament aboard the *Cherokee*."

Admiral Fitzwilliams looked toward the chairman for permission to speak. Receiving a slight nod, he turned to look squarely at the president. "Mr. President, I can state without reservation that no nuclear weaponry of any kind existed aboard the *Cherokee* outside of its propulsion system. Under no circumstances could a reactor problem have resulted in an accident and subsequent detonation of this nature. Mr. President, the *Cherokee* and the *Northland* were deliberately and intentionally attacked and sunk."

"I will accept that as a given, and we will proceed from that basis." Turning to Austin, the president continued, "General Austin, any word on Prince Andrew's status?"

"At the moment, sir, it is still in the search stage. No location has been identified, but we hope for some breakthrough momentarily. His coordinates were made available by our tanker."

"Fine. Ambassador Prescott has provided me with the Iraqi Options Proposal, prepared by your staff. I find the premise interesting, and in the light of current events, somewhat clairvoyant. Would you please elaborate on the relationship that may now exist between conclusions drawn in the document and the present situation?"

O'Brien found himself distinctly uncomfortable as General Austin began to brief the president on the anticipated actions of the Iraqis. As Austin concluded his remarks, all waited for the president to respond. Eastman, still standing, turned his attention to O'Brien. "Major, my grandaddy used to tell me a story about sled dogs in Alaska. He said that if you weren't the lead dog, the view never changed. He forgot to tell me, however, that once you were the lead dog, you might not like the view, and it wasn't always possible to get back in the pack. Major O'Brien, considering the conclusions you reached in this document over six weeks ago," he said, waving O'Brien's proposal, "we both find ourselves in such a situation. In about thirty minutes, the world's press will want to know what this lead dog sees ahead. You seem to have been able to see some things others didn't while you were still in the pack. Would you be so kind as to provide me with your opinion as to how this all fits together, now that we have the benefit of hindsight as regards Salimar's intentions?" President Eastman paused, but before O'Brien could speak, he added, "You will see from my conclusion that I have accepted your original premise that Iraq is behind this, even if it seems well outside their sphere of influence."

Major O'Brien stood, as much from nervousness as from the fact that President Eastman was still standing. "Sir . . . Mr. President, what we are able to analyze in the Office of Strategic Analysis comes as a result of information made available to us from the Joint Chiefs staff and from the intelligence agencies." This he said as much to cover his embarrassment in front of the Joint Chiefs as to give himself a few additional moments to compose his response. Picking up, O'Brien carried on, "I see three possible courses of action for Iraq from this point.

"One, they could continue to beat the drum against the U.S. through those nations opposed to our policies and those who generally remain neutral. Their premise would be that in a tension-reduced world, peace-loving nations have no need to parade around the world with their nuclear arsenal, causing fear and potential catastrophe wherever they go. Sir, if he is successful in this endeavor, he would eventually provide enough logic for a peaceful solution with which all but the staunchest of our allies would find themselves in agreement.

"Two, he could continue to promulgate covert terrorist actions against the U.S. through surrogate groups, embarrassing us where he found the opportunity. This course of action would, at the least, cause us to maintain a higher state of readiness at all installations, including individual ships at sea.

"And third, he could possibly use the excuse of this nuclear 'accident' to openly attack our units in the Middle East on the premise that they are a threat to the region's safety and are no longer needed to enforce the terms of the United Nations agreements, since Iraq only wants peace and tranquility in the area. Mr. President, this option is fairly low on the list because it offers the least immediate return for Iraq, and Salimar knows he can't trade blows with us, even if the world develops sympathy for his actions."

O'Brien paused, not sure whether to provide recommendations or suggestions, or whether to conclude his presentation.

Sensing O'Brien's reluctance, President Eastman interjected, "Major, you've been in this office before, I believe, as a young man?"

"Yes, sir," O'Brien replied, surprised.

Eastman was much older than O'Brien, and of the same vintage as most of the general officers in the room. His position as president carried with it an air of respect, for age as well as for office, and he lectured the assembled officers in that tone. "Gentlemen," he said, ignoring Clarene's presence as the only woman in the room, "I do not intend to go down in history as the second president to use nuclear weapons, accidental or otherwise. I want the answers to this riddle, and I want them now." Turning his attention back to O'Brien, he continued in a somewhat softer tone, "Do you think your father won the Medal of Honor by being cautious when the situation demanded action?"

O'Brien was taken aback, first by the president's knowledge of his father's Medal of Honor so many years ago, but second by his raising the issue as a challenge. "No, sir, I have always believed my father saw his duty and took no particular care for the personal consequences of his actions, other than to do what he could to avert further loss of life." O'Brien continued to feel distinctly uncomfortable, especially in the presence of General Jones, for whom this revelation was proving most interesting.

"Well, Major," the president said with a hint of a smile, "I have a sense that some of that Kiwi blood still courses through your veins, which, in light of the *Northland*'s unfortunate destruction, provides you with a dual responsibility to contribute to the solution of this dilemma. Continuing my earlier analogy, Major, are you familiar with the Iditarod Race?"

"Yes, Mr. President," O'Brien mumbled as he mentally shifted gears, "the thousand-mile dogsled race in Alaska." The president certainly had a way of keeping one off balance, O'Brien thought.

"That's right, Major. During that grueling thousand and forty-nine miles, which usually takes ten days to two weeks, the lead dog is called upon to perform, but without the pack pulling for the entire thousand miles, they would never reach Nome. You understand my meaning, Major?"

"I believe so, sir."

"Then please continue."

O'Brien glanced at General Austin, who provided a reassuring look. "Mr. President," O'Brien continued, "my original premise in the Iraqi Options Proposal indicates that the longer we stay in an enforcement role in the Middle East—policemen if you will—the higher risk we run of eroding all support we ever had to correct Iraq's original moves against their neighbors. Each incident regarding a U.S. plane being shot at, and our retaliation against the radar installation or whichever target we choose, brings us further down the road toward being seen as the resident bully. Sir, the Romans functioned in that role for several centuries and never achieved any degree of acceptance."

O'Brien could sense that the general officers present were beginning to get tired of being lectured by this young major, and he moved to conclude his remarks. "Mr. President, the immediate objective is to clearly demonstrate to the world that this was no nuclear accident, that the *Cherokee* positively had no weapon on board, and that U.S. credibility is intact. Captain Shelley Molloy, an exceptional young officer on my staff, summarized to General Austin just as we left the office to come here: We're quite certain who, and we have a reasonable certainty of why, we just need to find out how. Mr. President, if you can give us the time to determine how Salimar accessed nuclear weapons, we can take the necessary measures to avoid any further such action."

As O'Brien concluded his remarks, a presidential aide entered the room and handed the president a message form. Eastman briefly looked it over, and a smile crossed his face. "Gentlemen, Clarene, we have just been advised that Prince Andrew and the American crew of the helicopter have been rescued from their life raft by New Zealand air-and-sea rescue forces. I'll call John Blankenship as we break up this meeting." Relief was evident on the faces of the Joint Chiefs of Staff when they heard the news—they had felt responsible for his safety during the transport from New Zealand to the vessels, as he had been aboard a U.S. Navy Sea King helicopter.

The president thanked O'Brien for his remarks and asked the Joint Chiefs if they had any further contribution. He then thanked them for coming, and they rose to leave. Following their departure, the president again sat down to consolidate his thoughts with Clarene Prescott. "Well, Clarene, where do we go from here?"

"Mr. President, General Austin seems to have placed his trust in this young major, and you know I have developed a confidence in Austin's judgment. We don't have many options at this point. Like it or not, we are involved in a fire-suppression mission, and in this instance your dogsled story won't stand. The 'pack' out there in the press room intends to eat the lead dog alive!"

"Thank you for your vote of confidence, Madam Ambassador," the president said to Prescott. As he rose to prepare for the coming address to the nation, he added, "I believe that some of my predecessors have not found it necessary to be eaten so long as they had trusted servants to feed the pack, or perhaps I should say to feed *to* the pack. Maybe the president should rely on his trusted and experienced national security advisor to 'feed' the pack," he said with a grin. Considering the gravity of the loss of the two crews, Eastman felt somewhat relieved that he would not have to add His Royal Highness, Prince Andrew of Great Britain.

Out in the foyer, the chairman of the Joint Chiefs talked briefly with General Austin while Major O'Brien waited. General Jeremiah Jones, commandant of the Marine Corps, walked up to Major Zachariah Daniel O'Brien and put forth his massive hand, which O'Brien took in a handshake. "Major," General Jones said, his piercing eyes boring into O'Brien, "the Marines are always looking for a few good men. I'm pleased to see you come from good Kiwi stock. You know, as a very young private I arrived with the Second Marines in Wellington in '42. Under slightly different circumstances, O'Brien, you might have even been my son," he said with a twinkle in his eye. "If you ever seek a real challenge . . . ," he offered. Turning to a serious vein, General Jones added, "You've got a task on your shoulders, son, tracking down the root of this devious attack. I don't envy you. Anything, and I mean anything, that the Marines can do to assist, you call me personally. Understood?" he said, looking directly into O'Brien's eyes.

"Yes, sir," O'Brien replied. "Understood."

Washington, D.C.
National Security Agency
August

Walking back to General Austin's office, Major O'Brien stopped to telephone his office to tell his staff to stand by until he returned. In the general's office, Austin hung his hat on the rack and sat behind his desk. O'Brien took a chair opposite him, seemingly drained by the meeting. "General," O'Brien began, "you invited me to see where the buck stops. It seems to me that the president bucked it right back to us."

"Would you trade places with him right now, and face the press?" asked Austin.

"No, sir, I believe I'll stay in the pack, so to speak." O'Brien moved to the issue at hand. "General, the Air Force at this moment is taking air samples in the vicinity of the explosion to try to pinpoint the origin of the weapon. It's going to be hard with no ground residue remaining, at least until some fallout reaches Chile. Of course, the Chileans might not be too helpful, and we can't blame them. I'd like to begin by trying to trace backward to determine how the weapon was delivered. We could search for missing aircraft, small vessels, and so on, but it's going to be pure detective work at this point."

"You're right, Major, but we don't have the liberty of unlim-

ited time. I'll coordinate with the CIA and advise them where we
will concentrate our attention. Your office will assume responsibility for the South Pacific. Assign the required tasks and areas of
responsibility among your staff. Find the method of delivery,
Zach. We've got to give the president some ammunition with
which to restore American credibility. This is going to get ugly
internationally before it gets any better. The only bright light I see
is that Andrew wasn't on board. The repercussions if he had been
killed, I don't care to imagine."

O'Brien returned to his office, and for the next several hours
into the early morning, pausing only to watch the president's
press conference, he and his staff worked to flesh out a workable
investigative operation. They needed to provide the highest probability of obtaining information in the least amount of time. When
they were through, they left, returning to their homes for a few
hours of sleep before departing for various parts of the world,
south of the equator.

General Austin placed a call to Clarene Prescott, made a few
suggestions, and requested that she ask the president to pave the
way for O'Brien with the prime minister in New Zealand. She
agreed with the plan and passed on to Austin her appreciation for
the efforts of his staff during the meeting. "The president was
favorably impressed with O'Brien's candor," she said, "considering the delicate nature of the meeting. The fact that he was willing
to express recommendations other than 'charge' in the presence
of the Joint Chiefs spoke volumes, and at that point the president
needed to know someone in the military could exercise restraint."

In an unusually informal manner, Prescott closed with this
personal comment. "Bill, the president's really in a hole on this
one, and prior to your arrival in our meeting, the Joint Chiefs collectively were ready to go back to Iraq and destroy it. That would
just make us look more the bully. I need the benefit of your thinking this time because the military establishment is going to close
ranks and press for action. Can I count on you, Bill?"

General Austin reflected for a moment on his own career,
which he felt had stopped at his third star, perhaps because he did
not always follow the military tradition of "forceful action" as

being the only proper response to aggression. "Ambassador, Major O'Brien has my confidence, and he was speaking for this office at my direction. Accordingly, we will provide you with all the assistance this office can generate." General Austin broke his own code of always addressing his superiors by their title or rank and closed with "You do what you need to do, Clarene, and trust us to stand behind you."

"Thank you, Bill. Keep me informed as you progress, and please express my appreciation to your young major."

Washington, D.C.
White House Press Room
August

For several months the president had been receiving critical review over his military retirement system proposals and his attempt to reform a program that, for many years, had been the most lenient retirement program available in the nation. It seemed that each time a politician had attempted to revise the program, they had only encountered more legislation assuring in perpetuity the right to retire after twenty years of service. No change had ever been successfully implemented. Like many political issues, it was always easier, however, to say or do nothing than it was to attempt change. And so the status quo had remained. Bill Eastman and his wife, Jean, were determined to leave senior citizens, including the military, a secure retirement system as their legacy to the nation. It was a noble cause; nevertheless, it had been the source of ample criticism.

This evening, however, the president expected no questions on retirement. Rather, he was more concerned that his own retirement would possibly be hastened by the meeting. Clarene Prescott had not been joking when she said the press intended to eat the lead dog alive. Eastman delivered his opening remarks in the form of a report to the nation on the facts as they were known. He started by informing the nation that our First Alert Tracking System at Cheyenne Mountain and Omaha had reported what appeared to be a nuclear explosion approximately twenty-five hundred miles west southwest of Santiago, Chile, over two thousand miles north of McMurdo Station in the Antarctic, and about eighteen hundred miles southeast of New Zealand. The only known traffic in that area at the time was the USS *Cherokee,* a United States guided missile cruiser, and the HMNZS *Northland,* a New Zealand frigate. He also reported the news that Prince Andrew's helicopter crew and the prince had been rescued by New Zealand forces. The rescue had taken nearly nine hours because that part of the South Pacific ocean was quite isolated.

Regarding the explosion, he reported that not much was known regarding the type of weapon, but the U.S. had investigative teams headed that way as he spoke. He discounted rumors about submarines and missile exchanges between U.S. ships and accidental discharge of nuclear weapons. He stated emphatically that no nuclear weapon was on board the *Cherokee* and that the mission of the ship, to visit New Zealand, was of paramount importance to the peaceful diminution of nuclear threat. He expressed his appreciation for the trust the New Zealand government had placed in receiving a United States warship for the first time in over ten years.

The president also expressed his deep sympathy for the families of the crews from the USS *Cherokee* and HMNZS *Northland.* He said memorial services would be held in both nations in honor of those who gave their lives in the cause of peace, and he asked his fellow Americans to trust their government until the source of this dastardly attack was discovered. He promised to leave no stone unturned in the search for the perpetrators. He added that the United States would exercise restraint in dealing with the situation because what the perpetrators wanted was blind retaliation and a widespread reaction. He closed by reminding people that the world had changed considerably over the past fifty years, and not every enemy was willing to stand up across the field in an honorable fight.

"Nevertheless," he said, "that does not detract from those who are called upon to preserve the freedoms we have come to expect. 'Freedom isn't free,'" he quoted, "and many honorable men and women have paid the price of that vigilance. The crews of the *Cherokee* and the *Northland* have joined the list of those who have given their all."

Clarene Prescott and the president's chief of staff were waiting when he concluded, and they walked down the corridor with him to the Press Room. They reassured the president about his presentation, and as they entered the room, flooded with lights, they took up their positions on either side of the podium, with the chairman of the Joint Chiefs immediately behind.

The president began, "Ladies and gentleman, you have all heard my opening statement to the nation, and I'm certain you understand that highly technical questions will not serve any purpose tonight, as we are still evaluating what little information is available. We can however repeat our statement concerning our adamant stand that no nuclear weapon was aboard the USS *Cherokee,* and a reactor problem would not have resulted in such an explosion. Please try to limit your questions to enable everyone to have the opportunity to participate."

By tradition, the first question at presidential press conferences belongs to the senior correspondent, in this case, Alice Krenshaw from UPI. She rose and began, "Mr. President, ever since the USS *Maine* blew up in Havana harbor in 1898 under suspicious circumstances, to the contrived Gulf of Tonkin incident in Vietnam with the USS *Turner Joy* and USS *Maddox,* plus the Iran-Contra scandal, the military has sought to mislead the American people into believing what they thought was necessary to justify military action. In light of the radioed distress messages reporting a fire and reactor problems on the *Cherokee,* which was received in Chile and several outposts in Antarctica, why should the American people believe tonight that the government is completely blameless in this latest, and perhaps most disastrous, tragedy?"

President Eastman's heart sank, and he realized the lead dog had just lost his hind leg. The questions only got worse from there. All decorum and protocol were lost in the frenzy to expose this administration as nothing more than a repeat of other deceitful administrations that had led the American people down the garden path.

This peculiar American institution of exposé had reached new heights, or perhaps, as President Eastman was thinking, new lows. The pride and honor of being president of, arguably, the world's leading nation were lost in the scurry to defrock its leadership. It was as if the senior levels of the news profession sought to outdo one another in their "tabloid" headlines. It played right into the hands of the one man for whom criticism of leadership meant instant death.

For the following several weeks, international response would follow the course set by American journalists. One intrepid journalist fighting against the tide had paraphrased excerpts from Ezra Taft Benson, secretary of agriculture under President Eisenhower. He had written in his newspaper column, "We have discovered the only enemy capable of defeating a democratic society, and that is 'the enemy within.'"

CHAPTER TWELVE

Wellington, New Zealand
The Beehive
August

PRIME MINISTER ONEKAWA had just reached his office when his secretary advised him of a call from President Eastman. "Put him through, Mary," he said going to his desk.

"Mr. Prime Minister, this is Bill Eastman. It is a sad reason to extend this call, and I would prefer that we had met under more favorable conditions. The only positive aspect of the entire event is the safe return of Prince Andrew."

"That's true, Mr. President. Any further information on the cause of this tragedy?"

"I'm sending my representative down to meet with you if you can provide the time, and he will brief you on the issues before us. We have transmitted to our ambassador certain details he will bring to your attention this morning."

"Excellent, Mr. President. You can understand we have been

having our own discomfort from particular constituencies. We'll have Greenpeace on a local news show tonight. This sort of thing is right down their alley. Nothing quite as dramatic as your press conference last night, however."

"Yes, a particularly feisty group when they want to be, Mr. Prime Minister. I would appreciate your giving what support you can to our liaison, Major O'Brien. I believe you have met before. I'm hoping his Kiwi blood will help him obtain the benefit of the doubt until we can resolve this issue to everyone's satisfaction. Nevertheless, we would like to keep his presence and mission confidential until he can surface with some information."

"Mr. President, we will do everything we can to assist. Thank you for the call. I will keep in touch should we come up with anything of importance. Good day, Mr. President."

"Good evening, Mr. Prime Minister, thank you for your understanding."

As Prime Minister Onekawa replaced the receiver, he called out to his secretary, "Mary, see if Dan Hegarty can step in for a moment, please."

"Certainly, Mr. Prime Minister," said Mary as she picked up her phone to call.

Dan Hegarty was chief of Security Intelligence Service, New Zealand's small but highly efficient internal investigative unit. Together with the New Zealand police, they had surprised the world and particularly the French with their ability to ferret out the actions of several French intelligence agents who had tried to thwart the efforts of the local Greenpeace operation. The French had never expected to be caught blatantly carrying out open terrorism in a neutral country, but the SIS and police had risen to the challenge, and the result was embarrassment for the French government and the resignation of several French ministers of government.

As Hegarty entered the prime minister's office, he knew what was up. The airwaves had carried nothing else for the past twelve hours. "Dan," the prime minister began, "it looks like you're the man of the hour again. I've just spoken with President Eastman. He's sending a man out to try to get to the bottom of this issue.

I've been around long enough to suspect everything and everyone, as I would surmise you do also in your line of work, but I
believe Eastman is telling the truth about the weapons the ship
was carrying, or I should say not carrying. But, and it's a big but,
Eastman may not know the truth. If his military has him fooled,
we might never know. I want you to stay close to this issue, Dan.
The man you will work with is a New Zealand citizen as well as
an American. His name is Zach O'Brien, and he's an air force
major. Give him what support you can, but give me your evaluation of him and let me know what you believe is the real purpose
behind his investigation. I want to know if they intend to white-
wash this thing. I want to know why the boys on the *Northland*
died, and I darn well intend to find out."

Auckland, New Zealand
The Pulham News Hour, TV One
August

Following another of the interminable news flashes, this one
showing Prince Andrew arriving at the hospital for a check and
visually showing him in good health, the announcer concluded
his remarks by informing his audience that they would be rejoin-
ing the Pulham News Hour in progress. Jeff Pulham had as his
guest the director of Greenpeace for South Pacific Operations, in
New Zealand for a conference coincident with the visit of the
American ships.

"Your plans, then, were to protest the arrival of the American
vessel, starting at Christchurch?" Pulham asked.

"Yes, Jeff, we were in total disagreement with the proposed
visit, feeling that nuclear propulsion was nearly as dangerous as
the weapons, at least to the long-range health of New Zealand citizens. But perhaps this incident is timely in the sense that the
world will see what we have been trying to tell them for so long."

"How do you mean?"

"Well, Jeff, for over twenty-five years, Greenpeace and other
environmentally conscious organizations have told the world that
the French nuclear testing in the South Pacific was dangerous.
This explosion today, as horrendous as it is to the families of the

poor crewmen, was no greater, in fact smaller, than most of the
tests conducted by the French. If it took the lives of the crewmen
to highlight that to the world, it is indeed unfortunate, but demon-
strative of our position."

Somewhat stunned, and having expected a vitriolic attack on
the United States, Pulham hesitated, at a loss in implementing his
normal thrust-and-parry approach. "Do you mean . . . uh, are you
trying to say that, uh, that the loss of these two ships was no
worse than the French nuclear testing?"

Fully in control now, the Greenpeace director continued.
"Absolutely not. You've taken my comment out of context. I said
that the weapon, or perhaps I should say its 'yield,' at least from
early reports, was not larger, and perhaps was even smaller, than
the ones the French have been testing. The deaths of the crews
are abhorrent, but the explosion still serves to demonstrate our
point: nuclear testing must stop."

"Well, thank you for your comments," Pulham stuttered. He
had not expected this to go quite the way it had, figuring a rousing
show designed to castigate the Americans for their deceitful possession of nuclear weapons on board the *Cherokee*. Clearly,
Greenpeace had conferenced on this issue and decided to take the
long view rather than charge America with negligence. Did they
know something that he didn't know? Pulham wondered.

Woodbridge, Virginia
August

It was nearly two A.M. when O'Brien left the loop and entered I-
95 heading south. I-95 was a main north-south corridor on the
east coast of the United States, and even at two A.M. it had steady
traffic. As he drove, he tried to reflect on the events of the past—
what was it?—twelve hours since they had received the first
reports of the explosion. It seemed as if they had been at it for
weeks already. Americans were used to immediate response and
quick solutions to most things they saw on the news, but he
doubted if many people realized how vast the distances were in
the South Pacific Ocean. The triangle within which this explosion
had occurred placed it far from any land mass. The Air Force had

an aircraft on the scene for observation within four hours, but it would be several days before a U.S. vessel could examine the scene, if indeed there was anything to examine.

President Eastman had been a real surprise tonight, Zach thought. He had been able to maintain some degree of pleasantry in his meeting with the Joint Chiefs, and he had even surprised Zach with his recitation of Dad's award ceremony, but there was no room for pleasantry in the face of those intrepid guardians of truth and the right to know. Zach reflected on his mother for a moment, and her feelings about the press. She had taught him as he grew that they were a necessary part of a free society but that most seemed overzealous in their pursuit of the "story" as opposed to the "truth." Truth that didn't titillate, or take front-page headlines, was boring, and there was no story in it. Ah, but a good scandal, now there's news! He didn't envy President Eastman his "lead dog" position.

As he turned into his driveway, he saw the light was still on in the kitchen. He pulled into the garage, closed the automatic door, and entered the kitchen. Alison was reading the paper and listening to the continuing news from CNN on the small television on the counter. She stood up in her bathrobe and smiled at him. He looked weary, she thought. Without words, she put her arms around him and just held him for some moments.

This was his refuge, Zach thought. Whatever evil coursed through the world, and there would always be someone to perpetrate evil, his home and his family provided the refuge he needed to recharge his batteries and to recall why he opposed evil in the first place. Evil took many forms. To the religious, it was the influence and power of Satan bent on destroying the good God would have people do. To others, it was simply one person trying to put something over on another for his or her own personal gain. Sometimes that meant stealing a purse from an old lady to get fifty dollars to buy drugs, and sometimes it meant detonating a nuclear device and killing hundreds—and potentially thousands, if situated in a populated area. Such men would always be with us, Zach thought, but not tonight, not in this house.

"How about some poached eggs on toast, sweetheart?" Alison asked.

"Yes, thank you."

Alison could see his haggard look and the deep concern in his eyes. The news had been continuous since the first accounts starting coming in. "I'm surprised you were able to come home. How's the president holding up?

"The press ate him alive, Alison. No mercy."

"All those poor men on the ships. All those families. All those children without fathers." She felt the tears start down her face as she prepared the eggs. She was thinking privately, as millions of military wives had done for centuries, that her husband sat before her this time, but another time was always possible, and then . . .

Zach saw her tears, rose from the kitchen table, and went into the living room to the table next to his chair. When he returned, he was carrying the Book of Mormon. "Alison, all day since I heard the reports of the explosion, this scripture has been running through my mind. It still doesn't justify what happened, and perhaps it doesn't even relate, but for me, it puts some perspective on it. I have always been amazed at this story and how we just gloss over it in church. The magnitude of what happened to these men and their wives and children is virtually unbelievable. It somehow explains . . . not explains, actually . . . well, just listen:

"'And it came to pass that we did march forth to the land of Cumorah, and we did pitch our tents around the hill Cumorah. . . . We had gathered in all the remainder of our people unto the land of Cumorah. . . . And it came to pass that my people, with their wives and their children, did now behold the armies of the Lamanites marching towards them; and with that awful fear of death which fills the breasts of all the wicked, did they await to receive them.'

"Imagine that, Alison, their wives and all their children with them. And it wasn't the wicked who were *coming* with the Lamanites, it was the wicked *among the Nephites* who were waiting for the approaching armies and death.

"'And it came to pass that my men were hewn down, yea,

even my ten thousand who were with me, and I fell wounded in the midst; . . . and we beheld the ten thousand of my people who were led by my son Moroni. And behold, the ten thousand of Gidgiddonah had fallen, and he also in the midst. And Lamah had fallen with his ten thousand; and Gilgal had fallen with his ten thousand; and Limhah had fallen with his ten thousand; and Jeneam had fallen with his ten thousand; and Cumenihah, and Moronihah, and Antionum, and Shiblom, and Shem, and Josh, had fallen with their ten thousand each.'

"This is just amazing. Listen to this, Alison:

"'And it came to pass that there were ten more who did fall by the sword, with their ten thousand each; yea, even all my people, save it were those twenty and four who were with me.'

"Alison, in that last short verse, *over one hundred thousand people are reported dead.* I can't remember ever hearing the full magnitude of that battle until one day I added up the ten thousands. Two hundred and forty thousand people, nearly a quarter of a million people, plus their wives and children, and the interesting part, considering that this was hand-to-hand combat with swords, is that no mention is made of the Lamanite deaths. They must have had close to equal numbers. This might have been the largest single battle in the history of the world, and it goes virtually unnoticed in the end of the Book of Mormon."

Alison placed the eggs before her husband and sat down at the table, taking his hand in hers. "I'm afraid I don't understand the relationship, Zach."

"Perhaps there is no direct relationship, but the scripture kept coming to me today. I kept thinking that the relationship might be like a warning: unless we control these things so they don't get out of hand, the Lord has shown us what can happen. If those many people can be killed with swords, imagine the destructive power from our nuclear weapons. If we don't find a way to turn our thoughts back to him, we're as vulnerable as the Nephites were, no matter how 'promised' our land is supposed to be."

Alison nodded. "I can see that. But the men on these ships belong to our time. Their families are here, now. I know that Mormon's battle was real, but from the way the scriptures tell the story, no one was left to mourn. Somehow these families, today, have to understand why their husbands, fathers, sons, and brothers died. Someone has to tell them."

Zach lowered his head and nodded. "I know. We have been assigned to do exactly that—find out how and why. I think we know why, and who. Most of all who. But we must discover why and then how, so the world can understand that we didn't let those men die through our negligence." Zach's appetite was gone now, but he slowly ate the eggs Alison had prepared, continuing to read the scriptures.

Several hours later, as light crept through their upstairs bedroom window, Alison cuddled closer to Zach and lay silently. The closeness they had always shared was needed now—feeling each other's presence, knowing they were each alive, caring and, perhaps most of all, drawing comfort from each other in the face of this catastrophe. As the dawn came and they woke to face the reality of the day, Zach stroked Alison's hair and whispered of his love. Alison was sure of Zach's love whether he was next to her, as he was now, or halfway around the world, as she was sure he would shortly be. But for the moment they were together, and for this morning at least, they were one.

London, England
Queen Anne Hotel
August

Michelle woke before dawn and lay thinking. How her life had changed again in so short a time! Last evening she was flying to England to be with Cameron, scared, nervous about the reunion, but calm and comforted immediately upon feeling his arms around her. Then the news broadcast. Was it real, had it really happened? Her subconscious wanted to tell her otherwise, but she knew if she turned on the television, it would still be there. She and Cameron had watched it nearly all night until she had fallen asleep on the couch, exhausted. Before she fell asleep, there had been no word on Prince Andrew, although it had been known that he was not yet on the ships when the explosion had occurred. His helicopter had simply disappeared from radar.

Michelle couldn't fathom it. Why was she singled out for such sorrow? Was she destined to lose everyone she loved? Could she avoid such agony by simply not loving? All these thoughts raced through Michelle's mind as she lay waiting for the light to enter her room. Cameron had literally carried her into the bedroom after she practically passed out. He must still be on the couch, she thought. Her thoughts drifted to her father and how she had first learned of his injury. She had been working when she received a call from her mother . . . *her mother!* In her confusion and grief, she had completely forgotten about her mother. She must be frantic by now. Michelle had lost her father and her brother, but Mum had lost a husband and a son. What time was it now in New Zealand? Eleven or twelve hours ahead, five thirty A.M. by her watch . . . it must be coming up on six o'clock in the evening in Auckland. She had to call Mum.

Quietly, so as not to wake Cameron, she used the phone at the bedside and asked the hotel operator how to get an outside overseas line, and then she dialed the number direct. After three rings, the phone was answered. "Hello," the soft voice said.

"Mum, it's Michelle. Is it true?"

"Yes, Michelle," her mother said, her voice breaking. "Are you still in London?"

"Yes, Mum, but I'll be home as quickly as I can. Why, Mum, why?"

"I don't know, Michelle. I'm still trying to understand it myself. The others are coming up as quickly as they can. Let me know when you'll arrive in Auckland so I can meet you."

"Oh, Mum, he was so young. He didn't deserve this."

"I know, so was your dad. Michelle . . . "

"Yes, Mum."

"I need you this time, it's so . . . "

"I know, Mum, I'm coming."

Michelle hung up the phone and let the tears flow again. She had cried through the night at the shock of her brother's death, but now she recalled her earlier tragedy. They were living in Christchurch, and Michelle had just turned nineteen. Her mother had called at work to tell her that her dad had been injured in a

boating accident. Mum would be flying up to Auckland to meet
him at the hospital. She had no idea how serious the injury was,
but she promised to call as soon as she knew anything. Later that
evening, while the three sisters were frantic without news, Mum
had called to tell them all to come up on the first flight and to
bring their grandmother with them. It's serious, Mum had said,
but she didn't know, or at least she hadn't told them any more.

They had arrived in Auckland the next morning and gone
straight to their dad's hospital room. Even as she recalled it now,
nearly eight years later, she shuddered at the memory of seeing her
father in the hospital bed. Mum had been calm and reassuring, but
Michelle had seen in her eyes the resignation that comes from
knowledge. Her mum's spirituality had brought her through that
crisis, but her dad's death had made Michelle wonder how people
could believe in a God who would do such a thing. It had angered
Michelle. Her father had been so fit, so vibrant, and he had so much
to live for, with a family who loved him. And now her brother . . .

She was so lost in her thoughts that she didn't notice
Cameron come up behind her and take her shoulders. She reached
up and placed her hand over his without speaking.

"They found Andrew's life raft and rescued the crew from the
helicopter," Cameron advised.

"I'm glad for them," she murmured. "I'm going home,
Cameron."

"Yes, I understand . . . Michelle, I do love you. I know that
now, and I want to be with you. Forever."

"Cameron, we can't—I just can't think of that now. I should-
n't have come. I've got so much to do—I've taken so much time
away from my business. We should slow down, I mean we
should . . . "

"I know you're upset, Michelle. I'll do what I can to help. I
just can't leave right now. Nine other men are depending on me."

"No, no, of course. I didn't mean you should come. Just take
me to the airport, and I'll catch the first flight home."

"I'll call you as soon as you get home, Michelle, and then
when I get back—"

"I don't know, Cameron. I've got to think, I need to . . . think . . . " Her voice faded away.

Driving to the airport, Michelle and Cameron were quiet, each lost in thought. As Cameron left her in the waiting lounge, he tried to hold her and tell her again that he loved her, but he could sense that Michelle had withdrawn. He was confused by her reactions. All he wanted to do was support her in her distress, but she had turned cold. He kissed her cheek softly and left the lingering impression of his fingers on her face as he turned to leave. As he walked to the escalators, he wasn't able to see the tears forming in Michelle's eyes. But then, neither could Michelle see Cameron's eyes.

Moscow, Russia
The Kremlin
August

Looking out the window of his office, Ivanovich Romanov, president of the Russian Republic waited for the director of the KGB to arrive. *As if I didn't have enough to deal with,* he thought. *The entire future of the Russian people depends on our ability to establish some kind of workable economy, production, manufacturing—all of which takes money. And we don't have any. Here we are with our hand out to the West. How many of the former leaders of the Soviet Union saw the same disaster over the horizon and continued to spout the same rhetoric and five-year plans?*

Sergei Andreyev entered the president's office, fully aware of the content of the meeting. Even in financially strapped Russia, CNN brought the latest news, and while the Soviet Union had dismantled politically, the apparatus of military might remained in place. They had detected the explosion in the South Pacific simultaneously with the Americans.

"Good morning, Mr. President. And how are you this fine morning?"

"None of your wit this morning, if you please, Sergei," replied Romanov. "The Cold War ends, and tensions regarding mutual destruction cease, and then some madman ignites the flame again. Madness, Sergei, madness."

Ivanovich Romanov, engineer, and Sergei Andreyev, engineer, had been fellow classmates at Sverdlovsk University in the old days. Both had achieved some distinction and risen to political power under the old system. The recent changes that had swept through Russia surprised all of them with the furor of its speed and magnitude. Held together by sheer might and forceful control, the Soviet Union had finally opened the doors, and everybody had simply left. For a while, it seemed as if no one was on duty. Romanov had brought some stability, but he, more than most, knew he still had to defeat a strong element of hard-liners who sought to regain control. Who'd have thought that he would have gained his greatest popularity by defending the status quo and preserving the seat of power for Gorbachev? Now everyone was unsure of his roles and his respective loyalty, but Romanov and Andreyev felt that their association was on firm ground, and they held two of the more important and powerful positions, if such could still be said to exist in the Russian Republic.

"Our hands are clean, Ivanovich my friend. I can find no implication of former Soviet involvement, though," he hesitated momentarily, "we know how often private 'arrangements' were made under some of our former glorious leaders."

"Yes, Andrei, that's what scares me the most." Romanov moved close to Andreyev and said, "We must know, Andrei. We must look in all the closets."

"Yes, my friend, I will see to it." He turned to leave and asked, "Will you speak with Eastman?"

"I must. We must support him in this . . . even if he is guilty. You understand?"

"Yes, my friend, yes."

Wellington, New Zealand
The Beehive
August

Major O'Brien arrived in the company of the American ambassador to New Zealand, who was going to provide Prime Minister Onekawa some information that the Americans had assembled in the short time since the explosion. The prime minister had sev-

eral members of his staff present, including Dan Hegarty, whom
O'Brien recognized from his earlier visit. They had not actually
met, but O'Brien had briefly stopped at SIS when he was coordi-
nating the original visit of the *Cherokee.*

"Good morning, Mr. Ambassador. It's very good of you to
come so early this morning."

"It is our pleasure, Mr. Prime Minister. The president asked
me to brief you on certain background matters that we have not
yet made public. As you know, we absolutely deny the presence
of any weapons of mass destruction on the *Cherokee.* The United
States would not have participated in any plan that would have
sought to deceive the people of New Zealand. This reconciliation
has been too long coming, Prime Minister, and we want to assure
you that we approached it in good faith."

The prime minister nodded his acknowledgment. "I understand that and have full faith in the United States' intentions, Mr.
Ambassador. Tell us what you know of this incident."

"It is our belief that the current leadership in Iraq generated
the momentum to bring this plan to fruition. As yet, we have no
direct link, and we've been unable to confirm Salimar's access to
the weaponry, but we are working on that as we speak. Major
O'Brien has been sent by the president to coordinate with your
office, and hopefully with your security services. We would
greatly appreciate your involvement in every step of this investigation."

"That is our intention, Ambassador Huston. We are glad to
be of assistance. Mr. Hegarty here will work with Major O'Brien,
and they can keep both of us informed of their progress."

"That is the president's intention, Mr. Prime Minister."

"Excellent," said Onekawa, rising to conclude the meeting.
"Dan, you get with Major O'Brien here and see if you can work
out a schedule to put you both together."

Hegarty rose, as did O'Brien, and they left while the ambassador concluded his remarks to the prime minister. In Hegarty's
office, he offered O'Brien a cup of coffee, which he declined.
O'Brien took a seat opposite the desk, and Hegarty sat on a chair

against the wall, eyeing O'Brien like a cop, determining what method of interrogation would best serve his purposes.

"O'Brien, you should know at the outset that I neither believe nor disbelieve your innocence in this issue. It's my feeling that the U.S. military may have pulled the wool over Eastman's eyes, and your country could be guilty as charged. They'd never admit it if they were," he said, more for shock effect than for information.

"Hegarty," O'Brien said, looking him straight in the eyes, "you're absolutely right. If we had carried a nuclear weapon on that vessel and it had exploded, taking your crew with ours, we'd never tell you. It's that simple. The answer is also just as simple, as I see it. You have to decide who you want to believe, and then set out to find the facts to support that belief. If you prove yourself wrong in the process, so be it. I will approach it that way. I want to believe we were the victims of a terrorist force, but if I discover my military leaders were guilty, what do you think that will do to my belief in my own system? I want them to be innocent, but I will not cover it up if they're not. I'll have no choice but to resign. Should that be the case, I will lose two countries, so you see I have more to lose than you do. I need you along to be the impartial detective. I need your objectivity, and if and when you see me stray from the facts we discover, speak up, immediately."

"Okay, O'Brien. If you follow that path, I'll support you all the way. But I want you to understand, if for one moment I think you're hiding or covering up anything, I'll blow the whistle on you instantly."

"Agreed. Now what say we work out a plan to go about this investigation. The first thing we need to know is how the weapon was delivered to the ships. No aircraft other than our tanker and Prince Andrew's helicopter were on radar for the two hours prior to the detonation. We have confirmed that fact from all available radar installations that covered the area. We need to conduct a search of vessel traffic in the area for several days prior, port of departure, arrival, and so on. Any anomalies will help to lead us to a track. I think we have to proceed under the assumption that whatever vessel delivered the weapon went down with the naval vessels. It couldn't have been a loose floating vessel, so we are talking about a kamikaze mission of some sort. Fanatics, Hegarty. Like those who operate in the Middle East. It's never hard for them to find someone who is willing to die with the explosion, as witnessed by the truck driver who took out the Marine barracks in Lebanon."

For most of the morning O'Brien and Hegarty continued to work out the required details. Shortly before noon O'Brien stood to leave and shook Hegarty's hand. By now they had moved to a first-name basis. "Dan, I appreciate your candor," O'Brien said. "I hope by the end of this investigation that three things happen. One, we discover the delivery method and the perpetrators. Two, that we can find a way to prevent further incidents, if such are planned. Three, that you can report back that the United States was not irresponsible in this incident, and as a result, you and I develop a good professional working relationship."

"That would suit me fine as well, Zach."

New York City
United Nations General Assembly
August

The floor was under the control of the ambassador from Iraq, Teraq Haquim. He had been speaking for nearly twenty minutes and showed no sign of weakening. Haquim was the fifth speaker of the morning, and all had been vitriolic in their denunciation of the United States and its callous disregard for the safety of mankind. Over the past seventy-two hours, a constant parade of nations had called for withdrawal of U.S. forces from territories now occupied. With the absence of the Soviet Union to threaten their peaceful existence, they saw this incident as an opportune time to also get rid of U.S. forces. Ambassador Haquim had been particularly vehement. In a time when world neighbors were looking to each other for peaceful solutions to age-old problems, the Americans continued to parade around the world, flexing their muscles and threatening everyone with nuclear weaponry that they had just proven was not stable and that they could not contain. "What if this had happened in some peaceful harbor? What if it had happened in Auckland harbor?" Haquim said, looking directly at Sir Geoffrey.

This special session of the General Assembly had been called to address the recent developments of the past forty-eight hours, ostensibly to seek answers to the causes and assurance that no further incidents could occur. In fact, it had been called by the third-world powers who sought once again a forum to humiliate the United States and rub their noses in the dirt. The opportunity did not come that often, and on previous occasions the incidents were relatively insignificant, worthy of little attention. This time, however, they had just cause, and they were going to make the most of it.

With his call for an outside investigation, the ambassador from the United Kingdom had tried to bring reason and calm to the session, but on this morning blood was up. The third-world countries, who felt that they had cause for retribution, were similar in their actions to the vultures of the press who had cornered President Eastman two days earlier.

Finally, Haquim began to close his remarks. "With reckless abandon these warmongers continue to flaunt their superiority. With starvation and internecine wars throughout the world, they chose to invade Iraq, though we had sought only to reunite our country. During the American Civil War who intervened to say the South had a right to be independent? Who forced the North to cease and desist from their compulsion to force some of the states to remain? Iraq sought only to accomplish the same, by unifying our country and freeing the people from the bands of one small family who had robbed and pillaged the resources of Kuwait for their own gain. It appears as if the United States sees equality as a trait available only to those who can achieve it with force. Iraq has been brought to her knees by these same people who would have us believe that their ship was on a peaceful visit to the blessed and tranquil New Zealand.

"I say no, we must not believe these aggressors. They must receive the same sanctions reserved by this body for countries who act against the will of the people. Iraq has been forced to comply with the mandates established by the United States. It is now time that they abide by their own rules. It is indeed a sad day for the human race, and we must look only to the military giant in whose grasp we remain for the answer." With a look of sadness for the ills of the world, as perpetrated by the United States, Haquim relinquished the podium.

The concluding speaker of the morning was the ambassador from the United States. As he took the podium, a silence came over the floor. How he would respond to this violent attack was of interest to those who supported the United States, as well as to those who had launched the attack.

For what seemed like an eternity, he scanned the audience, pausing to reflect on those who had spoken earlier. Then he addressed the audience, "Mr. Secretary General, distinguished ambassadors, and honored guests, the United States of America offers its most sincere sympathy to the New Zealand families who have experienced the loss of loved ones in this most tragic occurrence. In the cause of peace, they, along with the honored members of the American vessel, have served their respective nations and, indeed, the citizens of the world to the best of their abilities. These families may hold their heads high in honor of their sacrifice, for while the current view of this incident is one of shame, inflamed by those who would have you believe that negligence and abuse of power were the causes, the truth will yet survive. We will yet bring to light the cowards who perpetrated this heinous act, and their complicity will be laid bare before the world."

Looking directly at Ambassador Haquim and pausing for the audience to acknowledge his stare, he concluded his remarks, "We must search in our hearts for the truth, distinguished ambassadors, for as we have seen this day, very little of it has been allowed to escape the lips."

CHAPTER THIRTEEN

Tel Aviv, Israel
The Knesset
August

THE DEPUTY DIRECTOR OF MOSSAD had prepared his analysis for the briefing with care because he knew his conclusions would not be received well. The prime minister had ordered a reduction in all covert activities during the peace negotiations, and if the conclusions Ariel Rheinman had prepared were accurate, it could blow a hole in the hoped-for breakthrough. For nearly a year, the Palestinians had been at the negotiating table with the Israelis, and progress was finally within reach. That is, if one were to believe the promises made at these meetings. The real problem, as Rheinman saw it, was the extreme factions present on both sides of the issue. Hard-core Jews refused to compromise for land they had been developing since it had been captured several wars earlier. For the Palestinians, their hard-core groups were vowing to ignore any peace accords reached without their approval. The

Israeli-Palestinian dispute was, and had been for many years, a no-win scenario.

Since the Israelis viewed the PLO as the primary terrorist group responsible for so many atrocities, they had refused to even recognize the PLO as representative of the opposition. Now there were multiple splinter groups that made the PLO seem moderate in comparison. The leader of the peace movement, Hamil Aziz, had for years promised annihilation of the Jews and the return of the Palestinian homeland. Now he was sitting across the table, talking like a diplomat. Then the American ship was destroyed by a nuclear explosion. Rheinman didn't believe in coincidence, and he was still alive as a result. This meeting would be tough to conduct, and even tougher would be the attempt to persuade the prime minister when he could smell peace.

Prime Minister David Rashorn arrived in a white, short-sleeved shirt and khaki trousers. Israeli politicians seldom wore the suit and tie favored by the Western world. The climate was more conducive to casual attire, and perhaps so was the Israeli temperament.

"Good afternoon, Prime Minister," greeted Rheinman.

"Shalom, Ariel. And how is the guardian of our frontiers today?"

"Worried, Prime Minister. Worried."

"I believe it comes with the territory, my dear Ariel. I suffer from the same malady. Is this worry something we should share, or is that a foolish question?"

"Two issues bother me, Prime Minister. One, we are quite certain the Americans did not have an accident as claimed. They have been the victim of terrorists, and the Butcher is somehow involved." The Israelis had taken to calling Abdul Salimar "the Butcher" in private circles. He continued, "We cannot identify how just yet, but we have several sources working on it. The pressure on the Americans is mounting to remove all forces from the Persian Gulf, and word we get from Washington is that withdrawal is under serious consideration. They don't want to be forced out, but even allies are pressuring them to reduce the visible presence. Their departure, I need not remind you, will leave us once again on our own."

"Ah, Ariel, we have been there before, have we not? But the peace accords are progressing well, and maybe, just maybe, God willing, we will be able to establish some degree of mutual acceptance. I sorrow for the Americans, but they have long escaped the wrath of the villain. Perhaps in some small way this will help them to see our plight with more understanding."

"Perhaps, Prime Minister, perhaps. Yet if the peace accords . . . " He paused, for this was the news he knew Rashorn would not be pleased to hear. "We have reason to believe if they are concluded successfully, Aziz will be killed."

"Ariel, people have been trying to kill Aziz for years, and some of the attempts were even fabricated to bolster his image as a live martyr. What is so different this time?"

"His own people, his own inner circle," he said with resignation.

Within the intelligence community of the Middle East, it had been understood that as factions split within former allies, differences would eventually widen, and elimination would be, and had been, the result. This was to be accepted, but the inner circle of the leading faction of the PLO leadership had been united in its intended purposes, even as they moved toward conciliation.

"Prime Minister, should the agreement be reached and signed, the document would be so much paper if it were immediately disavowed and the signatories assassinated. We must proceed carefully. I am here to ask your directions on our actions. We cannot attempt to warn him, because we do not know who on the inside to trust. Not yet. We are still working on it. Approaching him directly would be met with disbelief at such a critical point in the negotiations. It is a very delicate matter."

"Ariel," the prime minister said with disappointment, "this was to have been a good day."

"Yes, David, it was, and we will do our best to assure the rest of our days have a similar opportunity. But with regard to our peace concessions, there will be those on all sides who will demand that we honor our word, regardless if the other side repudiates their position. It will widen the gap even more, especially among our own people." Rheinman allowed the prime minister to consider his remarks and concluded, "On the other matter, what would you have us do about the Butcher."

"Only one thing can be done with him, Ariel, and that will have to wait. I will be with President Eastman and Aziz for the conclusion of these talks. I will speak with Eastman privately and assure him of our support in this *Cherokee* issue, but until you have more conclusive information, I will not discuss any danger to Aziz."

"Very well, Prime Minister. We will keep looking, and I will be in touch."

Royal New Zealand Yacht Squadron Marina
Auckland, New Zealand
August

"Mr. Rossiter, I'm sorry. We've just come up completely empty. Not a trace."

Rossiter was exasperated. "Mr. Pokere, you mean to tell me that not a single marina throughout the North Island sighted *Triple Diamond* during the entire two-week charter?"

"Well, sir, they've all reported negative sightings. The last confirmed sighting we have is the Fullers' catamaran out near Great Barrier the day the charter started. She was seen heading straight out to sea."

"What does Search and Rescue say?"

Pokere just shook his head. "Much the same, sir. You know they've been busy seeking information on the sinking of *Northland*."

Rossiter nodded. "OK, Mr. Pokere. Can you provide me a written confirmation of the efforts you've made to locate or trace *Triple Diamond,* for my insurance company?"

"Certainly, sir. Their agent has also been here looking for information. I told him the same thing."

"They're not too pleased with my claim, to say the least," Rossiter said, sighing.

"I'm very sorry, Mr. Rossiter. She was a beautiful yacht."

"Yes, she was. Turns out to be a very expensive charter."

Pokere had never seen Rossiter so dejected. "If we hear anything, sir. I'll contact you immediately."

"Thank you, Mr. Pokere. Thanks for your help."

"I wish we could have done more. With the *Triple Diamond* gone, do you want us to maintain your berth?"

Rossiter turned to leave the marina office. "Yes, please. I'll sort this out somehow."

"Right, sir, we'll take care of it for you. Good luck, Mr. Rossiter."

"Thank you."

Washington, D.C.
The White House Oval Office
August

Clarene Prescott walked with General Austin toward the Oval Office. They had reached their agreed recommendations and planned to present them to President Eastman, after which the meeting would expand to include most of the Joint Chiefs. Admiral Fitzwilliams was in San Diego on Navy business and would be unable to attend.

The Secret Service saw them through the entrance, and President Eastman came out from behind his desk to greet them. "Good Morning, Clarene, General Austin. Have you come to some conclusions you can share with us this morning?"

"Yes, Mr. President," Prescott replied. "I'm afraid the Chiefs won't like it."

"There is that possibility," he said with obvious concern. President Eastman always took great care with recommendations that concerned the military because of the bad press he had taken when running for office. During the Bush presidency, Vice President Quayle had taken considerable heat because he had chosen to serve in the National Guard during the war and thereby had avoided active military duty. Thousands of other young American men had taken the same route, but once again, the media had tended to focus on the most negative side of the issue. Quayle's problem had been small, however, compared to the roasting Eastman had received for his complaints about the short twenty years of military service necessary to receive a full pension, which he had publicly aired while serving as a senator from Florida. Florida was full of retired persons to whom Senator Eastman had been adamantly loyal. Most of them had worked long and hard to retire and had spent considerably more than twenty years to obtain their pension.

As president, Eastman still had to deal with the military leadership, who had long memories. Their loyalty to their commander-in-chief was unquestioned, but their opinion of his views was something different, and Eastman was careful when presenting something that went against their judgment. Women in combat had been an example. During the campaign, he had promised to remove all barriers to women's ability to serve in all positions in the military, but once he took office, he gradually moved to "study" the issue more closely, eventually opting to appoint a committee. That committee allowed the process to bog down in debate over physical capability and emotional stability, touchy issues to say the least. The committee appointment turned out to be one of those political decisions that attempted to give something to each but ended up infuriating both sides.

"Let's hear the results, Clarene, and we'll deal with the Chiefs when they arrive."

"Mr. President, nearly every world leader has taken a position on this issue. Very little equivocation. As expected, all of our usual adversaries demand the removal of military forces from their part of the world. Many of the usually neutral countries have assumed a posture of reducing our presence as well, although they are not blatant about it. They feel it would ease their relations with other countries and most likely would not hamper our position. However, certain of our staunchest allies have privately asked us to consider reducing the physical presence to give at least the appearance of moving to reduce the tension. Those in a position to know the facts are aware that we are not responsible for a nuclear accident, yet those who want to believe we are have convinced the rest of the world that we are covering up." Clarene hesitated at this point. "Mr. President, were I in their shoes, I might be concerned myself. We do not have an enviable track record of being honest about our past mistakes, including those actions we took to further our own ends. That was why Krenshaw's question was so telling during your press conference."

Prescott was referring to the earlier press conference ten days ago when Alice Krenshaw from UPI had opened her questions by citing several known deceptions that the American government had perpetrated on their own people in order to achieve desired military objectives. In comparison to other "democratic" countries, the only unusual thing about the practice of the American government deceiving the public was that the public was allowed to expose that deceit and that the messenger did not disappear after the episode.

Continuing, Prescott cited several leaders with whom she had spoken. "I reminded John Blankenship, Mr. President, where we had stood with respect to the Falklands, and he was decidedly uncomfortable. He has a general election coming up and is nervous. Notwithstanding the fact that Prince Andrew is all right, he was within thirty minutes of being on the *Cherokee*. That hasn't gone down well in Britain. He suggested that we could pull out temporarily, which he knows is so much eyewash." Prescott moved to conclude, "Mr. President, the truth that surfaces from this analysis is that we must take action to demonstrate to the world that we hear and understand their concerns. We believe that they are wrong and that the danger level will increase; nevertheless, it is our recommendation to you that we structure a pullout from the Persian Gulf visible to the world."

"Give in to Salimar, Clarene?"

"It's been a long fight, Mr. President, with many rounds left to go, I fear. Even the underdog scores some points from the referee during those rounds when the champ is conserving his strength. General Austin has some ideas that he would like to work on for your consideration. I believe they will preserve our options should the situation change dramatically."

"Can it get much more dramatic, Clarene?" Eastman asked rhetorically. He knew the answer.

"Yes, Mr. President, if we are not careful, it can get much more dramatic, and have dire consequences for the world."

"Peace with honor, again," Eastman said facetiously, referring to the agreement Neville Chamberlain, prime minister of Great Britain, had made with Hitler just before the outbreak of World War II.

"Peace with caution perhaps, Mr. President," Prescott added.

Turning to look at Austin, the president simply said, "General?"

Austin spoke for the first time in the meeting. "Mr. President, you are the commander-in-chief. The JCS will follow your orders, and I can assure you they will not like this recommendation to reduce, no eliminate, military forces from territory hard won. We've done it often, from the smallest piece of soil for which we spilled young American blood, only to return it a week later, to the largest of conflagrations, which we politically negotiated away after the battles. I'm sure you understand the military's position. We are always called upon to respond to a problem but never to be part of creating the solutions that conclude those issues. Such exclusion assures thereby the potential for return to the same issue some time later. Nevertheless, as unpopular as it will be with my contemporaries, I fully support Ambassador Prescott's recommendations. For my part, I will do my best to develop a scenario that will protect our options should the situation change."

Eastman knew how hard such a recommendation was for General Austin, and he could see the understanding in Prescott's eyes also. Austin's young son, a Marine Corps lieutenant, had been one of those whose life had been spent to gain a hill we gave back the next week. Useless, all so useless, Eastman thought. "General Austin, are you familiar with the expression 'They also serve, who only stand and wait'?"

"Yes, Mr. President, I understand the meaning."

"Perhaps it could be paraphrased metaphorically to say, 'They also serve, who serve.' Now that may seem redundant, but there is a philosophy that the higher one rises in leadership, the greater the service to others is demanded. Most government and military leaders fail to appreciate that premise. I believe this philosophy of service manifests itself in the military in such mundane practices as the privates eat before the generals, and so on. Do you see my point?"

"Mr. President, I have always been prepared to subjugate my personal preference for the good of the whole."

"I know that, Bill," the president said, calling Austin by his first name and assuming a softer tone, "and that is why Ambassador Prescott and I have developed such faith in your recommendations. We trust your judgment and know that you will provide your best effort, even when the decision, as in this case, seems counterproductive. Remember the 'Lead Dog' story I told O'Brien? What we didn't discuss was that way behind the lead dog and the pack was someone calling out directions, and so the sled team was actually being led from the rear. So it is with the American government system, of the people, for the people and by the people'—but only when the leaders are responsive to the people. With the support of people like you, General, and Ambassador Prescott, and young O'Brien, I intend to have such a presidency."

The president stood up and went to the speaker phone on his desk, pressing the button to connect him with his secretary. "Mrs. Clauson, please ask the Joint Chiefs to come in." Turning back to General Austin, he added, "General, put together a plan for us that will protect our options, and I'll handle the JCS."

"Yes, sir," replied Lieutenant General William Austin, deputy director, Intelligence, National Security Agency.

Washington, D.C.
White House Press Room
August

The hastily convened press conference had only a single announcement with no questions following:

"The president has announced that the United States will begin a removal of military forces from the Persian Gulf in an effort to reduce the growing concern for safety voiced by our allies in the region. The United States wishes to advise that it con-

siders this action premature and potentially dangerous, but in a
gesture of conciliation toward those who so ably supported the
coalition during the recent conflict, we have acceded to the
requests of those nations."

Baghdad, Iraq
Military Headquarters
August

Abdul Salimar strode into the room, resplendent in his military
uniform. He usually wore military attire instead of the Western
business suit, as it reminded his staff that he was in charge, not
merely the elected leader. General Alihambra came to attention
as Salimar entered the room, as did the remainder of the
Revolutionary Council, who were all present at this meeting. In
a most unusual action, Salimar moved to General Alihambra and
took his hand, shaking it warmly and then embracing the general,
kissing him on both cheeks.

"You have made your mother proud this day, General,"
Salimar said, "and the people of Iraq are in your debt." Moving
to his seat at the end of the table, he addressed the group. "Had
we more faithful generals such as him, we would be dining in
Kuwait City, as soon again we shall."

The meeting turned to the daily agenda, and several hours
later, dismissing the council, Salimar motioned for Alihambra to
remain. "General, the world's reaction has exceeded even our
expectations. We must proceed now, with all haste. How are the
preparations for our friend Aziz?"

"Excellency, all preparations have been made. It is somewhat
dependent on those within his circle, but all seems well."

"See it is done, Alihambra. This man could disrupt our plans
if he is allowed to arrange a new relationship with the Zionists.
You have done well so far, General, do not fail your people now."
Salimar proceeded to instruct Alihambra on his next assignment,
which included meeting with Wyndham again to advise him of
the next incident to be initiated. Growing bolder, Salimar wanted
to punish the British as well as continue to humiliate the
Americans. The plan included a second detonation in England,

about one hundred miles north of London near two U.S. Air Force bases located adjacent to one another.

"Let us test this Wyndham once more, General. See if he can produce two weapons, one for the English venture and one to be delivered directly to us. Move swiftly, Alihambra. Our glorious future awaits."

"Yes, Excellency, I move at your command."

Auckland, New Zealand
Devonport Naval Station
August

Over two hundred and fifty thousand people crowded the grounds at the Auckland Domain for the public memorial service for the crew of HMNZS *Northland.* Michelle felt it appropriate that the public service was being held here, in this park immediately adjacent to the Auckland Hospital where her father had died. It seemed such a short time ago since they had all come to the hospital, but she knew it had been nearly eight years. The service lasted somewhat over an hour with addresses by the prime minister and a series of dignitaries, including the Governor General Dame Tizard representing Her Majesty, Queen Elizabeth II. Prince Andrew had returned to Great Britain shortly after receiving a clean bill of health in the hospital, but not before thanking the New Zealand Navy for his rescue.

In spite of the somber, reflective mood, it was a beautiful day, and Michelle Duffield could not help thinking of the times she and Graham had been out on the yacht with Dad on days like this. Michelle had not developed a faith in the hereafter as her mum had, but if there were such a place, Dad had gotten his crew back in place, and he and Graham were trimming the sails together.

No political comments were made during the service about the United States or the growing suspicion that terrorists had somehow obtained a nuclear weapon and used it on the Americans. New Zealanders were grateful that if it had to occur, it had happened far from their shores. It could have been a lot worse a week later.

In the afternoon, a small, private memorial service was being held at the naval base in Devonport. Even that would not really be small, as two hundred and forty-two crew were on the *Northland,* and all of their families were expected to attend. Well over two thousand people were anticipated. Michelle, her two sisters, Graham's fiancée, Rachel, and Michelle's mother, Joanne, would attend together. As they drove to Devonport from downtown Auckland crossing the harbor bridge, Michelle watched the yachts on the harbor, subconsciously looking for *Triple Diamond.* She had not answered Cameron's messages on her phone recorder. She had not spoken to him since returning from England three weeks earlier, although he had repeatedly tried to contact her. She had even conducted her business from elsewhere, having her associate refer calls to her mobile phone as necessary. She just couldn't face him. She didn't know what to say or to do.

Admiral Sir Trevor Pottsdam, chief of defense forces, opened the services, paying tribute to the crew and their selfless actions. He covered the history of the *Northland* and the general purpose for New Zealand maintaining a defense force. "Military action," he said, "is seldom appreciated, rarely sufficient when applied, and absolutely indispensable when required. The *Northland* crew did not have a chance to face their enemy"—the first reference of the day made concerning the suspected cause of the disaster— "but their memory will be well served when the time comes for those who perpetrated this act to pay the price."

Michelle was mentally drifting, listening to the navy band conclude the service by playing the lilting strains of "The Navy Hymn." She reflected on the words "and those in peril of the sea" as she thought of her family's love for sailing. Lost in her reverie, she didn't notice as Cameron moved silently behind her, gently placing his hand on her shoulder. Michelle's mother saw him approach and smiled as he appeared.

"I've missed you, Michelle," Cameron said. Michelle was wearing sunglasses, and once again her eyes were hidden from his view. Turning to her mum, he introduced himself and offered his condolences on the loss of her son. The guests were beginning to stand and leave as Joanne moved with the other two girls to allow a moment alone for Cameron and Michelle. "Could we meet somewhere please, Michelle?" Cameron asked.

"We . . . ah . . . we have all the family up, Cameron. I'm not ready, I'm . . . really I'm not ready yet. I've got to sort this out."

"I understand, Michelle. I'll be there if you need me." Cameron turned and left, disappearing into the crowd before Michelle had time to think of any reply.

Later that evening at Joanne's home, Michelle was sitting on the deck, just watching the sunset, when Joanne came out to sit with her. Michelle's other sisters had gone to bed, for they would fly back to Christchurch early next morning.

"You've bottled it all up, Michelle," Joanne opened. "Would you like to talk about it?"

Oh, Mum, you've already got enough on your plate, and I haven't been able to sort out my own feelings, much less how to deal with his."

"Michelle, you're right, I've got enough on my plate—some would say more than a body should have to handle. But I hope the time never comes when I have too much happening to be a part of my children's lives. There is really only one question, Michelle. Do you love him?"

"I was certain of it when I saw him in the airport in London. Five minutes later my world had turned upside down, and as I thought more about it, I saw Cameron in the same light as Dad and Graham. I couldn't stand it—I just couldn't stand it again. I don't know how I'll recover this time. How do you cope, Mum? Everyone always sees you as so strong, so . . . *resilient* I believe is the word Tom uses to describe you."

"Tom has been a good husband to me since we married, though we certainly didn't have it easy in the early years. I don't believe he knows that part of my continuing resilience, if that's the right word, comes from him. When he met me, I had always found the necessary strength to handle the problems as life brought them to me. Since then, it has required a team effort, and I truly don't believe Tom realizes how much I rely on him for support."

"Mum, there have been times when I've been ashamed of

myself for my feelings about everything since Dad died. I was angry at Dad for leaving. I know that's a normal reaction, but I was even angrier at you when you married Tom and moved to the States. I couldn't understand how you could leave us too. The closer I get to thirty, the more I understand that you were still a young woman when Dad died, and sitting home, waiting for us to provide grandchildren seemed a dubious future. Still I was angry at you and your Mormon church, and it took a long time to let go of it. I don't even know if I have let go yet."

"I knew that, Michelle, and it pained my heart to lose you and the closeness we had for so long, but I knew you had to find out for yourself that you could still have a mum even if the picture we once had of our family had changed. I've always loved you girls and hoped someday that you could accept my decisions as I have accepted your decisions I didn't agree with."

"Mum . . . " Michelle lowered her head and breathed deeply, "Mum, I do love you, and I know that I need you to be here." Reaching for Joanne's hand, with tears once again forming, Michelle said, "I'm sorry, Mum, I truly am. I've always been afraid to lose those I love, and holding you away prevented that from occurring. Do you understand?"

Tears welled in Joanne's eyes also, and she replied, "Of course I do, Michelle. I can't really tell you how to deal with your feelings for Cameron, but I have learned one important lesson from losing your dad. I had thought about not sharing that feeling again with anyone, but I discovered it was foolish to live life through fear. Of course I lost your dad, but if we hadn't married, I would have never had him at all, and"—Joanne paused once again—"then I wouldn't have had you either. Michelle, if you love Cameron, and it appears to me that you do, it seems a great waste to lose him for fear you might lose him. Does that make sense?"

"Yes, Mum. It does." Michelle and Joanne sat quietly for some time as the sky grew dark. As Joanne rose to go into the house, Michelle spoke again. "Mum, do you think Graham is with Dad?"

"I'm absolutely certain, Michelle. I've been assured since the moment I heard the report."

Exasperated and confused, Michelle responded, pleading, "How, Mum? How can you be so certain?"

Joanne paused to consider her response, knowing Michelle's disregard for her religion and not wanting to offend her. "Michelle, I know because the Spirit bore witness to me, and because Graham wanted me to know."

Long after Joanne had retired, Michelle continued to wonder how her mother had always been able to see beyond with such conviction. In the absence of confirmation to herself, it had privately, and always silently, been pleasing to Michelle to have such comforting reassurance from her mother.

Persian Gulf
USS **Kennedy**
August

Rear Admiral Alberto Montoya, commander of all naval forces in the Persian Gulf, glanced around the small conference room on the *Kennedy,* observing the somber faces of his senior staff, including the commanding officers from each of the fourteen vessels in Task Force Victor. His pronouncement would not go down well.

"Each of you has been provided a copy of the brief statement issued by the White House earlier this week. There is no room for discussion. The CNO has directed immediate compliance, and that's what I intend to accomplish."

Captain Wilson Richards squirmed in his seat. "Admiral, mark my words, it's going to cost lives."

Montoya looked steadily at Richards, formulating his response. "There's no debate, Captain."

"I don't like it, Admiral. Not one bit."

"And you think I do?" he demanded. "Every man here feels the same. When in your illustrious career have you been given the option of only carrying out orders you liked?" Montoya was angry even though he knew Richards was only voicing what was on everyone's mind. "Now hear this, Captain Richards, and hear it well. The *Heritage* and every other ship in this Task Force will clear the Persian Gulf and deploy to Diego Garcia within seventy-two hours. Do I make myself clear?"

Frustrated, Richards had no options. "Aye aye, sir."

Softening somewhat, Admiral Montoya stood and quietly looked over the assembled officers. "During the past fourteen months of my command, it has been my honor to serve with the officers and men of Task Force Victor. As you all know, Captain Richards, soon to be Admiral Richards, will replace me in sixty days." Looking toward Richards, Montoya smiled. "Bull, when you assume command of the task force, and when the balloon goes up again, for I agree with you that it undoubtedly will, you can tell the president, 'I told you so.' But you'll have to stand in a long line to get to him."

"With all due respect, Admiral, the line I'm concerned about is the list of names we'll have to put on the next memorial wall."

CHAPTER FOURTEEN

San Diego, California
USS Pegasus
August

USS *PEGASUS* WAS A FORTY-EIGHT FOOT coastal patrol vessel in the service of the U.S. Coast Guard, berthed out of San Diego. She had been assigned many missions since her commissioning in 1951, but the past six years she had been involved in interdicting drug traffic flowing from South and Central America and had amassed an enviable record of captures. Yet her crew felt that their efforts to stem the flow of drugs was just a finger in the dike. The druggies were better equipped and better funded, and they had more manpower. It was in all respects a war, and contrary to most military situations in which the United States found themselves, the other side was winning. Still, some gains could be made.

They were escorting last night's capture into port. *Emiliano Zapata* had tried unsuccessfully to slip by their patrols during the early morning hours as the fog hung off the California coast. The speedboats that the *Emiliano Zapata* was supposed to meet had escaped, but they would be back, and their luck would also run out one day. Lieutenant Williamson was pleased with this haul— on the *Zapata* were several holds full of marijuana and significant amounts of cocaine. His assignment was about up, and he was not looking forward to his next duty at Coast Guard Headquarters, Washington. He loved the sea, and he would prefer to remain in command of the *Pegasus*.

As they tied up and turned over the examination to the shore crew and the DEA boys, Williamson began to clean out his cabin of personal effects. However small and old *Pegasus* was, she had been his for the past eighteen months. He had come to feel his personality mesh with the ship, as he was sure previous skippers had felt. It was like leaving one's family to depart the ship. He could never feel this way toward his new command—his new desk command would leave much to be desired. The Coasties belonged at sea, as did all true sailors. He'd be back.

Washington, D.C.
National Security Agency
August

General Austin, I have Captain Adams from Coast Guard Headquarters on the line for you," Alice said.

"Thank you, Alice, please put him through." Austin seldom had much to do with the Coast Guard. For the past two weeks his mind had been filled with strategic withdrawal and contingency plans and with reports from O'Brien's "Irish Mafia" as they scoured the South Pacific turning up small clues as to the method of delivery used to sink the *Cherokee* and the *Northland*. Lieutenant Savini had gone to Chile to see what he could find. It seemed a dead end when he had not discovered any vessels either missing or gone long enough to have left Chile and met the naval vessels in the right area. Savini had discovered only one unusual event, but that had occurred the evening before the explosion, when a privately chartered Lear jet had gone off course and ended up way out to sea southwest of Santiago, in the area of the *Cherokee*. General Austin couldn't make any connection with that flight; still, O'Brien's team had recorded it as they had dozens of other pieces of information in this giant puzzle.

"General Austin speaking. Captain, how may I be of assistance?"

"General, we've turned up something on the west coast that might be of interest to you, and then again it might be another dead end. But I thought you should make that determination. Several days ago, one of our cutters interdicted a drug run from down south, and during the routine investigation of the ship, we discovered that she had an unusually high radiation count in one of her holds. Not high enough to be of short-term danger to humans, but definitely something of interest was in that hold. Our lab boys have requested assistance from Lawrence Livermore Lab up in Tracy. They should be finished tomorrow. The commandant suggested we bring you into the picture since you're pursuing the *Cherokee* incident. May be no tie-in, General, but again, that's for you to decide."

"Thank you, Captain. I'll get back to you later today. I'd like to have someone stop out there and see what conclusions the Livermore scientists reach. Please pass on my appreciation to the commandant for his information."

"Yes sir, General. Have a good day."

Austin got off the phone and walked to the foyer for a cup of coffee, thinking about how this might relate. Moving back to his office, he stopped at Alice's desk. "Alice, see if you can track down our wandering Kiwi. Last time he called in, he was in Wellington."

"Certainly, General. He sent a fax this morning with his itinerary. Let's see, one day ahead, eight hours back." As Alice figured the time difference, she grumbled that everyone should be required to be on the same time, knowing full well that half the world would have to be day sleepers for that to occur. "He should have arrived back in Auckland this morning, General. He's been covering the major harbor and marinas with Dan Hegarty from the New Zealand Security Intelligence Service."

"See if you can reach him for me, please."

Austin returned to his office and began to mentally add up

some of the clues. They didn't make a picture yet, but maybe
O'Brien and Hegarty had turned up something more. The real
problem on his hands was the operational nightmare the president
wanted in the form of a plan for strategic withdrawal from the
Persian Gulf area, with protective measures in the event Salimar
got feisty again. And he wasn't getting much cooperation from
the JCS staff over at the Pentagon on this assignment, though, he
had to admit, he really hadn't expected much help from them.

"General," Alice called over his intercom, "I've located
Major O'Brien. He'll be on the phone in a moment. They went
to get him."

"Thank you, Alice." Austin waited a moment before O'Brien
came on the line.

"Good afternoon, General Austin," said O'Brien. "I'm just
about to wrap it up here and head back. Couple of minor issues
but nothing concrete so far."

"Zach, plan to stop over in San Diego for a day or so, and
check with the Coast Guard there. I'll coordinate from here, after
you let Alice know your new flight schedule. They've confiscated
a drug ship with some radiation count on board. The lab crew
from Livermore has gone down to check it out. They should be
done by the time you arrive. Just a gut feeling, Major, but I think
it will tie in somehow."

"Right, General. I'll reschedule and check with Alice.
Anything from Chile?"

"Small bits, but we'll piece it all together when you and your
staff get back. On that other issue we discussed the other day, give
some thought to the chessboard. Understand?" Austin was speaking obliquely to the issue of moving military units from the
Persian Gulf and their earlier conversation with President
Eastman, but doing so over an open communication line was
risky, so he avoided any direct comment.

Following a slight hesitation, O'Brien replied, "Understood,
General. See you in a day or two." O'Brien had worked with
General Austin long enough to develop an excellent ability to
exchange thoughts without really saying anything discernible to
outsiders.

Auckland, New Zealand
August

O'Brien hung up the phone and went back to Hegarty. "I'll be off this evening, Dan. Can you conclude the review of marinas and let me know what transpires?"

"Right," replied Hegarty, "want a ride back to your hotel?"

"Give me a minute," O'Brien said. He went inside the marina office and made a local phone call, after which he had Hegarty drop him off downtown on Queen Street. Leaving the car, Hegarty shook his hand and commented, "It's been enjoyable working with you, mate. Keep in touch."

"I will, Dan. You can count on it." O'Brien entered the sliding glass doors and waited about five minutes in the lobby of the Fay Richwhite Building until Cameron Rossiter appeared.

"I didn't expect to hear from you today, Zach. How's the Yankiwi doing?" Rossiter said with a grin.

"Don't stress the 'Yank' part so loud, Cameron—your stock will go down. We're not really on top of everyone's favorite list just now." O'Brien had seen the negative side of the world press coverage increase anti-American feeling not only in New Zealand, but, via CNN in his hotel room, he had seen the results all over the world.

They left the building and began walking down Queen Street toward the restaurant. "Yeah, you're right. Making any progress on improving that status?"

"A little at a time, but I'm certain we'll get results eventually. At the moment, that's just faith speaking, and not hard evidence."

"Faith precedes the miracle," Cameron quoted to O'Brien's surprise. "That was the title of the book you sent me, wasn't it?"

"Do I spy a budding convert, Mr. Rossiter?"

"Not exactly, Mr. O'Brien, but I thought if I were going to deal with religious foreigners, I'd best learn to speak the lingo."

They laughed and then walked in silence for a short while before O'Brien spoke up, "Actually, Cameron, this has been a dreadful assignment. Trying to piece together the method of operation and identify the terrorists have been top-priority issues with President Eastman and my boss." O'Brien followed Rossiter into the restaurant and waited for the waiter to seat them. Zach moved to change the subject in which he had been totally immersed for the past several days. "And how's Michelle these days?"

Cameron looked down at the table. "Perhaps you didn't know, Zach, but her brother was the signal officer on the *Northland*."

O'Brien's eyes opened wide. "I had no idea. It always seems to come down to a personal tragedy in the end, doesn't it? Is she holding up well?"

"She's withdrawn—she won't allow me to contact her. She's frightened and confused. Just when she needs someone the most, she's shut me out. But enough of that," Cameron said, wanting to leave the subject. "How are Alison and your children?"

"They're quite well, thank you. Alison wanted me to thank you again for the wonderful weekend on *Triple Diamond*. We haven't enjoyed anything so much for a long time. Going out again this weekend?"

"Nope. I'm jumping out of airplanes this weekend."

"Come again?" O'Brien asked.

"My weekend Territorial Force activity. You are speaking to one of New Zealand's finest. I'm sure you've heard the expression, 'Who dares, wins.'"

O'Brien was incredulous. "You're in the New Zealand Special Air Service?"

"Lieutenant Cameron Sterling Rossiter, at your service, Major."

"Will wonders never cease? Brothers in arms, so to speak."

They talked for the rest of the hour. After Cameron left for afternoon meetings, O'Brien remained for a while and then returned to his hotel room and called Alison. He would be home soon, he said, and suggested that she give Michelle a call when she had a moment, advising her about Michelle's brother. O'Brien began to pack his bag and consider the impact of the pieces of this international puzzle, which, individually, looked insignificant. Somewhere in that puzzle, a picture will emerge, he thought as he called the airlines.

"Air New Zealand, international reservations. May I help you?"

Moscow, Russia
The Kremlin
August

"President Romanov, Admiral Orchenko is here for his appointment."

"Send him in, please." Ivanovich Romanov was locked in a battle with his Parliamentary opponents, including his vice president; and so far the military had supported Romanov. He had no idea what this Orchenko wanted, but when he had requested a private meeting of the utmost urgency, Romanov had thought it wise to hear him out. "Good morning, Admiral, and what brings the navy to the Kremlin with such haste this morning?"

"Good morning, Mr. President. Truly a matter of some urgency that I believe will be critical to your current decisions. Perhaps, Mr. President, if I start at the beginning . . . " For nearly an hour Admiral Orchenko described Khrushchev's plan of retribution and how those who knew had been eliminated in one sweeping plane crash. From what Admiral Orchenko had been able to determine, it seemed that only three people had remained alive when his uncle had died, and he had been able to confirm the deaths of two, the other committee member and Khrushchev. A Captain Gregorio Valasnikov was unaccounted for since he had been sent to England and assumed a false identity.

Ivanovich Romanov listened with rapt attention, until he interrupted. "Admiral, if you would be so kind as to wait for a moment." Romanov rose and went to the door of his office, asking his secretary to locate Sergei Andreyev, KGB director, and ask him to please come immediately. Returning to Orchenko, he asked, "Admiral, would you like some tea while we wait?"

Replaying the history for Andreyev, Admiral Orchenko knew he had surfaced an item of significance, just as he had thought. Leaving the diaries, Admiral Orchenko departed with the deep appreciation of President Romanov and with strict orders to reveal this finding to no one else. In spite of the changes that had swept the Soviet Union, the Russian penchant for secrecy remained a firm vestige of government.

After Orchenko had gone, Romanov and Andreyev discussed their options for some time, before arriving at a plan of action.

"I agree, Ivanovich, but why the United Nations?"

"Because, my friend, we cannot go straight to the Americans this time. We could wash our hands of this ancient plan, but the stain would remain. They will of course know in time, but we must preserve our options and solidify our economic assistance quickly, Sergei. No, the New Zealand ambassador will fill our need, and he has as much interest in finding the perpetrators as the Americans. They lost their ship also, Sergei. When they caught the French, they handled it with great care. I believe we can trust them to bring this to the attention of the Americans. Eventually, I will explain it to Eastman after it is over.

"We could just remove the remaining weapons quietly. I have agents who could . . . "

"No, Sergei, the Americans and New Zealanders must see for themselves where these weapons are and how long they have been there. It is important that they understand how old this thing is and that we had no part. They already have concerns about control of our current weapons after the breakup. We must be able to prove that these are not our weapons, at least not current ones that we could have lost during the political division. You understand?"

"You will speak with our U.N. ambassador?"

"Today. And Sergei, find this Captain . . . Valasnikov, if he still lives."

Auckland, New Zealand
August

Dear Michelle,

You have been constantly in our prayers since we learned that your brother Graham was aboard the Northland. Somehow the tragedy took on a much more personal feel once I learned that. I can't help but wonder how you are bearing up and how the rest of your family is coping. The Duffield family certainly have had their share of such losses, and my heart goes out to you. Know that we will continue to pray for you and those you love that your suffering will be bearable.

Michelle, I feel impressed to tell you that you need to grieve for
Graham and you need to separate losing him from losing your
Dad. I know the struggles you have been having with your decisions as regards Cameron and what part he could or should play
in your future. I feel that you may shy off any commitment to
Cameron because of the need to shut out of your life any further
opportunity for loss and pain. Unfortunately we do not get to
choose the experiences we have, if we did we would choose all
of the great ones and leave the suffering and loss to someone
else. It is through the tough experiences that we grow and learn
compassion for others and thereby progress in this life. I am sure
that you are a far different person than you would have been had
life stayed rosy and secure with all of your family around you.
What I am trying to say is that these experiences are ours whether
we like and want them or not. They help us to become the
people we are and to face further experiences in life that will
come our way. We cannot postpone living our lives because we
might not like what it holds.

You need Cameron at your side more now than you ever did. You
need his strength and comfort, you need the person he is to help
you become the person you need to become, you need to make
a commitment to him for whatever length of time you and he are
given to spend together. None of us knows what life holds in the
future, but we need to take hold of the opportunities which present themselves right at this moment and do the very best we can
with them. I feel that you and Cameron have a great deal to offer
each other and it would be foolish to miss out on that because
maybe you might lose him some day. Perhaps Lord Tennyson
said it best, " 'Tis better to have loved and lost than never to have
loved at all." At some time in our lives, be it sooner or later, we
will all feel the pains of death and separation—that is a part of
living. I know that your family has suffered much more in their
lives sooner than some others, but we will all have to face up to it
and do our best to carry on.

I also know that Graham and your Dad will be rejoicing at their
reunion, just as poignantly as you and your family are suffering at

this moment. Their joy will be great, and if you could focus on that aspect of the tragedy it might help you to move on and heal. Michelle, heal you must. You must do right by yourself if you are to love others. You owe it to your Mother, who got back up and dusted herself off and got on with her life after your Dad died, to the memory of Graham and the good times you spent together growing up, to Cameron who is your future and your children's future, and to yourself. The last person is the most important one in the plan of things. Turn to Him, let him feel your pain and sorrow, let him reach out to you and comfort you and help the healing. If you close up and shut all of this away, you will suffer and your life will suffer and your family will suffer, and the suffering has been great enough already.

I say these things because I care for you very much and I see you as a strong individual who has struggled valiantly with life's traumas. Both Zach and I have talked much about how we could best help you in your time of need, and I feel impressed that this letter is the best way I can give of myself right now. Others will offer comfort and take care of your temporal needs at this time but I feel that your emotional and spiritual needs are great and have to be tended to also. Thus I pray I have been able to help with them. Know that you are constantly in our thoughts and prayers. Our love to Cameron and feel free to show him this letter if you feel so inclined.

Love,
Alison

Geneva, Switzerland
August

And was His Excellency pleased with the results of our little endeavor, General?" Stephen Wyndham asked.

"Very well done, Mr. Wyndham. Most satisfactory to all concerned. Except of course to those who are used to delivering the crushing blows. Very well done, indeed." General Alihambra had been in Geneva for two days, and again, as before, he had arranged a sizable deposit to Wyndham's account prior to their meeting, in time for Wyndham to confirm the delivery.

"Now, what is it that His Excellency would have us do this time?"

General Alihambra smiled. "His Excellency feels that while the Americans deserve his full and undivided attention, he must not neglect their British cousins. Consequently, we request your assistance in preparing a small picnic, perhaps for His Highness, Wee Willie. He will be attending a county fair north of London in late September. Perhaps he could be, shall we say, overcome, by the heat of the day?"

"I see," said Wyndham, somewhat surprised. "That, as the Americans say, is a different kettle of fish. You wish another incident, similar to the last, to occur in England coincident with Prince William's country visit, am I correct?"

"Precisely, my dear Mr. Wyndham. Precisely. Can you make the arrangements?"

Something was different about Alihambra, Wyndham felt. He was . . . perhaps *exuberant* would be the right word. Wyndham knew that Salimar could be a tough taskmaster, and perhaps Alihambra was riding on a high after successfully pulling off this last assignment. He was stretching things a bit, Wyndham thought, to go for the English heir to the throne.

"That poses significant problems, General. Specifically, I have made it a rule not to conduct 'business' on my own turf, if you understand what I mean."

"Yes, we considered such a well-founded concern on your part." Smiling, Alihambra continued, "Your deposit was somewhat larger than you anticipated, was it not?"

Wyndham considered his options, watching Alihambra carefully. This would probably be his last assignment, after which he would leave England and find a new home and a new identity. "Indeed it was," he responded. "Perhaps we can accommodate your needs, General," Wyndham said deferentially while he kept his eyes on the weapon he knew was under Alhambra's waistband, "Fortunately you have deposited just enough to cover the additional expenses. How foresighted of you,"

With a great laugh, Alihambra said, "I somehow felt you might be so inclined, Mr. Wyndham. It is a pleasure doing business with you. And for the other item. His Excellency proposes to procure directly from you, as convenient, the means to conduct one further incident that will be planned and directed internally. For this consideration, one last payment of fifty million U.S. dollars will be made again into your account, totaling one hundred and seventy-five million U.S. dollars for your services."

"A direct buy this time, with delivery where?"

"You will be advised. Can it be arranged?"

"Yes, we can arrange to facilitate your needs."

"We must make sure that none of our friends feel left out of our considerations, Mr. Wyndham. They must all feel equally cared for," General Alihambra said with relish.

Washington, D.C.
National Security Agency
August

Precisely at 6:30 A.M., Major O'Brien walked into his office in the National Security Agency. He knew that General Austin was generally at work by seven, and he wanted a few moments with him to prepare his briefing. He could see by the staff status board that all his staff had returned and would be arriving shortly. They would convene a brain-storming session this afternoon.

General Austin arrived a few minutes before seven and stopped at Zach's office on his way in. "Welcome home, Major. It's been quiet around here with your whole staff gone. Peaceful actually." He smiled. "Give me thirty minutes, Zach, and then let's try to put it together."

O'Brien finished summarizing his list of items and spent the last few minutes talking with Lieutenant Savini and Captain Molloy before heading for Austin's office. Their trips had produced little in the way of hard evidence, and it was beginning to look like the puzzle pieces came from different boxes. Just as he was about to leave his office, his secretary, Jean, told him he had a call. "Jean, please tell them I'll call back later this morning," he said as he headed out of his office.

"It's Captain Adams, at Coast Guard Headquarters, Major. He says it's urgent."

"Right. I'll take it in my office. Put it through, please." O'Brien returned to his desk and waited for the phone to transfer. "Major O'Brien speaking."

"Good morning, Major, Captain Adams here. I spoke several days ago with General Austin regarding our discovery out in San Diego. I understand you made the recent visit to ascertain the connection, if there was one, between the *Emiliano Zapata* and your investigations into the *Cherokee.*"

"That's right, Captain. It seems clear that some radioactive material was in that hold, but as yet they cannot determine specifically what it was. Has something else turned up?"

"Indeed it has, Major. I hope it's the clue you're looking for. The *Emiliano Zapata* was commissioned in 1967, but it has operated ever since out of Yokohama, Japan, as the *Kamitsu Maru,* last bound in early July for Auckland, New Zealand, with a load of electronic gear. She hasn't been seen since she left Auckland, destination Western Samoa. That is until she turned up in San Diego as the *Emiliano Zapata.*"

O'Brien let out a long whistle. "Captain Adams, if the National Security Agency had a 'Man of the Month' contest, you'd win hands down. Thank you for calling. Can you put that on paper and have it couriered over to us, or better yet, I'll send someone over to pick it up. Again, my sincere thanks, Captain."

"The Coast Guard is here to serve, Major. Glad we could be of assistance."

O'Brien jumped up from his desk and headed for Austin's office. "Jean, get someone to run over to the Department of Transportation, Coast Guard Headquarters, and pick up a document from Captain Adams. Give it about an hour for them to prepare the papers."

"Right, Major, I'll get it before I go to lunch."

General Austin was talking on the telephone when O'Brien arrived, grinning from ear to ear. Motioning for him to take a seat, he concluded his call and looked at O'Brien quizzically. "You look like the cat that ate the canary. Has the other shoe dropped in your search?"

"General, all of the resources at our command sometimes go for naught until a piece of intelligence falls into our lap by accident. There was really no reason for the Coast Guard to connect their drug raid with our search, but someone was just clever, and put two and two together."

"Would you like to explain that, or are we going to play Twenty Questions?"

"A small Pacific freighter named *Kamitsu Maru* left Yokohama in early July, bound for Auckland with a load of electronic gear. After departing Auckland she was bound for Samoa and wasn't seen again, until she turned up last week in San Diego, as the *Emiliano Zapata*."

"Bingo," said Austin. "I felt a connection. Still not solid enough, but it will open the door, and we can fill in from there. Somehow, that ship delivered the weapon to the South Pacific and got it in the path of the *Cherokee* and the *Northland*. One more link to discover, and we'll pin it down. We've still got to find a way to make the world believe it, however. It's too convenient as it is. Let's summarize what we've got."

O'Brien rose and went to the general's white board, which he often used for small briefings held in his office, and began to list items they knew. "One, we have two ships nearly two thousand miles from the nearest landfall; two, no debris of any consequence remaining; and three, no radar track of any aircraft in the area for three hours on either side of the incident, other than our own."

Austin interjected, "The JCS ruled out the possibility of someone else having a Stealth aircraft, at least someone who both has nuclear weapon technology and would want to use it on us."

O'Brien continued, "The small possibility of a submarine exists, but *Cherokee* would have had considerable advance warning, unless her listening ability had been impeded. So the method of attack must have been a vessel, or vessels, that appeared harmless. The taped copies we have of the supposed transmission from the *Cherokee* are of doubtful origin as well. No contact designator was used, and even if an emergency existed, the radioman would not have thrown all caution to the wind. In all probability the distress call was false and did not emanate from the *Cherokee*. So, what does that leave us?"

Austin added, "Have you considered the possibility that a timed device was placed on board *Cherokee* during one of her stops in South America?"

"Yes, and it's also highly unlikely, even with a new crew. Captain Molloy went to the two stops while Savini was in Chile. She reported there were no indications from our resident agents, either CIA or sister agencies from abroad, of any apparent hostility. The conclusion, which brings us no closer to the facts, is that a small, nonoffensive vessel approached *Cherokee* and self-detonated in range to eliminate *Cherokee, Northland,* and themselves. How many crew would be willing to commit suicide, or more importantly, what is the minimum number of crew able to sail such a small vessel?"

"OK," said Austin, standing up, the piece we seem to have in hand is how the weapon got to New Zealand. Aboard the *Kamitsu Maru.* Track her back, Major. Examine her cargo and intended recipients. That seems something the SIS can do for us in New Zealand. How has your SIS contact been?"

"Helpful, sir. Hegarty's a good man, but wary of our credibility."

"I don't blame him, Zach, do you?"

"No, sir, and I just spent eight days trying to improve his view of us. He's coming around, but we need something hard and fast to show him. New Zealand will be the key to the international community believing our claim that *Cherokee* was clean. If they announce to the world their belief, no one else would continue to disbelieve our version. Except of course our Iraqi 'friends' who know the truth, and their cohorts."

"Right. Keep on that, Major. Now, let's shift our thoughts to the operational relocation of assets currently in the Persian Gulf. I've worked most of it out, and the key is in keeping quick reaction forces relatively close at hand. Review my draft this morning, and we'll see Prescott this afternoon to run it past her."

"Yes, sir," replied O'Brien. Turning to leave he added, "It's good to be home, General."

"Bring any scones this time, Major?"

"No, sir. I didn't even let the folks know I was there until the last day. They drove down, and we had dinner just before my flight left for Los Angeles."

Austin rose and addressed Zach seriously, "Major O'Brien, I know how important this is to you and the severe blow it has dealt to relations with the Kiwis. We will leave no stone unturned to rectify that situation, for the good of our country, of course, and our position in the world community. But also because I know you would like to be able to go home with your head held high. We're innocent this time, Zach, and as you so often point out to us, 'The truth will out.'"

"Thank you, General. It is important to me. Very important."

CHAPTER FIFTEEN

Auckland, New Zealand
September

CAMERON ROSSITER WAS QUITE PLEASED with himself today. After presentations and training covering several months, he had finally closed a new account for sixty PC work stations at a national bank chain. The deal would mean about four new staff members and a service contract over the next twenty-four months. Driving north through the commuter traffic, he thought about his evening class at the local community college. He was taking Japanese in an effort to present himself on a more equal footing with the Japanese businessmen who came to New Zealand. They all seemed to speak some degree of English, and to eliminate their edge, he felt that he would have to learn to speak Japanese. He wasn't finding it easy.

Arriving home, he commenced to change clothes and think about a bite to eat before leaving for class when the telephone rang. "Hello, Cameron Rossiter," he answered.

"Hi there. I'd like to speak to Captain Hook, please," Michelle's soft voice said.

Cameron was instantly alert, elated at Michelle's call. "I'm sorry, ma'am. He fell overboard and was eaten by the croc, but I can assure you our present crew can handle any request to your satisfaction. Care to come aboard?"

"Is it a dinner cruise?"

"Well, ma'am, dinner is a distinct possibility, but the cruise will have to be a review of the brochure for our new vessel. The old one seems to have gone missing."

"So I heard," Michelle continued. "Suppose a landlocked lass brought fish and chips in a door-to-door service? Would that meet with your approval?"

"Sounds great. About forty-five minutes?"

"See you then."

Replacing the receiver, Cameron forgot all about his class and began to consider the reasons behind Michelle's call. He had begun to think that she had completely eliminated him from her life. He quickly swept through the house, picking up any remaining clothes and papers, giving it a tidy appearance. He had finished showering and changing clothes when the door bell rang.

"Fish and chips, anyone?" Michelle said with an embarrassed grin.

"I've prepared a place on the deck," Cameron replied, gesturing toward the back of the house

After placing the food on the table and arranging a couple of chairs for them, he took her by the hand and looked into her eyes. "I've missed you, Michelle."

"I've had a lot to sort out, Cameron. Please don't be hurt or angry with me."

"I'm not angry, Michelle, just confused."

"Me too—that's why I'm here tonight. Perhaps together we can sort things out."

"Great! Let's eat, and then we can sit in the spa and hopefully reach some understanding."

"If we sit in the spa, understanding might be the last thing we reach. Maybe we'd better just sit on the deck tonight," she said while laughing.

They ate, making small talk and discussing how their businesses were going. Like Cameron, Michelle had landed a contract she had been working on for some time, and they both congratulated each other. Michelle was obviously nervous, but she held her own in the conversation.

After they finished eating, Cameron went inside, returning with a small blanket, handing it to Michelle. "Thought you might get a little chilly this evening."

"Thank you, Cameron. It is cool tonight." She paused for a few moments, and Cameron allowed her to collect her thoughts without interruption. "What happened to *Triple Diamond?*"

"They really don't know yet. It just seems to have disappeared, last seen passing Great Barrier Island on the first day of the charter. The police haven't been much help, and the insurance company doesn't want to know me. But that's not why you came over, is it?"

"I really don't know how to begin."

"Why don't you just tell me you love me and couldn't possibly live without me anymore."

"That's exactly what's wrong, I'm afraid. Afraid that if I allow myself to love you, I might have to live without you. Cameron, I'm sure you've figured out some of it. My father loved the sea, and I lost him. My brother was a naval officer, and I lost him. And the man I have fallen in love with also loves the sea, and he loves to sail it alone. Cameron, I haven't recovered completely from the loss of my father, and Graham . . . " She paused. "I just don't know how to handle it."

"Did I hear you say you loved me?"

"Cameron, don't tease me. You know how I feel. I know you do. I've never been able to hide it from you, or for that matter, you from me. I've just tried to put it away, forget it, and move on, but I can't, I just can't. I do love you." She reached for his hand. "My mother finally put meaning to it the day of the memorial service. She said, 'It would be a shame to lose him for fear you might lose him,' and it all seemed so clear that what I was doing seemed foolish. Then my pride kept me from contacting you, until I received another letter from Alison, which made me decide to call you."

"I knew your mother was a bright woman, Michelle. It seems to run in the family, doesn't it? And I'm going to have to give Alison a big kiss, whatever Zach says." He came over to sit on the edge of her chair, still holding her hand. "And what have you decided to do, Michelle?"

"Cameron, if you still want me, I intend to have you for today, and then for tomorrow, and then for the day after tomorrow, and then if I don't have you after that, I will have had you for all those days in between. That sounds logical and bright and hopeful, but it frightens me. Do you understand?"

"Of course I do. Life comes with no guarantees, but it does come with promise. You told me once that your mother has a strong faith that things are meant to be, and we must adjust to the hardships that life brings. I can understand that, I truly can. Life has been kind to me as a result of my father's hard work, but it could have been different. I've never thought we had any special gift bestowed on us." He moved to take her face in his hands and looked softly into her eyes. "I do love you, Michelle, and of course I still want you. Today, tomorrow, and for all the tomorrows we are allowed."

Tears were beginning to run down Michelle's cheeks as Cameron kissed her. She buried her head in his shoulder and allowed him to hold her once again. She remembered how safe she had felt, if only momentarily, when he had met her at the airport in London. For that fleeting moment, until the newscast had shattered their lives, she knew he was hers and she was his, and now, in his arms, she felt that way again. "Cameron, I want to love you as Alison loves Zach. They're special people. I feel it."

"I think I understand the feeling, Michelle. I've spent time in their home with their children. It has an atmosphere of love, but what we should look for is what's right for us. They didn't build their family on anyone else's but on the way they needed each other. We'll find ours, Michelle, I promise you."

Michelle sat back again and looked at Cameron. "I've been

writing to Alison, and she has helped me sort out some problems in my thinking. You know, about the issues we discussed at dinner the night before you left for England."

"Have you come to terms with your mother's and father's disagreements?"

"Probably not, but at least I know neither of them was wrong—in the sense that one did the wrong thing. Mum discovered something her life needed. I no longer feel it was in place of us—her family I mean—but I did for a long time. Her new church seemed to replace us, and I resented it. Now I see how a marriage can be if both parties have the same beliefs, or in more general terms the same direction. Do you remember our talk about direction?"

"Of course I do. I've been thinking about it too, but I don't know if religion is the answer."

"Neither do I, but to clear this issue from my mind once and for all, I've got to know exactly what it is my mother sees that has captivated her for so long." Michelle rose, and went to the railing overlooking the city lights. "I can't ask Mum though, I've got to learn from someone else. There's too much emotion behind us to discuss her church. You know, I tried to find out about the Mormons once, or I should say, Graham and I did. We asked a Catholic priest, and we also asked him what the relationship was between my mother and father now that he had died, and where it left us children."

"What did he say?"

"He said the Mormons were not to be believed, and according to the true Catholic church, there was no marriage between my parents now. It ended with my father's death. It had a cold finality to it. I was left feeling, I don't know, sort of left out." She paused again for some time and turned to look at Cameron. "Cameron," she asked, reaching for his hands and pulling him up from the chair, "will you investigate this with me, and help me put some objectivity to my prejudices?"

Cameron smiled and lowered his head to kiss her neck. "Of course I will, Michelle, but you can't ask a Ford dealer what he thinks about Hondas."

"Huh?"

"I mean, if you want to find out about Mormonism, you can't ask a Catholic priest, or an Anglican minister for that matter. They'll present their views, and that's understandable. Ask the Mormons directly, and either accept or reject their information as you decide, but you can't really expect someone from another religion to give you an objective opinion." He watched her for some moments. "There is one other thing."

"Yes, I think I know what you're going to say."

"Perhaps, and you have to be prepared for this possibility, you may discover that your mother was on to something. Have you considered that?"

Again, Michelle was quiet for nearly a minute. "Yes, I have. And it frightens me. It had so much power over her. She changed completely, and it affected all our lives. I don't want to change, Cameron—I like my life."

"Maybe," Cameron spoke with compassion, "she didn't want to change either. It could be that what she found was just so compelling that it changed her life without her permission. Believe me, I'm not saying she's right, and for all we know, they might have some excellent system for brainwashing people, but there have been things in my life that I was unable to deny, even though I didn't want them to be that way. You have to be prepared for that possibility. I'll do this with you, Michelle, because I can see how important it is to you, and because"—he paused to take her in his arms—"I can see how important you are to me. Together, we'll see what it's all about."

"Cameron," Michelle said hesitantly, "what if only one of us . . . " She halted, afraid to even speak the words.

Cameron held her tenderly and spoke gently close to her ear. "Then we'll have to be honest with each other . . . like your parents were."

"That's what I'm afraid of," she said softly.

Cameron took Michelle's hand and guided her back to the deck chair, sitting next to her and looking at the harbor and city lights. They were quiet for some time, just holding each other in the chair, Cameron stroking Michelle's hair and watching the few vessels on the harbor as the evening progressed. Finally Michelle spoke, "Do you remember how you first asked me out? You know, 'How spontaneous are you, Ms. Duffield?' Do you remember that?"

Cameron laughed at the memory. "I certainly do. I remember that entire day like it was yesterday."

"Well, it's my turn. Tomorrow evening I'm flying to Christchurch for the weekend. My sister recently had a baby, and I want to go see him. I'd like you to come." She smiled as she delivered the challenge.

"Done," said Cameron. "My mother will praise your glory for bringing her son for a forced visit. I guess this is the show-and-tell time for family, huh?"

"It's time, don't you think?"

"I do indeed."

Once again they were quiet for some time, just holding and thinking how nice it was to be back together again. Quietly in her heart, Michelle gave her own thanks to Alison for her advice and concern. Michelle knew that Cameron was too important to her future to lose him over unwarranted, or even for that matter, justifiable fears. Her mum and Alison had both given essentially the same advice. It had worked. "Cameron," Michelle spoke up, "I think I'm ready for that spa now."

"Great, your suit's still in the guest room. I think I might look around for any sign of Captain Hook too," he jested. "It's been lonely without him."

Christchurch, New Zealand
September

Arriving early in the afternoon, Cameron's father, John Rossiter III met them at the airport and took them to the Rossiter home in the fashionable Westmoreland suburb overlooking the city. Michelle liked Cameron's parents, John and Sarah Rossiter. Sarah sized up Michelle quickly, and favorably. She saw in Cameron's demeanor a different attitude toward Michelle, and in fact he was somewhat nervous, Sarah thought as he introduced Michelle.

"So your parents come from Christchurch too, Michelle?" Sarah asked.

"Yes, my mum was born on the west coast, but she grew up in Riccarton. Dad was born in Christchurch."

"And where is your mum now?"

"After Dad's death, she remarried a few years later and moved to the States for a while, and now she lives with her husband in Auckland."

"How convenient for you. Do you see her often?"

Cameron gave his mother a look that said, "Don't push it, Mum."

John saw the interchange and smiled to himself. It was Sarah's first opportunity to be the protective mum for her oldest son. "So, Michelle," he commented, "Cameron tells us that you're ready for the America's Cup crew."

Michelle threw back her head, laughing, "Hardly, Mr. Rossiter, but my father and brother did pass on some of their sailing knowledge and, I guess, some of their love for the sea."

"There are much less productive activities one could pursue. At least sailing provides an appreciation for nature, not to mention a good suntan."

Looking toward Cameron, John continued, "How long you down for, Son?"

"Just the weekend, Dad. We go back on the Monday five A.M. flight."

John raised his eyebrows and joked, "Whew, that's early. Just take the keys and leave the car in the airport car park. Your mother will take me out to get it later, at a more civilized hour."

Cameron also laughed. "Right, Dad. Speaking of your car, I'd like to run Michelle over to her sister's for a while, and then I'll be back later this evening. I'd like to meet her family too, and see this new nephew Michelle's been crowing about."

"Oh, did your sister just have a baby, Michelle?" asked Sarah.

"Yes, and I've only seen pictures."

"Do you like children, dear?"

John quickly interjected, "Who doesn't, Sarah? You kids run along and we'll see you again tomorrow. It's been very enjoyable meeting you, Michelle. Cameron's not very informative, as you can imagine."

As they rose to leave, Sarah added, "Michelle, how about a nice dinner on Sunday afternoon, your sister and her husband too, of course?"

"Thank you very much, Mrs. Rossiter. I'll ask them this evening and let you know tomorrow if that's all right."

"Certainly, dear. And please call us John and Sarah if you feel comfortable with that."

"Here's the keys to the Porsche, Cameron. Take care of my 'baby,' will you?"

"Of course, Dad. You worked pretty hard to get it, so I'll try not to smash it while I'm here."

Once they had reached Michelle's sister's home, the cooing and gurgling began.

"Oh, Jackie, he's absolutely adorable," Michelle cooed. "Don't you think so, Cameron?"

"He's just wonderful," Cameron replied awkwardly.

"Men don't have any understanding of babies, do they, Jackie?" Michelle said to her sister.

Cameron could see that Michelle was indeed "clucky," which was the expression he thought the women used.

After they had talked for a while, Cameron said he'd better get back to his parents before it was too late. "I'll be back tomorrow about noon, Michelle. Will that suit?"

"Sure. Maybe we can take a run out to Sumner Beach and see if the winter fools are still swimming."

Cameron stood to leave. "It's been very nice to meet you, Jackie. You certainly have a lovely son."

"Thank you, Cameron," Jackie said, smiling. "Maybe tomorrow when you return, you can hold him and try it out for size."

"I sell computers, Jackie. Does he come with an owner's manual?"

"Not hardly. I believe the standard package includes one crying, messy, and hungry miniature human, with two ignorant parents standing around wondering what to do."

"Well, if that's all, I can handle that. It sounds just like a couple of my staff."

They all had a good laugh, and Michelle walked Cameron out to his car. "Thank you, Cameron."

"For what?"

"Just thank you. For everything."

"My pleasure, I can assure you," he said. "See you tomorrow." He kissed her good-bye and drove back to his parents, arriving about 11:30.

Surprisingly his father was still up, reading. "Thought you'd be long gone, Dad," he said.

"No. Your mother has gone to sleep, but I'm still reading. Nice woman, Cameron."

"I think so too, Dad. She's, well, she's kind of grown on me rather quickly."

"No one said it had to take forever, you know. You're old enough to know your own mind."

Cameron sat down on the leather lounge suite, removed his shoes, and leaned back against the cushions, letting the effort of the day drain out of his body.

John watched his son and was silent, but to invite conversation, he marked his page in his book and placed it down on the table next to his chair. "Care for a cup of coffee, Cameron?"

"That would be great, Dad."

Returning with two cups of coffee and a piece of Sarah's sponge cake, John sat down again in his chair and waited for Cameron to talk. John didn't have to wait long.

"Dad, you remember that discussion we had several years ago about value systems?"

"Some concern on your part, as I recall, about honesty in business I believe."

"That's right, but the lesson applies to a much broader spectrum, doesn't it?"

"I believe it applies to life in general. Why? Is something wrong?"

"It's not so much that something's wrong, but Michelle and I have had several discussions about directions, and the necessity of both people in a relationship moving in the same direction. Some of my thoughts have paralleled our discussion on value systems." He paused to nibble on his mother's cake. Cameron had always been able to share with his father and respected his advice. He was fortunate, he thought, for this had allowed them to develop a friendship as well as the father-son relationship. Cameron continued, "Dad, Michelle's parents, that is her mum and her deceased father, were married for about fifteen years with an excellent relationship and common values. But when Michelle was about fourteen, her mum investigated religion and, out of the blue, joined the Mormon church. Do you know anything about them, Dad?"

"Certainly do. I've had several Mormon associates over the years."

"Well, as Michelle puts it, that decision by her mother completely changed the direction of their lives. The father was adamantly opposed to the religion, and the mother wouldn't give it up, which made it tough on the children. They chose to follow their father's lead. Seven years later, he was killed in a yachting accident, and a few years later, their mother married an American, also a Mormon. That kind of locked up her religious affiliation."

"What's the issue, Cameron?" John asked.

"Michelle is afraid of commitment without knowing how unified the direction, or value system, of each party will be. We both have recently met an American couple. I've told you about him. He works for White House intelligence, and he's the one who arranged the visit of a U.S. naval ship to New Zealand. Anyway, they're also Mormon, but Michelle sees them really happy after fourteen years of marriage. She's confused because she has always been able to blame the Mormon church for her parents' division, and now along comes this seemingly perfect marriage, claiming the Church as the reason. I can understand her confusion."

"Are you serious about Michelle, Cameron?"

"Right to the heart of the matter, eh, Dad? Yes, I am, and that's why it's so important to resolve this issue. Do you feel that you and Mum were going in the same direction in the early years?"

John Rossiter III paused, leaned back in his chair, and contemplated his answer. What a struggle they had had when he first started. Working nights, hosting meetings for his fledgling network marketing program. "Cameron," he began, "if it weren't for your mother's belief in my dream, I would never have achieved it. It's that simple. She supported us, I mean even financially for some time, and then with you as a baby, she kept things humming while I went out with nothing but dreams and pictures on the wall of things we hoped for. She could have said, 'Just work more hours at your job, or concentrate on feeding us, not on your Porsche.' But she didn't and we succeeded. I mean that literally, Cameron, *we* succeeded, not me."

Cameron had never heard his father tell this story, and it fascinated him to hear of his parents' early struggle, while his own life had seemed to come gift-wrapped.

John went on, warming to his topic. "I think that it truly doesn't matter what direction a couple is moving in, as long as they're moving toward it together. The value system one chooses in life is indeed important, and the Mormons I have known have set a tough road for themselves because they set very rigid standards in a world where standards are often set by plurality. Truly, I firmly believe that it is not as important what value system you choose as much as it is how you live up to that value system. Situational ethics permeates our society, and by that I mean most people choose to believe what is popular at the moment. That allows them to do whatever they want. Setting a standard and then honoring it when the going gets tough are the true tests of values. The term is integrity, I believe. If, as you say, Michelle's mother maintained both her commitment to the marriage and her new commitment to her religion in the face of family opposition, then I take my hat off to her. It's not an easy road to ride. Now"— he leaned forward and looked steadily at Cameron—"if you think your old man is going to tell you and your young lady how to develop this kind of directional guidance, you're wrong." He smiled.

Cameron's face lit up with a bright grin. "I know, Dad, 'all the advice I want, but the decision is mine.' I remember the rules."

Picking up his coffee cup and plate, Cameron headed for the kitchen. "Thanks, Dad." Returning from the kitchen and starting up the stairs, Cameron looked at his father again. "Dad, I'd like you to know that I admire what you and Mum were able to build for us, and the unity I have always seen in your marriage."

Cameron went up the stairs toward his room, leaving John Rossiter III leaning back in his chair, reflecting on this new, and unusual, compliment from his son. Having set his own values early in his life, John had tried to instill them in his son, or at least an appreciation for the necessity of some value standard, even if it wasn't his father's. But he had seldom received those rare and priceless moments a parent treasures when the child, now adult, takes the time to thank and honor the tutor. John was filled with pride, and he remained basking in his love for his son, his wife, and his life for some time.

After another day of relatives, beach walks, and visits to old haunts, Michelle was ready at 4:15 in the morning on Monday when Cameron arrived in his father's Porsche to drive to the airport. Their flight back to Auckland was nearly full from the early morning business commuters. At the Auckland Domestic Terminal, they took a taxi into the city. "Dinner tonight?" Cameron offered.

"At home," Michelle said. "Seven o'clock, my place."

Kissing her good-bye as she got out of the taxi at her office, he held her hand a moment as she stepped out. "Thanks for the invite and the weekend. You didn't steal your nephew and carry him back in your suitcase, did you?" he teased.

"I'll wait for my own, thank you," she said, smiling as she left. "See you tonight."

As Cameron rode the taxi down Queen Street to his office, he pondered the weekend and his father's advice. It was true, he and Michelle would have to seek and discover their own direction and

value system. Life, and certainly marriage, was too dangerous
without something to grasp, and two hands, or four in the case of
a marriage, were needed on the handle. How Michelle's mum had
discovered her values and whether or not they were appropriate
for Michelle he didn't know, but together they would find out.

New York City
United Nations Building
September

Leaving the committee meeting room, Sir Geoffrey Holden,
ambassador to the United Nations from New Zealand, felt
drained. It had been a long week and it had taken all his strength
to deal with the many ambassadors who had pleaded with him to
publicly denounce the Americans for their obvious negligence
and the totally unwarranted pain they had caused to so many New
Zealand families by the loss of their loved ones. He had maintained a steady posture of waiting until the investigation had been
completed and the causes of this unfortunate incident were determined.

In the foyer, he met the lovely young woman who served as
the public relations assistant to the new Russian ambassador.
"Good morning, Natasha. And how are the people of the North
faring this fine day?"

"Quite well, Ambassador, apart from limited food supplies,
no petrol for the vehicles, when of course one can be acquired,
and an unknown future government structure. Otherwise, we are
quite stable," she said, smiling broadly.

"Well, Natasha, you are not functioning as an 'Intourist'
guide this morning," Sir Geoffrey said with reference to the
Russian National tourist bureau.

"No, Sir Geoffrey, candor becomes one, don't you agree? But
only behind closed doors, of course"—again with a smile.
"Speaking of tourist agencies, have you had time to see any of the
New York sights yet?"

"Very little, I'm afraid. Since my arrival we have been, shall
I say, involved."

"Yes, I can imagine," Natasha opined. "The best view of the

New York harbor is found from the Staten Island Ferry. It goes right past the Statue of Liberty, you know. That was France's gift to the United States after their revolution. Ah, the glorious revolution, seen by each country as their salvation and deserved freedom, while they continue to see all other revolutions as anarchy. But then I am drifting from our conversation. Let's see, where was I? Oh yes, the Staten Island Ferry. It's about a twenty-minute ride each way, Sir Geoffrey, and best seen in the waning light of sunset, about five o'clock. A truly marvelous view and most informative when viewed with friends." She smiled again. Shifting to the plural, she concluded, "We hope you will find time on your schedule to permit this most worthy and enlightening view of New York. Oh, and be sure to obtain one of the world-famous hot dogs with sauerkraut. The best in the world, so I am told."

Sir Geoffrey was still trying to fathom her comments as he bid her good-bye. "Thank you, Natasha, for your insight. I still believe you were misplaced, however, and should be in the Bolshoi. You clearly have the grace and composure necessary for the artistic enlightenment of mankind."

"Why thank you, Sir Geoffrey, but there are many ways in which we can provide enlightenment, are there not?"

"Indeed so, Natasha, indeed so."

Sir Geoffrey continued back to his office, puzzling over the meaning of the apparently random information he had received. At his desk, he looked over his messages, then made his decision. Picking up the phone, he called Lady Mildred. "Good afternoon, dear. How has your day gone?"

"Why, Geoffrey, what a surprise. To what do I owe the honor of this unexpected call?"

"I thought I had been neglecting my duties as your husband leaving you alone in this magnificent city. I called to offer you the opportunity to show me some of the sights this afternoon."

"And what shall we see, my dear?" Lady Mildred asked.

"I thought the Statue of Liberty would be most enthralling as the sun sets, as viewed from the Staten Island Ferry. Shall you meet me in front of the building in, say, forty-five minutes?"

"That would be wonderful, dear," she said cheerfully. She had been on a number of peculiar "sightseeing" trips with her husband since coming to New York, and she had endured them all with good humor.

"Don't forget a warm wrap, Mildred. It can get chilly on the harbor at night. See you shortly."

Sir Geoffrey and Lady Mildred Holden walked the last several blocks as they exited their taxi near Battery Park at the south end of Manhattan Island. The ferry terminal was crowded with people jostling to reach their ferry, although at rush hour they were only twenty minutes apart. Thousands of New Yorkers rode the ferry into work each day, leaving their homes early in the morning, riding the Staten Island Rapid Transit train system down through the Island to the ferry terminal in Richmond and then taking the ferry twenty minutes across to Manhattan. Those lucky enough to work close to the Manhattan terminal walked to work, while others again boarded either the subway or bus to their jobs. The financial district of New York, including Wall Street and the twin towers of the World Trade Center were within walking distance of the terminal.

Sir Geoffrey and Lady Mildred moved through the struggling crowd and found seats in the inside compartment filled with people reading newspapers and magazines, doing knitting or crossword puzzles, or listening to battery-powered headsets, anything designed to lessen the drudgery of commuting back and forth to work each day for the better part of an hour each way. As the ferry departed the terminal, Sir Geoffrey offered to obtain a hot dog for Lady Mildred. "Oh, no thank you, Geoff. I'll leave that particular epicurean delight to your strong stomach. Just an orange juice for me, please."

At the counter, Sir Geoffrey requested one hot dog and two orange juices from the vendor, who raised an eyebrow when he heard the Kiwi accent. "Where ya from, Gov'ner?" he said with a clipped brogue.

"Down south," Sir Geoffrey said with a smile.

"Right," said the vendor, "I knew youse wasn't from here."

Obtaining his food, Sir Geoffrey started to depart when a distinguished gentleman spoke up with another distinct accent. "Don't forget the sauerkraut. It makes the combination special," the man said in a Baltic staccato.

Sir Geoffrey recognized him immediately as the Russian ambassador to the United Nations but did not address him specifically.

"Thank you, sir, I'll have a 'go' as we say down south."

"You'll find it most pleasurable, and you'll be able to inform your friends of your new discovery." He moved to leave and added, "and don't forget the view of the Statue from the starboard side. It's most breathtaking."

Returning to Lady Mildred, Sir Geoffrey excused himself. "I believe I'll step outside to have a look at the Statue of Liberty as we pass. It's much too cold out there, dear. Please don't bother to come, I'll be back shortly."

On the deck, Sir Geoffrey went to the rail and watched as the Statue approached. Quietly the Russian ambassador moved alongside Sir Geoffrey and began to comment on the Statue. "Symbols mean different things to different people, don't you agree, Sir Geoffrey? At different times the meaning can even change as a result of new knowledge. We once had a leader whose view of the world was somewhat different than today's leaders. Such people often leave a legacy, which sometimes is not the kind of legacy one wishes to inherit. In fact, one might even consider it a dangerous legacy."

Through the remainder of the ride to Staten Island and through most of the return trip, Sir Geoffrey listened as the story was unfolded to him. As the ferry approached the Manhattan terminal, the ambassador concluded his remarks. "So, Sir Geoffrey, while a New York hot dog may not be the gastronomic delight one finds in a good French restaurant, it does bring with it certain enlightenment not found elsewhere."

"Sir, it was a meal worthy of the experience, but perhaps one best kept within the family, so to speak."

"Exactly, Sir Geoffrey, exactly. Good evening to you, sir."

Returning to the cabin, Lady Mildred rose clutching her coat.

"Did we have a good time, dear?" she asked with a raised eyebrow.

"I should say, my dear, that New York provides the opportunity to meet all sorts of interesting people, and the hot dogs are quite an experience."

Early the next morning before leaving for work, Sir Geoffrey placed a call to Auckland. A sleepy voice answered the phone, "Hello."

"Cameron, my dear boy. How are you this bright morning?"

Recognizing the voice, Rossiter replied, "It's midnight and it's raining here, Sir Geoffrey."

"Now that's too bad. It is crisp and clear here in New York. I'd love to show it to you as I promised. Tomorrow if possible, dear boy."

Rossiter hesitated before replying, "I'll see what I can do, Sir Geoffrey. May I call you later?"

"Of course, Cameron. Oh, and Cameron . . . I haven't called."

"I understand, Sir Geoffrey. Good day."

"Good day, Cameron. Thank you."

Washington D.C.
The Mall
September

"Major O'Brien, there's a Mr. Rossiter for you on line two."

"Thanks, Jean," O'Brien said as he picked up the phone. "Cameron, this is a surprise. How's the weather in Auckland?"

"I've no idea, Zach. I thought it was my turn to drop in for lunch, so I'm just down the street from the White House. Got time for a bite to eat?"

"Yes, certainly. Give me about thirty minutes and I'll meet you. Where are you?"

"Let's meet by the Vietnam Memorial in the park. I've always wanted to see it, and then we could walk through the Mall to the Lincoln Memorial. What better guide than a member of the inner circle.'"

"Cameron, not to burst your balloon, but I more often go in

circles than participate in the inner circle. Meet you at the Wall at 12:15."

O'Brien stopped by Captain Murphy and Lieutenant Savini's office to advise them he was rescheduling their meeting for 2:30 and left for the park. *What was it, only about a week since I saw Cameron?* O'Brien thought. *He didn't say anything about coming to the States.*

The usual line of tourists waiting to tour the White House extended around the perimeter fence. People never tired of seeing their country's history in action. Each hoped for a quick glimpse of the president or Jean, but were seldom so fortunate. O'Brien always approached the Vietnam Memorial with reverence, and he never failed to be impressed by the number of people who tarried. On several occasions he had seen Alice, General Austin's secretary, eating her lunch there, and on one occasion he had seen her consoling a woman about her age who was crying. Over twenty years had gone by since this unpopular war had ended, yet people continued to come and stand with awe at the list of honored dead. Veterans who gave their lives and their families were not concerned with the political popularity of the war, rather the sacrifice of their loved ones. However reluctant they had been to go to war, they had in the end sacrificed their lives in the call of duty to their country. Many times O'Brien had thought how close it came to having his father's name on this wall, and how fortunate his father was to have survived the ordeal. Most of the rescue crew had not come back and were now listed on the Wall—a fact he and the elder O'Brien had thought about on more than one occasion.

As he walked along the wall, he saw Cameron standing between two observers, one of whom was wearing a beret and an old military field jacket. Zach waited for him to finish his conversation before saying hello.

As the viewers moved away, Zach headed his way. "G'day, mate," Cameron said in a lilted Australian brogue.

"And a top o' the morning to you too," Zach replied, trying to duplicate his best Irish brogue. "How long will you be in town?"

"Just a day or two. I only decided to hop over yesterday, and

I flew into New York this morning. That was an interesting chap," he said, referring to the man who had just left. "He said he comes here every month and talks to his old platoon mates to let them know what he's doing. He said he wouldn't be here if it weren't for them."

"That's not an unusual story, Cameron. The dedication some of these veterans and relatives feel is truly amazing, and it's been well over twenty years for most of them." O'Brien spied a street vendor with hot dogs and motioned Cameron in that direction. "This is our answer to fish and chips. If you think those things in New Zealand that say 'American hot dogs' even come close to these, I'll eat a jar of marmite, heaven forbid," O'Brien said, laughing. They got a couple of hot dogs and Cokes and moved to sit on one of the park benches. At lunch hour, the park was full of people coming and going, with no one taking particular notice of anyone else. It was an excellent place to have a quiet conversation. O'Brien quickly wondered how many clandestine conversations had taken place here, just out of reach of the White House.

"Cameron, my instincts tell me this meeting has a purpose," Zach opened.

"I suppose that's why they have you assigned to intelligence. A mutual friend has come into some information, the source of which he is presently unable to reveal, and he felt unable to deliver the message himself because of his visibility. He said you would probably guess the source, but for the time being, he wanted to maintain the confidence he promised. I knew when he first arranged for you and me to meet, he had a reason beyond accommodations, but I don't think even he knew what would transpire." Cameron was watching everyone who passed and holding his conversation each time someone got close.

"Cameron," Zach said gently, "only a third of Americans work for the CIA, and most of them play golf on Wednesday afternoons. We're safe here."

Cameron realized he appeared overly cautious and laughed. "I guess I've been watching too many Jack Ryan and James Bond movies. What Sir Geoffrey says is 'historic information' has come to his attention, and he has asked me to transfer it to you. He feels he can give you about a forty-eight hour lead before he feels it necessary to pass it on to the prime minister. He feels you deserve that, and he would like to begin to repair the damage to relations between New Zealand and the United States. He feels that if you bring this to the New Zealand SIS first, followed by his report, it will lend credibility to your intentions."

Turning serious, O'Brien viewed Rossiter professionally. "I can see that reasoning. Are you aware of the nature of the information?"

"Yes, the only material written down are four obituaries, which he said were of utmost importance to the overall message." Cameron began to reveal the story as relayed to him by Sir Geoffrey only hours before he caught the shuttle to Washington. He could see that Zach was greatly impressed by the story.

"Cameron, do you understand the significance of this information?"

"Not all of the background means much, but certainly it demonstrates that someone with knowledge of this past action obtained access to the location of these nuclear weapons and used one to destroy the two ships."

"Exactly right, and from the information provided here, three more are up for grabs, if they're not gone already. What a clever idea, and virtually no chance of being discovered or disturbed. A cemetery! Amazing!"

O'Brien added to Rossiter's knowledge with the new information. "We know the ship that carried the first weapon to New Zealand in July—the *Kamitsu Maru,* with electronics gear on board. How it got to the *Cherokee* and *Northland,* we still don't know, because it's still afloat under a different name."

Cameron looked up at Zach. "What was the name of that ship?"

"*Kamitsu Maru,* out of Yokohama. Why, do you know her?"

"Zach, I'd have to call my office to confirm, but I believe that was the name of the ship that delivered a special purchase of computers I ordered last June. The fellow required that shipment be on one of his vessels, for freight costs, he said. I've been trying to reach him for about two weeks. He arranged for a couple of his business friends to charter *Triple Diamond* in late July for two weeks, and it hasn't been seen since. Since there's no accident report, the insurance company has been giving me lots of problems as well."

All at once everything coalesced in O'Brien's mind, just as if someone had entered a dark room, and the lights had been turned on. He thought out loud, "The other shoe just dropped."

"What's that?" asked Cameron.

"Oh . . . ah, nothing. Just a saying."

"What kind of average speed could *Triple Diamond* make?"

"About six knots, maybe seven."

"That's too slow." O'Brien's mind was racing now and ideas were forming as fast as he could discard them. "Did *Triple Diamond* have a retractable or dismountable keel?"

"Yes, but you'd have to take her out of the water for—"

O'Brien interrupted, "Cameron, did you rent a car?"

"Yes, I did, and I booked into the Sheraton."

"Well, book out if you can, and be at 1521 Lakewood Drive, Woodbridge, Virginia, tonight about six for dinner. I've already called Alison to expect you. It's about a forty-minute drive, barring traffic jams. No buts, and no excuses." Standing to leave, O'Brien became brusque. "I'm really sorry, Cameron, but I've got to get back to my office. You've just shed some very important light on this whole issue. Can you find your way?"

Cameron rose and smiled. "Aye aye, Captain. Excuse me, Major."

Washington, D.C.
National Security Agency
September

"Alice, you are beautiful this afternoon. Is the general in?"

"Why thank you, Major O'Brien, I've just had my hair . . . Major?" O'Brien went flying past her desk before she even had time to announce his presence to General Austin.

"The other shoe dropped, General." O'Brien was breathless, having practically jogged back from the meeting with Rossiter.

"I suggest, Major O'Brien, that you put your shoes back on and start from the beginning."

"Yes sir. They picked her out of the water and carried her to the spot. Then they left her with only one or maybe two crew. I know, I've sailed on her. She's able to be crewed by one. Cameron's done it many times between the islands."

Austin was becoming exasperated by now. "Major O'Brien, intelligence officers who speak unintelligibly end up as infantrymen in Greenland. Do you get my meaning?"

"Yes, sir. From the top." Zach took a deep breath and tried to regain his composure. Over the next fifteen minutes he laid out the scenario as best he could, with a few missing gaps of unknown information.

General Austin had always been a quick decision maker, and as O'Brien had been talking, he had been making notes. "Major, this is how we will handle it from here," he said in a directive tone. "First, contact Hegarty. I want him directly in this from the start. Second, coordinate a 'Prime Directive' flight out of Andrews for the next five days, multiple destinations in Asia and Europe. Routing will be Japan, Omaha, England, and Spain, in that order. Have Hegarty meet you in Japan and take him with you from there. I'll get the president's authorization for the flight priority. Third, notify Jameson at CIA of the trip. He'll want to go as well, and have him put a couple of men on each site until you arrive. No contact and no notification of anyone. Just observe until you arrive. Fourth, call Colonel O'Malley on the JCS staff. Have him coordinate for a nuke ops team to meet you at each destination. I think that covers it. I'll brief Prescott and she can have State coordinate with the other countries. If our analysis is right, we'll find Japan empty, but we still need to show Hegarty the origin and confirm the exhumation timing. You're right, Zach. It was a brilliant plan, and it's fascinating that it still applies thirty years later. Let's get these other three weapons, Major, before any more innocent people die. And Zach, good job."

"Not guilty again, General. It fell in my lap, courtesy of the meeting you arranged for me with Sir Geoffrey Holden."

"Maybe so, but you put it all together. About him . . . Sir

Geoffrey. He's got his head on the block. Let's justify his judgment."

"Exactly what I intend to do, General. I'll be in touch each step of the way."

O'Brien left the office as General Austin began to dial his phone. "This is General Austin. Is Ambassador Prescott available, please?"

After a brief pause, she came on the line.

"Clarene, I think the boss deserves some good news, don't you?"

CHAPTER SIXTEEN

———————

Northern Japan
Small Private Cemetery
September

DAN HEGARTY ARRIVED with one of his associates, Hamish Docherty, and they met with O'Brien prior to going to the cemetery. The groundskeeper had been notified they were coming, but he had no knowledge of which plot they would be excavating. Meeting with him that morning would confirm what O'Brien already knew. The plot had been excavated about eight weeks earlier, but O'Brien wanted Hegarty to confirm that for himself.

In the car on the way to the cemetery, O'Brien gave Hegarty the background on the original Soviet plan. Hegarty was amazed. "Such a detailed, extensive plot," he said, "and all to humiliate the West, specifically the Americans. Makes me glad I live where such intrigue isn't part of my everyday life."

"I understand that, Dan. But before you allow that thought to make you complacent, remember the world has gotten smaller, and every country has some responsibility, even if they would like to remain above the fray. The boys on the *Northland* would attest to that."

"I suppose you're right. We can't sit back and watch the big boys play, can we?"

"Not if we want to assure our security. It takes all of us working collectively to keep the bad guys from taking over."

The groundskeeper was surprised when they requested information on the particular plot they had listed. Through the translator from the embassy, they were told that a young couple had disinterred their parents in mid-June to relocate them. He had heard no more since then. At O'Brien's request, he showed them the site. Clearly the earth had been turned recently. The nuke ops team leader took readings from the earth nearby and nodded to O'Brien to confirm that readings indicated something emitting radiation had been in the area. O'Brien thanked the team leader for his quick response. The team leader, Major Henry, said, "If this was what I think it was, Major O'Brien, I wish we could have gotten here sooner."

"So do I, Major," said O'Brien solemnly.

Leaving the cemetery, O'Brien asked Dan about the investigation into the disappearance of *Triple Diamond.*

"No leads, Zach. It just seems to have vanished."

"*Evaporated* would be a more appropriate term, Dan. And it was such a beautiful yacht."

"That's right," Hegarty said. "You know Rossiter, don't you?"

"Yes, we've become friends, but that didn't prevent me from considering the coincidences involved in his computer order coming in on the *Kamitsu Maru,* and his yacht being the delivery vehicle. Have you completed the background check we requested on him?"

"Nearly. He seems clean enough. As an SAS officer, he has been subject to extensive background checks throughout his service. I think he was just convenient."

"Yea. A shame too. He's having difficulty trying to convince the insurance company about the loss of his yacht. That's a couple hundred thousand to replace it."

"Maybe that's somewhere we can help, Zach."

"I know he'd appreciate any assistance he can get," O'Brien said as they rode to the airport. "On to Omaha then, Dan. Been to the States?

"Once, about ten years ago."

"I'm afraid we'll have to miss the obligatory Disneyland trip this time."

"New Zealand's already had her ride, Zach. Now it's time to make the other guy pay for the ticket," he said, referring to the *Northland.*

Omaha, Nebraska
September

The Air Force VIP jet landed at Strategic Air Command Head-quarters, Offutt Air Force Base, Nebraska, about 9:30 A.M. Waiting for them were the base commander, Colonel Borello, and the SAC deputy chief of staff, Lt. General John Tolyan. Even though O'Brien was traveling in civilian clothes, he saluted General Tolyan, identified himself, and made the necessary intro-ductions. "General, this is Dan Hegarty, chief of New Zealand Security Intelligence Service and part of the prime minister's staff. Perhaps you know Mr. Jameson from Washington," O'Brien said without identifying his association with the CIA.

General Tolyan shook hands and motioned for his driver to prepare to leave. "Know exactly who you are, Major. Your boss and I go way back. I believe we have everything laid on for you, including the nuke ops team, which hopefully will be required. I'd hate to think this one is missing also. We've had the site under observation for about forty-eight hours. No inquiries have been made, but it doesn't look like it's been disturbed for years."

"General, that would make my day."

"Mine, too, son. Let's get cracking."

They drove about forty-five minutes into the countryside to a small, rural cemetery. The groundskeeper had been alerted by the local funeral home that some folks would be coming to discuss exhumation, but again, he had not been advised of the particular site. He expected a few family but was surprised by the two military staff cars, a large, military moving van, and about a dozen men in protective clothing with electronic instruments. Pete Garrison, local groundskeeper, had never been able to figure out his VCR, and he tended to shy away from electronic equipment, fearing someone might ask him to give them a hand. He checked his interment list for the plot, listed as Grace and Henry Adamson, buried 14 November 1963. He gave them a small map, with the site highlighted in yellow marker, "Section F, Range 3, Plot 13."

The nuke ops team began to take readings immediately upon arrival at the site. "Clearly been something here, General," the team leader said. The moving van opened, and a small excavator was unloaded and began to carefully remove the earth from the grave site. Fifteen minutes later, the excavator moved aside, and several men in protective clothing entered the grave site and worked carefully with shovels around the partially unearthed caskets. The two caskets were lifted one by one and loaded onto the moving van, and the excavated earth was loaded onto a dump truck and taken away. The entire operation was over in about forty minutes, and within seconds they were all driving back toward Offutt AFB.

In the security of the base, the caskets were opened, and what emerged confirmed the validity of Sir Geoffrey's message. Khrushchev's Silent Wind had been thwarted, at least on this one occasion. Standing silently in the presence of such destructive power, O'Brien thought of the men aboard the *Cherokee* and the *Northland* and of how such a weapon had quickly but surely ended their existence.

General Tolyan broke the silence. "In 1964, two young lieutenants were assigned to Offutt Air Force Base as new pilots. Perhaps," he reflected, "Generals Austin and Tolyan might have ended their careers somewhat sooner had this devious operation emerged as planned." For the first time, O'Brien recognized that as he had explained the timing and location of these weapons to General Austin several days earlier, he must have come to the same conclusion.

The general offered accommodations for the night in the base

VIP quarters, but O'Brien declined. "We'll have to sleep next week, General. We'll catch what we can on the flight. If we leave now, we can refuel at Westover, and be at Lakenheath by tomorrow morning."

"Right, son. I'll contact that old warhorse you answer to, and I'll have everything ready at Lakenheath when you arrive. As Austin relays it to me, Major, you've done a lot to begin to restore U.S. and New Zealand relations, even if they don't know it yet."

"General, I'm just along for the ride. Others have made the discoveries, and Mr. Hegarty is along to ascertain our good faith and establish our credibility with the prime minister."

By the time O'Brien landed in England the next morning, General Tolyan had reported to Austin the designation of the plutonium in the weapon and confirmed its Soviet origins. They had reminisced about their early unknown brush with death, and like most warriors had dismissed its relevance. "Bill, you've got a pretty good staffer in O'Brien, it seems. Humble kid," Tolyan said.

"I think he knows his worth, John, but he's got enough Kiwi in him to keep him humble. He might actually be the right combination of capability and aggressiveness as a Yank, and quiet confidence and humility as a Kiwi. His father is an impressive man. Were you aware his father is a retired U.S. Army colonel who took the 'Medal' out of Vietnam?"

"No, Bill. Good stock, eh?"

"The best, but let's keep him in the dark about that for awhile," Austin joked.

Turning back to business, General Tolyan concluded his remarks. "We'd better hope we can pick up two more of these monsters in England and Spain."

"Yea, but I'm not holding my breath, John."

Lakenheath, England
September

Arriving at Lakenheath Air Force Base reminded O'Brien of his Irish holiday only eight months ago. They had spent some time in London as well, but he had not gotten as far north as Lakenheath, about ninety miles north-northeast of London. Once again, they were met by local military commanders, and in addition, both Special Branch of Scotland Yard and Special Air Service (SAS) Captain Scott.

They were escorted to the base commander's office, where they were informed that the local police had advised them that the site they were interested in had been excavated only five days earlier. Given the recent retrieval, it had been decided not to visit the site with a complete crew as had been done in Japan and Omaha. The terrorists might still be in the area, and they didn't want to alert them that the authorities were aware of the contents of the site. A quiet couple had strolled through the cemetery with a hidden Geiger counter, which once again registered remaining traces of radioactivity. The Chief Inspector from Special Branch informed O'Brien that an investigation had begun and they were in the process of tracing the movements of the "remains." The usual thorough methods of tracking known terrorists and unsavory characters were being followed, but the added precaution had been implemented to restrict those in the know to Special Branch and SAS personnel. Local police in each district were not involved at this time.

O'Brien requested time with the wing commander and the base commander, Hegarty and the chief inspector from Scotland Yard. Once they were alone, O'Brien informed the group of the original intent of the plan. It seemed logical to conclude that while the Soviets or Russians were most likely not involved any more, the purpose of the explosion had been the same: humiliate the United States and cause removal of weapons. Therefore, concentrating the search near U.S. facilities that had nuclear weapons stored would produce the most likely results. O'Brien tactfully but strongly recommended to each military commander that they not issue a full-scale alert, which might scare off the terrorists and leave their weapon available for another day. They were in agreement, and as the meeting concluded, Captain Scott, British SAS, was introduced to his American counterpart with whom his team would conduct searches of the area around the American bases.

O'Brien called General Austin, who was fully aware of the developments. Together they decided it was imperative to get to

Spain immediately. They were only days behind the group, and they might get in front this time, as they apparently had in the U.S. General Austin said it seemed clear that the group was recovering all weapons from their original sites. Major O'Brien noted that the terrorists might be racing to recover the last weapon if they had found the Omaha grave excavated, which would have tipped them off that the authorities were on to them. With only one more site to visit, time was running out, and now they had at least one nuclear weapon missing and potentially targeted.

Rota, Spain
September

The Spanish grave had been excavated thirteen days earlier, they were told. Without the ability to control the situation as well as they could in England, they returned to Lakenheath and offered the full assistance of the military to the SAS and the Special Branch of the British police. It was appreciated, they were told, but too much attention drawn to the investigation would hamper their ability to ferret underground for information. Some facts had turned up, and they were following up on some clues. The chief inspector said he personally would brief Mr. Jameson, who decided to remain in London at the embassy.

With nothing more to accomplish, O'Brien returned to Washington with Dan Hegarty, who spent the next three days being shown the operation at the National Security Agency. From the New Zealand Embassy, Hegarty made contact with the prime minister, who by now had come to believe the Americans had been telling the truth about *Cherokee.* They were all, unfortunately, unable to issue press releases or make the facts known, since two weapons of mass destruction were still missing. Silent Wind still had life.

Tunis, Tunisia
September

Flying high over the Mediterranean, Hamil Aziz, leader of the Palestinian organization, had a lot on his mind. In the past week, he had concluded a tentative peace accord with the Israeli foreign minister, met with several heads of state to obtain their commitment for financial support for the new Palestinian state, and met with President Eastman in the United States. But perhaps most significant and certainly the most dangerous, he had shaken hands with the Israeli prime minister on worldwide television. He knew that gave comfort and a more secure feeling to most of the world's leaders that some accord had been or would be reached, but he also knew, for those dedicated to the annihilation of the Jewish state, as he had been for most of his life, it meant trouble.

Aziz had been in the forefront of the struggle against the establishment of Jews in Palestine as far back as he could remember. The multiple wars over the years had been helpful for bringing the cause of the Palestinians to world attention, but in each case, the Israelis had merely solidified their position further by defeating the attackers and actually taking more territory in the process. The war Aziz had been involved in had never ended; in fact, it was continuing to this day in spite of his changed directions. By day and by night, clandestine actions had been his stock in trade. Trading hit-and-run attacks with the Israelis had been costly, but there were always dedicated, or perhaps fanatical, young men willing to trade their lives for the restoration of their homeland.

Actually, throughout history, what better motivation had existed? Recovery of one's homeland was paramount to all peoples when they felt they had been deprived of such ownership. It seemed, however, that the Palestinians could not understand that the Jews saw it the same way and felt they had, from their perspective, historical records to prove their claim, in the form of the Bible.

Whatever the strategy, it had become clear to Aziz that eradication of the Zionists would not happen through six-man raids into Israel and blowing up school buses to make their point. Now that the agreement had been reached with the Israelis, and generous funding had been promised by those neighboring nations wanting some stability, he had only to convince the hard-liners in his own organization of the merits of the plan.

The plane began its descent for Tunis, where he would be met by loyal followers. They planned to coordinate for several days and then meet with some of the various factions to try to obtain their support for the new accords. It was not an enviable task, and one which seemed more formidable than dealing with the opposition. There was an air of having sold out that did not sit well with Aziz, for all things considered, even his enemies had seen him to be an honorable man who had strongly believed in his cause and had been prepared on many occasions to die for it.

They taxied to a private part of the airport where three black cars waited for his party. Aziz climbed into the lead car, which left immediately, followed by the other two. Outside the airport, the three cars played leapfrog for several miles, until it was not certain to anyone watching which car contained Aziz. These maneuvers had been a part of his ritual forever, it seemed to him. He didn't even take notice of them anymore. Five miles from the airport they approached road construction, which caused them to slow down somewhat from the rapid movement favored by security personnel. Aziz glanced up from his papers to notice the construction equipment lined up silently alongside the road, without any workmen present. Curious for a midweek, he thought, but perhaps a work stoppage had occurred in his absence. He certainly had not had time to keep up on local news these past three weeks.

The entourage rounded a bend and began to accelerate as they came to the end of the construction. In the lead car, the front-seat passenger turned to view the following cars. The line of barrels marking the construction route, painted orange, had kept the two lanes of traffic separate for the past two miles, although traffic was extremely light this morning. Looking forward, the security guard in the lead car saw the remaining barriers coming to an end. His car passed the barrels until about twenty from the end, he saw a single green barrel, watching it closely until his car passed and the second car approached. In his hand he held what looked like a small transistor radio, with the small antennae extended.

Aziz looked up again, seeing the end of the construction approaching, the rows of orange barrels sliding past his window.

He casually glimpsed the single green barrel as it approached the front of his car. He felt the car rise first, before he heard the report of the explosion, and then it was black. When the car came to rest on its back, the three occupants were all dead, killed almost instantly by the intense explosion, saving them from the agony of the now-burning car.

The other two cars stopped immediately, the occupants jumping out to see what they could do to rescue their leader. The front-seat passenger security guard from the first car was also out immediately, running in the direction of Aziz's car. In his hand was an Uzi submachine gun, the transistor radio now gone. Many other assassination attempts had been made on Aziz over the years, but he had always been protected by the loyalty of his followers. From their perspective, they were still loyal, not to Aziz but to the cause for which so many of their brothers had given their lives. Aziz had raised money to promote the founding of the new homeland, much more than they had been able to raise, but the funding they had been promised was more important. It was guaranteed for the support of their continuing cause. It was for the eradication and elimination of the Zionists. A worthy cause indeed, they thought, and one to which they remained loyal.

Braintree, England
September

Try as they might, they had been unable to deter Princess Diana from attending the fair with Prince William. Prince Harry had not been scheduled to attend and was remaining at home. The chief inspector had counseled with Her Highness's security people, who were only too glad to cancel her appearance, but she would have none of it. She usually got her way when she insisted.

Two days before, O'Brien had been notified, as had Hegarty in New Zealand, and they had flown over for the final part of the search. British SAS had discovered the location of the terrorist team in a small abandoned farm house near Braintree, some distance from the community of Mildenhall and the American Air Force base that they had surmised would be the target. Several men had come and gone during the time they had been observing, and they were hoping to catch them all together and complete the capture. Princess Diana's insistence on attending the fair had put a crimp in that plan. There were not going to allow Prince William to place himself in danger, and so they had scheduled the raid for dawn the day before the fair.

The chief inspector and Captain Scott, SAS, had reasoned that the weapon probably would not be armed if they did not intend to use it until the next day. However, it could also be at another location, and from the pattern of coming and going, not all of the men would be present when they raided. They had counted five, all totaled, and at the moment three were in the house.

In the late evening hours they began to surround the house. Major O'Brien and Dan Hegarty were present in an observer role. The unknowns were considered. How many men they would face was defined, but whether the weapon was in place was unknown, as was its status should it be there. Utmost caution had been instructed, and the usual pattern of quick entry, stun grenades, and shooting to kill anyone not on the insertion team had been modified. If possible, they would try to take the terrorists alive. Standing by was a nuke ops team from the U.S. air base should their luck hold and the weapon be recovered.

At 0415, six SAS were in place at front and rear entrances, with side windows covered by additional SAS troops. Inside, two men slept, and the third was reading as the assault began. Captain Scott entered through the front door and immediately found himself face-to-face with the first terrorist, who dived for his pistol. Scott put two rounds through his forehead by instinct, and even though his weapon had a silencer, that was the signal for the remainder of the SAS insertion team to enter. The two sleeping terrorists opened their eyes to discover six SAS men, faces covered in gas masks and goggles staring down at them, motioning for them to turn over and lie face down. The assault was over in less than ninety seconds, with two men in custody and one dead. No injuries occurred to the assault team, and the "contained" signal was given. The U.S. Air Force major in charge of the nuke ops team entered the house with his team and began a room search for the weapon, which was discovered in the basement, unarmed and awaiting final assembly. In three more hours, Gregory Farnsworth-Jones was due to arrive to complete assembly and prepare the timer, as he had on the *Kamitsu Maru* several months earlier. Without the telephone call from the occupants, now in custody, he would never arrive. Before daylight, the nuke ops team had the weapon removed, and the SAS had the terrorist group in a secure detention facility under questioning. O'Brien was on the phone to General Austin advising him of three down, one to go. Silent Wind still had life, but for now they had thwarted the plan to extend the retribution to England, and with the two terrorists in custody, perhaps they could learn more about the nature of the fourth target.

Prince William and his mother attended the fair the next day, oblivious to the nature of the threat, and the twenty-two thousand people who decided to attend the fair were able to peacefully return to their homes, ignorant of the fate others had planned for them that day.

CHAPTER SEVENTEEN

───────────

Wellington, New Zealand
The Beehive
October

DAN HEGARTY HAD AN APPOINTMENT with the prime minister this morning to brief him on what the New Zealand press had named "The *Northland* Issue." He knew the truth now, and soon the prime minister would also, and of course those military leaders in positions that required their understanding. But the press could not be advised of the discoveries until the remaining weapon had been recovered, and that might not be such an easy task.

As he waited, Admiral Sir Trevor Pottsdam, chief, New Zealand Defence Forces, entered the foyer just as the prime minister's secretary rose. "Admiral Pottsdam, Mr. Hegarty, the prime minister will see you now," she said pleasantly. They entered Onekawa's office, Hegarty deferring to Admiral Pottsdam. Prime Minister Onekawa came out from behind his desk to greet them. "Good morning gentlemen. Dan, I've invited Sir Trevor to sit in as you brief me, so that he can decide what action, if any, is necessary to put this issue to rest. Please be so kind as to fill us in on your trip."

"Thank you, Prime Minister." Turning to the admiral, Hegarty acknowledged his presence with a slight nod. "Good morning, Admiral. During the past week I have traveled with Major O'Brien to each of the four sites listed on Sir Geoffrey's report. I should indicate here, Prime Minister, that Major O'Brien was in touch with my office nearly two days before the report from Sir Geoffrey arrived. I think they advised us immediately after they discovered the issue. In summary, I believe Major O'Brien's statement that the *Cherokee* was clean."

Onekawa spoke up. "Yes, Dan, Sir Geoffrey told me he felt the Americans were on to the same information and intended to act on it. The Russian ambassador knew the Americans would know shortly, but he still wanted to go through Sir Geoffrey."

Hegarty continued, "In Japan the weapon was, of course, gone. We discovered intact the placement in Nebraska, but both England and Spain contained recently excavated graves. The British Special Branch conducted a quiet investigation, and as you know, they were successful in recovering the weapon and capturing two of the terrorists. The Spanish authorities were less cooperative, and we have some concerns about recovering that weapon. It most likely is out of the country by now."

Onekawa turned to the admiral and asked, "Admiral, what is the feeling in the Forces at present?"

"Prime Minister, the upper echelon is aware of the facts as we know them, at least our belief that the Americans did not have a weapon on board the *Cherokee*. Even with our limited knowledge of applied nuclear physics in a military environment, we know the type of explosion that occurred does not happen because a ship fire consumed an unactivated nuclear weapon. However, the ratings are still grumbling about the Yanks and their know-it-all attitude. Once the situation is cleared up, and we can present the story, it will sort itself out."

"Dan," Prime Minister Onekawa said, "will Special Branch

continue to accept our involvement and keep us informed if they find out anything from the terrorists?"

"They've been pretty good so far, Prime Minister, but actually we are getting most of our current reports from O'Brien and his office at the National Security Agency. Special Branch has kept them fully up to date."

"I see. How were the *Cherokee* and *Northland* approached without any concern on their part?"

"We've pieced it together as best we can from the information at hand. A Japanese freighter, the *Kamitsu Maru,* brought the weapon from Japan in a normal load of cargo for New Zealand firms. Sometime before their arrival, a small group of terrorists disguised as businessmen on holiday chartered a local Auckland yacht, the *Triple Diamond,* for a two-week pleasure cruise. It was outfitted for ocean travel and could be sailed by a single crew member as well. We have talked with the owner, who confirms the charter and the capabilities of the yacht. The *Kamitsu Maru* put back to sea supposedly bound for Western Samoa. The next time anyone heard from her was under her new name *Emiliano Zapata* when she was captured in a drug raid off San Diego. What we think happened is that the *Kamitsu Maru* met the yacht *Triple Diamond* at sea, lifted her out of the water, and took her down near where she could be in the path of the *Cherokee* and *Northland.* A Lear jet tracked the navy ships just prior to the rendezvous to coordinate the course. Then as *Triple Diamond* met the naval vessels, she either radioed for assistance or simply approached, and before they knew they were in danger, someone detonated the weapon. We believe *Triple Diamond* sent the false radio signals prior to the detonation. Some of the events may have transpired differently since no evidence remains from any of the vessels, but that scenario covers the most likely events."

"Good, Dan. You're satisfied that O'Brien has been straight with you?"

"Yes, Prime Minister, I believe he was quite embarrassed by the event and the position it placed him in regarding his dual citizenship. This reconciliation was important to him. That's why his boss, General Austin, placed him in charge of the project."

"Yes, I can understand. I'm pleased your evaluation was positive. Please keep me abreast, Dan, and also advise the admiral if anything new develops. Oh, and Dan, please pass our appreciation on to O'Brien. I'll be in touch with President Eastman shortly."

"Certainly, Prime Minister."

Woodbridge, Virginia
October

"Hello, O'Brien residence," a young female voice said.

"Hello. Is your father home, please?"

"Yes, he is. May I tell him who's calling?"

"Cameron Rossiter, from New Zealand."

Pat placed the receiver on the kitchen counter and went to the stairs. "Dad," she hollered up the stairs, "it's for you. New Zealand."

"Thanks, Pat," Zach replied. "I'll take it up here. Please hang up the other phone."

"Hello, this is Major O'Brien."

"Lieutenant Rossiter, here, sir," Cameron said, sounding very formal. "You have been ordered to report to the island of Kauai, state of Hawaii, for training exercises during the week surrounding New Zealand's Labor Day. Are you able to arrange suitable transportation and time commitments, sir? Accommodations have been arranged for you and your wife."

"Who dares, wins, right?"

"Absolutely. How about it, can you and Alison join me and Michelle next week in Hawaii for a brief bit of well-earned R&R? I understand you've rounded up all the 'caskets' you can find and now it's a waiting game."

"Do I have twenty-four hours to accept these unanticipated orders, Lieutenant?"

"Certainly, sir. We'll await your reply. Hope you can make it. Michelle suggested it and thought it would be a great time to just kick back and relax."

"Sounds magnificent. I'll call you tomorrow, same time."

"Roger, Major," Cameron said, continuing the military charade. "Talk to you then."

Zach hung up the phone and walked down toward the bathroom where Alison was bathing four-year-old Kate. Standing in the doorway, he watched Alison wipe the splashed water from her brow and try to keep Kate still long enough to dry her off. Alison noticed Zach in the doorway, just smiling at her. "What?" she said, curious and knowing Zach's funny smile.

"You look haggard and tired, Alison. I think you need a rest."

"What?" Alison said, confused.

Kauai, Hawaii
October

"Zach, this is magnificent," Alison said. The condominium was lovely at the Pona Kai Resort on the outer island of Kauai. As Zach and Alison drove their rented car into the parking area, he followed the signs for the 'check in' office. After asking for the Rossiter cabin, they drove toward the beach, and in the last row of individual cabanas, they found number five.

Zach turned into a parking space, and as Alison was getting out of the car, Michelle came running out of the cabana with a broad smile on her face. "Isn't it lovely here, Alison? We're going to have a ball."

Alison pushed her sunglasses up on her head and embraced Michelle warmly, the two women holding each other for several moments, allowing unspoken appreciation to exchange through expressed affection. "It's so good to have you and Zach with us, Alison," Michelle offered. Cameron was only a few moments behind Michelle, giving Alison another hug and whispering in her ear, not allowing the others to hear.

Behind the car, taking the luggage out of the trunk, Zach watched the greetings, feeling pleased that it was obvious Alison's letters to Michelle had made them fast friends. "Excuse me, madam," he said to Alison, "will that be all, or will my services be required any longer?"

With a laugh, Cameron said, "Feeling a bit left out, are we, old chap? What say, ladies, shall we let him stay for a while and see if he can make himself useful?"

Alison, literally beaming at the unexpected joy of the reunion, took two steps to Zach, reached up, and kissed his cheek. "I think we might find him quite useful. Quite useful, indeed. Let's keep him."

With that, Michelle stepped to Zach and also gave him a hug and a kiss. "If ever this lady tires of you, Zach, I understand you have excellent credentials as husband and father, and I'm sure we could find someone to give you shelter."

"Well, I can see I'll have to keep my wits up this week. It looks like three to one at the start." He smiled, lifting two suitcases and moving toward the cabana.

Walking on the beach that evening, all four carried on a bantering conversation without any serious issues, merely content to be in each other's company once again. Once in the cabana, Cameron reminded Zach to set the alarm for five fifteen. "What?" cried Zach. "I'm on vacation!"

"Right you are, Zach. And it starts tomorrow on the first tee at the Princeville Oceans golf course, about forty minutes north of here at six-thirty. Absolutely magnificent views of the ocean, mountains, and Hawaii at its best, and then later in the week we'll try the new Jack Nicklaus course at the Sheraton, also among the top golf courses in the world. Surely you didn't think my talent was limited to yachts?"

"What about the girls?"

"That little round, bright, and warm ball that comes up in the East and goes down in the West will keep them company on the sand, twenty yards away from the cabana. We've been in winter for four months, and Michelle is dying to change the color of her skin for a while. How about Alison?" he asked.

"Oh yeah. She likes to bask in the sun also. OK, you're on. See you at five fifteen," Zach replied.

The next day, Cameron found himself quite surprised at Zach's golf skill, and Zach eventually took him two and one in a match play setup. Cameron had gotten ahead one hole early in the game, but Zach was playing with rented clubs and hadn't found their feel yet. It was, as Cameron had said, a beautiful course. Only once during the round did anything substantial arise in their conversation, when Cameron offered his appreciation for the written communication between Alison and Michelle. "It really has been what she's needed to see things from a different perspective," Cameron commented.

"In your opinion, Cameron," Zach asked, "what's at the heart of her concern?"

Cameron thought for a few moments, selecting an eight iron in the process for his approach shot on the fourteenth. After placing the ball about twenty feet from the pin, he climbed back in the cart and drove toward Zach's ball. "In summary, without going over most of the background which you probably know from her letters, she has three basic fears. First, the men she has loved, father and brother, both died young, leaving a void where most people have a support structure throughout their lives. That she has to deal with internally. Second, she has to come to terms with what it was that changed her mother so much. That one she's been able to shut away and reject because she didn't need it to live. She's now coming to understand that she needs to address that issue and find out what it was, and that brings us to the third fear. Since she and I have contemplated a marriage and life together, she has asked me to investigate your religion with her, in quest of her mother's reasoning. I think she just wanted some support initially, but now she's reasoned it out. Three things can happen. Both of us think it's hogwash." Cameron paused, embarrassed by his phrasing about Zach's religion. "Pardon the expression, Zach."

Zach just smiled. "Go on."

"That would be no problem, because it would leave us where we are now and would eliminate the question she had about her mother. They just had different views, both quite acceptable. The second possibility is that we both find it's wonderful, as you and Alison do. That also is great, because it gives us both a new value system to appreciate and a common direction."

Zach began to nod his head. "I can see where this is leading— the root of all Michelle's fear."

"Correct," Cameron nodded. "Perhaps only one of us will find it acceptable, and she will repeat what happened to her mother's marriage."

On the fourteenth green, Zach lined up his twenty-one foot downhill putt and stroked the ball, watching it curve through the break, angling toward the hole while Cameron's eyes grew bigger, since they were even in their match through the thirteenth. The ball brushed the edge of the cup, gently fell toward the hole and picked up momentum from the centrifugal force, lipping out after running the full rim of the cup, and returning toward Zach to stop four inches from its destination, having traversed the distance and returned toward its owner.

"Man," Cameron exclaimed, "that was a heart stopper. But," he said, beaming confidently, "I'm still alive with four to go." Zach birdied fifteen and seventeen to take both holes, finishing two up with one to go, and Cameron graciously conceded defeat.

Driving home, Zach put closure on the issue. "Will you risk the multiple outcomes by having a look, Cameron?"

"I don't think we have a choice, Zach. Our life together will be clouded if we don't clear the air on this issue that's dogged Michelle's thoughts for so long."

"Right across the street from our resort . . . " Zach began.

"I know," Cameron replied. "We've seen it. We'd be happy to attend your church with you on Sunday." He smiled at Zach. "It's a place to start, I suppose."

"But you have a degree in child psychology," Michelle said as they lay on the warm sand in front of their cabana. "How can you let your career just go by?"

Alison smiled, having heard this question many times over the years from those who felt, or, more appropriately stated, who had been convinced by public sentiment and women's groups, that their lives were wasted staying home taking care of the house and kids. "One reason I took the degree program I did, Michelle, was to assure myself that it could be put to use both as a profession when that seemed appropriate and as a mother each and every day. It's very helpful. We could talk about it for hours, but I think an article I read in *Readers Digest* years ago went right to the heart of the matter."

Michelle rolled over to "brown" the other side for a while, sipping on her drink and adjusting the hat to shield the sun from her eyes. "Tell on, teacher," she said humorously.

"A woman who had earned her MBA from some Eastern university and had entered the corporate world was doing quite well and rising toward middle management, with a bright career ahead. But the biological urge to have children came, and she convinced herself that she could do both. She had the baby, missing only about six weeks of work, and then returned to work, her mother taking care of her daughter during the day. All went fine for a while. Then when the daughter was about three, the woman's mother died, and she had to start looking for another child care situation.

She went about it in the same methodical manner she had learned to pursue at work. Investigate this, evaluate that, and so on. She listed the things she wanted to give her daughter—coaching, vocabulary growth, environmental concern, values like hers—and all the things we want to teach our children to make them like us, or hopefully better. Michelle, she came to the conclusion that the child care offered was just that, child care, not nurturing. Her conclusions, using all of her skill as a managerial analyst, were simple. All the elements needed for the maximum potential growth of her child, mentally and physically, could only be provided by the person who cared for her the most: her mother! She betrayed her women's movement, at least in their eyes, and her female friends at work were astonished when she resigned, but she reached the decision regarding what was important to her."

Alison reached for her drink and sat up to put more suntan lotion on her lighter skin. Michelle also sat up, and they watched out on the water for a while as the surfers and boaties went about their playtime, taking in the good life that Hawaii has in such abundance.

"However," Alison added, "never think I am saying that one

must choose, because I believe it is possible to do both if the support structure is available. I teach slow-learning kids in the elementary school two afternoons a week, when Kate is in pre-school. I hope never to lose what I have learned and to be able to put it to use in a practical, professional situation. But, and this is quite important to me, our children are the more important of the two, and should I be required to choose, they would come first."

Michelle thought for a moment before responding. "My mother was always home when we got there," she said almost as an afterthought. "Yet, she was and still is as professional a businesswoman as I know." Only the sound of the ocean and the children playing down the beach interrupted their thoughts. "Alison," Michelle started, "could . . . I mean, did Mum's church teachings . . . " She paused, trying to formulate the question developing in her mind. "I mean, could her new beliefs have . . . "

Michelle looked at Alison, who was gently smiling, saying nothing. Softly and knowledgeably, Alison just nodded her head in agreement and smiled at Michelle. "It's a value that we all hold most important, Michelle. If your mother had the skills you say, and they were recognized as such by others, she nevertheless saw her children—you, Michelle," she added for emphasis, "as more important than her own progress. Perhaps today she is not as far ahead as she could have been, but," and she paused to let Michelle race ahead with the conclusive thought, "you are!"

The week went all too quickly for both couples. Golf, luaus at the hotel, guided tours to the Grand Canyon of Hawaii, including a visit to the spot where Captain James Cook had visited the Sandwich Islands, the name by which Hawaii was known for several centuries, and of course simply lying on the beach and doing nothing at all. Two days before their week was up, they returned to the main island and toured the facilities there. Pearl Harbor was an emotional experience for Zach as he contemplated those who had, as had happened so often in the course of history, given their lives that fatal morning in 1941 for the freedom of their brothers. It always moved Zach to visualize the sacrifice that people made so that their fellow humans could continue in freedom. A wonderful day was spent at the Polynesian Cultural Center, two hours from Honolulu, and that evening at the airport, they went their separate ways, vowing to consider this an annual opportunity to recharge their batteries.

At church the previous Sunday, Cameron and Michelle had been quiet, and during the vacation no pressure was applied to their investigation. Zach felt certain, however, that circumstances allowing, Cameron would bring this issue to a head to free Michelle of the bonds her fears and anger had placed upon her. For himself, Cameron felt that if these values had the ability to unify one marriage and sever another, they were worth investigation. Something was there, good or bad, and he was determined to discover what it was. In the meantime, the O'Briens were good friends, and he felt certain that would not change even if he and Michelle investigated and rejected their spiritual values. It was clearly important to Zach and Alison, but they had given no indication of judgment regarding the possible acceptance or rejection by Cameron and Michelle. That made it all the more intriguing.

Baghdad, Iraq
Military Headquarters
October

General Alihambra did not look forward to telling His Excellency of the failure of the English incident. No matter how many successes, only one failure was often enough to end one's career. And the end of one's career in Iraq meant the end of one's life.

Abdul Salimar, Supreme Leader of the Iraqi people, arrived at the remote site by helicopter. Alihambra was waiting. They were to inspect units of the Republican Guard and to discuss with the battalion command their particular mission. Alihambra had decided to complete the inspection before advising Salimar of the turn of events.

Colonel Wadi greeted General Alihambra, and they both waited for the helicopter with His Excellency, visible in the distance. As soon as the craft set down, Salimar departed the aircraft, and Alihambra and Wadi saluted. "Greetings, Excellency," Alihambra offered. As usual, he could detect no emotion or intent in the Leader's face, and he wondered if perhaps he already knew of the failure.

"Colonel," Salimar said as he strode toward the vehicles, "do you understand the nature of your assignment?"

"Yes, Excellency. The 212th Battalion of the Republican Guard will conduct this exercise in preparation for future assignments. We are to develop a plan to assault, capture, and hold the imaginary oil pipeline, including a pumping station and sections of the pipeline five kilometers on either side of the station. We are to hold until relieved or ordered forward. My company commanders understand, Excellency."

"Good. Show me!"

As Salimar watched, the forward elements of the 212th Battalion began a mock assault on the facilities chosen to represent an oil-pumping station. Throughout the army, Salimar had personally visited with units to observe their understanding of their particular assignments in this war-games scenario he had been formulating. Commanders knew the nature of their assignments, and none were ignorant of the intended purposes, but as yet no one had spoken aloud of the venture, beyond the theoretical. It was an exercise, but one in which His Excellency took a personal interest. Therefore, it was important. The fact that these exercises had increased significantly immediately following the American withdrawal from the region and the Persian Gulf missed no one's attention. They were building up again, and it wasn't to bluster. Iraq was on the move, and they all felt certain the "coalition" would not be reformed this time. Besides, they would not repeat their mistake of moving too slowly and not far enough. This time, Iraq would succeed.

As the battalion completed its mock assault assignments and Salimar grunted his approval, General Alihambra broached the subject of the English incident. "Excellency, the English venture has resulted in the capture of the item and two of the three men by the SAS. Wyndham was not among them." He waited for response.

"Wyndham is free?"

"Yes, Excellency."

"He has served his usefulness, General," Salimar said with a look that indicated his meaning.

"I will see to it, Your Excellency," Alihambra said, wondering when the time would come when he too had served his usefulness.

General Alihambra would immediately set about to remove Mr. Wyndham, alias Farnsworth-Jones, but he would be too late, for others also had learned of his part in this venture, and they would play their hand sooner. Alihambra would take credit, however, as the story was relayed to Abdul Salimar. One never missed an opportunity to take credit for successful assignments, nor failed to divert blame when possible. Team play was not considered a virtue.

Chapter Eighteen

Washington, D.C.
National Security Agency
November

MEETING WITH HIS STAFF, Major Zachariah Daniel O'Brien had come to the conclusion that he had a great team. Their combined skills and background had been exactly what he had been looking for when he reviewed several hundred personnel files to staff this office. General Austin had instructed him to develop a team capable of considering each perspective, as the Office of Strategic Analysis, National Security Agency, would be called upon to provide contingency plans independent of the Pentagon, who would, of course, be preparing their own. It did not endear O'Brien to the JCS staff when their plans or conclusions did not concur with NSA conclusions. Each office had been required to support its conclusions. O'Brien didn't actually mind his ideas being reviewed by others whose job it was to discredit them. Someone in an enemy headquarters would be responsible for the same job:

find the flaws in his plans. He believed that the final product would be a better one, and someone further up the chain than he would be able to pull together the best of each effort. The American serviceman would be the beneficiary, and one life saved was certainly worth someone's plan being revised.

Captain Shelley Molloy was the cultural expert and regional geographer. She had taken a doctorate in political science with a Middle Eastern specialty from Yale. Her contribution was invaluable to the brain trust side of the equation. Captain John Francis Murphy was an experienced recon Marine who had commanded a company during Desert Storm and who had a perspective of the final assault and the foot soldiers' requirements. Added to his master's degree in Middle Eastern languages, he provided a perspective necessary to any team preparing contingency plans for an operation in the Persian Gulf. His relationship with Molloy, who generally looked upon foot soldiers the way computer nerds looked at football players, had developed as he had rewritten several of her computer analysis programs and had improved their output.

And then there was Savini, the brash, young Italian fighter pilot. Vincento Savini had surprised them all when O'Brien had brought him onto the team. Twenty-seven years old, qualified naval aviator, flying F-14 Tomcats, with one kill to his credit in Desert Storm and the cockiness expected. What had floored them all was the revelation, several months after his arrival, that he had taken a law degree from NYU in the top five percent of his class. What was a law graduate doing flying fighters? No one had really gotten a satisfactory answer yet, but they kept trying.

O'Brien was pleased with his team. For the past several weeks they had been working on the contingency plan the president had directed General Austin to prepare. It had already gone through several iterations. Austin was not the kind of general who took other people's work and bucked it up the line with his signature on it. Staff did much of the slog, but he had imprinted his mark on the entire plan, and O'Brien felt that Austin had every right to claim it as his own work. The direction Austin had provided had clearly marked the final product, and shortly they would be briefing the national security advisor, Clarene Prescott, prior to making a presentation to the president. Time was running out, O'Brien felt. Iraq would not miss this window of opportunity. If only they could find the fourth weapon, they could openly identify to the world the original plan and erase this stigma of negligence remaining from the *Cherokee*. In the meantime however, they had to proceed with hands tied. The American military had been there before, O'Brien recalled.

New York City
United Nations Building
November

"Ah, good morning, Ambassador, how nice to see you this morning," Sir Geoffrey smiled at the Russian ambassador as they entered the General Assembly floor.

"And a fine morning to you too, Sir Geoffrey. How are the Kiwis this day?"

"We are well, Ambassador. Having found the pleasures of a New York hot dog to my liking, I have taken the occasion to sample several others, equally tasty. There is one yet, I'm told, available only in *Spanish* Harlem that rivals the street vendors. It's hard to locate one, but I must seek it out at the first available opportunity."

"If you're not careful, Sir Geoffrey, they'll make a New Yorker out of you before long."

"The Americans are a most forgiving and tolerant people, Ambassador, allowing each to retain his own identity. However, one can only tolerate so many hot dogs before the taste is gone and the appetite wanes."

"I fully understand, Sir Geoffrey. A good day to you, sir."

Sir Geoffrey moved quickly to his seat, having delivered his appreciation and the necessary information. Diplomats worked in strange ways, it seemed, again bringing to mind Sir Geoffrey's favorite quote, of his own origin: "Seldom do the purposes for decisions conform with the reasons presented." It seemed to parallel the present situation.

London, England
November

Gregory Farnsworth-Jones left his office fully intent on spending the weekend on the southern coast, relaxing with friends. Since the loss of the Mildenhall weapon, he had felt some concern that the British authorities would be able to track him, but he had been careful never to deal directly with the field team. On those brief occasions when he had met with them, he had been disguised and had used his Stephen Wyndham alias. He was beginning to actually feel safe, although he might have some problem with Alihambra regarding the payment he had received. Even if he had to return some of the money, he had been well paid for his efforts.

In the car park, several people were moving toward their vehicles, hurrying to end their workweek. A young couple were preparing to enter their car, parked next to his, and the woman was having some trouble with her portable pram. As he moved past her to enter his car, she brushed the folding pram up against his leg, pinching his calf in the process, inflicting a small stab of pain. She offered her sincere apologies, and he helped her place the pram in the trunk of her car. As he drove from the car park, the young couple drove off in the opposite direction. Clumsy woman, he thought, and no baby as well.

As he drove home, he lowered the window, feeling somewhat hot, even though it was November. The perspiration began to form on his brow, and by the last intersection before his street, had he not known the way, he would have noticed that he was unable to focus enough to read the street sign. In the house, he started to change clothes, preparing to shower and head off for the rendezvous with his friends. Perhaps if I just lie down for a moment, this dizziness will fade, he thought. Why am I suddenly so hot? That flu virus has finally gotten me, and on the weekend too.

Lying still on the bed, resting, Gregory Farnsworth-Jones left the cares and concerns of his workweek behind him. Over the next two hours, he left all other cares behind him as he slowly departed this earth for that journey all make eventually. He had much to answer for at his next stop. His housekeeper found him there, Monday morning, dead of heart failure according to the coroner, time of death approximately two days earlier. One might have hoped that Silent Wind had claimed its final victim, but Farnsworth-Jones had only been the messenger of death, as had the young couple with the pram, from the Russian embassy. A new architect now had possession of the last vestige of the original plan, and this architect equaled several other historical figures in the destructive scope of his plans.

Baghdad, Iraq
November

Seventeen Generals had convened for the strategy session with Abdul Salimar. As November drew to a close, plans were being finalized for the exercise, tentatively scheduled for late December. No one actually had any remaining illusion that it was only an exercise, but the charade would continue as long as His Excellency declared it such.

General Alihambra outlined the roles each division would play and the coordinated efforts of their supporters, for this was to be a joint exercise, on several fronts at once. A grand scale this time, with far-reaching objectives. Again no one was under the illusion that once captured, such territory could be held against the forces that could be arrayed. But would they be arrayed again? And even if they were, it would be too late. If required to retreat, complete and utter destruction would follow them. When they had been required to depart Kuwait in '91, they had shown the world through hundreds of oil wells burning what devastation looked like. This time it would be thousands. That price would not be paid by the rescuers, and certainly Iraq would be able to negotiate a suitable ending this time. But still, coalition forces might not be able to be assembled again this time, and then . . .

CHAPTER NINETEEN

Washington, D.C.
White House Situation Room
December

PRESIDENT WILLIAM EASTMAN was seated at the head of the table. Around the table were several Cabinet officers, including the secretary of defense, and the secretaries of the Army, Navy, and the Air Force. The Joint Chiefs were present, along with senior officers of the CIA, the various military intelligence units, and Clarene Prescott, national security advisor to the president of the United States. Lieutenant General William Austin, deputy director of Intelligence, National Security Agency, was standing before the assembled group, prepared to deliver the opening remarks. Major Zachariah O'Brien was present, assisting General Austin with briefing materials.

"Mr. President, gentlemen," and turning towards Clarene Prescott, "Ambassador. All branches of the military service have contributed to the contingency plan we are about to review, and while not all are completely satisfied with the final product, it has achieved consensus as the most workable scenario available to us in light of current knowledge."

That was an understatement if ever there was one, the president thought. Eastman had been party to political bickering for many years while a senator from Florida and during his term as president, but no politician need take a back seat to posturing generals. Turf protection was sacrosanct to a far greater degree than division of labor was to union officials. It had truly amazed President Eastman that General Austin had been able to obtain any degree of consensus on this plan, for which Austin had given full marks to Major O'Brien. What happened, Eastman thought, between the time a young, brilliant officer like O'Brien had the ability to grasp the whole picture without parochial protection for his particular service, and the time they eventually became generals, scrapping tooth and nail for their particular plane or ship budget? It seemed if the Army had their way, the Navy would still be under canvas sail, and the Air Force would again be called the Army Air Corps. This attitude affected all the services, but Eastman had to admit, when they finally were up against it, they coalesced into one efficient fighting unit, as they had in Desert Shield/Storm in 1991. Perhaps Congress and the budget process were the only enemies they couldn't agree how to fight.

Austin continued, "Clearly from recent intelligence, Salimar is on the move again under the guise of routine maneuvers. He might be flexing his muscles to remind his neighbors who he is, but we do not have the liberty of assuming that degree of innocence. We have assumed, for the purposes of this contingency plan, several things: one, that Iraq will again move to recover territory they continue to feel is theirs; two, that we will receive urgent pleas for assistance from those countries so affected; and three, that coalition assistance will be much more difficult to acquire. We can also assume several other points. Namely, that they will not make the same mistakes they did last time by not moving fast enough to achieve their ultimate objectives. Remember, they were under the assumption last time that the United States would not move to counter their movement, and consequently they felt they had plenty of time to achieve their objectives. Also, to assure Arab support, they will do everything necessary to involve Israel, and the recent assassination of Hamil Aziz has left the PLO leaderless for the present. With no one recognized to talk for the Palestinians, the peace talks have halted. And finally, until information to the contrary occurs, we must assume that Iraq has possession of, or access to, the one remaining tactical-stage nuclear weapon. That makes them a formidable opponent regardless of how many tanks we destroyed in '91. If they have that weapon, gentlemen, make no mistake, they will not hesitate to use it!"

Austin waited for comment, and when none arose, he continued. "The contingency plans are in three phases: one, projected moves by Iraq; two, current disposition of our available units; and three, recommended countermoves in the event of action by Iraq." For ninety minutes, Austin outlined ground, air, and sea forces in their current configurations and proposed movements necessary to counteract any thrust by Iraq. "We have them at a disadvantage in several areas, gentlemen, but primarily in regards to their knowledge of our disposition. We have kept the chess pieces moving, and with Somalia, Bosnia, and other trouble spots, we have been able to keep rapid deployment forces at the ready. In summary, we could have a fairly stable defensive perimeter established around his forward thrust lines and control of the air within seventy-two hours of any attack. The scale of his attack would, of course, affect our ability to contain the advance. If there are any questions, we will now entertain them."

Several issues were discussed for the next fifteen minutes, but most in the room had already seen the draft paper on the contingency plans and were familiar with their particular roles.

President Eastman closed the meeting. "It would be my fervent hope that this has all been just an exercise to hone those skills which will never be brought to bear. I thank you, gentlemen and Ambassador Prescott, for your dedicated effort. This country stands where it does because of the dedication of those willing to serve its needs, and when necessary, as your predecessors have so often proven, to sacrifice all for freedom. Let's hope that we can partake of a joyous Christmas season with 'peace toward all.'"

As they all departed, Austin motioned for Major O'Brien to remain for a moment. "The president wishes to speak with you, Zach."

O'Brien wondered what the president wanted, but he was getting used to Eastman's surprises. When the others had left, only Eastman, Austin, Ambassador Prescott, and O'Brien remained.

"I have been informed of the results of your investigation, Major," Eastman said. "We, all of us, and to a greater extent your fellow citizens who will never know of your participation, are grateful. Upon the recommendation of General Austin and Ambassador Prescott, I have sent your name to the Senate for below-the-zone promotion to lieutenant colonel. Merry Christmas, Major," Eastman said, smiling.

"Thank you, Mr. President, thank you very much."

Walking back to his office, O'Brien expressed his appreciation to General Austin for his support.

"It's well deserved, Zach. What you've done is important, but I feel somehow that we will yet have much to do before it's over."

"I agree, General. Let's hope we can get through the holidays peacefully."

Woodbridge, Virginia
December

O'Brien arrived home from work exhausted but elated. He had spent several nonstop days preparing for the briefing General Austin had just given. It went well, he thought, as well as could be expected. Once again, in the background was the ever-present unspoken battle between air power and ground forces. The Air Force had felt in 1991 that if they had been given more time, they would have completed the job themselves, while senior Army commanders were certain that no enemy could be defeated until the ground troops had actually "taken" the objective. The argument would continue, for it presented no easy solution and changed with each battle situation.

O'Brien was home now, and Christmas was approaching. He

knew it was a dangerous time in the Middle East, but perhaps they would have a few weeks' reprieve. "How's the woman of the house?" he called out.

"Glad to see her man," Alison said as she came into the room. "And how is the president today?"

"Still juggling personalities and trying to keep everyone happy. The 'lead dog' constantly has someone nipping at his heels," O'Brien replied, continuing the president's analogy of several months earlier. "Any mail, Alison?"

"On the hall table, dear. I think you might like the Kiwi letter," she said, smiling broadly.

"Oh, something from Mom and Dad?" he asked, picking up the several letters and quickly sorting them for the foreign stamps. He found the letter but recognized it was not from his parents. It had an Auckland return address. "Looks like an announcement envelope," he commented out loud. "Well, I'll be darned. Somehow he overcame her fears, and now he's gonna bite the bullet. That's great, honey. I'm really happy for them."

Alison came and put her arms around his neck, kissing him softly. "I've spoken with Michelle twice in the past several weeks. She really loves Cameron but is so frightened of her losses. She said her mother told her it made no sense to lose him for fear she might lose him."

"I've told you before, Alison," he said, holding her face in his hands, "you should always listen to Kiwis. They have good sense."

"Yes, dear," she said condescendingly as she turned back toward the stove. "They've chosen late February. Think we might be able to go?"

"I'd like to," he mused. "Depends on current events."

"The world will never revolve around our needs, Zach. We should plan for it, and be prepared to back out if required."

"You're right. I suppose we could use my pay raise to pay for the trip."

"Your what?" Alison asked.

"My pay raise, darling. You know. That amount of money one makes as a result of career advancement for recognized performance."

"But you just had your annual pay raise in October with the new budget, small as it was."

"Yeah, you're right again. I guess I'd better call the president and tell him I've had my pay raise and he should withdraw my promotion from the Senate."

Alison turned from the stove and flashed a bright smile, glee written all over her face. "Oh, Zach. Really? Lieutenant Colonel O'Brien?"

"In the flesh, my dear, so treat me with respect, please."

"Then we can go to Auckland for the wedding?"

Once again Alison had won. "You make the advance reservations, and we'll tell Mom and Dad in the next letter."

Again Alison came over, stirring spoon in hand, with flour on her cheek, and put her arms around Zach's neck. "I thought we might call them tonight."

"That's one of the reasons why Mom loves you so much, Alison."

"And why do you love me so much," she teased, caressing his hair.

As Zach went into the lounge to read the remaining mail, Alison returned to the stove and continued preparing dinner, thinking about the kind things Michelle had said during their conversation. Alison wished them well, and she would do all she could to continue to respond to Michelle's questions about how she and Zach had achieved such a loving relationship. She began to hum the hymn she had been teaching the children last Sunday, "Love at Home." It wasn't hard to develop such a relationship, she thought, but it did require both parties' efforts. It pleased Alison that Michelle had the courage to tell her that she had recognized something different about her relationship with Zach. If it showed to others, it must be working.

Auckland, New Zealand
Papakura Army Camp
December

From thirty thousand feet, free-falling, Captain Joshua Armstrong could barely make out the army camp, south of Auckland. They had taken off in a Royal New Zealand Air Force Orion from the air force base at Whenuapai, north of Auckland, earlier in the day. His four five-man patrols were completing a week of training exercises prior to the Christmas break. This final movement, the HALO, or high-altitude, low-opening parachute jump, would complete the training cycle.

It was exhilarating to free-fall from thirty thousand feet, waiting to open the parachute and float the final several hundred feet into the target. Special insertion could be accomplished this way, with limited ability on the part of the enemy to observe the drop.

Captain Armstrong had been in the New Zealand Special Air Service unit for five years. SAS units worldwide were linked in a brotherhood of training and mission, which in recent years had been limited primarily to counterterrorist activities, such as the one the British 22nd Regiment had carried out on the Iranian terrorists holed up in the Iranian embassy in London in 1980. Two primary roles occupied the training of SAS troopers: Special Forces, which provided the capability of intelligence gathering in a military environment or battlefield situation, and Counter Terrorist, providing the training necessary to combat hostage situations, takeovers, hijackings, etc.

Since the Second World War, commando units of the British Commonwealth had carried out hit-and-run missions and formed small patrols to gather intelligence regarding the capability and disposition of the enemy. The Special Air Service had evolved from this background. New Zealand's SAS had experience in the Malayan jungle in the fifties, Thailand in the early sixties, Borneo in the midsixties, and Vietnam during the late sixties and early seventies. Their history was a proud one, as most elite military forces can claim. Within New Zealand, the political climate was generally peaceful, and the propensity for a hostage situation was limited; nevertheless, training continued and the New Zealand Special Air Service Group had maintained itself as an elite force, capable of being sent anywhere in the world on a moment's notice.

Captain Armstrong was particularly proud of his four five-man patrols. With the exception of a few relatively new men, they had worked together for several years. The Territorial Force, New Zealand's equivalent of the Army Reserve, which included an SAS component, augmented their ranks on occasion and could double their number if necessary in an emergency. Following this jump, the men would report back to Papakura Army Camp for several days' routine before slowing the pace for the Christmas holidays. Armstrong eagerly anticipated the break. Being in the field limited his fatherly opportunities, so he was looking forward to the time he would be able to spend with his wife and three children. Following the holidays, he was off for training in England. He would be attending a specialized course in England with the British 22nd SAS Regiment, which should prove invaluable.

CHAPTER TWENTY

Iraq–Saudi Arabia Border
January

AT 0200 ON THE MORNING OF THE 17TH, forward elements of the Iraqi army were being airlifted by helicopter to multiple sites along the Trans-Arabian Pipeline, intent on capturing oil facilities and pumping stations at Rafhah, Shu'bah, Qaysumah, Al Wahriah, and An Nu'ayrihah. Other elements, including armor remaining from the 1991 campaign, were pursuing a rapid thrust down the coastal highway, intent on capturing everything between the Iraqi border and the pipeline and securing all facilities in the triangle.

At Shu'bah, eight men were on station that morning. Seven were peacefully sleeping, and one was on watch at the control panel in the pumping station. At least, he was supposed to be on watch. It often became quite boring overnight watching the gauges that never seemed to move. Mohammed was reading a novel when he thought he heard the sound of a helicopter

approaching, but at this hour of the morning? Soon several helicopters were heard, and Mohammed stepped outside to see what
was going on. The first helicopter had landed and the six-man
team had disembarked, headed his way. He called out to them
before falling in a hail of bullets. Quickly and efficiently the first
helicopter team, followed by four more helicopters, left their
thirty-man assault unit in place, before returning to Iraq for their
next drop. The facility was secured as the teams went from room
to room rounding up the startled men, tying their hands behind
their back, and leading them out into the desert. Twenty minutes
later, the assault team returned alone.

Unit commander Captain Hamadi directed assignments to
secure the perimeter and establish mortar and automatic weapons
emplacements. Within two hours, the facility had been ringed
with explosives, and a defensive perimeter established. Captain
Hamadi reported Shu'bah secure.

Further to the east, Colonel Wadi commanded Operation
Bright Spear, a forward thrust that included the deepest penetra-
tion of the invasion plan and that was spearheaded by his own
212th Battalion of Republican Guard. He pushed his tank column
as hard as he could. They had to reach their objectives in the first
six hours, before clear daylight allowed Saudi aircraft to mark
their positions. As with Shu'bah, helicopter assault teams had
secured the facilities during the early hours of the attack, and
Colonel Wadi had the job of reinforcing and holding the captured
facility.

The 212th was headed for the control terminus on the coast
at Ras Tannurah, just north of Bahrain. Pipelines throughout the
region terminated there, and it served as the controlling facility
for the entire eastern region, including an offshore link to Abu
Shafah, an island loading station for oil tankers. An enormous
facility, Ras Tannurah processed over four hundred thousand
barrels of crude oil per day. It was the southernmost extent of
the planned invasion and, Colonel Wadi knew, impossible to
defend either from the air or sea, but his orders were specific.
His job was to hold until relieved, and he intended to do just
that.

His column had encountered virtually no resistance, and they had rolled steadily down the highway, making good time. They arrived just before dawn, having secured several other pumping facilities along the way. Wadi's command consisted of the 212th Republican Guard Battalion, two companies of infantry, and twenty-six Russian-built M-72 tanks. Other units under his command had dropped off at earlier facilities on the drive south.

Colonel Wadi directed the mining of the approaches to the facility at Ras Tannurah and the placing of explosives throughout the terminus. Ras Tannurah alone would burn for years should it become necessary to abandon the effort and retreat—a holocaust of untold proportions should the order come.

Iraq–Kuwait Border
South of Al Basrah
January

Republican Guard units had broken through the small border patrols, which offered virtually no resistance, and the Guard was now racing down the highway toward Kuwait City. Helicopter assault units had already landed in Kuwait City, and they had immediately captured the communications facilities, while additional special operations units had as their targets several officials of the government, members of the Royal Kuwaiti family.

Waking to the crashing sound of Iraqi troops, the foreign minister, Prince Rasheed, watched as his family members were gathered in their night clothes. They were blindfolded, had their hands tied behind their back, and were led away in the dark. Household servants were unceremoniously shot where they slept or when they came to offer assistance to the family.

The scene was repeated in approximately fifteen households throughout Kuwait City as senior government officials and their families were quickly rounded up and herded into trucks for transport to an unknown destination. Salimar had returned in vengeance.

Washington, D.C.
White House Situation Room
January

The first units involved in the invasion crossed the Iraqi border approximately 6:00 P.M. Washington time, on Saturday evening, 16 January. By 7:30 P.M., Lieutenant Colonel O'Brien had been notified and was driving north on I-95 toward his office, wondering how broadscale this assault would be. He arrived a few minutes before 8:00 P.M. to find General Austin already in place and O'Brien's staff beginning to arrive. He immediately went in to General Austin's office to get the latest information and found Austin heading out.

"Good you're here, Lieutenant Colonel. Leave word for your staff, and come with me. Tell them to relay any information to us in the White House Situation Room."

Arriving in the Situation Room, O'Brien acknowledged the presence of General Jones, Marine Corps commandant, and Admiral Fitzwilliams, chief of naval operations. Several Cabinet officers had arrived, including the secretary of defense. Neither Clarene Prescott, national security advisor, nor the president had arrived yet. The president was en route by helicopter from Camp David, and Ambassador Prescott was in California. She would not be back until the following morning via Air Force transportation being arranged.

Admiral Fitzwilliams was the senior officer present, and he began to brief those who had arrived. "What information we have is very sketchy and only about an hour old," he said. "The initial reports came in just after 6:20. The Saudis reported air action by Iraqi aircraft against their oil facilities below the border and in the northeastern corridor, coordinated with armor and infantry assaults. They have scrambled their air units to respond, but secondary reports indicate that the Iraqis have achieved a foothold. About fifteen minutes later, the Kuwaitis reported that both ground and air assault operations had commenced against the undefended positions in the north and west of Kuwait City. This looks like a joint effort to occupy both targets at the same time. It would seem that the Iraqis are not limiting their incursion to Kuwait this time."

General Austin started to ask a question just as the president entered the room, and everybody stood up. President Eastman moved to the head of the table and took his seat. "Gentlemen, it seems that our exercise several weeks ago will not be limited to the theoretical. Admiral, could you please bring me up to date?"

Admiral Fitzwilliams re-covered the ground he had provided for the small group. At the conclusion of his remarks, the president was beginning to ask a question when General Austin was called to the phone by one of the aides in the Situation Room. He placed his hand over the mouthpiece and interrupted the president, "Excuse me, Mr. President, I believe you should hear this first hand."

"Put in on the speaker, General Austin," Eastman said.

Austin replaced the receiver, and some static came over the speaker in the room. "This is the president, go ahead," Eastman said.

"Mr. President, this is Lieutenant General Tolyan, Strategic Air Command Headquarters. At 8:16 P.M. Washington time, we received advance warning from the Israelis that they were putting their defense forces on full alert and calling reserves to active duty immediately."

Silence prevailed for the next few moments as everyone considered the magnitude of the rapidly developing situation. The president spoke first, "General Tolyan, what actions have you initiated?"

"Mr. President, we have issued a DEFCON TWO at this stage. No signs of action appear to place U.S. forces in any immediate danger at present, but DEFCON TWO will put most of our bomber force in the air and enable us to evaluate the situation while they approach their turnaround points."

During the conversation between the president and General Tolyan, Admiral Fitzwilliams had gone to the telephone and was now back at his briefing position at the head of the table. The president continued, "Thank you, General. Keep us advised, and we'll maintain an open line." Turning to the growing group, as

General Cagney, Army chief of staff, had arrived, the president surveyed the room. "General Austin, which of our contingency operations would you feel most applies to the situation in which we find ourselves?"

"Mr. President, in all cases the initial moves are identical, and we can implement those immediately while giving ourselves the time to determine the specifics of the attack. We had already considered the possibility of Iraq launching a multipronged attack. The most pressing problem now, Mr. President, is how to prevent the Israelis from launching their own preemptive air strikes against Iraq. That would immediately escalate the event and potentially bring in some of the other Arab states on Iraq's side."

Turning to Fitzwilliams, the president nodded. "Admiral?"

"I fully concur with General Austin, Mr. President. It's a repeat of the 1990 intentions, but on a larger scale. Salimar will still want to involve Israel to gain the support of his neighbors. I have alerted our naval installations on Diego Garcia and in the Eastern Med and ordered the *Kennedy* to put to sea immediately, accompanied by her task force. Holding the Israelis in check will be the most important event to keep this from escalating beyond control."

The president noticed Colonel O'Brien whispering to General Austin and addressed them, "General Austin, what do you or Colonel O'Brien have to add?"

"Sir, Colonel O'Brien just mentioned that Salimar most likely has the fourth, and final, missing nuclear weapon. It is our opinion that Salimar will use this weapon as a political tool, sticking with conventional weapons, including perhaps the biological components we were concerned about in 1991, unless we force his hand."

"Yes . . . well," the president intoned, "convincing Israel to hold back if they know he has a nuclear weapon might not be so easy. They are famous for preemptive reasoning to eliminate their potential problems."

General Cagney spoke up, "Sir, the Israelis came quite close to using their tactical nuclear weapons in the Yom Kippur War in 1973. The Syrians had attacked them on the Golan Heights and had decisively beaten the Israelis early on. The Israeli defense force informed us that they were left with no choice but to use what they had code-named the 'Samson Option,' basically several nuclear drops on enemy positions, trying to force the U.S. to resupply their arms quickly. We resupplied them immediately."

"But they weren't imminently threatened with nuclear weapons that time, were they?" the president asked.

"No, sir. Still, they will require us to assure them of our total support if we are to stand any chance of getting them to hold off a preemptive strike," Cagney concluded.

The president rose to leave. "Perhaps I should call Prime Minister Rashorn immediately and see what their position is at present. Carry on, gentlemen. I don't think we'll be going home for a while." The president left to place a call to Prime Minister Rashorn, and Admiral Fitzwilliams continued to coordinate the meeting. Turning to Lieutenant Colonel O'Brien, General Austin leaned over and said, "This time Salimar didn't open with a pawn, did he? He drove straight out with his knights and his bishops. The chessboard is clearly in action now, Colonel. I think the Kiwis might like to be in on this one as we move our own chess pieces. What say you give them a call and invite them to the party?"

"My pleasure, General," O'Brien said as he rose to leave the room.

Over the next thirty minutes, the remaining members of the Joint Chiefs arrived, as did senior officials from the CIA and military intelligence agencies, until the Situation Room contained about thirty people, ten or twelve of whom were positioned around the conference table, with the rest updating map emplacements and manning communications. Information was beginning to flow fairly steadily at this point.

The president returned to the room, and again everyone stood or ceased what they were doing at the moment. "Gentlemen, I will be in and out of here for the immediate future, and I would appreciate it if everyone carried on with his duties in a normal manner—if, indeed, anything about this situation could be considered normal."

Admiral Fitzwilliams continued as senior officer, as the chairman of the Joint Chiefs had been on an inspection tour in Georgia, and no one expected him for several hours yet.

President Eastman advised the group regarding his talk with Prime Minister Rashorn. "The Israelis had been aware of the recent increase in troop movements but had not anticipated such a full assault. The prime minister assures me that they will not immediately retaliate, but if any action is detected against Israel, his people will be calling for blood, and his military will be leading the crowd. What the U.S. does is important to them, just like last time." Eastman turned to Admiral Fitzwilliams and motioned for him to continue.

"Mr. President, we have alerted all air forces within striking range. We will be able to obtain complete air supremacy within twenty-four to forty-eight hours, but the *Kennedy* is not going to be on site for about four days. With aerial refueling, she will be able to launch air strikes within about twelve hours, however. We also can deploy units from the European theater by refueling as well." The admiral turned to General Austin. "General, could you provide an overview of 'Desert Boomerang' for those who were not part of the original briefing? Please cover what actions will take place in each phase over the next several days."

Austin spoke as he rose, "Certainly, Admiral. Mr. President, gentlemen, our initial response is, to be air power, with which we can halt the advance of forces until we have ground forces in place. This phase can be brought to bear, as Admiral Fitzwilliams has indicated, almost immediately. From first reports, Iraq is going for the oil facilities. If I were planning their operation, I would have planned on immediately losing air supremacy, so my ground forces would have to take their objectives within twelve to twenty-four hours. That is quite possible given the close proximity of Saudi oil fields. We should assume that Iraq clearly knows they will be unable to hold the ground acquired in this assault. He probably is counting on one of two things. First, that perhaps we will be unable to reconvene the coalition forces and achieve some Arab unity to condemn this action. If I were Salimar, I wouldn't have counted on that. Secondly, he knows that we will remember what he did in 1991 during the retreat, and he only had access to limited oil fields at that time."

General Austin paused for a moment to briefly look through the contingency plans in front of him. "Mr. President, on page seventeen of Colonel O'Brien's report, later code-named 'Desert Boomerang,' you will find the option I believe is the primary thrust behind this invasion. With your permission, I suggest Colonel O'Brien brief us on his analysis in this area."

Eastman nodded his approval, and gave a small smile toward O'Brien, who rose to move to the head of the table.

"Thank you, General Austin. Mr. President, gentlemen. Over the past hour I have been reviewing the initial field reports and constructing a small area map of reported incursions. Salimar is clearly going for control of the oil fields, pumping stations, and the Trans-Arabian pipeline. In a nutshell, he intends to take the oil fields and hold them, daring us to take them back. We know what he is willing to do if we launch a ground attack to recover them, and air attack by us once he had occupied the facilities would achieve the same negative results. The strategy pointed out in Desert Boomerang is to capture as much as he can and negotiate his way back to what he wanted in the first place. If we disagree and try to force him out militarily, he torches the oil wells, hundreds more than he did last time. Again, if he can drag Israel into the battle, he will gain Arab support.

"The most important remaining issue is the distinct possibility that he has control of the remaining nuclear weapon from the Silent Wind plan. Considering the type of weapons we have recovered from the cemeteries, Salimar does not possess a delivery system to mobilize such a weapon. That limits him to physical placement and reduces the possibilities. However, we don't want to force his hand on that issue. If that premise is correct, the only immediate optional response from us is containment. That, in any event, would be the first objective.

"In 1990, we took about ten weeks to get most assets in place, a remarkable achievement. This plan calls for sufficient containment forces in place within four to six days, followed by logistical supplies. Elements of the 82nd Airborne have been retained in Somalia, along with two battalions of the First Marines. Two more battalions of Marines are with the fleet at Diego Garcia. The 101st Airborne we have had on exercise in Europe and peace-keeping missions in Bosnia. These lead elements can be in place within the next forty-eight hours, but they will only be supplied for about three days. Logistical support is available, and reloca-tion will begin immediately."

The president rose and moved to the large-scale map on the wall in front of the briefing table. Colonel O'Brien sat down, and the room was quiet for several minutes while the president just reviewed the map. He faced the group in the briefer's position. "How many times have we heard during various seminars and from educational institutions that 'those who do not learn from history are destined to repeat it'? Two years ago we had in one place the largest gathering of troops since June '44. We just didn't finish the job, did we? I guess Kennedy stood here and wondered whether the other guy would launch a nuclear strike first during the Cuban crisis."

Looking directly at each of the Joint Chiefs of Staff, Eastman was directive in his comments. "We have to outthink Salimar, gentlemen, and I need your assistance to do it." Addressing the secretary of state, he continued, "Arrange the contacts with all former coalition members, and let's see if we can restructure the former alliance. Admiral Fitzwilliams, implement the initial phase of Desert Boomerang, and I'll stay in touch with the Israelis. Thank you all, gentlemen. I believe we will earn our pay this week."

Indian Ocean
U.S. Naval Installation, Diego Garcia
January

Newly promoted Admiral Wilson Richards, until recently captain of the USS *Heritage,* had assumed command of Task Force Victor, with his flag aboard the *Kennedy.* The *Heritage* remained a key task-force vessel, along with thirteen other ships of the line. Task Force Victor had until now been assigned temporary duty at Diego Garcia and in close proximity in the Indian Ocean. Of the fourteen vessels assigned to the task force, six were at Diego Garcia, and eight were within six hours sailing. Two hours earlier, Admiral Richards had received a flash priority message from Admiral Fitzwilliams instructing him to proceed at flank speed to Station Zebra, a previously designated location identified in the plan for Desert Boomerang. Station Zebra was located at the southern entrance to the Persian Gulf, within quick striking range of Iraq. Admiral Richards had been there before.

Operational orders had been transmitted to all vessels of the task force to rendezvous en route for a commanders' conference. That would take place about nine hours hence. Richards was ready and had been ready for some time. His gut had told him Abdul Salimar would not hesitate to move once he had a clear path. The U.S. Navy's evacuation of the area some months earlier following worldwide political pressure had eaten at Admiral Richard's soul. It was Vietnam all over again, he thought. We had it won. Decisively. Then we gave it away, and more important, we were forced to leave with our tail between our legs. Yes, it was Vietnam all over again. Now it was time, once again, to call out the dogs of war and unleash the fury of U.S. air and naval power, something Richards firmly believed in. During the next several hours he would refine his battle plan according to constantly arriving information to his combat information center and then meet with his commanders.

Richards thought momentarily of Captain Bernard Johannsen and the new command USS *Cherokee* he had so deserved. Barney would have loved to be in on this one, but in his absence all commanders in Task Force Victor would remember. And Salimar was going to find it hard to forget as well.

Kuwait City, Kuwait
January

As General Alihambra walked into the room, the soldiers came to attention immediately. Five soldiers were in the room, wearing camouflage fatigues and rubber gloves. Scattered around the floor were electrical wires and rubber matting. Alihambra spoke to the captain in charge and, satisfied with his answer, glanced around the room once more before leaving. In the center of the room, three people, including Prince Rasheed, hung upside down from chains wrapped around their ankles, naked and blindfolded. Electrical wires were attached to their earlobes and chest. One of the three was unconscious.

The captain spoke to Prince Rasheed in the middle, "The General has asked about your accommodations, and whether you find everything to your satisfaction. He is pleased to be back in beautiful Kuwait. He regrets to inform you that you cannot be allowed to die, for you must serve as host to other visitors who will also come to enjoy your hospitality."

To his left, Rasheed's eighteen-year-old son hung silently, listening to the sounds and movement of which his blindfold denied view. On his right, Prince Rasheed's wife hung unconscious, unable to withstand the agony of her own torment and her awareness of the pain inflicted on her son. For five hours they had hung this way, occasionally being jolted with electricity to hasten their discomfort. The Iraqi captain knew their internal organs could not withstand this inverted position much longer or they would begin to hemorrhage internally and die. He would lower them soon, but for the moment he was content to seek the limit of their endurance.

CHAPTER TWENTY-ONE

Wellington, New Zealand
Headquarters, New Zealand Defence Forces
January

ADMIRAL SIR TREVOR POTTSDAM had convened the senior military officers from all branches of service for this meeting, after which the military had been requested to make recommendations to the prime minister about New Zealand participation in what the press had been calling "Gulf II." Admiral Pottsdam had little doubt about the military position, but he had requested a thorough analysis of the available capabilities, however small the contribution. Following the revelation concerning the origin of the weapon that had destroyed the *Northland,* Pottsdam was certain that each branch of service would want a piece of the action. He couldn't blame them, and he knew public support would be overwhelming, so the politicians would most likely agree.

General Douglas, Army chief of staff, Admiral Wilson, chief of naval operations, and Air Vice Marshall Young, Air Force chief, were present, along with representatives of certain special operations groups. At the request of the prime minister, Dan Hegarty, chief of security of the intelligence service, was also present. Admiral Pottsdam opened the meeting. "Gentlemen, I believe we've been here before on the same issue. Perhaps this time we will have the fortitude to see it through."

In 1991 New Zealand had contributed a medical detachment and some military transport aircraft to the coalition. With a total defense force of only eight thousand army personnel, four thousand air force, and four thousand navy, New Zealand was not in a position to add significantly to the numbers that had been sent, and this time was no different, apart from the desire to avenge the *Northland*. "I have received your written recommendations, gentlemen, and I believe we have consensus on the level of our participation in this effort. Today we will refine our recommendations to the prime minister. Bear in mind that whatever effort we mount must be available immediately and on site within the next seven days for land and air forces and as soon as possible should we decide to send a naval contingent."

Admiral Wilson, chief of naval operations, spoke. "Sir Trevor, the Navy respectfully submits that our participation is absolutely essential to the morale and welfare of the officers and ratings." With conviction in his voice, he continued, "Admiral, the men and women of the *Northland* deserve nothing less."

"Hear, hear" echoed around the table as the other service chiefs voiced their support for Admiral Wilson's plea.

Admiral Pottsdam nodded his understanding. "Your ardor is commendable, Paul, but can we respond in time?"

"Admiral, it's about a two-week trip for a frigate, but even if we arrive late for immediate action, we should be part of the joint effort." He continued, savoring the moment, "Fortunately, the *Southland* sailed nine days ago to participate with the Aussies in exercises in the Indian Ocean, west of Perth. That puts her within four days of the U.S. task force assembling north of Diego Garcia."

A soft murmur and some chuckles around the table followed Admiral Wilson's comments, and even Admiral Pottsdam found himself smiling at this information. "Paul, what a fortunate situation to find ourselves in, and how timely the joint exercise."

"Yes, Admiral," he said with a broad smile, "perhaps fortune is indeed on our side this time."

"More likely a crusty old warhorse with a nose for trouble," replied Pottsdam. "Right, then, let's outline our commitment. Air Force?"

Discussion continued until the New Zealand Defence Forces had prepared a recommendation for the prime minister consisting of one Army battalion, supported by light artillery, two squadrons of transport aircraft, the frigate HMNZS *Southland* from the Navy, and a joint service medical detachment as per the original deployment. Something near twenty percent of New Zealand Defence Forces were offered for commitment to Desert Boomerang, a greater commitment than any other country had provided in the previous engagement, and one worthy of the response necessary to honor the crew of HMNZS *Northland.*

"One other issue, gentlemen," Admiral Pottsdam continued, "the prime minister has spoken with President Eastman, who specifically invited New Zealand to participate in this venture. I have been contacted by Lieutenant General Austin, the president's national security advisor for intelligence. He requested we entertain a special request from President Eastman's original liaison, Major O'Brien. Actually, General Austin informed me that O'Brien had been promoted to lieutenant colonel. Dan Hegerty of SIS has worked with Colonel O'Brien and spoke with him this morning. Mr. Hegerty."

Hegarty rose from his position at the back of the room and walked to the head of the table with Admiral Pottsdam. "Gentlemen, the prime minister has asked that I make Colonel O'Brien's request in his absence. A special operations mission is anticipated sometime in the next several days or weeks, and O'Brien specifically feels that New Zealand should participate." Turning toward the left side of the room, Hegarty addressed a lieutenant colonel sitting quietly against the wall. He wore the distinctive sand-colored beret of the SAS. "Colonel Yorgasen."

Yorgasen had risen through the ranks of the SAS from his

earliest missions against the Indonesian Army in Borneo, followed by service in Vietnam. At his name, Colonel Yorgasen stood and responded, "Sir?"

"Colonel Yorgasen, Colonel O'Brien has requested the participation of the NZSAS—specifically, two five-man patrols prepared for immediate relocation to Bahrain in preparation for a direct-action mission to be determined later. Can your group field two teams immediately?"

Colonel Yorgasen stiffened and responded, "I'm afraid we couldn't possibly be ready, sir . . . in less than two hours," keeping a straight face as he said this.

Hegarty liked this man immediately, and he felt O'Brien would also. "Excellent, Colonel. With your permission, Admiral Pottsdam," and turning to the senior army officer, General Douglas, "and yours, sir, Colonel O'Brien has one other request: the voluntary recall of a Territorial Forces SAS officer, Lieutenant Cameron Rossiter. It was Rossiter's yacht, *Triple Diamond,* that was used to deliver the weapon to the *Cherokee* and the *Northland.* O'Brien feels Lieutenant Rossiter deserves in on the show."

Hegerty waited for their response. Admiral Pottsdam looked at Colonel Yorgasen and then General Douglas. Both men nodded their agreement, and Admiral Pottsdam moved to close the meeting. "Gentlemen, I believe that covers it. It has been nearly fifty years since we had a cause as just as this one. Godspeed to us all."

Washington, D.C.
White House Oval Office
January

"Clarene," the president addressed the national security advisor, "I wish this call were to Margaret Thatcher instead of John Blankenship. He's got difficult issues to deal with, just holding on to the reins of his office."

"Yes, Mr. President," replied Clarene Prescott. "But I believe he'll come through. He knows the impact of Britain remaining on the sidelines, in spite of their posture in Bosnia."

"Let's hope so. If Britain decides to sit this one out, we have no hope of bringing in the rest again."

The president's secretary buzzed through on his intercom. "Mr. President, the prime minister's secretary is putting the call through to him now."

"Thank you," he replied. "Well, here goes my pitch, Clarene."

After a brief pause, John Blankenship came on the line, "Hello, John, Bill Eastman here. How are things in the mother country?"

"Stressful, Mr. President, with the usual clamoring for change."

"Yes, the mandate never lasts past the first significant issue, does it? John, I'm sure you know the reason for my call. The gravity of the present situation demands that I get straight to the matter at hand. It appears as if the colonies are looking for assistance again. Can we count on Britain to lend her considerable weight to the effort?" Eastman smiled at Clarene Prescott. He knew his direct approach did not fit the general diplomatic pattern of oblique reference to what one wanted. He had previously discussed with her his feelings that such oblique inference was what had gotten them into the Gulf war initially because Abdul Salimar had misunderstood American intentions concerning his incursion into Kuwait.

Prime Minister Blankenship responded, "Bill, we have been discussing it with the ministers, of course, but a bit more time to consider seems appropriate."

Eastman recognized the equivocation in Blankenship's voice. It was akin to the "bandwagon" effect in politics. "Let's see what everyone else does" was the motto, and if it appeared a popular thing, jump on the bandwagon and pretend you were there first. "John, this certainly may drag on as these things have a tendency to do, but success or failure and the length of the effort will be determined in large part by how quickly we respond to curtail his advances, and most important, by what resolve we show again. Salimar is counting on our inability to reconvene the kind of support we did previously. Perhaps even more important, to keep the

Israelis from taking unilateral action, they must be assured that the West will do all it can to reverse this situation. If they move on their own, John . . . well, I need not tell you how that could escalate things." In an attempt to bring the issue home, Eastman added, "John, the Commonwealth family has been injured, as you know. And," referring to Prince Andrew's narrow escape, "it certainly came close to affecting the mother country in a most personal way. The Kiwis are prepared to do their bit, which considering their size, is a significant commitment. We need Britain, John, and we are asking for your support."

Prime Minister Blankenship was not used to such direct pressure, but Eastman felt it imperative to force an early decision.

"Mr. President, I will again discuss it with the Cabinet this afternoon. We will get back to you quickly."

"Thank you, John. My regards to your family." President Eastman replaced the receiver and turned to look out the window of his spacious office, contemplating the call. Clarene Prescott remained silent momentarily. Turning back to his desk, Eastman pressed the intercom to his secretary. "Jean, see if you can reach Margaret Thatcher for me, please."

Clarene's eyebrows went up, and then a smile crossed her face. "Going for help, Mr. President?"

"We need resolve, Clarene. Blankenship has it, but I think it needs a shove in the right direction. In any event, it can't hurt to ally our forces with strength, and whatever else people may think of Margaret Thatcher, she earned the title 'Iron Lady' for action, not equivocation."

Washington, D.C.
National Security Agency
January

For fifteen minutes Lieutenant Colonel O'Brien had been informing Austin of his meeting in New York with Sir Geoffrey Holden and Ambassador Haquim. O'Brien had gone to New York at the request of Sir Geoffrey and, at his request, had taken Mr. Jameson from the CIA.

General Austin couldn't believe what he was hearing.

Evidently the meeting, held quietly in a private residence, had produced the shocking revelation that Haquim wanted to defect, which had floored both O'Brien and Jameson.

"General, it's the break we need. He can provide a great deal of inside information, but he's scared to death. Justifiably, I might add."

"What did he say was his primary motivation?"

"He admitted Iraq's complicity in the *Cherokee* and *Northland* attack, and he was afraid that Salimar was planning on using the remaining weapon against Israel. He feels that his participation in such wholesale slaughter is not conscionable and that even his life was not worth continuing to support such a regime. General, I asked him why he had taken so long to reach this decision, since Salimar has been perpetrating horrendous acts for years. His answer surprised me and showed that he had been doing his homework on us as well."

"I don't understand," Austin said.

"He asked me if I was a religious man and what church I attended. By his response after I told him, I knew that he already knew the answer but that he intended to trap me in my own question. When I said I belonged to The Church of Jesus Christ of Latter-day Saints, he asked, 'Doesn't your church teach you to obey the laws of the rightfully installed government, regardless of your country of citizenship?'" O'Brien paused and shook his head. "He had me, General. He knew what I believed, and he was posing the question, 'At what point does one decide that his government has gone beyond the bounds of acceptability and that moral law overrides the government policy?' I've debated that issue many times in church as well. Haquim finally felt that point had been reached, and he acted."

"How did you leave it?" Austin asked.

"We finally convinced him to remain in his position at the U.N. until we could come up with a solution that would assure his safety. He still has a wife in Baghdad, and she is his greatest concern. General, I believe he can provide some significant insights and perhaps the answer to this dilemma. I have a couple of ideas but request your permission to do some background work first before presenting them for consideration."

"All right, Colonel. Be careful, Zach. From this point on, his life is quite literally in our hands, and Salimar wouldn't hesitate to end it if he felt Haquim a threat."

"Will do, sir. I'll be back with some answers in the next forty-eight hours."

Returning to his office, the first call placed was to General Jones, commandant of the Marine Corps. "Commandant's office, Master Gunnery Sergeant Winters speaking, sir."

"Sergeant Winters, this is Lieutenant Colonel O'Brien, National Security Agency. Would it be possible to speak with the general on a matter of some urgency?"

"Hold one, sir."

O'Brien made some penciled notes during the hold and asked his secretary to have Captain Murphy come in if he was available. Sergeant Winters came back on the line, "Colonel, I can put you through."

"Well, Colonel, I'm certain you didn't call to advise me of your well-deserved promotion. Perhaps you felt my offer of a place in the Corps with 'a few good men' was too good to pass up."

"General, I'm not sure my qualifications would suffice for the Corps, but I'm honored to have been considered. Actually, sir, I called to request a private meeting with you on a matter of urgency that is also time-sensitive. I need to take you up on your offer of assistance from the Corps. Would your schedule permit a meeting with me and Captain Murphy of my staff? You might recall, sir, Captain Murphy is my Middle East area specialist, as well as an experienced Marine recon company commander."

"Know all about Murphy, Colonel. Two-thirty this afternoon too late?"

"Excellent, sir. We'll be there."

As O'Brien completed the call, both Captain Murphy and Lieutenant Savini walked into his office. O'Brien smiled at Savini, who had the biggest grin anyone had seen in months.

Zach knew what was coming, but he had no intention of stealing Savini's thunder.

"Colonel," Lieutenant Savini said, "it is my duty to keep my personnel file correct and up to date, and therefore I request permission to add this insignificant document to its contents." He placed a single sheet of paper on O'Brien's desk, which O'Brien dutifully took to read. At the top were the words "Physical Profile, Change Form." The important information was located bottom center on the page and indicated that the flight surgeon had given Lieutenant Savini all "1s" in his physical profile, thereby signifying that he had recovered from his back injury and was returned to flight status.

"Congratulations, Lieutenant. Have you preflighted that 'DESK, METAL, 27X60,' to which you have been assigned?"

Savini realized that O'Brien had known of the outcome prior to his presentation, and his smile broadened. "No, Colonel, the desk is not flight worthy, but"—he made a long pause—"NAVPERS advises that a carrier, the USS *Rushmore,* is en route to the Persian Gulf and also assures me that I can join her in Spain before she transits the Suez Canal. Rumor has it that they have extremely flight-worthy F-14 Tomcats on board, waiting for some young 'Wiseguy' to dust off the seat. There's one hitch, Colonel."

O'Brien feigned surprise and looked at Captain Murphy. "Here it comes. Murphy. Are you in on this too?"

Captain Murphy put both hands in the air in mock surrender and said nothing.

"Let's have it, Savini."

"Colonel, the quick transfer requires commanding officer approval, and if you recommended approval, and General Austin concurred . . . "

"Lieutenant Savini," O'Brien said in a mock official tone, "please proceed to the desk of the deputy director, Intelligence, and check with his secretary, Alice. I believe she has some papers in her out basket for you, signed by one Lieutenant Colonel Zachariah O'Brien and by one Lieutenant General William Austin, requesting the immediate expulsion of one Lieutenant

Vincento Savini from the confines of his imprisonment at the National Security Agency.

"*Mamma mia,* fantastic, Colonel. *Grazie, grazie, grazie!*"

"Once is enough, Lieutenant." Reaching his hand out, O'Brien added, "Congratulations, Vinny. I think the aircraft carrier USS *Rushmore* could use 'Wiseguy' right now, perhaps more than we need you at the NSA. You'll be missed."

As Savini left to collect his marching orders, O'Brien came out from behind his desk, grabbed his hat from the coatrack, and looked at Captain Murphy. "John, you're not quite so lucky. All I could arrange for you was a personal meeting with the commandant of the Marine Corps right after lunch. Get your hat. The good news is, I'll buy you lunch on the way."

This time Murphy was astonished and once again held his hands up in surrender, this time for real. It was not often a lowly Marine captain met the commandant and left with his skin in place.

Washington, D.C., the Pentagon
Office of the Commandant of the U.S. Marine Corps
January

Master Gunnery Sergeant Winters stood and came to attention as O'Brien entered the office. "Lieutenant Colonel O'Brien and Captain Murphy to see the commandant."

"The commandant is expecting you, sir. Please be seated, and I'll let him know you're here." Sergeant Winters went to the door, knocked, and entered, returning in a few seconds. "Please step this way, gentlemen. Would either of you like coffee? The commandant will be having a fresh cup."

O'Brien appreciated the way in which Sergeant Winters advised them of the general's preferences. O'Brien didn't drink coffee, but it was a no-no to order a cup if the senior officer being visited didn't also participate. Captain Murphy responded, "I'll have a cup, but the colonel will pass." Murphy had been working with O'Brien for nearly two years and knew his preferences.

Entering the office, General Jones came out from behind his desk to greet them. As in the president's office, O'Brien was awed by the man. His reputation belied the fact that he was most gracious, treating O'Brien with courtesy. His office was a museum of military paraphernalia. A tattered Japanese rising sun flag hung from one wall, and below it on the credenza was a Japanese ceremonial sword. A Vietnamese peasant hat, conical in shape, rested on one table. O'Brien felt that by walking around the room, he could probably trace the history of the Marine Corps, at least since 1942.

General Jones grasped O'Brien's hand in his paw, or so it felt to O'Brien. "Welcome, Colonel O'Brien. It's good to have you visit." Moving to Murphy, who was standing as straight as he could, General Jones also shook his hand. Continuing to clasp the hand, the general looked into Captain Murphy's eyes for a quiet moment and said, "It's a pleasure to meet you, Captain. I'm pleased to see you're wearing your Silver Star."

Taken aback, Murphy stammered, "Thank you, General. It's . . . ah, the men deserve the credit actually."

"Don't they always? Nevertheless, don't make light of the awards your country sees fit to present to her fighting men. Too many of them didn't live to see the results of their actions. Spending twenty-seven days behind enemy lines gathering intelligence data was quite a feat. Be proud of your deeds, son."

"Yes, sir, General." Murphy actually blushed a little at the comment and instantly decided he would follow this man anywhere. How had he so quickly discovered his part in Desert Shield? Murphy wondered.

"Be seated, gentlemen," Jones said. "Colonel, how can the Marine Corps be of service to the NSA?"

"Thank you, General, for meeting so quickly with us. General Jones, I would like to request the assignment of two small recon squads, about six men each, one for primary and one for backup. The mission would entail immediate movement to Bahrain where we would train, at least to the extent we understand the mission, and be instantly available for the mission when the word comes. I have two New Zealand SAS action squads en route already. This operation will entail one Kiwi and one U.S. squad, a total of about fifteen men.

General, I am not at liberty to share the nature and source of the information to be provided, but we have a direct line to someone who will be aware of Abdul Salimar's movements, and we intend to be in place at the right time when informed. The mission has General Austin's approval, but he has limited the dissemination of information for reasons I am certain you will understand. Until this moment, I have not advised Captain Murphy of why we are here, but I would like him to lead the recon team. Overall mission responsibility will be placed with the Kiwi commander, again for reasons we cannot discuss. Truly, sir, I am sorry for the direct request without much background, but it is essential to the mission to include this unit."

"No apologies necessary, Colonel. I've gone blind before, and probably will again. Captain Murphy, as you know, all recon missions of this nature are volunteer. Are you prepared on the spot to make that decision?"

"I trust Colonel O'Brien, General. I'm ready."

"Good man, Captain," Jones commented. "And you, Colonel O'Brien?"

Smiling, O'Brien replied "Yes, sir, I'll be along for the ride. That's why I require Captain Murphy so badly. I need him to bring me out alive."

General Jones stood, at which both visitors instantly took to their feet. Jones looked at Captain Murphy. "Do you know the men you want, Captain?"

"Yes, sir. I could form two squads," Murphy replied.

"Inform Sergeant Winters, and he'll cut the orders. And Captain, bring this 'wing wiper' back alive. There aren't many men outside of the Corps I find worthy of merit, but I've gotten attached to this young fellow." With a wink at Murphy, he added, "He can't be blamed if, in the ignorance of his youth, he chose to attend the wrong military academy, can he?"

Turning toward O'Brien, General Jeremiah Jones, commandant of the Marine Corps and Medal of Honor winner at the age of sixteen, extended his hand again for O'Brien's, grasping it firmly, "*Semper fi,* Colonel O'Brien, *semper fi.*"

Woodbridge, Virginia
January

When Zach arrived home, Alison was gone with the kids to a skating party arranged by the church. Zach went upstairs and showered, thinking constantly about how he was going to tell Alison and the kids that he had to go away again for a while.

He heard the garage door closing as he was getting dressed, and then a little voice as four-year-old Kate ran up the stairs: "Dad, I skated around the entire rink without falling!"

"Well, come and tell me all about it," he said, picking her up in his arms and starting back down the stairs. Spying Alison, Zach walked toward her and gave her a kiss. "Good activity?" he asked.

"The usual," she replied. "Tommy Jackson teasing all the girls and Millie acting the fool. Youth activities would be great if we could jump all the kids from twelve to sixteen and skip the years in between."

Zach grinned.

"Have you eaten?" Alison queried.

"Grabbed a sandwich at the shop on the corner as I left work. I knew you would be out. I'm fine, thanks anyway." He paused and set Kate down. "Maybe some . . . " he silently mouthed the words *ice cream,* "after bedtime."

"What? What are you going to have after we go to bed, Daddy?" Kate asked.

Alison smiled. "If you'd whispered, 'We'll do the dishes after bedtime,' she would never have heard a thing."

"Right," Zach said. "Alison, I'd like to call a family council this evening, for just a few minutes."

She looked at him inquisitively, and then at the grandfather clock in the hall. "Better get going then. It's almost bedtime for Kate and Michael."

In the family room, the kids gathered around on the floor, and Alison busied herself sorting clothes from the day's washing, while sitting on the couch.

"I have a family issue to discuss with everyone," Zach started. "First, does anyone have any family business?"

All were quiet. Monday evening was the normal family business meeting, just prior to family home evening, where each took their turn planning a home-centered activity.

"OK. You're all aware of how late I've been working each evening for the past week or so. I apologize for that and especially to you, Pat, for missing your school band concert."

"It's OK, Dad," Pat said, all adultish, "I know you would have come if you could."

Zach smiled at his oldest daughter and winked at her. "Right, Pat. Everyone is going to have to chip in with chores again for a while. I'll be going away for a couple of weeks the day after tomorrow, and I'm not certain when I'll be back, but I'll try to stay in touch whenever I can." He glanced at Alison, who continued folding clothes and maintained a composed look on her face. She could be so stoic, Zach thought, and hard to read sometimes.

"Where are you going?" Michael asked.

"Just to another military base, Michael. I can't say exactly. In fact, I don't know exactly," he said truthfully.

"All the soldiers are going to Iraq again. Are you going with them?" Michael continued.

"All the soldiers have important jobs, Michael, and they'll miss their families also."

Pat joined in the inquisition, allowing Alison to keep in the background. "The news said we had to fight the Iraqis again, Dad. Will you be in danger?"

"Lots of good soldiers, men and women, will be there to support each other, Pat. We always try to keep danger to a minimum." Zach was cornered now, and he had to extricate himself gracefully without alarming his family. He knew that one of two things would happen when the kids went to bed and he and Alison were alone. She would be quietly angry at his decision to participate in the operation, or . . .

"Dad has responsibility for lots of soldiers, and it is important for them to know that he cares about them and believes in what they're doing. His place is with his men," Alison said to the kids softly. "Do you understand that? He loves us very much and does everything he can to protect us."

Michael jumped up, startling everyone with his abruptness. "I don't care," he exclaimed. "I don't want Dad to love us."

Pat and even little Kate's eyes opened wide.

"Why ever not, Michael?" Alison said. "You know Dad loves you."

"Yeah, and Jesus had to die because he loved me too," he cried, running out of the room.

Zach stood and started to follow Michael, then stopped to turn back to the girls. "Michael's just upset. He knows I love all of you. Don't worry about him—he'll be fine."

With eye contact, Alison suggested that Zach go to Michael and that she would take care of the girls.

Zach knocked on Michael's door, opening it slowly, and found Michael on his bed, playing with a transformer robot. "Can I come in?" he asked. Zach sat down on the side of Michael's bed. "Which robot do we have here?" he asked.

"GobaTron," Michael replied.

"Michael, I understand your fears. I have fears too. You know I could never stop loving you, don't you?" Michael was silent, continuing to fiddle with his robot.

"Michael, do you remember when we talked about the stripling warriors? They all went off to war, and the Lord protected them, didn't he?" When Michael didn't respond, Zach persisted, "Didn't he, Michael?"

Finally, Michael slowly nodded his head.

"Jesus came to earth specifically for the purpose of saving us. He knew when he came that he would die for us. That's not my mission, Michael. I will do everything I can to return to my family. I love you like Jesus loves us, but I don't have to die for you like he did. Do you understand that?"

Michael slowly looked up at his dad. "Will you take GobaTron with you, Dad? He always wins."

Zach smiled, reaching for the robot. "Yes, Michael, I'll be glad to take GobaTron with me. Will you do something for me? Will you give me a hug big enough to last for the next couple of weeks?"

Michael raised up on his knees on the bed and slowly put his arms around his dad's neck. "I love you, Dad," he said.

With glistening eyes, Zach held his son close and spoke into his ear. "I know you do, Michael. And I love you. Always."

After the kids were asleep, Alison returned to the bedroom, coming up behind Zach while he was brushing his teeth. "It's OK if you love *me,* Colonel O'Brien," she said, putting her arms around him from behind and looking at him in the side mirror. "Come home to us safely, darling. We all love you and need you."

Zach turned, toothbrush in hand, and held her close for the longest moment without another sound between them.

Baghdad, Iraq
Military Headquarters
January

Three Air Force generals were gathered around the table while His Excellency presented his desires, or, more appropriately, his demands. "When you advised me to ground our aircraft during the last campaign to avoid having them blown out of the sky by American and British air power, they did little good to our cause, did they not? If aircraft sit on the ground, we might as well not have them. You will follow the plan I have outlined, and you will succeed. Is that understood?"

All acknowledged their agreement verbally and with nodded affirmation. Who was brave, or perhaps foolish enough, to question the Leader? The fact that two of the generals present at this meeting had not been generals merely three years ago during the first Gulf war was evidence enough to them that changes came swiftly to those who did not succeed. The earlier generals had, in fact, not been seen or heard from since shortly after the war, but no questions had been asked regarding their whereabouts.

Salimar continued, "I want every aircraft necessary for the success of this mission assigned immediately. Timing is absolutely critical. You must arrive at the appointed hour, or our advantage will be lost. I don't care how many aircraft come back. If they are not successful, I want *none* back. *Do you understand?*"

"We will succeed, Excellency."

"Good, see to it."

CHAPTER TWENTY-TWO

Suez Canal, Egypt
USS Rushmore
February

STANDING AT THE RAILING of the USS *Rushmore,* Lieutenant Vincento Savini knew that this was where he belonged. Three days earlier, he had caught the mail courier from the coast of Spain as *Rushmore* had traversed the Straits of Gibraltar, and then he had reported in to the commander of the air group. One more Tomcat driver aboard. Following his check ride, he had obtained full flight status once again and been assigned to the "Black Diamond" F-14 squadron. His squadron leader was pleased to have a Gulf war combat veteran in the crew, and he had been assigned flight leader, responsible for four Tomcats.

Sailing through the Eastern Med, Vinny knew that they were nearing the battle zone once again. Tomorrow morning they would transit the Suez Canal, and after that, it was all go. Combat patrols, ground-support missions, and the exhilaration that goes with supersonic speed and instant decisions. "Wiseguy" was home.

Yet what was it that bothered him? Feelings not present before plagued Vinny as he stood looking out at the evening sky. In Desert Storm, Vinny had been the first in his squadron to bring down a MIG, in fact, one of only two they got. The rest of the vaunted Iraqi Air Force flew to Iran and were impounded by their former enemy. In that earlier engagement, Vinny had acted on instinct really, and the elation he felt had buoyed his spirits for weeks. He loved the quiet adulation of his fellow pilots, most of whom, like him, were young and impressionable. Their esteem had carried him through the remainder of the air war and had also impressed his commanders, who always looked for leadership qualities. If one's peers looked up to you, then something could be gained by giving responsibility to that person, and so Vinny had been given flight leader status and other unassigned leadership roles, all of which he accepted. But he was still bothered by something.

At NSA he was part of the "Irish Mafia." What would they call themselves now that he was gone? he wondered. The Irish Mafia had constantly tried to get him to talk about his law degree and his leaving it all to become a pilot. As friendly as he was with others, few made it inside Vincento Savini. His law degree meant nothing to him. It had been obtained at the insistence of his father as a rite of passage, something akin to "take out the garbage and finish your homework before you go out to play ball," a chore to be accomplished before life started. Well, he had satisfied his father and had taken top honors in his class, graduating in the top five percent. That, Vinny had told himself, would get the "old man" off his back.

His father hadn't known about his acceptance of a commission in the Navy until he showed up in uniform one evening, the last evening that Vinny had seen his father. He'd been thrown out amid a tirade of verbal abuse about wasting his life and the hardearned lessons his father had tried to pass on to him. The Navy had become his family after that, and a good family it was too.

His peers treated him as an equal, and to some, a leader. For the first time in his life, Vinny felt, what was it . . . wanted!

But something was still wrong. Almost a year earlier while on routine patrol over Iraq, flying off the *Enterprise,* Vinny had been shot down in one of those rare episodes that Salimar had orchestrated to keep tensions up. He could recall the trail of the missile as it sought him and literally chased him all over the sky—like his father had chased him when he was young, and he had run to avoid the stern lesson his father intended to teach him. And like his father, the missile had caught him. He and his radar intercept operator had successfully ejected, but the memory was seared into his mind. He would never forget the sight of that missile coming at him as long as he lived.

In the recesses of his heart Vinny knew what was wrong but didn't want to let it out. The Navy had trained him, spending hundreds of thousands of dollars to put him at the controls of a multimillion dollar aircraft, and now as flight leader that responsibility was tripled with three other pilots and aircraft under his charge. Vinny had those qualities the Navy looked for in its officers. He had courage and leadership ability, he was responsible, he understood duty and commitment, and since that day over northern Iraq he had added one more element. He had added fear!

Before dawn, the *Rushmore* prepared to enter the Suez Canal. Security was tight. Advance helicopter gunships would patrol the banks of both sides of the waterway to spot terrorists or potential trouble, and the USS *Puyallup,* a missile-equipped destroyer, would take up defensive duty at the mouth of the Canal. The Suez wasn't long, but maneuverability was impossible during this phase of the transit. An aircraft carrier was about the largest ship able to transit the Canal. Vinny and his flight were assigned northern patrol, remaining out over the Mediterranean to prevent attack from the sea, while other aircraft would guard additional sectors of the passage.

Ninety minutes later, *Rushmore* was well into the Canal, and four F-14s under Vinny's command were out over the sea on patrol. An E-2C Hawkeye was overhead with radar control.

Skyhawk had been tracking a flight of Syrian aircraft for the previous half hour and the Israeli response. This feint, designed to approach but not cross the Israeli border, had been diversionary to alert Israeli aircraft and draw American attention away from the Iraqi mission, even now skimming the wave tops of the Mediterranean Sea after crossing low across Syria.

"Bluebird Leader, this is Skyhawk. We have four bogies approaching from the west on two seven five degrees, range sixty miles."

"Roger, Skyhawk, will investigate. Bluebird out," replied Vinny. They turned west toward Libya to investigate the intruders and immediately picked them up on their Hughes AWG-9 weapons control system. Closing in on the four aircraft at a speed of over nine hundred miles per hour, Vinny picked up the missile launch as fast as Skyhawk could transmit.

"Bluebird flight, we have missile launch, I say again, we have missile launch. Arm and engage," Vinny instructed his flight. They were not yet in visual range, but Vinny could feel the adrenaline beginning to pump through his system. "Fight or flee" was what the medics had told him. The body's natural reaction to danger provided the added boost to do either, depending on the makeup of the individual. Vinny had always fought, but what now?

Without thought, his instincts took over, and he began to track the incoming missiles and search for a target. Instantly his fire-control system found and locked onto an incoming aircraft. The inbound missiles had not targeted his aircraft, and he maneuvered to make his shot. Free of the necessity of evasive action, he launched two Sidewinders at the target and watched as they both impacted, destroying the target. He could see his wingman also engage, taking out one other intruder. The remaining two aircraft turned immediately and ran.

"Skyhawk, this is Bluebird. We have two, repeat two splashed, with no friendly damage."

"Roger, Bluebird. Skyhawk confirms two bogies down."

Still unobserved, the Iraqi aircraft approaching from the north were at wave-top level and eighty miles distant. Forty miles had been the order. Get within forty miles and launch. All twenty-eight of the French Mirages carried Exocet missiles, with an effective range of forty-five miles, one of the most feared by naval vessels. The USS *Stark* was witness to the power of an Exocet, as was the British Destroyer HMS *Sheffield* during the Falklands war.

In the first Gulf war, Salimar had not used his air force to any extent, the reason still not being clear except the knowledge that it was no match for allied air power. This time he had decided it was as useful blown out of the sky as it was being safe on the ground, and he had ordered one massive strike. His capture of all assigned targets prior to intervention of U.S. air power made him bolder. If they struck back, he would ignite the Middle East with an inferno never before seen. This air strike was to be bold, imaginative, and foolhardy. He knew it could cost him most of his air force, but only one Exocet had to get through while the *Rushmore* was in the Canal, and that was possible no matter how strong the opponent. It was an odds-on gamble.

"Bluebird, Skyhawk. We have twenty-eight, I repeat, twenty-eight inbound bogies north and east of your location." Vinny knew instantly the feint from the west had been to draw them off. They went to afterburner and came back east to defend the mouth of the Canal. Elements of his squadron came from east and west of the carrier, but caution required retaining some aircraft for protection in case this approach was also diversionary and another attacking force came from another direction.

"Skyhawk, we have them on scope. Engaging now." Vinny had bagged one bogie on the diversionary run, but his thoughts were not on how many kills he had but the helplessness of the *Rushmore* in the confined spaces of the Canal. If it was hit there . . .

At forty-five miles from target, the twenty-eight Mirages gained altitude and almost simultaneously launched twenty-eight French-made Exocet missiles. Bluebird flight was closing, as well as four Tomcats from the east bank of the Canal and their assigned patrol zone. The Tomcat's weapons control system is capable of tracking twenty-four targets and initiating attacks on six of the intruders at the same time. The human element could never achieve that degree of complexity.

As soon as the Exocets were launched, the primary target became the missiles rather than the attacking aircraft, all of whom had turned immediately upon release. Each Exocet carried three-hundred-and-sixty-pound blast fragmentation warheads and traveled at just under Mach 1. They would travel the forty miles from launch to the *Rushmore* in just over three minutes. Launch from the USS *Puyallup* was immediate, and forty-eight SM2–E standard missiles were fired, targeted on the Exocets.

The threat was real and immediate. Vinny was aware it had come from the sector he had been assigned to protect. His flight of four Tomcats had targeted and locked onto incoming Exocets and had launched their Sidewinders to intercept. All totaled, nearly one hundred missiles had been fired against the incoming threat of twenty-eight Exocets, but targeting from multiple defensive systems, many had locked onto the same Exocet, and so, while all defensive missiles had targets assigned, not all incoming Exocets had been accounted for in the barrage. This was what Abdul Salimar had counted on. Two Exocets passed the interception point and were six miles out when the anti-aircraft systems on the *Rushmore* came into effect. Approaching directly from the rear, flying south down the Suez Canal toward the tail of USS *Rushmore,* one final Exocet was downed, but the missile from Iraqi Captain Shamir's Mirage cleared all fire and impacted the *Rushmore* directly below the flight deck, resulting in a massive fire below the rear deck and crippling the rudder control mechanism. USS *Rushmore* slowly moved off course and pushed her way up into the west bank of the Canal, thereby blocking passage of any other vessel for the indefinite future. Salimar had gambled and won against the most powerful navy in the world.

Auckland, New Zealand
February

Rossiter's secretary, Jenny, walked into his office and announced the arrival of his visitors. "Mr. Rossiter, a Mr. Hegarty and a Colonel Yorgasen are here to see you."

Rossiter didn't know Mr. Hegarty, but he certainly knew the name Colonel Yorgasen. What could they want? he wondered. "Colonel Yorgasen, how nice to see you. Please, come in and have a seat."

Yorgasen was in full uniform, and Hegarty in civilian clothes. The colonel spoke first. "Lieutenant, let me introduce Dan Hegarty of the Security Intelligence Service, from Wellington." Cameron's ears perked up as Yorgasen used his rank of lieutenant, as opposed to his name.

"Very nice to meet you, Mr. Hegarty. I've spoken with some of your staff on the disappearance of my yacht."

"I recall. Have we been able to help with the insurance issues?"

"Yes, indeed," Rossiter replied. "I'm well on the way to obtaining a replacement. Thank you for your efforts."

"Thank Colonel O'Brien, Mr. Rossiter. He suggested to me that there was a problem where we could possibly help. We were glad to do it."

Colonel Yorgasen reentered the conversation to ask, "Lieutenant, how did your annual encampment go this year?"

Rossiter was certain the colonel knew the answers but followed his lead. "For a part-time warrior, sir, I believe it went well."

Colonel Yorgasen switched to Rossiter's first name. "Cameron, I'm certain you can perceive that this is something more than a social call. We have all been invited to a party—an SAS party, by specific invitation of someone I believe you know. Lt. Colonel Zachariah O'Brien."

"Yes, sir. We have formed an acquaintance over the past year. And where would this party be, sir?"

"As you might expect, Lieutenant, the reception will be held overseas, and it includes a rather cosmopolitan grouping, including Colonel O'Brien."

"And the date of the party, Colonel?"

"Quite short notice for an invitation, I'm afraid. The reception line begins tomorrow."

Rossiter felt he'd been railroaded, but he also felt he knew the reason. "Does the guest of honor have any knowledge of the whereabouts of my yacht, sir?"

"I wouldn't be at all surprised, Lieutenant. Not at all. The rest of the team has left already. My aircraft will be departing tomorrow at 10:00 A.M. from Whenuapai. I would enjoy your company, if it meets with your pleasure."

"Yes, sir," Rossiter said somewhat reluctantly.

Colonel Yorgasen and Hegarty rose to leave, exchanging handshakes. Rossiter again thanked Hegarty for his assistance with the insurance issue and told Colonel Yorgasen he'd meet him in the morning. After they left, Cameron told Jenny that he didn't want to be disturbed. He closed his door, turned his chair to look out his expansive window on the harbor, and began to think what all this quick movement meant. Why had O'Brien asked for him specifically? Obviously it had something to do with the fact that *Triple Diamond* had played a large part in the *Northland* disaster, and perhaps O'Brien felt that he deserved a shot at those who had stolen it from him. It was a dangerous way to get revenge. On the other hand, he was, after all, a member of the Territorial Forces, and New Zealand had elected to join the effort in the Gulf. His SAS status had assured him a place on the available list, so a military call up for Gulf action was likely anyway.

But what about Michelle? She was not going to take this well. Their wedding was only three weeks away. How could he break the news to her gently? What a mess! But he didn't have the normal time to consider each angle. He had to pack immediately and leave in the morning. He reached for the telephone and dialed Michelle's number.

"Corporate Services, Michelle speaking, how can I help you?"

"You can't imagine how you've already helped me, Ma'am," Cameron joked, "but if you would like to do me the honor of having dinner with me this evening, you could be of even more service."

"It would be my honor, sir. Is it formal, or fish and chips on the deck again?"

Cameron knew that if they were alone at his home, Michelle

would have a tougher time keeping her composure, and so he quickly decided they should go out to a public restaurant. "Informal, in a public place of your choosing," he replied.

"I'll be ready at seven," she said, "and I'll have a place in mind by then."

"See you later." As an afterthought, and thinking he would miss her as she hung up, he added, "Michelle, you still there?"

"Yes."

"I love you."

"How nice to hear it. Thank you. I'll whisper my reply in your ear later. 'Bye."

This was going to be tough, Cameron thought as he drove home. He had called his director of operations and placed responsibility on him for running the business for the next several weeks. He didn't know how long he'd be gone, but he would try to keep in touch. Arriving home, he began to think of the things he would need to bring. Not much actually. Several changes of uniforms, mostly fatigues. By six he was finished packing, and he took a shower before picking up Michelle.

Michelle also showered and was dressing while watching the six o'clock news. The involvement of the New Zealand forces in relocating to the Gulf was a constant item. For New Zealand to mount such a large effort was big news. HMNZS *Southland* had arrived on station with the naval forces in the Persian Gulf, and the announcer was reporting the relocation of elements of the army combat teams and air force transport units. All this effort, Michelle thought, to avenge Graham and his shipmates. The premonition that had bothered Michelle all day didn't offer much comfort. How many other sisters, mothers, and wives . . . or fiancées would have to mourn their losses?

Cameron arrived promptly at seven, and Michelle was ready and waiting. They drove across the bridge into Auckland toward the city center.

"Where to, Ms. Duffield?"

"I thought the Sheraton would be nice."

"Oh, it's formal after all," Cameron teased.

"All farewell dinners should be formal, Cameron," she said softly.

Shocked, Cameron remained silent.

Michelle continued, "When do you leave?"

Not sure how to respond and caught off guard, Cameron fudged his answer. "What do you mean, leave?"

"Cameron, I'm sure we don't have much time. Please be honest with me."

Cameron marveled at her intuition. How had she known? Considering for a moment, he determined that Michelle had been braver than he himself would have been. They would have gone most of the evening before he felt the time was right, if ever, to bring up the depressing subject. "Yes, you're right, Michelle. You do deserve that, don't you. I'm sorry. I was just afraid of broaching the subject. I leave tomorrow morning. How did you know?"

"I put two and two together. Alison called last night and told me she wasn't sure they could attend the wedding. Zach had been called away for a special reason, and she was worried. He couldn't tell her where he was going or when he would be back. Of course she didn't mention you, but watching the news tonight, I just had a feeling."

"Michelle, I'm truly sorry. I was visited this morning by Colonel Yorgasen and—"

"Cameron, it's all right. Remember? Today, then tomorrow, and then the day after tomorrow. For as many tomorrows as we have." Michelle paused, struggling to maintain her composure. "When I was hurt and confused at the memorial service, you didn't argue. You just said, 'I'll be there when you need me.' I'm saying the same thing. I'll be here when you get back, and we can pick up our life together then."

Cameron was astounded by her acceptance of what he had expected to be a very difficult piece of news to deliver. They were both silent for several moments, and as they came off the harbor bridge, he reached out to take her hand. "I do love you, Michelle," he whispered.

"I know, Cameron, and I love you, always."

Dinner was an afterthought. They went through the ritual of eating, trying to be pleasant and talk about work, the O'Briens, and general issues, but the cloud hanging over their future was Cameron's imminent departure. In such a short time together they had already been separated for over a month; now neither knew how long this parting would be. Neither one was willing to entertain the thought it could be forever, yet Cameron had already begun to think since Colonel Yorgasen's visit this morning about his own mortality. He was so young, his life was in order, and he had attained financial success at an early age, a fact that always amazed him. To lose it all in a war halfway around the world seemed unthinkable, yet here he was, donning his greens and flying off to battle. Was the loss of a yacht worth all of that? But of course, it wasn't just the yacht, was it?

"How are you going to handle the postponement of the wedding?" Cameron asked. "What was it we sent, a hundred and seventy-five invitations?"

"I'll get Mum's advice. She's a whiz at that stuff. That's no problem. The problem is the invitation to the groom. Where can I send yours?" Michelle knew full well that he wouldn't be able to tell her anything about where he was going, but she felt she had to ask.

Cameron just smiled lovingly at her and reached across the table for her hand. "I don't need an invitation, Michelle. The look in your eyes tells me all I need to know.

"Cameron, I won't get maudlin, but I want you to understand something. I *need* you to come back to me."

Cameron spoke not a word. Michelle's emphasis on her needing him to return was comment enough.

Michelle continued, "Perhaps it's unfair, but all I ask is that you take no unnecessary chances. No John Wayne stuff, please."

Trying to make light of the possibilities, Cameron came back with "Not to worry, Michelle, I'm just a Territorial Forces officer. They'll probably have me passing out toilet paper from some supply depot hundreds of miles behind the action."

"Cameron, your word. I want your word," she insisted.

"Michelle, I . . . I have to go where . . . well, you understand, don't you? I'm under orders."

"Who dares, wins. Right? The blasted SAS motto. You all run around the bushes acting like little cowboys, and that's fine for exercise, but this is real, Cameron, this is dangerous. I want your word that you will try to be careful."

"Michelle," he responded, finally able to give his word to something he could control, "I promise to be absolutely careful in everything I do. I know this is real. But I want you to think about one thing, even if it's painful for you. It was real for Graham and his shipmates too. We're going for them as well."

She just looked away into space and left his comment unanswered. Finally Michelle broke the silence, taking Cameron's hand once again. "I'll be here when you return," she said, smiling. "I love you deeply, Cameron. I know that now. I almost let it slip away from us through my fear. I admit that I'm afraid, but I will not be ruled by fear. Just come back to me, Cameron. Just come back."

Rural Iraq
Field Military Headquarters
February

"We have plucked the eagle's feathers," boasted Salimar to his generals. They will, of course, retaliate with another abuse of their power, but we have shown the world how a small country, dedicated to its goals, can bring the warmongers to their knees."

They were meeting in a remote village in Iraq, away from the Baghdad center, which the Americans would surely hit with cruise missiles and air attacks. Salimar had survived as long as he had by always being cautious about his routine—where he slept, where he met—and he had often changed his plans at the last minute to confuse even those who were aware of his plans. The success of the raid on the American aircraft carrier going through the Suez Canal had exceeded all their expectations, except of course, Salimar's. "How many planes did we lose, General?"

"Excellency, fifty-two aircraft took part in this mission, and only nine failed to return. Your strategy was brilliant, Excellency, brilliant."

"The men on this raid will receive our highest honors, General. See to their comforts and pleasures. We will yet have purpose for them again," Salimar directed.

"It will be done, Excellency."

"Tonight, I address the nation to tell of the brave deeds of our airmen and of the swift victories our forces have taken against those who opposed us last time. Allah be praised."

"*Allah akhbar,*" his generals voiced in unison.

From another remote site that afternoon, Salimar taped a message to be delivered to his people that evening and, by a CNN pickup, to the world. Taunting the U.S., he extolled Iraq's victories and the reunification of their land under Arab leadership. He called upon his Arab brothers to unite in common cause against the aggressor and reestablish the true religion throughout the land. For nearly ninety minutes, Salimar harangued his way through denunciations of imperialist aggression, words that had been virtually memorized over the years by third-world countries to describe the Western superpowers and the way they oppressed the smaller nations. His conclusion, however, was chilling. With oblique reference to the recent nuclear explosion, he promised the world that Allah was behind their purpose, and he would not allow them to fail, whatever was required to achieve the ultimate victory. Were they to be overwhelmed by the allied forces of evil, life as it was known in the Arab world would end. Oil would no longer be needed, and it would be put on the altar of sacrifice to the greed of Western nations, for whom it meant life itself.

The Western leaders listened closely, with interest and a great deal of concern.

Iraqi–Saudi Arabian Border
February

In just over two weeks, a virtual stalemate had occurred on the battlefront. Once initial advances had been made by Iraqi forces and initial objectives had been achieved, they had stopped in place. President Eastman had worked long and hard to achieve Israeli restraint, and both sides had reached tentative agreement in this area. The Israelis for their part were content to hold their forces in check, since the Americans had been pleading for restraint to the point of political blackmail regarding resupply of weapons.

In Saudi Arabia, U.S. forces had quickly been airlifted in to develop defensive perimeters three miles back from the Iraqi front lines. Small recon efforts had been mounted, but other than occasional firefights, no major engagements had been fought. The air war, however, continued in Iraq, with U.S. forces effecting interdiction missions to thwart the resupply of Iraqi forces in Saudi Arabia. This would eventually take its toll, but that would take some time.

Allied military headquarters in Riyadh had not received ample direction from Washington regarding their long-range objectives, but they had plenty to accomplish just reestablishing supply lines to troops in place and increasing strength to facilitate another ground campaign, should it prove necessary.

One small group located in a remote part of Bahrain felt they possibly had the ability to bring the entire operation to a successful conclusion, but as yet they had not been able to obtain the necessary information to make it happen. In the meantime, they waited and continued training, exercising, and preparing for their eventual mission, which they knew would come.

Slightly north of Bahrain, Iraqi Republican Guard Colonel Wadi retained control of the massive oil-pumping facility at Ras Tannurah. Since early on the morning of the invasion, he had solidified his position, and the entire facility had been ringed with explosives. Pictures of this self-destructive measure had been forwarded to arrive at Allied military headquarters in Riyadh, with a full explanation of intended retreat or surrender directions given to the defending forces by Salimar himself. Colonel Wadi had made it quite clear to Allied authorities that his men knew they could not go home unless their mission had either been achieved or they had completely destroyed the facility.

In Washington, D.C., President Eastman had formulated several potential operations with the Joint Chiefs of Staff. He would begin to enact these plans shortly, but for the present he waited. The chiefs could not understand his reluctance, attributing it to his lack of military service and lack of understanding of the need for decisive, quick action. But the president yet had one ace up his sleeve, and together with Clarene Prescott and General Austin, they knew peace could be achieved if the forthcoming information were timely and the subsequent operation successful. They could break the back of this stalemate once again, with minimal loss of life.

CHAPTER TWENTY-THREE

Bahrain, Saudi Arabian Peninsula
Headquarters, Detachment Twelve
February

DETACHMENT TWELVE WAS ENSCONCED in makeshift tents in a remote area of Bahrain, about twenty miles from the city. Isolation was intentional to keep their presence quiet as long as possible. They looked like any other military outfit, and knowledge of their composition had not been distributed. In fact, at this point even Allied military headquarters neither knew of the nature of their intended mission, nor was aware of their joint American-Kiwi makeup. General Austin had received his directions from the president, and he was directly in charge of this operation.

The senior officer on the scene was Lieutenant Colonel Yorgasen, New Zealand Special Air Service. Lieutenant Colonel O'Brien was present, but he had turned over command of the field operations to Colonel Yorgasen, who would plan the actual insertion when the information was received. O'Brien remained

the link to Washington and to the source of information,
Ambassador Haquim. This fact was known only to General
Austin and O'Brien. A daily briefing was held each evening after
training.

The first evening, Colonel Yorgasen addressed the group. At
the end, he turned the meeting over to his American counterpart.
"To conclude, Colonel O'Brien has a few words. Colonel?"

O'Brien surveyed those in the mess tent, which was the only
facility large enough to gather the detachment together. Twenty-
seven men comprised Detachment Twelve. Yorgasen and
O'Brien were in joint command—the former, operational; the
latter, tactical, with the final go/no-go decision solely at O'Brien's
discretion. Officers included Captain Murphy and Lieutenant
Nelson from the U.S. Marines, and ten enlisted noncoms comprised the remainder of the U.S. soldiers. Captain Joshua Armstrong and Lieutenant Rossiter, plus eight various ratings
comprised the New Zealand contingent. In addition they had one
Kiwi armorer to keep weapons in operating condition and two
medical personnel, also Kiwis. Colonel Yorgasen had tentatively
developed the operational format, putting Captain Armstrong in
command of the team to be inserted, which consisted of a Kiwi
five-man patrol, including Lieutenant Rossiter and three ratings,
plus Captain Murphy and four other Marines. O'Brien's presence
on the insertion team had not been decided, but General Austin
had been against it when first discussed. Eleven men would make
the raid, two five-man squads of SAS and Marines, plus one
medic. Twelve, if O'Brien went along.

"Thank you, Colonel Yorgasen," O'Brien began. "I'll try to
be brief. It's an honor to be with such a select group of men. We
are here in this joint operation because of the mutual loss to our
two countries and in respect for the seven hundred and ten men
and women who paid with their lives. It falls to us to be the force
by which the crews of these two ships will be avenged. As yet,
I'm not able to divulge the nature of our intended mission. Let me
just say that we have the capability of actually ending this disastrous situation with a minimum of bloodshed."

O'Brien had learned over the years that many military men

professed no particular religious preference or creed but that, almost to a man, they honored those who died defending their nation. Respect for those who died in the service of their country and, by extension, in the service of their fellow men was a military tradition. O'Brien sought to unite these men in purpose by reminding them of the origin of Detachment Twelve.

"Some of you have just arrived this morning," he said, smiling at Lieutenant Rossiter, "and will be briefed by your respective team leaders. Suffice it for now to say that we welcome you to Detachment Twelve. You have been handpicked for your specific skills. Until we receive further information, we will not be certain of the size and disposition of the final assault team, so all units will train on the assumption that they will take part in the mission, as well they might. Again, I am proud to be a part of Detachment Twelve. That's all I have to say at this time, Colonel Yorgasen. Thank you."

Yorgasen stood again. "Thank you, Colonel O'Brien. Representing the NZSAS, let me say we are proud to combine with the U.S. Marines. My father had the pleasure of serving with the Marines in '43. At least here in Bahrain, we can keep you away from our New Zealand women," he said with a smile. Laughter rippled throughout around the room, and Yorgasen concluded, "After we eat, there will be officers call at 1900 in the command tent. That will be all, gentlemen." All stood as Yorgasen and O'Brien left the tent, and then they dispersed to their respective tents.

Outside, Rossiter approached O'Brien and saluted, which Zach returned, followed by a handshake. "I want to thank you for your gracious invitation, Colonel," said Rossiter with a grin.

"It's the least I could do after such a lovely weekend on your yacht."

"You're right about that, sir; it's the least you could do," Cameron added with humorous sarcasm. Actually, on the flight over, I began to warm to the challenge. It's true I've maintained my Territorial Forces association, but I've never thought of myself as a soldier."

"Cameron, I'm sorry about disrupting your life, but I truly felt you would want a part of this, considering how they used your resources to deliver their horrendous message. Also, Lieutenant Rossiter, I apologize for the necessity of using rank and formality structure in—"

Cameron interrupted with, "No problem, Colonel, I fully understand. We are in a small, elite unit, and command structure is necessary. Think no more about it, please."

"Thank you, Cameron," Zach said. "How's Michelle? I don't see any bruises on you for postponing your wedding."

"She was truly amazing. She knew and understood before I had developed the courage to tell her."

"Remarkable, these women, aren't they? We couldn't do as well without them, yet they seldom seem to understand our need to be a part of a military operation such as this. I sometimes wonder who they think would do it if we didn't. Perhaps someone else's husband and father, I guess." They continued walking toward the tent area, entering the tent Rossiter had been assigned to share with Captain Murphy. Colonel Yorgasen had billeted the officers with their respective counterparts, as opposed to keeping SAS together and Marines together. Captain Murphy had not returned to the tent, and O'Brien and Rossiter were alone.

"So tell me, how did you change your wedding plans?" O'Brien asked.

"Open for the present. Michelle will reschedule when I return. She's worried, Zach." He paused, then added, "Sorry, Colonel."

"Cameron, I believe between the two of us we can judge our relative privacy and revert to our friendship when away from the troops, don't you?"

"Right. Anyway she's scared of losing one more person she loves. Quite justified, I might add. I'm even scared of losing me. How about you, Zach? Are you afraid of death?"

"No, I can truly say that I'm not."

"You mean to tell me that dying doesn't frighten you at all?"

"Oh, by all means, dying terrifies me like it does everyone else," O'Brien admitted.

"We're going around in circles here. You've got me confused."

"Let me explain. You asked if I were afraid of death. I'm not.
Truly. But I am certainly, like most men, quite afraid of dying, or
more specifically, the method of dying. Many of us are fortunate
enough to die peacefully in our sleep, but others die in horrible
accidents or in war. But Cameron, that's entirely different then
death. For me, death brings with it things that I know. I know
where I am going after death. Don't get me wrong. I'm not saying, I'm 'saved' in the religious sense, and I certainly will have
to stand judgment at that time, but I live my life with an understanding of where I came from, why I'm here, and where I'm
going after death. Being a military man most of my adult life, I've
looked upon death as a form of 'reassignment.' Can you understand that?"

Cameron was silent for a few moments. "I guess it is the act
of dying that we're really frightened of, but even on the other side
of that, wherever that is, how does one obtain such a certainty of
death and its purpose?"

O'Brien realized that Cameron had given considerable
thought to his possible death since his recall only two days before.
"Given the limited diversions available to us in this sandy par-
adise," O'Brien said, gesturing at the desert surroundings, "I think
we might have time to discuss that while we're here. For now, let
me just say that for me, death is not the worst enemy I can face.
Not being ready for death is of far greater concern to my peace
of mind. I'm not talking about some existential philosophy,
Cameron. It's just simple, daily living."

"I suppose it takes a rather strong man, or constitution, to face
death with that degree of certainty."

"I don't think so. I'll tell you what I think is a strong man,
though. I have a vivid picture in my mind of looking at a paint-
ing when I was a young boy. It was a warrior, muscles rippling
on his arms and a sword standing next to him. I can still recall
how he appeared to me at that young age. He was the epitome of
strength, and like most kids, I wanted to be like him, to be a
strong warrior. It wasn't until I was a teenager that I noticed

something else about him. I saw another copy of the picture in one of my books one day, and this time what I noticed was that he was on his knees. For most of my youth, I had formed an impression of the strongest man I could imagine, and I later discovered that while he was indeed a warrior, his strength came from the fact that he was praying. The image, and the lesson, never left me.

Wanting to give Cameron some time to think about his comments, O'Brien changed the subject. "How about a few miles around the desert, my friend, where we can jog some sand into our toes?"

Cameron rose up and smiled. "You're on, Colonel. Let's find out what that big desk you sit at has done to this 'Washington Warrior.'"

"Lead on, Lieutenant. Perhaps this old man can open your eyes a bit."

"Is that a physical or a philosophical challenge, Colonel?"

"A bit of both, Lieutenant, if you're up to it."

Moscow, Russia
The Kremlin
February

Ivanovich Romanov's secretary addressed the small gathering around the table in the Kremlin.

"Mr. President, I have President Eastman on the line."

Speaking through interpreters, both President Romanov and President Eastman had arranged a discussion to conclude the pressing issues of Russian involvement in the Middle Eastern crisis. Some days earlier in another telephone discussion, both presidents had discussed the prior Middle Eastern crisis when Russia had supported but not participated in the military action against Iraq. Eastman had gone boldly to Romanov to directly ask for his intervention in resolving the current issue. British Prime Minister John Blankenship, aware of the possibility of Russia's entry into the coalition, had quickly acknowledged British support for a quick and peaceful solution. British forces had once again been directed to provide support for the military actions now building in the Middle East.

Russia's entry would shock if not overwhelm Iraq, formerly a client state of the Soviets.

"Put it on the speaker, please," Romanov said. "Good morning, Mr. President. I have General Sovensky present for our discussions as agreed."

"And a good morning to you also, President Romanov," Eastman responded. "General Rothschild, our chairman of the Joint Chiefs, is with me. Have you come to any conclusions regarding the options we discussed earlier?"

"Indeed we have, Bill," Romanov said, shifting to informal conversation. "We have also discussed the matter with the Turkish premier, and they are prepared to collaborate with us on the issue. We must have reasonable assurances, however, that our vital interests in obtaining a continuing supply of oil will be a priority issue in the conclusion of this unfortunate episode."

"Of course, Ivanovich. We can be certain that unless we stop this madman somehow, we will all find ourselves being warmed by the hearth instead of the furnace."

Eastman knew that for several decades, the former Soviet Union had sought for ways to have guaranteed access to Middle Eastern oil. This military effort would offer them the opportunity to have a presence in the northern Iraqi oil fields. General Sovensky addressed his counterpart.

"General Rothschild, we have received your intelligence estimates and satellite photos. They corroborate our own information and will assist in planning our effort."

"Thank you, General Sovensky," replied Rothschild. "You should have little if any opposition in the north. All forces and supply routes are, of course, concentrating on the south. Will you be able to attend our strategy session in Riyadh in two days?"

"We will be there, General, with a prepared operational plan."

President Eastman concluded. "Ivanovich, this is an historic occasion once again. It seems the Russian and American peoples are destined to support one another during the crises. It is a shame we spent fifty years in between being suspicious and distrustful."

"We agree completely, Bill. Perhaps you and I have the opportunity to correct that situation, do we not?"

"Let us hope so, Ivanovich. Good day to you."

"And to you, my friend."

Riyadh, Saudi Arabia
Allied Military Command Headquarters
February

Under the strictest secrecy, the Russian and Turkish military leaders attended the strategy session held in Riyadh to coordinate the efforts by American, Saudi, and Israeli forces. The presence of Israeli forces was a first, and it had been viewed with some trepidation. As yet, other Arab nations had not joined in the second effort to curtail Iraq's military adventures partly because of the Israeli involvement. Of course, that had been Salimar's intent initially. Political efforts to reconvene the coalition were ongoing, but fear had been present when other Arab states had seen that Iraq possessed nuclear weapons of their own.

U.S. General Charles Winston Powers had become the commander of Central Command, and as such he was in charge of all military operations in the Middle Eastern theater. He held the position General Norman Schwarzkopf had held in the first edition of Desert Shield/Storm. Desert Boomerang afforded Powers less political support than Schwarzkopf had possessed, but the Saudis were totally cooperative again, as the sovereignty of their nation had been violated by armed troops and the economic stability of their oil facilities hung in the balance. General Powers began the briefing.

"Gentlemen, the map before us shows the current disposition of invading forces and our containment perimeter. For nineteen days now, we have maintained an uneasy quiet, with only our air actions bringing any opposition. The Iraqi Air Force has not challenged us other than on individual occasions and, of course, the surprise attack on the *Rushmore* in the Canal. The *Rushmore* was provided emergency repairs and escorted through the canal into the Red Sea five days after the incident. Specifically, gentlemen, we have a stalemate on our hands. Any attack on the facilities occupied by the Iraqis will result in their total destruction. The president and Saudi leaders are attempting to resolve this issue politically to avoid that eventuality. In short, Salimar may well pull this off and retreat to the positions he wanted in the first place."

Looking around the room, General Powers could see the frustration. He continued, "We are not, however, without options to exert pressure on the opposition. General Sovensky from the Russian military command and General Kahmil from Turkey are here to outline their plan for assistance from the north. That move, gentlemen, would be totally unexpected by the Iraqis. They are prepared to brief us on their intentions, and collectively, we will formulate a supportive effort to cover their moves. First, however, we would like to obtain a quick briefing on the Israeli situation." Nodding to the Israeli participants, General Powers turned the floor over to them.

A simple briefing was delivered in which known facts were simply reiterated. No direct action had occurred against Israeli forces, but they were fully mobilized and prepared for immediate action should it be required. Considerable pressure had been brought upon the Israeli government by the U.S. for restraint, and so far the agreement was holding.

General Powers rose again to give the floor to the Russians. "General Sovensky?"

The Russian general, speaking surprisingly good English, began to outline the strategy of a northern invasion of Iraq. Intending to take key cities and airports, they did not intend to confront military forces directly, merely to open a second front in the north, giving the Iraqis something else to think about and to apply some pressure on their supply lines. It was expected that the move would be totally unanticipated. The wholehearted support of the Kurdish people, including military units, was offered, and a new political division, as had been sought for so long, was under consideration, with the Turks also having an opportunity to resolve their Kurdish problem.

Concluding his remarks, General Sovensky asked for questions.

"What is your timetable, General?" Rothschild asked.

"We have been formulating this operation for ten days, and we are now prepared to initiate in seventy-two hours. It is a forty-eight hour operation if opposition is as anticipated and allied air cover is provided by units in the south."

"Excellent," General Powers said. "Gentlemen, that concludes our briefing if there are no further questions." As the men rose to leave, individual conversations developed. An Air Force lieutenant general who had not spoken during the meeting moved to meet with General Powers.

"Sir, I'm General Austin, National Security Agency. One of my staff officers was not cleared for this meeting and is outside the meeting room. Might we have a word with you privately?"

"Of course, General. This way, please." Powers had never met General Austin but had been advised by the chairman, JCS, that Austin would be out to see him and expected his visit. Stepping outside the briefing room, Colonel O'Brien joined Powers and Austin. In General Powers's quarters, he offered his visitors a seat. "Coffee, General, Colonel O'Brien?"

"Yes, thank you," Austin replied. "None for the colonel."

Addressing his aide, Powers asked for coffee and then dismissed him. Powers, Austin, and O'Brien were alone, and Powers spoke first. "General, I trust the president has something up his sleeve which has prevented him from moving on this stalemate?"

"Precisely, General. Our information is extremely sensitive, and I will be unable to share with you the source of that information."

Powers raised an eyebrow but motioned Austin to continue.

"General, we have placed a small, mixed force of U.S. Marines and New Zealand SAS in Bahrain for the purpose of carrying out a special mission which, if successful, will end this stalemate and allow us all to go home once again. I understand that sounds highly improbable, but I can assure you it is plausible, given the source of our information."

General Powers was no fool and quickly addressed the issue. "You're going after the Butcher?"

"Yes, General, we are, but it is our specific intention to cap-

ture him as we did Noriega in Panama. In his present role and by
his own definition, Salimar falls in that unique category of military leader as opposed to political leader, and as such he is a
viable target even under our American restrictions against targeting foreign political leaders. However, this operation is under the
command of New Zealand forces, and American control is limited to the go/no-go decision."

"I see. And if he declines to come politely?" he queried, getting right to the heart of the matter.

"It completely depends on Salimar, but we will do all in our
power, short of endangering our insertion team, to bring him out
alive."

"That's a tough order, General. How can we be of assistance?"

"As I'm sure you're aware, that's why we're here, General
Powers," Austin explained. "We have about thirty men, which
tentatively will be split into two groups, one for insertion and one
to support recovery. When the word comes, we anticipate that we
may have a short time frame. All I can say, General, is that we
have access from the inside to Salimar's movements. We intend
to be in the right place at the right time. We will require some
diversionary effort during the insertion, transport by helicopter to
the drop zone, and a diversion again at extraction. Anticipated
point of action will be Kuwait City, so your diversionary effort
can be planned around that area. We may have to actually wait in
seclusion in Kuwait City, and we have arrangements that will
make that possible. In fact, the planned operations just discussed
in your briefing in the north, General, may be an excellent time
to insert our team. The drop zone will be about eight miles outside of the city. Would you be able to plan a diversion to coincide
with the planned operation up north?"

"I'll handle that, General, we've got plenty of diversions to
arrange. One more wouldn't be a problem." Addressing O'Brien,
General Powers asked, "Will you be the contact here, Colonel?"

"Yes, sir, I will. Our group is called Detachment Twelve, and
the code word for the operation is 'Rainbow.' I'll contact you
with that code designation as my authenticator."

General Austin stood and offered his thanks for the time and the support, again offering his apologies for the inability to provide further clarification. "President Eastman is very cautious regarding the protection of this source for reasons of his own, to which even I am not privy."

"Understood, General Austin," replied Powers. "Thank you for your briefing. Please let us know if we can provide any further assistance." Austin and O'Brien started to leave, and General Powers added, "Best of luck, General, I sincerely hope you succeed. I'd like to take all these boys home alive once again. Colonel O'Brien, I'll look forward to your contact. I'll advise my aide to have your message delivered immediately upon receipt of your authenticator designation."

"Thank you, General Powers."

Austin and Colonel O'Brien left Allied military headquarters and started for the airport. Austin was returning immediately to Washington and O'Brien to Detachment Twelve. "Zach, we have arranged several designators for future communications. Our source is Skylark, the target is Erebus, and the operation is Rainbow, as you know. We'll use the Baseball Diamond for position designators."

"I understand, General."

Ambassador Haquim had been code-named Skylark shortly after the decision to leave him in place. President Eastman had actually met with Ambassador Sir Geoffrey Holden and Ambassador Haquim privately, after which Eastman insisted upon the operation being arranged with Haquim in place at the UN without removing him for protection. Austin didn't know why, but he agreed that as long as Haquim could remain in place safely, the information forthcoming would be much more valuable.

"Any word on timing, General?" O'Brien queried.

I should hear from Skylark shortly. In seventy-two hours certain military actions will occur in the northern sector. It seems to me an excellent opportunity to insert Rainbow and wait for the call. You should be relatively safe in the locations arranged, but the length of the wait will be unknown."

"Right, General. I'll plan accordingly."

"Zach, one other thing. I know you feel responsible for including Rossiter in this operation and risking his safety. I don't intend to preempt your decision regarding your participation in this operation. That call will be yours."

"Thank you, General. I've given it considerable thought. I want to discuss it once more with Colonel Yorgasen, and then I'll decide."

"Fair enough. I'll contact you immediately when we hear from Skylark." Austin looked at O'Brien for a quiet moment and thought briefly of his own young son killed in the Vietnam campaign and the senselessness of young men dying to keep tyrants like Abdul Salimar from controlling the world. Austin shook his hand warmly. "Godspeed, Zach."

"Thank you, General," Zach said, stepping back and rendering a respectful salute as they separated.

Eastern Turkey
February

Throughout the afternoon, small bands of Kurds had casually entered the cities in the normal process of bringing products to market and obtaining supplies. By evening, several hundred Kurdish guerrillas had infiltrated near the initial targets, awaiting the signal from invading forces from Turkey. Russian military forces combined with Turkish elements were positioned on the Turkish border. Military units had been there for several weeks, massing shortly after the war began. They had not been seen as a threat to Iraq but simply as precautionary moves prudent for any government on the border of a nation at war.

At 2300 hours the airlift began. Kurdish rebels were signaled to cut communication lines and to secure radio and television outlets. Military outposts were sabotaged to preclude immediate response, although military presence was limited to reserve units comprised of old men and the infirm from the last war. Russian military components of the 42nd Mechanized Rifle Division were airlifted by helicopter to Iraqi cities of Al Mawsil and Kirkuk. Swiftly they overwhelmed opposition with minimal resistance.

Turkish forces supported by armor units rolled eastward

toward the small cities in the mountainous areas, where advance airborne units had been transported by helicopter and also had secured all communication stations. Allied air power had provided diversionary attacks on Baghdad with little damage but much confusion as to what was happening. By dawn, a secure foothold was established, and throughout the day and evening, Russian armor continued south and east from the Turkish border to establish a firm perimeter running across the northern sector of Iraq, with the mountains in between being controlled by Kurdish units that had been calling them home for generations. By daylight of the second day, the invading forces were firmly in control of the northern sector of Iraq, and Salimar was essentially surrounded. The noose had been put it in place, but it was not yet tightened.

Bahrain
Detachment Twelve Headquarters
February

At 1500 hours, Detachment Twelve was assembled and provided its first comprehensive briefing on the mission at hand. All were in a state of readiness and tired of waiting for the go signal. O'Brien provided the briefing before turning operational command over to Colonel Yorgasen.

"I know all of you are aware of the reasons for tight security these past few days. It is time to explain to you the nature of our mission. Detachment Twelve will be inserted into Kuwait to await contact regarding the movements of Abdul Salimar. It is anticipated he will pay a visit to the captured Kuwaiti leaders in the near future. Our purpose is to capture him if possible. We are not to needlessly risk lives to accomplish a capture if it seems impossible. We may have to wait several days in a secure location in Kuwait City, provided by Kuwaiti underground. Our mission, code-named Rainbow, will divide us into two elements, one for insertion and one for recovery support.

"The insertion team, Rainbow Blue, will include Captain Armstrong, Captain Murphy, and Lieutenant Rossiter, plus SAS squad A and Marine squad A. I will accompany Rainbow Blue, but Captain Armstrong is in operational command. Recovery will be Rainbow Yellow, commanded by Colonel Yorgasen, and will include Lieutenant Nelson and SAS squad B and Marine squad B, as well as both armorers and our medic.

"For our Kiwi members, the baseball lessons this past week have not been for fun only. We will follow the Baseball Diamond location format. Our starting point in Saudi Arabia will be Home Plate, the drop zone for Rainbow Blue will be First Base, destination will be Second Base. We will hold at Second Base until the final mission is activated. Once the mission is activated, Rainbow Yellow will transport to the recovery point at Third Base. Successful completion of the mission will see Rainbow Blue reach Third Base, after which the combined operation will be designated Rainbow Green and will return to Home Plate. Our time has finally come, gentlemen. May God be with us on this mission."

At 1900 hours, Colonel O'Brien directed a radio message to Allied military headquarters, Riyadh:

EYES ONLY * CINCCENCOM

RAINBOW PLUS FIVE * EXECUTE

Transport from Bahrain to Home Plate arrived at 1930, and Detachment Twelve departed. They arrived at 2045 and began final preparations, checking and double-checking gear. At 2400 hours, Rainbow Blue was transported by helicopter to First Base, accompanied by four Apache helicopter gunships. Air activity was heavy, and the night sky was filled with illuminated tracer rounds. Rainbow Blue reached First Base and was met by Kuwaiti soldiers, who had stolen an Iraqi military truck. Blue loaded gear into the truck, and the helicopter transport departed, leaving them alone, eight miles south of Kuwait City. They had about three and a half hours to reach their destination before daylight.

Captain Murphy spoke fluent Arabic, although the Arab lieutenant dressed in an Iraqi uniform, who was directing the Kuwaiti squad on the stolen truck, spoke perfect English. The truck was outfitted in the rear like a hospital ambulance with stretchers arranged on both sides. Squad members filled the stretchers, covered with blankets, and the remainder sat on the floor, wrapped in bandages to look like wounded Iraqis returning from the front.

The Arab lieutenant, who identified himself as Lieutenant Anwar, approached Colonel O'Brien.

"We will take the direct route into the city, and you will be safely in your hiding place until the word comes. Skylark sends his regards. He will be in touch shortly."

O'Brien was startled by the use of the code name Skylark. "Who are you?" he asked.

"One who is tired of the bloodshed, Colonel. One who risks all on your success. And one who is nephew to Skylark."

"Then you are actually an Iraqi officer?"

"Yes, Colonel."

"Where is Skylark?" O'Brien asked.

"I don't know" came the answer.

"Lieutenant, you understand the success of this mission depends on our unobserved insertion to the safe house. If we are discovered beforehand, even if we get out safely, Erebus will never arrive at his intended destination."

"Yes, Colonel, we are aware. I have several men planted at security posts, and we should be able to get through checkpoints quickly and quietly."

"Right," replied O'Brien, "let's get underway. It's your mission now, Captain Armstrong."

"Yes, sir," Armstrong responded.

Kuwait City, Kuwait
Second Base
February

Rainbow Blue arrived without incident at 0215, having passed straight through several checkpoints en route. Lieutenant Anwar—O'Brien didn't know if that was his true name or not—had passed them through with ease. They had been taken to a large, residential home with a courtyard. Toward the rear of the house, they had been led down a small stairway under the kitchen floor to a fairly spacious room, set up with six cots, ample food, and stocked with English magazines.

Its drawback was that it had only one way in, and thus only one way out. If Lieutenant Anwar were not who he said he was, or were leading them into a trap, they were sitting ducks in this location. O'Brien and Armstrong discussed their options but decided they had no choice. They had to trust the young lieutenant. If he were Haquim's nephew, they would be all right. O'Brien activated his radio and reported to Home Plate the arrival of Blue at Second Base at 0230. All they could do now was wait.

Washington, D.C.
National Security Agency
February

Clarene stopped in to see General Austin as she left for an appointment. "Any word, Bill?"

"O'Brien's at the destination, but as yet I haven't heard from Skylark. It's a waiting game now, Clarene." The closeness of their efforts over the past several weeks had brought them to an appreciation of each other, and they had continued the use of first names.

"Bill, if I didn't know differently, I would think you had your own son in there."

"That apparent, is it? He is important to me, Clarene, but the decision was his. Basically, he's an intelligence officer and a fighter pilot, not a warrior, but he developed this mission and arranged for his friend to accompany it. He felt some sort of obligation to go, I suppose. For whatever reason, they seem to have gotten in with no problem. Now it's just a waiting game."

"Is Skylark in place?" Clarene asked.

"He got a message to us yesterday. He's been summoned back to Baghdad."

"And you let him go?" Clarene asked.

"He insisted. He said it was the only way he could provide accurate information."

"He may be braver than the soldiers, Bill."

"Yes, sometimes courage goes unsung. But if he is successful, he will have saved many lives, and we will be in his debt."

"I only hope he remains alive so we can repay him," Clarene added.

"I hope they can all be alive."

"Amen, Bill. Amen."

CHAPTER TWENTY-FOUR

Kuwait City, Kuwait
Second Base
February

ON THE MORNING OF THE SECOND DAY, O'Brien began to wonder again about Lieutenant Anwar. Surely if he had been so inclined, they would have been picked up by now. O'Brien and Rossiter were sitting together, playing cards and waiting. Captain Armstrong had arranged a watch schedule, with two men upstairs in the house, positioned in a front room with a view from both directions of the adjacent street. Others had been assigned sleeping shifts, and the twelve men had been required to "hot bunk" in the six accommodations. At noon, O'Brien and Rossiter had replaced the two on watch and gone upstairs. The house was vacant, other than two servants who had been present when they arrived, but they had seen no one since that time. The house seemed vacated.

In place upstairs, with a good view of the street, Zach and Cameron settled in for their four-hour watch.

"There's an old saying among pilots," O'Brien began. "Flying is thousands of hours of boredom, punctuated by a few minutes of terror. I suppose for special force raiders, the waiting serves the same purpose."

Cameron looked up and down the street before replying. "I've never been on a mission with the consequences of this one. In qualification training in New Zealand, we had to avoid capture while obtaining an objective over several days as individual units. I was captured and 'interrogated' by the police. They tried to make it unpleasant, but my resolve was strengthened by the realization that they couldn't do anything serious to me. Psychologically, it makes quite a difference. Interrogation here would certainly mean something different."

O'Brien nodded his head as they kept their eyes on the road out front. "No doubt about it."

For the next two hours they alternated sitting by the window while the other lay on the large bed in the room getting a few restful moments. Zach was on watch when Cameron spoke again. "Our discussion on death the other day has given me much to think about, Zach. I suppose if you don't think there is anywhere to go after dying, it makes it all that much more terrifying. One could say, "It's over," and there's nothing to worry about. It certainly makes you cling on to life a little harder on this side, but I can understand your proposition and the comfort it brings you to have a belief in where you are going."

"And you?" Zach asked.

"Undecided. But I do have another question for you, from a different perspective. If you believe in religious principles, how can you contemplate the requirement to kill someone, such as may be necessary on this mission?"

Cameron had posed a question that many others had asked Zach over the years. As soon as they discovered he was "religious," they assumed that he had no business in the military or in a role potentially requiring action and perhaps aggression. Zach smiled as he checked the approaches to the house again. "Ever read the Bible, Cameron?"

"Oh, maybe in church in my early years, or hearing something on television. Not actually read, I suppose."

"Cameron, the scriptures are full of the Lord's army following his directions, with people being killed, and righteous people being required to kill those who thwarted the Lord's purposes. It's interesting how people often look at the difference. My experience has been that if someone is potentially required to kill an enemy and he professes no religion at all, he can be assumed to be tough and manly in the act. But if he's religious, attends church, and tries to treat people gently, he's seen as a religious zealot. Somehow it diminishes his justification for serving a military role. It's a double standard. The fact that I try to live most of my life peacefully and treat people with respect, even though I might be required to kill the enemy today or tomorrow, doesn't present me with a dilemma."

Cameron rose and came to the window with Zach. "I suppose it is difficult to be accepted. In meeting you, I expected someone . . . I don't know, perhaps pious. But you were a normal guy, laughing, joking, and had I not known you were a Mormon, I would have thought nothing further about your religion. Do you understand that?"

"I've heard it all my life, Cameron. Of course I understand. Those who practice religion by punctuating every sentence with 'Praise Jesus' are not more righteous than those who try to serve him quietly in their daily lives, but they do make it difficult for others to accept people who profess a religion. They expect them to be—what was it you said—pious, as you expected me to be. When I wasn't, it confused you."

"Yeah, I guess that's a way to explain it," Cameron mused. "So how do you live with the killing requirement, in this specific instance, for example?"

"Consider this for a moment, Cameron. Would you kill a man if he tried to slip into your parking space ahead of you?"

"Of course not."

"Right. But would you kill him if you found him attempting to kill Michelle?"

"If there were no other way to prevent her death, yes, I guess I would."

"Well then, you've answered your own question. Killing is justified only in defense of life and then, as you said, only when it is the only way to prevent the unwarranted death. I don't relish the possibility of killing, but as I see it, thousands may die if we have to go head-to-head again with Salimar. And if he unleashes his nuclear threat, which he will, the potential destruction is unthinkable."

Cameron thought silently for a few moments before responding. "We're taught to make that decision before we enter the situation. Thinking it through in the heat of action could cost your own life or those of your teammates. It kind of makes it premeditated, doesn't it?"

"No more so than deciding right from wrong before each decision we make each day. Situational ethics, or responding to each situation as whim demands, demonstrates a lack of determination. In short, Cameron, killing is wrong, but killing to prevent more killing I have determined to be right. In the absence of an angel appearing to advise me before each decision, I will have to live with my actions and await my own judgment when the time comes." Zach watched Cameron for a reaction, then added with a humorous touch, "Of course you have to believe in angels, Cameron."

Suddenly Cameron bolted upright. "Truck coming."

Instantly they were both alert and hidden behind the corners of the window, weapons at the ready. The truck stopped out front, and Lieutenant Anwar climbed out the passenger side, entering the house. Zach went back to the inside stairway from where he could see the front door. Lieutenant Anwar entered, saw Zach at the top of the stairs, and began climbing them rapidly.

"Greetings from Skylark, Colonel. We will receive a visit this evening from certain military leaders. They are coming to personally deal with members of the Royal Kuwaiti family. I will return to pick up your team at 2300 hours. We don't know exactly what time they will arrive, but they will go to the prison holding facility. He is never on a planned schedule, so we will have to wait on a back street. I have three loyal soldiers who will man the roadblock station to keep others away. It's the best I can do. Can you be ready?"

"We're ready now. We'll be ready when you come," Zach replied.

Anwar turned to leave. "Oh, and Colonel, the Russians and Turks have invaded northern Iraq. The Leader is threatening mass destruction of all the oil facilities under his control unless they withdraw. His visit tonight is to eliminate the Kuwaiti royal family no matter what happens. He wishes to 'personally attend' to the matter, as his message said. This will be your only chance, Colonel. Skylark has been called back from New York. He doesn't know why. You may hold his life in your hands also."

"We'll be ready, Lieutenant," O'Brien stated firmly.

As Anwar left, Captain Armstrong came out from behind his concealed location, where he had moved when he heard the truck arrive. O'Brien motioned to him. "2300 hours, tonight!"

"Right, Colonel." He turned to descend to the basement room to alert the team.

"Cameron, perhaps we will find out more about my resolve this evening."

"Who dares, wins, Zach," Cameron stated, quoting the Special Air Service motto. "Let's just be sure we do all we can to assure we are not prematurely 'reassigned,'" he said with a smile.

Zach laughed nervously. "Absolutely," he said. "I'm still not ready."

Washington, D.C.
National Security Agency
February

"Message just in, General," Captain Molloy said. "Rainbow Blue activated 2300 hours this evening. Rainbow Yellow will deploy 0100 hours for Third Base."

"Thank you, Captain."

Kuwait City, Kuwait
Second Base
February

At 2250 hours, the truck arrived and Rainbow Blue left the safe house. Lieutenant Anwar had no further information on the arrival time of Erebus. The streets were dark and silent, with no local traffic. They passed through the occasional military check-point, which the lieutenant seemed able to handle with no prob-lems. In the center of the city, the truck stopped, and Anwar spoke through the window in the rear of the cab of the truck.

"Colonel, we are approaching the prison. We will wait one block south, behind the vehicle repair facility. Your men must remain in the truck under strict silence. I have three men stationed at the end of the street to keep others out. I will be with them or in the prison until he arrives. Security is tight, but few soldiers will be present on the street. That is his way. He does not announce his arrival by many soldiers. I will check with you occasionally as opportunity permits."

O'Brien, Murphy, and Armstrong conferred briefly follow-ing Lieutenant Anwar's departure and reached several conclu-sions. At Armstrong's direction, two of the SAS squad slipped out of the back of the truck and were gone for about forty-five minutes before returning, signaling thumbs up. "Four vehicles, sir," they reported, "all disabled." They waited silently, watching intently through the windshield from the rear of the truck. Occasionally they could hear muffled cries coming from the building but could discern no particular sounds.

At 0245, three vehicles pulled past the cross street in front of their location and disappeared around behind the prison. Ten min-utes later, Lieutenant Anwar came out the front of the prison and walked to his men across the street. After assuring he wasn't being watched, he slowly made his way back to the truck and came around to the rear. "He has arrived, Colonel." Anwar paused briefly. "Skylark is with them and two other members of the Revolutionary Council. They will be made to participate in this slaughter."

O'Brien was surprised by the information, which somewhat changed the situation. A "friendly" was inside the target area, but none of the team knew what he looked like. He was likely to get killed by the assault squad. "How many soldiers inside with Salimar, and where are they?"

"Six are in the guard shack out back. Four guards are inside, plus Salimar, General Alihambra, and the three council members. They are in the basement. Inside the side door, move to the first hallway intersection and turn left. Down the stairs, second room on the left. You'll know where when you get there, Colonel," he said with disgust. "One guard is at the bottom of the stairs, and three others are in the room with Salimar."

O'Brien turned to Captain Armstrong and spoke so that the remainder of the team could hear. "We have a 'friendly' inside that I don't want injured if possible. When we enter the room, I will identify him by ordering him first to get up against the wall. Does everyone understand that? The assault team acknowledged. Captain, how shall we play it from here?"

Captain Armstrong had already formulated an operational plan in his head, and this changed it very little. "Six men inside with me, including you, Colonel. Captain Murphy takes his Marines around back to the guard shack. At the first sound of action, take out the guards, and return to the front to cover our exit. Four minutes inside, tops. Lieutenant Anwar, have the truck in front of the building after you hear action inside. Right, three minutes we go."

O'Brien opened his portable satellite radio and transmitted the signal, "Home Plate, this is Rainbow Blue. Rainbow active, I repeat, Rainbow active."

Captain Murphy and the Marine squad left the rear of the truck and began to work their way around the building to approach the guard shack from the rear of the prison. They remained in the shadows, unseen by the guards who were intent on instructions being given by their sergeant. It was not every day the Leader came to inspect.

At 0254, Rainbow Blue commenced their move to enter the building. The three guards provided by Anwar had disappeared, and Anwar remained in the truck as directed. Entering through the side door, one man remained at the first intersection, the other five moving towards the stairs. Looking slowly around the stair-well, Rossiter spotted the guard at the bottom of the stairs looking down the hall. His back was toward the stairs. Suddenly, they were all startled by the unnerving scream of a man in agony, and they understood what sounds they thought they heard while waiting in the truck. Rossiter moved slowly down the stairs, and as he reached the bottom step, the guard turned to face him, his eyes opening wide. He started to yell, and Rossiter smashed the butt of his rifle against his mouth, knocking the man to his knees. He struck again, behind the head, rendering the guard instantly unconscious.

Rossiter signaled the squad to advance, and they moved along the wall to the room. The screaming had stopped. Captain Armstrong motioned for Rossiter to move astride the door and positioned two men on one side, with three on the other. With his fingers, he gave the one, two, three count, and they burst open the door, entering the room in less than a second. O'Brien came in third, instantly glancing around the room to spot Ambassador Haquim. Shouting at all present, O'Brien pointed at Haquim, "Face the wall, *now!*" The Iraqis backed up toward the wall, with Salimar glaring and shouting in Arabic. One guard tried to reach a weapon in the corner, and Armstrong put three rounds into him from his silenced Uzi. Turning to face the wall, Salimar, General Alihambra, a soldier, the captain who perpetrated most of the torture, and the three members of the council, including Ambassador Haquim, were now silent.

Guarded by the squad, O'Brien glanced around the room at the gore. An unknown Arab was prostrate on a table, with electrical connections to his body and blood running from the table. O'Brien motioned for one of the squad to remove his shackles, but he was unable to stand alone. O'Brien assisted him while the two remaining SAS squad secured the Iraqis standing against the wall by fastening plastic strapping bands on their hands. The tortured prisoner stood slowly, trying to put his trousers on. Again O'Brien assisted him. He spoke in English, but haltingly, pausing for air. "I am—" He gasped, trying to catch his breath, "Prince Rasheed, Kuwaiti forei—" He was wracked with a fit of coughing, spitting blood on the floor. Finally the coughing subsided, and he was able to talk. "I am the foreign minister. Nine of my family are . . . are imprisoned down the hall."

Captain Armstrong motioned to one of the squad. "Find them, quickly."

O'Brien and Armstrong turned their attention toward Salimar, who addressed them in English. "You have the wrong man," he said. "I am His Excellency's 'double.' He did not come for this trip."

"Yeah, sure," O'Brien said. "Then you should enjoy a short vacation in the United States, and we'll have to try again." Unnoticed, Rasheed slowly moved toward the corner, stumbling somewhat to cover his movement.

"You're going on a little trip, Excellency. An all-expense-paid overseas trip. Would you like to come along, General?" Armstrong spat out to Alihambra.

General Alihambra looked around with his hands cuffed behind his back. "You'll never leave the city, you British scum."

Armstrong just smiled and said, "You should travel more, General. You'd be able to place your accents better."

Alihambra's eyes grew large as he looked over Armstrong's shoulder, causing Armstrong to look behind him. Rasheed had recovered the rifle from the dead Iraqi soldier in the corner and aimed it at Salimar.

For nearly three weeks these Iraqis had tortured Prince Rasheed and his family members. He was certain his son would never walk again without a severe limp, and his wife had been unable to even make a verbal sound for over a week. Her torture had no longer pleased the guards, since they could draw no reaction. Rasheed had anguished in his heart for her more than for himself, notwithstanding that what had been his daily fare was nothing short of horrific. He would bear his own scars, both physical and mental, for some time to come. He watched Salimar for the several seconds it took to assure that his captors were aware of what was happening.

The SAS squad members looked to Armstrong and then to O'Brien for directions, not wanting to shoot Rasheed. Their instructions had been to capture Salimar alive if at all possible, and they had achieved their objective to this point. Armstrong moved toward Rasheed, who turned the rifle in his direction. "No, the Butcher will not languish in an American jail, availing himself of world sympathy and becoming a martyr for his cause. He will die the ignominious death such a tyrant deserves."

As strange as it seemed to O'Brien, his thoughts ran to the language Prince Rasheed used, to his excellent command of English. O'Brien thought, for the moment they stood there, that it was, as the entire Gulf War II had become, a stalemate. The SAS squad couldn't shoot Prince Rasheed after just rescuing him, and he seemed determined to end the existence of his torturers in the next moment. Prince Rasheed now occupied the central role, and he had assumed, albeit temporarily, command of the operation.

With one final look directly into Abdul Salimar's eyes, Rasheed raised the aim of the rifle. "*Allah akhbar.* God is good, Butcher, and may he have mercy on you, for judgment day is at hand," he softly spoke and pulled the trigger. Two rounds entered Salimar in the back and the neck. Rasheed moved the rifle quickly toward Alihambra and shot him in the side of the head, followed by two more quick blasts to kill the captain who had tortured him for nearly three weeks. Less than ten seconds had elapsed since Rasheed had obtained the rifle, but he had eliminated all those who had so brutally tortured his family.

O'Brien recovered from his surprise at the source of the attack and moved to grab the rifle before Rasheed completed his sweep around the room. After wresting the rifle from Rasheed, O'Brien bent to take Salimar's pulse but found none. He could detect nothing from Alihambra and the Iraqi captain either.

At the first gunshot, the Iraqi guards out back came bursting out of the guard shack, and the Marines opened up on them. The Iraqis returned fire, dropping two Marines before all the Iraqis were down. Picking up their wounded, the Marines swiftly moved around to the front of the building and set up a protective perimeter. Captain Murphy and one Marine ran inside and down the stairs toward the room, quickly taking in what had occurred. The two wounded Marines were in the truck, providing cover, and two more were just inside the front door, watching the street approaches.

Downstairs Captain Armstrong broke the tension. "Right, people, let's move it."

O'Brien had thought how to handle the situation of Haquim and tried to make eye contact. "Get these people out of here," he said to Rossiter, positioning himself so that he blocked Haquim's exit and thereby ensuring he would be last. He whispered to Haquim as the others left the room. "Will you be all right here?"

"Yes, Colonel. I'll be fine now. You must leave quickly. Thank you for my life."

O'Brien held his eye momentarily and said, "Thank you, Ambassador, for all of the thousands of lives you may have spared."

In the hall, Prince Rasheed, regaining his composure now, said, "We must take my family with us. If left, they will certainly be killed."

O'Brien quickly conferred with Armstrong. "We don't have room on the helicopters, but we must get them out of here. We'll figure out what to do with them down the road."

Pointing to the three Revolutionary Council members, O'Brien said, "Get these three out of my sight. In that room, and cuff 'em as well. Sergeant," he motioned toward the room they had just left, "bring the Butcher." The sergeant went back into the room and lifted the lifeless body of Abdul Salimar, and they began to move toward the door. They had been in the building less than three minutes.

At the entrance, the two Marines indicated they had seen headlights coming their way. Armstrong, followed by nine others—including three women, all of whom were helping each other to walk—emerged from the building and moved toward the truck. Sergeant Parker carried Salimar toward the truck Lieutenant Anwar had idling in front of the building.

"Load up, people," Captain Armstrong directed. In forty-five seconds, the Marines and Kiwis had loaded the Kuwaitis, plus the body of Salimar into the truck, and then they were rolling. In the truck were twelve members of Rainbow Blue, one Iraqi lieutenant, nine Kuwaitis, and the body of Abdul Salimar. As they drove away, O'Brien opened his portable transmitter again and initiated his message. If anything happened to Rainbow Blue and they were never able to report in person, he wanted Home Plate to know that Salimar was dead. The Iraqis might try to cover up the episode and pretend that Salimar was still alive.

"Home Plate, this is Rainbow Blue en route to Third Base. Rainbow plus Sunshine; repeat, Rainbow plus Sunshine," O'Brien reported, giving the success signal. "Rainbow includes Erebus, but Erebus is dead, repeat Erebus is dead."

They drove off into the night, waiting for the first checkpoint, which Lieutenant Anwar bluffed his way through, claiming that he carried a load of Kuwaiti prisoners bound for the detention camp located twenty miles out in the desert. The guard was somewhat suspicious, but it was three-thirty in the morning, and he was not brave enough to wake his lieutenant, especially when Lieutenant Anwar threatened to wake the officer himself and report the delay this private was causing his mission.

Kuwait Desert
Third Base
February

Colonel Yorgasen had been in place for about thirty minutes when he received the message from Home Plate. "Rainbow Yellow, this is Home Plate. Rainbow Blue reports Sunshine, en route to Third Base. Over."

"Roger, Home Plate, copy your message. Out," Yorgasen replied. He called out to those around him, "Look alive, team. They report success and are on the way." Yorgasen and two helicopters sat waiting to effect the extraction and provide the necessary cover if they were pursued. Four Apache gunships were overhead on the road from Third Base to Kuwait City.

Washington, D.C.
White House Oval Office
February

General Austin took the phone call himself from the message center at the Pentagon.

"General, this is Commander Nelson, Traffic Center. We have received a flash priority for you, sir. Reads: 'From Home Plate: Rainbow plus Sunshine. Erebus with Rainbow Blue. Erebus dead. Repeat, Erebus dead. Light casualties.' That's all it reads, General."

"Thank you, Commander."

Austin replaced the receiver and was silent for a moment. "Mr. President, Colonel O'Brien is en route from Kuwait City to the pickup point with Abdul Salimar. Sir, Colonel O'Brien reports that Salimar is dead. There are light casualties to the assault team at this point."

The president stood and walked toward his desk. "I'd hoped we could have concluded this without his death."

Clarene spoke, "Mr. President, we all knew he wouldn't come easily. There is a positive side to this. The finality of his death leaves no doubt to confuse his military leaders as to what they should do. If he were alive and captured, his generals would be concerned that if they ceased hostilities and we later returned Salimar, they would face repercussions. This way, if Skylark can gain control, we have a better chance of saving thousands of lives."

Eastman nodded agreement. "When will they reach safety, General?" the president asked.

"With no opposition, sir, they will reach the rendezvous point with the remainder of the team and the helicopters in about forty minutes. They will be under air cover from that point and should be safely back in Saudi Arabia in about another forty minutes."

"Can we depend on the report of Salimar's death?"

"We should see the body before announcing, sir, but Colonel O'Brien has reported Erebus as dead."

"Clarene," the president addressed his national security advisor, "we should prepare the necessary press releases before the Iraqis develop their own version of what happened. Also, prepare to notify all necessary governments and seek a cease-fire of this mess. If Skylark can pull off his end, we will be able to end this nightmare with no further bloodshed." President Eastman stood, causing General Austin to stand, and Eastman smiled broadly. "General, with sled dogs in the pack like Colonel O'Brien, this lead dog would challenge the Iditarod any day of the week. Well done. Mighty well done," said the president of the United States.

CHAPTER TWENTY-FIVE

Kuwait Desert
Third Base
February

Colonel, I have Fox Leader on the radio." The transport
chopper pilot was receiving a message from the helicopter gunships overhead.

"Fox Leader, this is Rainbow Yellow. Go ahead."

"Rainbow Yellow, we have one truck on the road toward your
position, no tail in sight."

"Roger, Fox Leader. Cover and allow safe transit. Continue
to watch for a tail."

"Roger, Rainbow. They're about nine miles away. Fox
Leader out."

Colonel Yorgasen directed the chopper pilot of the two waiting evacuation choppers, "In about ten minutes, rev 'em up and
prepare to get out of here." He quickly strode over to his squad,
forming a perimeter around the two choppers on the ground. Four

more of his ground team were about two hundred yards down the
road to ambush anyone coming in behind Rainbow Blue. "Listen
up, people. Rainbow Blue is about fifteen minutes out. Look
sharp and prepare to assist in the loading."

In a few moments they could see the approaching truck, covered by two Apache gunships. As the truck drove up, O'Brien
hopped out of the back and ran to Yorgasen. "We've got a problem on our hands. I've got twelve Rainbow Blue troops, nine
members of the Kuwaiti royal family, one 'friendly' Iraqi lieutenant, and one very dead Abdul Salimar. We're overloaded for
the choppers."

"That presents a problem all right," exhaled Colonel
Yorgasen.

As the unit unloaded the passengers, O'Brien and Yorgasen
walked over to the lead chopper pilot. "We're overweight with
our baggage, I'm afraid," O'Brien said. "We've got thirty-eight
people, and room for thirty, fifteen apiece."

The lead chopper pilot saw Colonel O'Brien's wings embroi-
dered on his camouflage fatigues and knew he was a rated pilot.
He thought for a moment and made his decision, hoping the
Colonel would understand the risk of loading too heavily.
"Colonel, I can take seventeen in each chopper and overload
slightly. Four will have to take the next trip. I'm really sorry."

"I understand, Major. Call in immediately once you're airborne and order one additional chopper ASAP. See if we can keep
a couple of gunships overhead for cover until they arrive."

"Will do, Colonel."

Yorgasen looked at O'Brien. "Zach, it's a tough call."

"Colonel, I know the operational phase isn't over, and you're
still in command, but I'm going to make this call myself. The
royal family must get out, and we must get Salimar out of here
also. We need to prove his death to the world. I'll call for three
other volunteers, and you get Rainbow Green airborne. I know
you want to stay, Colonel, but I would like you to successfully
conclude this mission." Without waiting for discussion, O'Brien
moved to the remaining team members on the ground. The squad
had been loading Kuwaiti royal family members on one of the

choppers, and they were nearly loaded. "We're overloaded, men. I need three of you to volunteer to stay with me until another chopper can arrive. It should be here in thirty to forty minutes. We don't have the time for discussion on the issue." Without a word spoken, all of the remaining squad members, Marines and SAS stepped forward. O'Brien smiled briefly, knowing the kind of men who had volunteered for this dangerous mission. "Right," he said. "Lieutenant Anwar, Sergeant Parker, and Captain Armstrong will remain with me."

Captain Murphy interrupted, "Colonel, with all due respect, I should stay. Besides, Colonel, I gave my word to General Jones I'd bring you back alive, and I have no intentions of facing the commandant of the Marine Corps alone." Zach smiled, nodded, and turned to Sergeant Parker, "Sorry, Sergeant, I'd better let this Marine warrior take care of me as General Jones ordered." Zach moved toward Colonel Yorgasen and saluted. "Time to get airborne, Colonel. See you in about an hour."

"Godspeed, Zach," Yorgasen replied, and he directed his men to board the helicopter.

Revving the engines, the pilot of the chopper advised that the gunships didn't have enough fuel to remain in place during the wait. The other chopper was ordered and had already lifted off, ETA thirty-five minutes. Just prior to take off, Sergeant Parker gave Captain Murphy a couple of automatic weapons in the event they were needed. Zach turned his attention to the task of defending the small ground installations for the thirty minutes necessary for their next copter to arrive.

Once airborne, Colonel Yorgasen called in. "Home Plate, this is Rainbow Green en route to Home Plate with thirty-four, repeat thirty-four. Rainbow Blue minus niner remains at Third Base. I say again, Rainbow Blue minus niner remains at Third Base."

"Rainbow Green, roger, we copy. Third chopper airborne, ETA now thirty-two minutes."

In ninety seconds it was deathly still in the desert. O'Brien commenced giving directions to the remaining team members, stopping in midsentence as he discovered Lieutenant Rossiter had remained.

"Lieutenant, explanations?" he demanded.

"Colonel, I asked Captain Armstrong's permission to replace him on this last leg. He has a wife and three children, sir. I just—"

"Establish a defensive perimeter, Lieutenant. We'll probably have company soon."

"Yes, sir." Looking O'Brien squarely in the eyes, Cameron smiled. "Thanks, Zach."

O'Brien, Murphy, Rossiter, and Anwar took up positions in the ground depressions dug by "Rainbow Yellow" during their wait. In Kuwait City, chaos reigned. The commander of the occupying forces had been alerted that His Excellency had been taken by commandos in a truck headed southwest of the city. No one bothered to tell him that Salimar was dead. Two trucks of Iraqi soldiers had already started to follow to try to catch the invaders.

At Third Base, O'Brien spotted the narrow slit lights of two approaching vehicles. They tried to conceal themselves lower into the ground, but they knew the fuel barrels scattered around the area would give them away. When the trucks were about three hundred yards from their location, Captain Murphy opened up with the M-60 machine gun, causing the front truck to veer off the road and come to a stop. The second truck also pulled over and the troops quickly climbed out, fanning out into the desert in a semi-circle, beginning to return fire. O'Brien called the incoming chopper to ascertain its ETA. "Rainbow pickup, this is Rainbow Blue, do you copy?"

"Roger, Rainbow Blue, this is Beagle Leader, we copy. What's your situation?"

" 'Beagle Leader, we are under attack. Two vehicles about three hundred yards northeast of Third Base. Anyone able to render assistance?"

"Hold one, Rainbow."

Beagle Leader radioed for overhead cover and contacted two F-15 Eagles returning from a night mission. "We copy, Beagle Leader. Snowbird here. Designate your target."

"Roger, Snowbird. We have four friendlies under attack waiting lift out. I'm eight minutes away. Can you assist?"

"Roger that, Beagle. Designate coordinates, please."

Beagle defined area coordinates, and the F-15s came in using night spotters to identify the trucks on the ground. One swift pass and the two trucks, plus about twenty of the Iraqis were no longer a threat to Rainbow Blue.

"Beagle Leader, this is Rainbow Blue. Thank those wing wipers for me and tell them they saved a dismounted Eagle driver. We are still under light fire, Beagle Leader. How far away are you?"

"Four minutes out, Rainbow. Hang on. We'll make one pass over the trucks, strafe the infantry, and turn to pick you up."

Spotting the approaching chopper, Lieutenant Anwar jumped up and ran for the drop point, crouching behind a barrel. Beagle flew directly overhead as planned, directing his fire at the remaining Iraqi ground troops. Fire continued from the Iraqis, and Anwar took two rounds directly in the chest and fell to the ground. Captain Murphy shouted to O'Brien that he would cover with the M-60 as the chopper landed. O'Brien motioned to Rossiter as the chopper came in to land, and they began to run in the direction of the chopper while Murphy kept a steady stream of fire in the direction of the Iraqis. The door gunner of the chopper also began to fire toward the Iraqis. O'Brien and Rossiter lifted Lieutenant Anwar and climbed aboard the chopper, shouting at Murphy, who couldn't hear them over the gunfire. Murphy saw they had made the chopper and left his position at a dead run. Fifty yards out, he dropped like a stone as mortar rounds began to land around the chopper.

"Colonel, we've got to get out of here, or they'll make mincemeat out of this bird with that mortar," the pilot shouted as he started to lift off.

O'Brien sprang to the cockpit and grabbed the pilot by the shoulder. "Set this thing down, *now*," he commanded. "He goes with us, or we'll all stay." The chopper settled back down, and Rossiter was out the door before the wheels touched down, followed immediately by O'Brien. They reached Murphy, who was nonresponsive. They couldn't tell if he was dead or not, but O'Brien lifted him, and Rossiter grabbed his other arm. Between them, they were dragging him towards the chopper when O'Brien was hit in the legs and collapsed. Rossiter dragged Murphy the remaining five yards, laying him inside the chopper next to Anwar. Rossiter followed the door gunner back outside to help him retrieve O'Brien, who was crawling toward the chopper. Once inside, the gunner began to return fire again, and Rossiter shouted, "GO, GO, GO!" as they lifted off. Small arms fire continued plinking off the fuselage of the chopper, but in moments they were clear and en route toward Home Plate.

Rossiter worked over Murphy's wounds, and he began to move, opening his eyes. O'Brien leaned over and, seeing Captain Murphy was alive, said, "Now what will you say to General Jones when you have to tell him an Air Force wing wiper saved the Marines?"

Murphy grimaced with pain and forced a smile. "I'll just tell him . . . I found 'a few good men' for the Corps."

The flight to Home Plate was uneventful, with Captain Murphy lying down, his bleeding now stopped by Rossiter's first aid. O'Brien and Rossiter sat with their backs up against the bulkhead, content to remain in silence and contemplation. Finally, about ten minutes out, Rossiter turned to O'Brien. "I would have to say, Zach," he said with a deadpan straight face, "that your parties are somewhat more exciting than yachting." O'Brien just looked at him, and slowly a laugh began to form in each of them, finally bursting forth and causing the door gunner to think to himself, "Crazy officers."

Just as the chopper was landing at Home Plate, Rossiter turned once again to O'Brien. "Zach, I've really enjoyed our time together," he said facetiously, "but the next time you hold a party, would you consider leaving me off the invitation list?"

Zach put his arm around Cameron's neck so he could help him up, flinching as the pain in his legs jolted through his body. "Ah, but, Cameron, I haven't told you the other story about the angel . . . "

Washington, D.C.
National Security Agency
February

Captain Shelly Molloy walked swiftly down the hall to General Austin's office and entered without knocking. "General, thirty-nine runs scored. Most important, nobody left on base, and the clean-up hitters just reached Home Plate. Captain Murphy is undergoing immediate surgery, but he'll be fine. Colonel O'Brien is also in surgery with two leg wounds, but he should be able to transport via med evac within a couple of days. A good mission, General."

"An outstanding mission, Captain. Perhaps one that will never be able to be told, but those who need to know will know. Thank you. Go home and get some sleep, Captain. All the boys are home safe."

"Yes, sir," she said and left his office.

Alone, General William Austin, deputy director, Intelligence, National Security Agency, had one more duty to fulfill. He reached for the telephone and dialed a number he had long since memorized. A sleepy voice answered the phone, "Hello."

"Hello, Alison?"

"Yes?" She bolted straight up in bed. "General, is that you?"

"He's safe, Alison."

"Oh, thank God," she said as the tears began to stream down her face.

"Yes, Alison. Thank God," as he replaced the receiver. *As we all should,* Austin thought.

Alison O'Brien slipped quietly out from under the covers, kneeling beside her bed to talk quietly and gratefully with her Father, thanking him that now, once again, her family would be together and safe.

Andrews Air Force Base, Maryland
February

As the giant C-141 medical evacuation flight taxied toward the hanger, Alison stood with her heart in her throat. She had, of course, been told that Zach's wounds were not serious and that he

would be just fine, but she worried that he might have asked
General Austin to minimize his injuries to spare her the worry
until he came home. General Austin stood together with Alison
and Jeanette Murphy, Captain Murphy's wife. The rear doors of
the plane opened, and medical personnel standing by on the tarmac began to deplane the wounded and injured members of the
flight. Not many wounded were aboard, as fighting had never
reached epic proportions during the stalemate.

Alison and several other wives and mothers waited, trying to
observe their particular family member. As a shiny green military
vehicle drove up, she noticed a tall, highly beribboned Marine
general officer exit the car, assisted by a lieutenant colonel wearing the shoulder insignia of general's aide. General Austin came
to attention and saluted the Marine general, who returned the
salute and smiled.

As the stretchers began to come off, the general's aide spoke
to the chief flight nurse, who pointed toward two stretchers being
lifted off by corpsmen. A young officer in camouflage uniform
and wearing a beret walked beside the stretchers. The aide walked
back toward the general and spoke briefly with him, after which
the general moved to intercept the two stretchers as they were
being taken toward the ambulance. As the general approached,
the young officer came to attention and saluted. Funny, Alison
thought, something must be wrong with his hand. As he saluted
he seemed unable to turn his wrist properly, and the palm of his
hand was facing forward rather than down, parallel to the ground.

Alison watched as the general leaned down to speak with the
men. She found it touching that a general officer would take the
time to come out to Andrews AFB to visit with his wounded men.
It was unusual, and perhaps his son or some relative was aboard.
She was surprised when the general's aide started toward her.

After saluting General Austin, he turned toward the ladies.
"Mrs. O'Brien?" and turning toward Jeanette, "Mrs. Murphy?"

"Yes?" the two women answered.

"General Jones has requested that you accompany me, if you
please."

Alison and Jeanette looked at each other momentarily and

followed the officer toward the ambulance. As she approached, she began to discern the features of the patient on the nearest stretcher, and quickly recognized the smile. "Zach," she cried out and ran the remaining ten feet and knelt at his side. Jeanette quickly moved toward Captain Murphy on the other stretcher.

Zach raised his head somewhat, restrained by the stretcher straps required during the flight. "Alison, may I present General Jeremiah Jones, commandant of the Marine Corps."

General Jones smiled at Alison. "It is my honor to meet you, ma'am. I am sure you are quite proud of this officer, Mrs. O'Brien. My only regret is that he is not one of my Marines." General Austin had also approached and been recognized by Zach.

"Thank you, General, I am indeed proud of him and intend to take quite good care of him now," Alison replied. General Jones moved away to speak with Captain and Mrs. Murphy.

Standing quietly off to one side, Alison had not yet recognized the young officer who had accompanied Zach off the flight. Zach smiled at Alison and took her hand as she walked toward the ambulance with him. As he was loaded into the ambulance, the young officer moved to enter the vehicle, "Excuse me, ma'am, I've been assigned to escort this officer until he is placed in proper care. May I now assume that I have fulfilled that duty successfully?" He began to laugh.

"Cameron!" Alison exclaimed. "What in the world . . . Zach, how did he . . . Cameron, what are you doing here?"

"As I explained, ma'am, my assignment was to see this officer safely home and place him into capable hands. I can see that mission has now been fulfilled." Alison wrapped her arms around Cameron and held him for some moments, whispering in his ear her thanks for bringing Zach home safely.

Kneeling by Zach, Lieutenant Cameron Rossiter, New Zealand Special Air Service, said his good-byes. "Zach, it has been . . . well, should we just say, it has been memorable. I'd better be on my way. I have a reunion of my own to arrange." Cameron offered his hand, which Zach took in both of his. "Thank you, Zach," he said with sincerity.

Cameron looked up at Alison, smiling, and then down at Zach once more. "Don't be a stranger, mate." he added, rising to leave. Coming to attention once again, Lieutenant Rossiter saluted Colonel O'Brien in the form British and all Commonwealth military do, with the palm facing forward, which Alison then recognized, smiling to herself about her mistake. General Jones and General Austin, watching this reunion from a few feet away, approached as they saw Cameron begin to leave. Cameron once again saluted the generals, who both returned crisp salutes.

"A good mission, Lieutenant?" General Jones said, pronouncing it "leftenant" as the British do.

"An excellent mission, sir, under commendable leadership." Looking toward Captain Murphy, he said, "Were it not for Captain Murphy covering our escape at Third Base, we would not be here to make our report."

"Thank you, Lieutenant," General Jones offered. "I appreciate your report."

Moving toward the ambulance, Generals Jones and Austin offered Zach their congratulations and prepared to depart. Alison and Jeanette had driven out with General Austin. "We'll leave now, Alison," Austin said. "It's apparent that Colonel O'Brien is in good hands."

As the ambulance drove off with the O'Briens and the Murphys, General Austin and General Jones walked back toward their cars. "So, you're changing Air Force blue for civilian gray, I hear," Jones commented.

Austin paused. "I think the time has come, General," he replied.

"I think perhaps mine has as well, Bill. I've worn Marine green since before I started shaving. It has been my life. When I see young men like O'Brien and Murphy, I realize in spite of the troubles we have, there will always be someone capable and ready to rise to the occasion. It's their turn, I suppose," Jones said nostalgically.

As General Jones entered his staff car, Austin saluted and watched the car drive away. Turning toward his car he looked out over the flight line and the aircraft arriving and departing. How often, he wondered, has the world turned on the actions of a small group of men, both good and bad? How often would we need to learn the lessons already learned by our forefathers? Entering his car and leaving the main gate, as the sentry saluted his vehicle, he was confident that no matter how many times the world would be required to retrace old ground, be it a hillside in Vietnam, or a sand dune in Kuwait, men of honor would rise to fulfill their calling. It had ever been so!

Auckland, New Zealand
February

"Good morning. Corporate Services, Michelle speaking. May I help you?"

"That's the sweetest sound a man could hear."

"*Cameron?* Is that you, Cameron?"

"Yes, my darling, it is indeed me."

"Where are you?"

"I'm in the airport lobby in Washington, D.C., at present."

"Are you coming home . . . when?"

"Not right away. I have a couple of things to do first."

"What? What do you have to do? Can't you come home soon?"

"No, I'm sorry, Michelle, I'm getting married tomorrow."

"*What?*" she cried. "What are you talking about?"

"I said I'm getting married early tomorrow morning to the first available girl I see getting off the Air New Zealand flight from Auckland to Hawaii."

"But, Cameron, we can't . . . I mean, we have to . . . Cameron, please, you're confusing me."

"Michelle," he said tenderly, "hang up the phone and then call Air New Zealand. You'll find a reservation under the name of Michelle Duffield on this evening's flight for Hawaii. If you inquire further, you'll find a return booking for Mr. and Mrs. Cameron Rossiter."

"But our wedding, our reception. We can't just—"

"Yes, dear, we can. We'll have any kind of reception you

want. Later. I don't want to spend one more day without you, Michelle. I love you. Do you understand that?"

"Yes," she replied, tears beginning to run down her cheeks.

"Just come to me, darling. We belong together."

"Yes, Cameron . . . Oh yes!"

Saudi Arabia
Ras Tannurah Oil Facility
February

Eight days following the Rainbow Blue mission, an Allied military procession under white truce flags drew near to the oil facility at Ras Tannurah and cautiously approached the entrance, manned by Iraqi troops. Colonel Wadi met the procession and accompanied them to the small airfield where four military helicopters waited. Ambassador Haquim was there to represent the government of Iraq, and an Army honor guard was formed up on the tarmac.

The U.S. military truck backed up toward the row of helicopters, and two groups of six highly polished Iraqi Army sergeants moved in formation toward the truck. Each group lifted a casket, each draped with the Iraqi flag, and slowly, in funeral step, moved the caskets toward the helicopters. Lieutenant Anwar and General Abdul Salimar were being received with honors. Lieutenant Anwar had died a hero's death in defense of His Excellency, and both were to lay in state in Baghdad for the next three days. The flight of helicopters lifted off, and they were soon joined by a flight of Iraqi fighters, given permission to fly in formation. The flight carefully avoided Kuwaiti air space and, following the Saudi border, turned north upon reaching Iraq.

Interim President Haquim delivered the appropriate words at Salimar's ceremony and waxed eloquent in support of the young lieutenant who lay beside him, stating that he had given his life for his country and in defense of the principles he stood for, that all Iraqis should remember his name. Haquim closed by saying that all men should take note of this occasion and remember the past so that they might learn from it. He knew in his heart that it had been said before.

EPILOGUE

Washington, D.C.
March

PRESIDENT EASTMAN CONTACTED the secretary general of the United Nations and requested he use his good offices to broker a ceasefire in the current crisis in the Middle East. The news of Abdul Salimar's death came as a great relief to the Western world, who thought they were going to have to deal with another Hitler. The ceasefire was quickly established, and plans were laid for the formation of a United Nations–controlled government structure in Iraq until proper authorities, as yet undecided, could be called upon to hold elections.

With the support of the Russian Republic and the United States of America, the United Nations appointed Sir Geoffrey Holden, ambassador from New Zealand and director of the New Zealand–based Organization for International Conflict Resolution, to coordinate the formation of an interim government structure in Iraq. Sir Geoffrey called upon the assistance of top

371

Iraqi government leaders, specifically, Teraq Haquim, previous ambassador to the United Nations, to head the interim government. Military leadership was restrained in the new formation, aided by the presence of Russian troops called upon to restore peace. A small unit of Russian troops, with the assistance of Iraqi military leaders, located and removed the one remaining remnant of Nikita Khrushchev's insidious plan to humiliate the Americans. The Khrushchev era was long over, but he had left a dangerous legacy that had threatened the world long after his demise. With the return of the fourth nuclear weapon to Russian control, Silent Wind was officially dead.

A proposition was placed before the United Nations General Assembly to form a new political division located in Northeast Iraq, to run along the 37th parallel from Syria to the Iraq-Iran border. The new political division was to be called Kurdistan.

Bay of Islands
New Zealand
December

A beautiful summer evening hung over the Bay of Islands as Clinton O'Brien, lieutenant colonel, U.S. Army, retired, stood over the barbecue. He watched as his family talked, played, and frolicked around the yard. Six of his eight children were home for the holidays, and with them came seventeen grandchildren. Down the hill, along the waterfront, Alison and Michelle walked along the beach, the family Cavalier King Charles spaniel running to and fro.

"We were so sorry to miss your reception, Michelle," Alison said, "but when we heard about your impromptu wedding in Hawaii, we were thrilled. Zach was still having therapy on his legs, but his wounds are healing nicely, and his legs are both functional. He's even been restored to flight status. The video of your reception was beautiful. Thank you so much for sending us a copy."

"We had a wonderful day," Michelle replied. "Cameron was so nervous. We had already been married a month. I couldn't believe it. You'd think after what they went through in Kuwait . . . "

"It's not the same to them, is it? Walking further along the beach, Alison watched as Michelle gently rubbed her stomach. Smiling a knowing look, she asked "What are you hoping for, Michelle?"

Michelle didn't answer for a few moments as they continued walking. "I already have all I ever hoped for, Alison," she said and laughed. "We'll know in June."

They continued walking, heading up the hill toward the house. "The boys never seem to be able to express their feelings about certain things, Michelle, but I want to tell you how grateful I am for what Cameron did for Zach in Kuwait."

"The way Cameron describes it, that is, when he talks about it at all, is that Zach was responsible for their safety."

"It doesn't matter, does it, Michelle? They were both there for each other, and we have them now. The world is right for a while because of them, and our world, yours and mine, is also right."

"Umm," Michelle thought out loud.

Zach and Cameron had been walking on the cliff top, reflecting on their time together and the events of the past year which had brought their families so close.

"I've been meaning to ask you, Cameron, how your investigation came out regarding value systems and Michelle's concerns?"

"We kind of got sidetracked, given the Gulf issues and the preparation for the reception, but we've decided that after the holidays we'll get serious again. The baby has started us talking once more about directions. You know how that happens."

"Indeed I do. I hope we were able to help. I also hope you know how important you and Michelle have become to our family. We've been really curious but at the same time aware that we didn't want to pressure you or make you feel it was more important to us than your friendship."

Cameron was a bit embarrassed, but he had come to understand the directness of this American whom he had come to like. "We feel the same, Zach. Whatever way it turns out, I know we will always maintain a friendship."

Cameron spotted the girls coming up from the beach. "So, where have you girls been?" he boomed from the top of the hill.

"Looking for a couple of good men," replied Alison. "Seen any?"

Zach and Cameron looked at each other with mock surprise. "Has she been talking to Murphy?" Cameron asked Zach, and they both laughed.

They all walked back toward the house. "Oh, by the way, Zach," Cameron said, "is it possible for you and Alison to drop by Auckland next Wednesday before you fly home?"

"We probably could work that in. What's up?"

"Just a little gathering," he said mischievously. "I've been requested to invite you to one of 'our' parties, which, I might add, are considerably safer than yours. Admiral Sir Trevor Pottsdam and Colonel Yorgasen would like to present you with a personal, sandy-colored beret. It seems they feel you deserve to be an honorary member of the 'Who dares, wins' club. Sort of a 'thanks, old boy' thing."

"Does this mean I'll have to jump out of a perfectly good airplane?" joked Zach.

He laughed. "Probably not this time. But you'll be back," he said with a hint of challenge.

Michelle jumped into the conversation. "It would also give you a chance to see our new yacht."

Zach's eyes grew a little more interested. "Great. What did you name this one?"

"We thought about it for some time, actually. It had to be something memorable, of course. We finally settled on a name I'm not likely to ever forget."

Zach held Cameron's gaze for a time, slowing developing a broad smile. "And the result?"

"Rainbow Blue."

White House Oval Office
Washington D.C.
January

"Ladies and Gentlemen, the President of the United States."

Bill Eastman, accompanied by his wife, Jean, strode into the room filled with people, to applause from those present. The room had about forty people, including Clarene Prescott, national security advisor; Lieutenant General William Austin; General Jeremiah Jones, commandant of the Marine Corps; and newly promoted Major John Francis Murphy, plus their families. Just prior to the president's arrival, General Austin had dropped a bombshell on Zach. Austin took Zach off into a corner to privately congratulate him on this very special day.

"I wanted to express my appreciation privately, Zach, and to tell you it has been a privilege and honor to work with you. The honor our nation pays to you today is well deserved," Austin offered with sincerity.

"That sounds almost like a good-bye, General."

"I suppose it is, Zach. I have tendered my resignation, effective in sixty days. Thirty-six years in this blue suit, and I'm proud of each and every day, and especially of the men and women with whom I've had the honor to work. The president will be submitting my name to Congress for approval as deputy director of the Central Intelligence Agency, effective in a couple of months when Bob Jackson retires."

O'Brien's eyes grew larger, and he whistled softly, looking around the Oval Office to be certain he hadn't disturbed the reverence in the room. "What a change! My heartiest congratulations, General. I've learned a lot these past few years under your guidance, and I would like to return the compliment. It has indeed been my honor to serve with you, sir."

Now it was Austin's turn to raise his eyebrows toward Zach. "If you're serious in that, Colonel, then I'd like you to consider coming out to the 'Farm,' as we refer to our place of employment." The "Farm" was a nickname for the CIA complex in Virginia.

"You mean—" Zach began.

"Yes, I do, but this is neither the time nor the place to discuss it. It's your day today, Colonel O'Brien, and Major Murphy's. Enjoy it, and we'll talk later if you're interested."

"Have Alice book the appointment, General," Zach said, smiling. "I'm interested."

The thought of this quick discussion flashed briefly through

Zach's mind, and he looked at Alison and his children, standing proudly in the front of the group as the president began to address the assembled people.

"It is a great honor we have this day to present our nation's gratitude to two of those who served her selflessly in the recent crisis. In the highest traditions of the United States Marine Corps, Major John Francis Murphy successfully performed his dangerous assignment without losing a member of his team. It is my honor to present to him his second Silver Star for gallantry in action." Major Murphy stepped forward, and the president pinned the Silver Star medal on his Marine Corps dress blues.

Turning to O'Brien, the president continued. "Twenty-seven years ago, a young boy was in this very room to observe the award of our nation's highest honor, the Congressional Medal of Honor, to his father, then Army Lieutenant Clinton O'Brien, for gallantry during the Vietnam crisis. Lieutenant O'Brien's rescue of a fellow airman, downed behind enemy lines, demonstrated to that young boy the reward of courage and an attitude of service to others. Today the recipient of that Medal of Honor has the privilege of watching his son also receive his nation's thanks. The tradition of 'service to others,' which this family has adopted as a motto, has been personified by both father and son. It would make this world a better place should other families find it in their hearts to adopt such a motto."

The president continued, "Lieutenant Colonel Zachariah Daniel O'Brien, for service to his country above and beyond the call of duty, has been awarded the nation's second highest award for gallantry, the Silver Star."

The president pinned the medal on Zach to the applause of the attendees, while the White House photographer recorded the event. Colonel O'Brien and Major Murphy had their photos taken with their families and the president, O'Brien being sure to include General Austin in the family setting.

Quietly standing next to her tall, very proud husband, Kathleen Flynn O'Brien remembered that day so long ago when her young Kiwi husband, Lieutenant Clinton O'Brien, had received his medal from President Lyndon Johnson. She had said her silent prayer at the time, "Grant us the strength to serve thee, Father, as thou wouldst have us serve." The O'Briens seemed destined to serve others, often at the risk of their own lives, but Kate was no longer afraid. If he had protected the two thousand stripling warriors as they went to battle in place of their fathers, he could have, and had, protected the O'Briens, father and son.

Kate's prayer had been answered. It was enough.

LIST OF ACRONYMS

ANZUS	Australia, New Zealand, United States Treaty Organization
AWACS	airborne warning and control system (EC3A aircraft)
CHARLIE	nickname given to Viet Cong soldiers
CIA	Central Intelligence Agency
CINCENCOM	commander-in-chief, Central Command
CNO	chief of naval operations
CWO	chief warrant officer
DCI	director of central intelligence (Central Intelligence Agency)
DCS	deputy chief of staff (on Joint Chiefs of Staff)
DDI	deputy director, Intelligence, Central Intelligence Agency
DDO	deputy director, Operations, Central Intelligence Agency
DEA	Drug Enforcement Agency
DEFCON	definite condition (five categories of increasing military alert)
HMNZS	His/Her Majesty's New Zealand Ship
intel	slang for intelligence information

JCS	Joint Chiefs of Staff (consisting of senior officer of each military branch)
KGB	Soviet Secret Police (Committee for State Security)
Lt.	lieutenant
LTJG	lieutenant junior grade (naval rank)
LZ	landing zone
NAVPERS	Naval Personnel Office
NSA	National Security Agency
NVA	North Vietnamese Army
NYU	New York University
NZ	New Zealand
OD	officer of the deck/day
OICR	Organization for International Conflict Resolution (fictional organization)
POM	prisoner of His/Her Majesty (Australian and New Zealand slang for British)
POW	prisoner of war
SAM	surface-to-air missile
SAS	Special Air Service (British and Commonwealth commandos)
SIS	Australian and New Zealand Security Intelligence Service
SPEC5	specialist five (military enlisted rank)
SSG	Strategic Security Group (fictional company)
USAF	United States Air Force
USMC	United States Marine Corps
USS	United States Ship
XO	executive officer (second in charge on U.S. naval vessel)